CW00501648

Beware
the horse with two legs

by

AJ Mitchell

Beware the horse with two legs

ISBN: 9798354550463

Chapter One

The Under-Secretary of State took his position before the despatch-box for the first time. This was a proud moment in Rupert Veneer's life. He hoped that his mother would see him on television although he doubted his audience appeal.

He remembered her words to him when he first took office, "Beware the horse with two legs, Rupert. Ride with him and you'll be sorry. Even an ass with four legs is more agile than a two-legged horse."

In heeding her words, he had achieved much in his short career. Within the political arena, it was not difficult to recognise deficiencies within a colleague and avoid them accordingly. However, today's deficient could be tomorrow's leader and therefore a certain fluidity in approach was essential to good career management. Flexibility was the Veneer keyword.

He took two, long and deep, breaths before speaking. He had been advised to do this by his mentor, the Right Honourable Michael Farrar MP, the Home Secretary.

"You'll be nervous at first, My Boy," Farrar told him. "The trick is not to let those nerves show. You must stand boldly and step up to the box. Open your book firmly and place your hands flat on the table. Lean slightly forward, so they take the weight. First give-away of a poor politician, shaky hands."

Rupert Veneer had listened carefully and followed the advice. He had positioned himself before the despatch-box without incident. His hands were firmly planted, either side of his notebook. They did not shake. The politician surveyed his surroundings, whilst gathering his composure.

It was late afternoon, and the House was virtually empty. Veneer's motion had been pre-agreed by all parties. Those present were purely to give the facade that the House of Commons was still a worthy body, credible to the electorate.

The Prime Minister's question-time had purged the Commons by the end of the morning session. Whilst the questions were pre-recorded, and the answers lacked spontaneity, it was the time to be seen. Any established Member recognised this and would only fail to appear through the most important of prior engagements. As the Prime Minister left the House on conclusion, so the rank and file departed soon after. It was an exodus. By the late afternoon, those present were either instructed to attend, or asleep at the bench.

"We are the party of Law and Order," Veneer heard his voice echo around the chamber.

His second breath had filled his lungs, but they emptied with the booming words. The large spectacles slipped slightly from a nose that was not built to support them. Veneer pushed them back with his thumb, over his bulbous eyes.

The Member for North Forsythe opened one eye at the words. He sat in the rear row of the opposition benches and had enjoyed a full luncheon, supported by much port. The wind rose in his gullet before his eye closed again.

Rupert Veneer had achieved a second electoral success. The party won a virtual landslide at the last election ensuring the safety of his marginal seat. He was pleased to have been returned to the Commons, securing his employment for another five years. With his appointment to the Home Office, he had graduated from a back-bench Member to Cabinet deputy.

Veneer was a graduate of Law and Politics at Keele University. He was the educated product of an educated man. His ability to speak publicly had been exercised through the college debating society. The party had seized the opportunity to recruit him soon after. Rupert Veneer was a loyal graduate both of college and party and developed his membership through backstage assistance. These efforts did not go amiss; the mid-term offer of candidature being an honour rapidly accepted. His surprise at election was well concealed.

Rupert Veneer surveyed the House from his position of power. The green, leathered benches, facing each other in a confrontational stance, could barely cater for two-thirds of those elected. It was fortunate that two-thirds rarely attended, thought Veneer. He was pleased with his audience of less than twenty Members, realising that he was fortunate there were not fewer.

Farrar had briefed Veneer, in short, as to the project. The aim was to reduce drug-related crime. The methodology was by research into a certain, group section as to why those offenders strayed from the line. Another quango was to be established. It would employ selected Members from all parties. It would be a source of easy revenue. There were no objections despite the fact that it had all been done before.

Veneer was now in his late-thirties and foresaw a rosy future in his chosen career. He was unmarried though not gay. His girlfriends had been few and those had been short lasting. The Under-Secretary was not a virgin though his sexual experiences were unworthy of mention. Whilst at home in politics, Veneer's social attributes were limited. He attributed this to his looks. His bulging eyes were sufficient to deter. He had been nicknamed 'Bug' at school, a name that had not, fortunately, followed him into politics.

Rupert Veneer's first presentation at the despatch box was, for him, a success. He continued for thirteen minutes and forty-seven seconds. A stopwatch accurately measured the time. He had planned fifteen minutes but rushed slightly due to nerves. The honourable Member for North Forsythe showed no further response. Veneer was asked just one question from the opposition bench.

"Is it not the case, Under-Secretary, that these proposals merely reiterate those put forward by our party, prior to the election? In short, you have poached these ideas from my, forward thinking, colleagues and merely re-packaged them as your own."

Veneer knew this to be true. "Not so, my dear Sir. These are new and fresh ideas aimed purposely at reducing the rising incidence of drug-related crime. Much effort has been put into these proposals to ensure they offer feasible options. They go far beyond any mishmash of ideas that your Party might have had prior to the election. I repeat again, we are the Party of Law and Order."

The honourable Member of the opposition re-took his seat. His position on the quango was already secured. He had nothing more to say. There was no further business. The Speaker called the House to a close. At this stage in the day, he was able to do this without loud verbal control. His voice was still hoarse from the morning session, as he repeatedly had to call for order to control those Members during Prime Minister's questions. With deliberation, Rupert Veneer secured his notebook and walked from the chamber. The Member for North Forsythe had not moved. The depth of his breathing broke the unnerving silence.

I lifted my foot to rest on the edge of the dressing room table. I had left the television on for company. 'An afternoon in the Commons' turned out to be the best programme. The hotel only provided terrestrial TV. I wouldn't have watched it if I'd had satellite. Still, it was only background. I glanced at the slightly overweight politician as he spoke. I did not appreciate the significance of the person, or the speech, until later, much later. I had other, more important things on my mind. I had to prepare thoroughly for the evening. I could not afford a mistake.

I slowly rolled the black stocking over my left calf, to my knee. I did not hurry, knowing that such sheer material would ladder easily. Ensuring that the lower leg was smooth and straight I completed the task before securing the stocking to the suspender belt. I did not like stockings. However, what they lacked in comfort, they made up for in man appeal, and that was what I was after that evening, a man, and one man in particular.

I looked at myself in the mirror. Katrina Marshall, undercover cop. My mirrored reflection showed a slim, twenty-five year old woman. I was more than thin, almost skinny. Some said emaciated but I disputed that. I had recognised eating problems as a teenager, all of them, in fact. I was better now; fit enough to become a police officer. My illnesses had taken their toll, however. I would never be fat.

My underwear was black, specially chosen for the occasion. I wore high cut, French knickers, which were trimmed in lace. A matching camisole, similarly trimmed covered my small, rounded, breasts. I did not wear a bra; I did not need to.

I placed the palm of each hand under my breasts and pushed upwards, exaggerating their form.

"I must have been at the back of the queue." I talked to my mirror image. I regularly did that. How sad!

I allowed my upper body to regain its natural shape and took my foot off the dressing table. I walked to the bed and picked from it a dark green silk shirt. I only partially buttoned it to allow the allure of the camisole to show. That was the idea anyway, who knows if it worked. A short black skirt barely covered the tops of my stockings. It was sufficiently shaped to absorb the contours of my hips whilst not so tight so as to reveal my underwear. I pulled it down a little anyway.

I sat on the stool to complete my make-up. I looked into the large, oval, mirror of the dressing table. My eyes were already deeply shadowed in black. I extended my eyelashes with mascara. I was generally impressed with my eyes. They were a part of me that had always looked good, although even they hadn't worked properly. Either large round glasses or contact lenses had been needed to support them for as long as I could remember. I paled my face slightly, highlighting my cheekbones and giving a haunting effect. This contrasted with the bronzed lipstick with which I coloured my narrow lips.

I looked at the face in the mirror. The face that looked back was not mine, however. This was not the Katrina Marshall that I knew and sometimes loved. The make-up heavily concealed my own features. I had fitted the auburn wig carefully to cover my own blonde hair. I would never have thought of doing so had it not been for the job. The long, curly tresses fell to my shoulders. Even my eyes had changed from their usual blue, due to the green contact lenses that I had inserted. Tonight, I would be Melissa Grant. It was Melissa who returned my stare. That bitch, Melissa; there were times that I hated her, yet times that I loved her. She was not like me, demur and sometimes slightly timid. She was strong, confident, yet always retaining a certain attraction that I found difficult to achieve. I looked at Melissa's nails. They were varnished to match her lipstick and were falsely extended into long talons. Melissa liked long nails. She never knew when they might prove useful.

I was nervous with that evening's date. Carlo Ramiro's car was due to collect me at 7pm. I had a quarter of an hour to finish Melissa's preparations. I was unhurried. I looked into the mirror. I was about to talk to my mirror image again. What was the matter with me?

"This better be all right tonight, Melissa." I told her. I slightly exaggerated my natural London dialect in contrast. "I'm not at all happy with this guy."

"Don't worry, have I ever let you down before?" Melissa replied with a slight Liverpudlian twist. I was pleased how natural it sounded. "I'll look after us both. I'll see you later on."

The internal hotel telephone rang promptly at seven. The receptionist spoke:

"Miss Grant, there's a car waiting for you at the front door."

"Thank you, please tell the driver that I'll be down in just a moment."

Melissa Grant picked up her handbag and a short black coat from the bed. The contents of her handbag were limited. She carried just her mobile telephone, a make-up bag, for any necessary repairs during the course of the evening and her purse with suitable proof of identity of my alter-ego. The purse contained appropriate credit and debit cards that any girl should carry together with a full driving licence. Certain other assets were hidden within the lining of the bag. I hoped they would be capable of transmitting appropriate messages to those outside.

She left the hotel room, briefly checking the interior before locking the door behind her. As she walked along the corridor to the lift, she pulled the sleeves of the coat over her arms. The lift took some seconds to arrive. She used the time to straighten her dress in the dull reflection of the aluminium door. It was time for Katrina Marshall to fade into the background although I would always be present to supervise Melissa's actions. We both shared my body and mind and I had no intention of allowing Melissa Grant to defile either. However, Melissa was a strong character and whilst I sometimes disapproved of her actions, I often had a sneaking admiration for her. I let her get away with far too much. One day I would correct the balance and draw her into line.

On her arrival on the ground floor Melissa walked confidently through the hotel foyer.

"Good evening, Miss Grant." The uniformed concierge greeted her as she approached his desk.

Melissa tossed the hotel door key to him as she passed. I was almost embarrassed as she left the hotel without response.

The revolving door to the street obstructed her passage. As she turned within it both she and I felt the cold of the autumn evening penetrate her limited clothing. The side street, off Piccadilly, was not busy and the black Mercedes was parked only a few yards from the Aphelion Hotel. She walked down the steps into the street and approached the car. The driver was a large Colombian. He was sitting in the driver's seat looking straight ahead. He made no effort to move. Melissa walked to the back door and opened it herself. She got into the car. It drove away from the hotel.

I could imagine Detective Inspector Duncan Trevellian's response as the Mercedes moved off and he had to spur his surveillance team into action.

"All units stand-by. She's just left the hotel, into the Mercedes. The car is on the move, travelling south, towards Piccadilly." He spoke into his car radio, transmitting his observations to the rest of the team. "Has someone got the eyeball?"

"I have control," answered one of his detectives.

Trevellian watched the maroon Ford Escort cruise, from a side turning close-by, in behind the Mercedes. He sighed and relaxed into his passenger seat. The take-off was always the most difficult part of these operations. One slip and the target could be lost. At least that had not happened. This was an important operation, which relied on them remaining in contact with Melissa Grant. They could not afford to lose her.

As the Mercedes swept through central London, travelling eastbound, Melissa relaxed into the soft leather interior. Whilst she made herself comfortable. I thought back to her initial meeting with Carlo Ramiro that had led to this evening's date. I had known of the party several days in advance. The invitation was not formal. We were aware that a certain flexibility at the door allowed entry to single girls. Melissa Grant successfully tested this flexibility and gate-crashed the party. The aim was to gain an introduction to Ramiro and Melissa had achieved that aim.

It was Ramiro's fortieth birthday party. Normally he celebrated his birthdays in some style, in his home country of Colombia. His family owned a large and sprawling ranch just outside Bogota. Birthdays, as with other festive occasions were of particular importance to the Ramiro family. Such celebrations were attended by every available relative, however distant. Carlo's ageing father, Paulo, carefully controlled the organisation of both business and social pleasure. He ran the family with a whip hand. After all, he was the originator of the family wealth.

Paulo Ramiro owned properties throughout the Western world. His industry spanned most developed countries, particularly the United States and Europe. Carlo had grown up within the family business and, as Paulo reached his sixties, he had allowed responsibility to pass to his son. This gave him time to concentrate on his prime interest. His racehorses were some of the finest in Colombia.

As Carlo's business role developed his family role had reduced. This was also affected by his preference to enjoy a socially upbeat way of life. His wealth allowed him the best. He ensured that he had it. For some years his primary residence had been a large apartment just off Miami Beach, Florida. Two weeks previously he had travelled to London to establish a more effective control at this lucrative terminal of the business empire. The lower echelon of drugs dealers contained remarkably fickle people. On occasion, a strict example of discipline was required.

Regardless of his business commitments, however, his birthday was not to be forgotten. A short telephone call between Paulo and Juan Marco, Carlo's aid, had decided the arrangements. Whilst it was simply too far for the Colombian contingent to travel, at twelve-night, British time, Paulo would be contacted by telephone in order that he could personally pass his best wishes to his son.

The party necessitated the closure of the Lanthanum Club to the general public. This was not a problem. The Ramiro's owned the club. It was situated just off Berwick Street in London's Soho and had become an important landmark with the City's more flamboyant occupants. This was partially due to the affluent ambience of the club. The easy availability of cocaine within the premises enhanced its attraction.

Chapter Two

Melissa Grant had arrived at the Aphelion Hotel on the afternoon of the party. My address as Katrina Marshall was not suitable for our double identity. Melissa had often used the Aphelion in the past. It protected my identity and was a convenient centre for her operation.

We had travelled by black cab from the hotel to the party at the Lanthanum. As the club became closer even Melissa's nerves began to show. Her hands shook slightly as she lit a cigarette with her flip-top, Zippo, lighter. I relied on the strength of her personality to see us both through. If she was worried, then I was more so. On occasions such as this I allowed Melissa's personality to guide us. Katrina Marshall slipped more into her sub-conscious.

Carlo Ramiro's reputation had travelled before him. I knew all about him. The importance of his family within the drug dealing fraternity was not something to be trifled with. Whilst no agency had succeeded with proof, intelligence gained by those agencies supported the family's worth. Of the few people that had crossed the Ramiro family, several had simply disappeared. One had subsequently been found, floating close to shore off Florida Keys. A British connection moved slowly along the Thames, towards the open sea, the weights securing him to the riverbed having broken free, and then there was the Colombian neck-tie, a punishment and death to be remembered.

The doorman at the Lanthanum had watched as Melissa's long legs emerged from the cab. If it had been me, I'm sure he would not have watched so intently. What was it about Melissa? I created her, yet I couldn't compete with her.

Melissa was aware that the doorman was the only arbiter of her entry to the party. When paying the taxi-driver she ensured that the attributes of her slender body were emphasised for the benefit of the doorman. With her back to him and keeping her legs straight she bent forward from the waist to look through the cab window. Her short, cocktail dress rode further up her thighs, her prominent posterior was not to be missed. There were times that she really pissed me off.

She walked towards the doorman slowly. Her handbag was slung, with both straps over her shoulder, in a casual manner. The speed of her walk was designed to enhance the sway of her hips. Her legs were lengthened by the high stiletto heels, her trim calves detailed accordingly.

"Hi, I've come to wish Carlo happy birthday. I've got a present for him." Melissa winked at the doorman.

"How do you know about the party?" His face remained impassive.

"Katrina told me about it. She's coming along later. She's going to meet me here."

Not a million miles from the truth, I thought.

Melissa had played a bluff. She hoped that the doorman would swallow the explanation without any more questions. He paused for a moment and looked Melissa up and down. He could not remember Katrina, but then he could not remember most of the girls that followed the Ramiro entourage. Here was another that obviously wanted to join. Melissa was apparently of the calibre required. I could see his mind slowly progressing. He was transparent. Perhaps if nobody else wanted her, she might go for him later, he thought.

"In your dreams," was my response. I didn't say it. This was Melissa's act.

"OK, go in." He stood to one side and allowed her to pass.

The club was thronged with people. As Melissa walked into the entrance, several heads turned to look at the newcomer. The Lanthanum was based around a single hall. A bar ran along the left wall. It was richly finished in mahogany. A decorative shelf above the bar supported glasses. The wall behind was mirrored to reflect the bottles in front of it. To the right of the bar were tables around which six people could sit. Behind these, towards the back of the club was a small, polished dance-floor. A group played on a stage nearby. The music was a mixture of Blues and Soul.

The atmosphere within the club was a heavy blend of perfume and smoke. I could detect the sweet, sickly smell of smoked cannabis. The mood was relaxed. A couple danced to the slow music. They hung in each other's arms, their feet barely moving. They danced from the hips; the movement more evident in the top halves of their bodies. They were locked together and danced in unison.

Melissa moved towards the bar. Although crowded, the queue for service was no more than two deep. She slipped between those waiting. She awaited the attendance of the busy barman.

"Scotch and water." She ordered on his arrival.

"Ice?"

She nodded. The drink was served in a large glass. She began to open her handbag in an offer to pay.

"It's on the house tonight, the Boss's birthday," smiled the barman.

Melissa took the drink and walked away from the bar. She threaded her way through the tables to reach the far wall. She rested against it for me to survey the crowd. I knew nobody. I was totally alone. I would have to correct that soon, I thought.

I had been uncertain whether to accept this assignment. I had been a police officer for six years and employed in undercover operations for four. My introduction to this shady side of police work was from a current boyfriend at the time. He was long gone and good riddance, Bastard! He was a police officer similarly employed, but not any longer. He was sacked for corruption, turned sides, rolled onto his back. He deserved everything he got; He was lucky not to have gripped the rails at the Old Bailey. It was a close count.

I had started on relatively minor operations, purchasing cannabis from street dealers. Having become a trusted member of the elite, Scotland Yard, team my employment had increased in importance and accordingly risk.

My team leader, Detective Chief Inspector Phil Shanks was sitting behind his desk, in the fifth-floor office, when I walked in. He saw me as a petite girl with long blonde hair. My large, round, red-framed glasses enlarged my blue eyes. I wore jeans and trainers. My check shirt was covered with a padded anorak. He did not fancy me, and I wanted to keep it that way.

"Katrina, meet Duncan Trevellian. He's a Detective Inspector on the drugs squad."

Shanks indicated Trevellian, who had been sitting behind the door, out of my sight. "He's got a job for you."

"Hello Katrina."

A long pause took place while he took the opportunity to examine me. I felt his eyes intrude into my very being. "I don't know if you've ever heard of Carlo Ramiro."

During his pause I took the opportunity to sit down. "He's the Colombian cocaine dealer, isn't he?"

Trevellian nodded. I looked at him as he spoke. In his mid-thirties, he was dressed in a formal grey suit and white shirt. Unusually, he wore the official CID tie, dark blue with thin white diagonal stripes. He had obviously dressed up for his visit to Scotland Yard. Trevellian was clean-cut with short, brown, brushed back hair. He looked fit. His face was slightly tanned. I liked what I saw but gave no indication.

"We've touched the edge of the Ramiro Empire on several occasions but all we ever get is bit part players. On a couple of occasions, we've taken out the odd kilo of coke, but whenever we've got close to the main team something goes wrong. We've got a snout working and he tells us that Carlo Ramiro is coming to London within the next week or so. We want to nick him with his pockets full. We don't want him getting away with it. That means we need somebody to get close to him. Phil, here, reckons that you're that person."

"Who's going to protect me?" I asked directly.

I wanted to know. My safety was the most important part of the operation, as far as I was concerned, and should have been the central issue, as far as anyone else was concerned. Unfortunately, this was not always the case.

"I am. I've selected my own team for this operation. Anybody who's slightly suspect is out. Each of them is sworn to secrecy, as are you and Phil. I can't overstate the risks, but we'll give you the best cover we can."

"What's Ramiro doing over here? I thought he was based in Miami?"

"He is. The British end of the business has been organised by Juan Marco, his sidekick. But he's not been over here permanently either. It seems like one of the employees has been taking the piss, creaming off the top of some of the deals. We believe that Carlo's come over to sort the problem out, to put the family firmly back in control."

"But Ramiro kills people, doesn't he?" I knew the answer to the question, as did Trevellian.

"I said there will be risks, you know them as well as I do. Are you in or not?"

I nodded. I appreciated the risks from the outset, but also the thrills. There was nothing to beat the adrenaline surge as the job came off. This one would be the pinnacle of my short career so far. The buzz would be enormous.

"We know that the Ramiro family has a warehouse down at Rotherhithe. It's a big place and always loaded up, so it will be difficult to search. We want you to place the drugs and put Carlo with them. What about it?"

I agreed without second thought. Unfortunately, I nearly always did. Undercover work was far more interesting than standard police work and I still needed to establish myself as one of the best. I could not afford to turn down a decent job and did not intend to do so.

With that agreement Duncan Trevellian went on to explain the occurrence of the birthday party and detail his general plan for the operation. The finer details would be down to me. I would be assisted by his intelligence. His information was good, his source reliable. This was the one opportunity he would have to break the Ramiro power-base.

Phil Shanks had said little throughout but watched the reaction of the two of us. He generally did this. He needed to know that his Undercover would be acceptable to the team and vice-versa. He would confirm later but I knew from that moment that Trevellian and I appeared to gel.

Detective Chief Inspector Phil Shanks was in sole command of his undercover team and selected its members. The archetypal policeman was of no use to him. He would be recognised as such the instant he was used. Shanks looked for the unusual, perhaps the defective. That's probably why he chose me. The selection procedure within the Metropolitan Police found a certain type to fit the mould of the uniformed constable. Many personalities slipped through the net, however, or many changed once established within the Service.

Shanks probably saw me as one of these. He had told me previously that he would not have selected me as a police officer. I was not physically impressive, nor mentally domineering. My timidity, he saw as an endearing factor. I refrained from telling him to shove the job up his arse. That would not have been timid, not an endearing factor.

Shanks had not been looking for police officers, however. His operatives could not afford to be identified as such by their targets. Apparently, I fitted the bill. He had pulled my personal record prior to selection and studied it closely. He was not concerned at my difficulties in passing the initial training, nor my noted lack of aggression. His own training emphasised different attributes and often totally contradicted those early techniques. He liked my musical flair. I played several instruments including rock guitar. I had been trained in dance at an early age, starting at an enforced ballet class as a five-year old. I hated it, but my mother would not listen. She drove me there after school, each Wednesday for two years, until she finally agreed with the teacher that I would never make a ballet dancer. However, I exaggerated my abilities and convinced Shanks that this drew me outside the standard personification of a police officer.

DCI Shanks was straightforward in his expectations. My undercover role required disguise. This would be achieved by the development of an alter-identity. Mine was Melissa. I grew to know her and like her, even sometimes to rely on her. Did I aspire to be Melissa Grant? I did not know, nor care. It worked for me.

Melissa sipped her drink as I looked around the club. Carlo Ramiro was easily identified. I had already seen his photograph. Duncan Trevellian had been in contact with the Miami police. They had e-mailed an intelligence photograph of Ramiro. The original was sent by dispatch.

"It was a good likeness." Melissa murmured to us both as we saw him.

Carlo Ramiro was a small man, just five feet eight. His weather worn skin took him beyond his forty years. The sun had aged him. His face was lined at the eyes and mouth. His hair had not receded. It was black and full, neatly parted to the left side. It was lightly gelled to keep it in place. Carlo sported a, carefully groomed, moustache, which emphasised his broad smile. He was dressed in a black evening suit with a hand-tied, silk, bow-tie. In his right hand, between his thumb and first finger, he held a large Colombian cigar.

Ramiro was surrounded by a crowd of well-wishers. Whilst some were apparently friends, there was no doubt in my mind that some of the girls were merely camp followers. It was this competition that Melissa would have to beat. I knew that she would achieve nothing by a direct approach. The girls would carefully protect their advantage.

Melissa looked around the club and spotted what she sought. The toilets were situated next to each other, close to the dance-floor. She emptied the remnants of her drink into her mouth and walked to the ladies' rest-room. Once inside she locked herself securely inside a cubicle. Here I was able to relax for a moment and calm my worn nerves. I regained Melissa's composure before leaving the protective enclave. Within the confines of the powder room, she checked and adjusted her dress and make-up. She left the toilet but did not walk far. I carefully chose her next location. It was in the direct path of those men using the toilet. They all had to pass her.

"I wish you'd get off my case." Melissa's Liverpudlian voice whispered to me, as we stood alone. "You haven't got the bottle for this sort of job. Why don't you just leave it to me?"

"Bugger off!"

This was the only response I could think of. I was not having that bitch tell me what to do. Melissa and I often had short arguments. I was pleased that I had always won so far.

I had selected Melissa's target. My observations revealed that whilst Carlo had an impenetrable ring around him his right-hand man was vulnerable. Juan Marco was younger than Carlo, in his late-thirties. He had worked for the Ramiro family since his youth. He was a trusted friend although still an employee. I knew all this through intelligence. Juan recognised his position. Whilst privileged, it was precarious, but he was careful to ensure it remained secure. Juan had arranged the party on behalf of Paulo Ramiro. Aware of Paulo's pedantic nature, he wished everything to be perfect. For several days he had busied himself, searching for that perfection. He stood at Carlo's side, providing drinks when his glass was empty and fending off the attention of unwanted guests. As the evening wore on, he began to relax. He was now beginning to enjoy himself. I learned this later.

Juan Marco emptied the remaining lager from his glass. He walked towards the toilet.

Juan noticed the auburn-haired, Melissa Grant, as he passed her. At that moment I wish he had noticed me. He didn't, he couldn't see past the disguise that was Melissa. Sometimes I regretted my job. She wore a short, burgundy red, cocktail dress. The thin gold chain showed her slender neckline in its best form. She was good. I wished I could have been better, but I wasn't. He entered the toilet and relieved the pressure on his bowel. On his return he was therefore more relaxed.

Melissa looked straight at him as he approached. I might have turned away.

"Great party!" A smile lit her face.

Juan slowed immediately. "Are you enjoying yourself?"

"Yes, It's great. I've been watching you. You've obviously put all this together for Carlo, haven't you?"

Juan was flattered that his efforts had been noticed. "Yes, it wasn't easy. It's taken days."

"You've done really well. Carlo should be honoured to have a friend like you. I know I would be."

"Thank you." Marco looked around. "Are you with anyone?"

"No, I'm here alone."

"Well, perhaps we could dance." Juan held out his hand to Melissa.

"I'd like that. I'm Melissa."

"And I'm Juan Marco, how do you do?"

Juan led Melissa to the dance floor. He too was dressed in evening attire. It set off his swarthy South American complexion. He was taller than Carlo, perhaps five feet eleven inches. He was clean-shaven, his face having defined lines. His clear brown eyes were piercing. He spoke clear, fluent English although with a heavy South American accent. I knew Melissa fancied him. I did too.

The dance floor was relatively empty, only two other couples braving the attention of others. The group were playing the old Wilson Pickett number, 'In the midnight hour'. Juan had clear rhythm. As we walked onto the dance-floor he turned to Melissa, spinning her under his arm as he did so. Being ready and alert she read his intentions and responded in a relaxed but stylish manner. She was a competent dancer who enjoyed the activity. Fortunately, I taught her all she knew. It was only occasionally that I thanked my mother for the ballet classes. This was one of those times. We fell into a slow, rhythmic jive, moving with the music, gently across the floor. I noticed as Carlo's attention was drawn to his friend's performance.

"Who is she?" he asked another guest. He received no useful information. He watched Melissa and Juan Marco intently.

I knew that the first dance was the most important. Whilst Juan's feet did not move much, his body swayed with the beat. This was perfect for Melissa. We were showing her for Carlo's benefit. She similarly moved from the hip, enticing Juan with her body. She bent her head back, highlighting the swan-like curves of her spine. In holding Juan's hand, she read his lead, turning and moving in response to his slightest gestures.

"You dance well," Marco complemented her.

"Thank you." Her smile was broad.

"And you are beautiful as well."

Melissa threw back her head, laughing in response. She held out her other hand to Juan. He took it and she slowly pulled him to her. Their bodies eased together, moving as one. Melissa put her arms around Marco's neck, although holding her head back to look him in the eye. I approved.

"You look good to me as well." She smiled.

I found out later that Carlo had been unable to identify the mystery girl that danced with his friend. Those he asked had no knowledge of her. Whilst Melissa was not the most beautiful girl in the room, she had an aura about her that attracted him. It was possibly the way she moved on the dance floor. Her body was slim, perhaps over-so. However, her expertise on the dance-floor was unmatched. She was clearly enjoying herself with Juan. He was impressed. He was determined to meet her.

Melissa danced with Juan Marco for several minutes. As the third number finished, she pulled back from him.

"Can we get a drink? I'm over-heating," she explained, wiping her forehead with the back of her hand but being careful not to disturb her make-up or my disguise.

"Of course." Juan led her from the floor towards Carlo. "What are you drinking?"

"Scotch and water please, with ice." Melissa could handle it, I couldn't. Sometimes I wondered why we were so different yet so alike.

"A potent drink," mused Juan.

"For a potent girl," smiled Melissa innocently.

The couple approached the bar. Carlo watched them with interest. They stood a few feet from him. As Juan Marco ordered their drinks Carlo moved to them:

"Will you introduce us, Juan?"

Marco turned to Ramiro. "Carlo, this is Melissa. I'm sorry, I don't know your surname."

"Grant," smiled Melissa as she held out her hand to Carlo.

She looked into his eyes. He held her eye contact. He took her outstretched hand and raised it to his lips. He kissed the back of her hand. As he lowered it, he gently stroked the back with his other hand. I cringed at his touch. Melissa's smile further enticed him. It was a half-smile, so alluring. Bitch!

"Your skin is soft, are your lips so?" His tone of voice was sensual.

I was tempted to tell him where to go. Had I have been Katrina Marshall, drinking in a pub, when approached with such a moronic line, I would have done so. I was not Katrina Marshall; I was Melissa Grant and I had a job to do.

Juan returned with the drinks, saving Melissa from an answer. She took the glass in her free hand, failing to release Carlo's grip. She prised their eye contact apart. She turned to Juan:

"Thank you."

If Juan Marco was disappointed, he did not show it. Carlo Ramiro was his friend and employer. They had been close for many years. This had been achieved by Juan serving his master and putting Ramiro's needs above his own. This case would be no exception. Whilst he was attracted to Melissa, Carlo's response needed no interpretation. He had claimed his right at his own birthday party. It was a right that would receive no argument from Juan. Marco turned smoothly away to engage one of the camp followers in conversation.

"Melissa, it is a nice name. I don't think we have met before?"

"No, but I've heard of you, obviously. By the way, happy birthday." She leant towards him and gently kissed his cheek. "I'm afraid I have no other present for you."

"Oh, but I think you have."

"Cretin!" I thought. Melissa said nothing.

The couple still held hands. It was evident to me that Carlo had taken the bait. Now, would he swallow the hook?

Just time now to gently reel him in, I thought. I hoped Melissa agreed.

"Will you dance with me?" She asked.

"I'd be delighted." Carlo put down his drink and they walked to the dance-floor.

The band was relaxing from vocal numbers. They retained a heavy blues beat in their slow, instrumental period. Carlo was completely different to Juan. He was not a natural dancer. His size and swarthiness went against him. He took Melissa in his arms from the outset, holding her left hand in his right. He would obviously take time to relax. She moved with him, allowing her body to mimic his movements. I began to feel the tension ease from him.

"I'm not a good dancer." He apologised.

"I think you're very good," Melissa flattered and flirted.

This pleased Ramiro. He did not like to be criticised, he liked to be complemented.

"Where do you come from, Melissa Grant?"

"Well, originally, from Liverpool, but I've lived in the South for many years."

"And what are you doing at my birthday party?"

"I intended to meet a friend here. She uses the club regularly and had been invited. It seems that she hasn't turned up."

"I'm here, Bitch!" I thought vehemently.

"I am pleased that she did not arrive. I might not have spoken to you." His English was good but heavily accented.

Ramiro released his grip on her hand and put both arms around her waist. She responded by putting her arms around his neck, allowing her head to fall onto his shoulder. Her high heels made her almost the same height as Ramiro. I was not therefore in the most comfortable position. I suffered in silence, I had to.

They danced together for over thirty minutes. Other guests had noticed the entrapment. A certain jealousy was evident amongst some of the single girls. Ramiro's friends were surprised that he had succumbed so quickly. The couple said little as they moved together to the rhythm. The band was aware of their principal, that evening, and recognised his needs on the dance-floor. The music remained slow and melodic. They finally left the floor. They walked together, bound as one. Carlo's arm held Melissa tightly. Her arm remained around his back. Carlo ordered drinks. Melissa sipped her third scotch and water. Maybe I could grow to like it.

"So why have you come to London?" She asked, trying to be merely inquisitive.

Wrong question, I immediately thought.

"Why do you ask?"

"I was just interested. You live in the US, don't you?"

"Business, purely business, but I have found some time for fun."

He laughed and kissed her lips. She responded accordingly.

"I know about your business, Carlo. I'd like to see more."

Had Melissa gone too far? It was certainly further than I would have dared go. I was nervous for her, but more nervous for myself.

"Maybe, we'll see."

The subject was dropped, but the idea had been implanted in Ramiro's head. They talked more generally whilst they finished their drinks.

"Do we have to stay here?" His thought was clear.

"What do you have in mind?"

"Come with me."

I was reluctant, I hoped Melissa similarly so. A haze of fear muddied my mind. Should she refuse, or should she go? I tried to analyse the consequences of each action. If she did not go with him, we stood to lose the advantage she had gained. If she went, she could put us both at unnecessary risk. I had not made her decision as Ramiro took her hand and led her to the rear of the club. We followed meekly and with uncertainty.

The door, close to the toilets, had 'Private-keep out' etched upon it. Another large doorman stood to one side preventing unauthorised entry. I had noticed the door earlier but thought little about it. Ramiro pushed it open and we passed through. We walked along a corridor, past the kitchens. Carlo stopped at a locked door at the end of the passage. He took a key from his pocket and opened the door. We walked into a large office. Carlo went to a centrally positioned, green-leathered, desk and turned on a curved desk-light. The soft light illuminated the room.

I looked around. This was obviously the club manager's office. It was tastefully decorated in heavy wallpaper. The carpet was colour co-ordinated and of rich quality. Similarly, no expense had been spared on the furniture. Behind the desk was a matching, leather bound, swivel chair. In the area in front of the desk was a coffee table and easy chairs. Fresh flowers languished in a vase on the table.

Carlo turned to face Melissa. She took his outstretched hands and allowed herself to be pulled towards him. He kissed her lips.

"Shit, what do I do?" I thought. I breathed in imperceptibly.

She responded, though avoiding the touch of his roaming tongue on mine.

"Thank you, Melissa." I could not speak my thanks. Carlo's lips were still exploring my own. Besides, if Melissa or I were to ramble incoherently, Ramiro would certainly become suspicious.

He stopped to remove his jacket. He hung it neatly over a chair and then walked back to Melissa. He kissed her again. My mind was racing. Typical of Melissa, she let me do all the worrying. At all costs she had to avoid sex with him whilst retaining the intimacy of their relationship. This was the only way that she would achieve the objective of the operation, to place him with his commodity, cocaine.

Melissa Grant felt the pressure of Ramiro's body. I felt it even more. She liked it, I didn't. She moved back slowly to avoid it, but only because I forced the issue. He moved with her. I suddenly found an obstruction that prevented further retreat. He had backed her onto the desk. His hands were exploring her body. I tried to tell her it was mine, but she just wouldn't listen. Her long fingers remained static on his back for fear of encouraging him further. I felt his hands run down the curves of her back until they were behind her thighs. He gently lifted her and sat her on the edge of the desk. Her legs were slightly apart, his body between them. His hand reached her inner thigh, above the upper limit of her black stockings. She placed her hand over it, stopping him from exploring further. She separated their lips.

"Carlo," she said softly. "Not tonight, I can't tonight." Her emphasis inferred an underlying reason.

He pulled her head back towards him. He kissed her again. He was aroused and did not want to stop. Bastard!

"Carlo, I can't tonight. I've deceived you slightly. I have an ulterior motive for being here. I'm also in the business, although to a lesser degree, of course. I need a new supplier. I was hoping that you might help me."

I improvised, but my efforts stopped Ramiro's activities. He looked at Melissa. He reached into the top pocket of his dinner jacket. Between his fingers he removed a small polythene bag. It was only two inches square. I could see a small quantity of pure white powder. I knew what it was.

"How about this," he asked. "Would this help?"

"Is that all you've got? I thought you'd got lots of the stuff." I hoped her eyes showed that she was joking.

"You'd be surprised at how much I've got." Ramiro boasted.

"I'd love to see, and maybe try and buy."

"Perhaps you will. But what about now?"

"Carlo, not now. Business first and then, who knows."

He paused and looked into her eyes. Melissa matched his gaze, showing sincerity.

"OK, next time, but it had better be." His emphasis on the latter words caused a chill to run down my spine. He put the cocaine back into his pocket.

Chapter Three

So it was that Melissa and I found ourselves in the back of the Mercedes, heading towards her date with Carlo Ramiro. He had taken her first rejection well. We returned to the bar of the club and continued drinking together. At midnight he received the telephone call from his father. This had pleased him. He was in a relaxed mood when we parted. Melissa left just after midnight, before the party finished. They kissed goodbye, the next meeting having already been arranged.

Duncan Trevellian was deeply concerned when I reported Melissa's progress the following day.

"Kat," he chose to shorten my name. I did not object though was uncertain both as to his familiarity and the sounding of my shortened handle. Did I look feline? I certainly hadn't purred at him.

"We can't let you go on with this. It's just too much of a risk."

"No, I think it will be OK," I tried to re-assure him. "Ramiro wasn't too bad. I was able to fend him off. After all, this is too important to call it off now."

"It is important, but not as important as you. What will you do next time? You've almost committed yourself, haven't you?"

"I reckon I can stall him all right. All I've got to do is to get him to take Melissa to the drugs and that's the end of him. It shouldn't be too difficult."

"I'm not happy with it." Trevellian's discontent could be seen in his face. He was trying to think of other options. There were none.

"Kat, you've got to be careful. At the first sign of anything going wrong you pull out. OK? And if you can't get out, you give the signal and we'll come in. Do you understand?" He was forceful in his final words.

Duncan Trevellian's serious attitude reflected his concern. It worried me. Was I in too deep? I nodded agreement. I did not smile. I threw up my dinner that night for the first time in ages. It was only a Big Mac, so I didn't feel it was wasted. It seemed natural to stick my fingers down my throat even though it was an experience of the past. I did it to relieve the tension. I don't know whether it worked or not. I resolved not to do it again, not regularly at least.

The Mercedes had rounded Hyde Park Corner and headed south towards Westminster Bridge. You can never rely on third hand information, but this is what I was told. I'm sure that certain aspects were left out, particularly when my safety was compromised. I didn't ask too many questions about events not witnessed by me and therefore I can only report the recounted facts of these matters.

From there the Mercedes turned left towards Waterloo and onwards to Southwark. Southwark Street caused the surveillance team their first problem. A traffic jam caused by unattended road-works blocked the narrow roadway. The following Ford Mondeo, manned by Trevellian's team, was blocked by a lorry. The Mercedes turned sharp right into a side road to avoid the congestion.

"I've lost him," came over the radio. "He's done a right. I've lost sight of him."

"Somebody get up there with him." Trevellian instructed.

Only a short delay occurred whilst the Ford manoeuvred into the side road. The Mercedes was, however, out of sight. The officers followed an assumed route but could find no trace of the car.

"Bomb-burst and find them," ordered Trevellian over the radio.

Trevellian's order followed its description closely. The team exploded from their organised system, searching all side and main roads for the vehicle. As a series of 'no trace' was reported to the Detective Inspector his confidence began to wane. He had pushed forward into Tooley Street towards Jamaica Road. He was coming to terms with the loss when suddenly the Mercedes emerged from a side turning, indicating to turn right before him. He promptly picked up his radio handset:

"Contact, contact. I have him, heading east in Tooley Street, all units come up quick."

Trevellian breathed a sigh of relief. He feared that they had lost the vehicle and with it the protection that I desperately needed. His concentration took him past the aged beauty of Tower Bridge without noticing. No other untoward incidents occurred during the journey.

In contrast, I had a pleasant, if nerve racking journey. We were south of the River Thames and travelling to the east of the city. This was an area that had been regenerated in recent years. The riverside had been developed with up-market bars and restaurants and HMS Belfast, a light cruiser built for the Royal Navy, was now permanently moored on the River Thames next to Tower Bridge. It was now open to the public and designed to encourage tourists to the area. The Shard at three hundred metres was one of the tallest buildings in London and dominated the skyline just off Tooley Street. Regardless the route was not the best-loved in London and the back streets remained uncertain areas for the un-initiated.

As the car finally stopped in a Rotherhithe side street, I felt my heartbeat surge. Melissa slowly leaned forward to open the car door. We stepped from the car. I suppressed the urge to look around, seeking my support. The driver pointed to a warehouse door to the right of the car.

"In there, in the office up on the right."

Melissa walked to the warehouse door, looking straight ahead.

"Upward and onward, girl," she whispered to me in her Liverpudlian accent. Her certainty gave me more confidence.

There was a wide, roller door for vehicular access and a small door to its right for pedestrians. She pushed the door. It was locked. There was a bell push at shoulder level. She pressed it. A loud bell rang within the warehouse. The door opened.

"Yes", said the man.

"Carlo Ramiro, he's expecting me. Melissa Grant."

"Miss Grant, come in." The door opened, and she walked through. "Go up the stairs over to the right and into the office above. Go right in."

I looked around. It was not a large warehouse although it was fully stocked with goods. I thought that it would certainly be difficult to search. I looked towards the steps that Melissa was expected to climb. They were open, wooden steps, leading to an office above. The office had large windows overlooking the warehouse complex. Vertical blinds hung at the windows. They were closed.

I assessed the opposition for Melissa. I could see few other people in the warehouse. The man who had opened the door remained at that position behind Melissa. Another four men stood as guards within the premises. I could not see if they were armed. One stood by a second black Mercedes that was parked within the roller door. Similar to the first, the tinted windows obscured the interior. Another three men were visible, working within the warehouse, moving the crates. Melissa walked to the stairs and began to ascend.

"Be careful," I told her as we walked up.

"I always am," was the certain reply.

On reaching the top of the flight of stairs Melissa walked to the door of the office. She tapped on it and looked through. Carlo Ramiro was standing by a desk, talking on the telephone. He waved her into the room. She walked in and stood close to the door. It was some minutes before the call was completed. Ramiro appeared to be speaking Spanish. I did not understand.

"Hello Melissa." Carlo put down the telephone and walked towards her. "It's good to see you again." He took hold of her hand and kissed it. "I'm sorry to have to bring you here, work you know. We'll go out to dinner later. You wanted to see the business did you not?"

"Yes, I did. I thought it would be more spectacular."

"Little in business is spectacular, Melissa my dear."

Carlo opened a drink cabinet against the wall.

"Whisky and water isn't it?"

"Yes please."

"But not today. You will have Aguardiente, a drink of Colombia."

He poured the drink and handed it to her. It was in a shot glass. He had poured himself a similar glass. Melissa briefly smelled the content. The aroma was of dark rum and aniseed. I assessed it as strong and decided to close Melissa's eyes as she swallowed. I failed.

"In one." Ramiro clinked glasses with Melissa.

Her eyes did not close. She held Ramiro's eye-line.

"Salud." She downed the drink in one as directed.

Regardless, the conversation was superficial and guarded. Neither was relaxed. There was something about Carlo Ramiro. He appeared colder, more calculating. I was particularly nervous, I felt the acid rise in my throat, my stomach churned, and I hoped he didn't hear the noise it made. My nervousness reflected in Melissa's behaviour. I shouldn't have let it.

"Are you all right?" Ramiro appeared concerned. I was not convinced.

"Yes, I'm fine." This was Melissa answering.

Carlo poured another drink. Melissa did not down it in one this time. As she drank it, I began to relax. This was probably due to alcohol absorption. It became clear that Ramiro wished Melissa to relax further. He produced the small bag of cocaine.

"Shit," I thought. Melissa did not respond.

"What about now. You said you want to try before you buy."

Melissa paused thoughtfully before finally nodding assent. "Why not, but with what?" She raised her hands to emphasise the question.

Ramiro looked around the desk. From one of the drawers he took a wooden box. He opened the lid. Inside I saw a small set of scales and other implements for use in the taking of drugs. The items were silver, or, at least, appeared so. Carlo took from the box a silver tube.

"This will do."

Carlo Ramiro opened the polythene bag with small scissors, from within the box, and carefully tipped the contents onto the desk. With the blade of the scissors he divided the white powder into two piles then spread it into two parallel lines. He held out the tube.

"No, you first", Melissa told him.

Ramiro held the tube to his nose. With the other hand he blocked his unused nostril and then snorted the coke through the tube into the other. He held it out to Melissa. She took it from him and copied his actions. As she did so Ramiro turned to wipe the cocaine remnants from his nose with his handkerchief. As Melissa snorted through the tube my hand covered the cocaine track. Ramiro did not see as Melissa swept it to the floor rather than inhaling it. This was an exercise that I had practised many times in the past to protect my cover. I had never expected to execute it.

"I'd call that an unacceptable waste, Mr Ramiro."

The voice was unfamiliar to me. Melissa turned quickly, leaning back against the desk as she did so. In the doorway of the small room, leaning against the surround and with arms crossed, over a blue overcoat, I saw a man I had not seen before. He was, perhaps, fifty years of age, although looking older. A wry smile cracked his lower jaw, beneath the blue homburg hat. His tie was loosened. He looked drunk, or drugged, perhaps both. A swirl of panic clouded me. I suddenly foresaw horrible consequences.

The effect of the cocaine did not make Carlo incoherent. Nor did it lessen his authority.

"You could have knocked."

"I was about to, but you were busy."

"And what, may I ask, is unacceptable waste?"

"Your girl here, she obviously wasn't impressed". The man walked further into the office as he spoke.

"Your cocaine's now firmly embedded into the floor, currently under the sole of her shoe."

He had reached Melissa and confronted her. She did not move. Her eyes affixed on his, I later remembered the granite grey of his eyes. He was the first to look away. He took Melissa's arm and prised her from the spot. He reached to the floor and firmly drew his index finger across the thin carpet. He displayed the white dust it had attracted to Carlo Ramiro.

"Most expensive yard of carpet I've come across."

"So, my dear Melissa, you deceive me."

Carlo Ramiro was less than pleased. Melissa did not respond. I could not assist her.

"She tells me that she deals in our product, my friend, that she is seeking a new supplier. It seems now that she might not be telling the truth."

"I wasn't lying, Carlo." Melissa Grant did not finish her explanation.

"Shut up." Ramiro turned and pointed a shaking finger at her. "You will not speak until you are spoken to."

"Bastard, bastard, bastard." I was now seriously concerned. I did not speak aloud.

"Then who was your previous supplier?" Homburg's question was direct.

I thought for a moment. "You know better than to ask me that, and I know better than to answer."

Homburg raised an eyebrow. "Cute. She knew the answer to that question, Mr Ramiro. However, there is something wrong. I've met many dealers and this girl is not one of them. She wouldn't be here alone.

talk business; I don't think so."

"Perhaps you're right, my friend."

Ramiro reached to the side of the drink cabinet where a pre-prepared envelope was resting. He picked it out and handed it to the man.

"Five thousand, check it. You have been useful to me and also today. I hope you will continue to be so."

The man opened the envelope and ran his hands over the money. Satisfied that it was genuine he opened his coat and put the envelope in the inner pocket of the suit that he wore beneath. Ramiro poured two large glasses of Scotch. He doused one with water. He gave one to Homburg, the other he held out to Melissa.

"Take it," he instructed. "You will need it later."

I took the glass in a shaking hand and held it tightly. It did not help. Homburg received his gratefully. He said little. He did not have to. The slate grey of his eyes reflected the personality within.

"Thanks for the present."

"No problem, but you have outstayed your welcome."

"Oh shit," I murmured to Melissa, as she was again left alone with Ramiro. The look on his face clearly identified his annoyance. Could we retrieve the situation? I doubted it.

"Carlo, please listen to me," Melissa pleaded as he approached her.

I was frozen to the spot. There was little room for manoeuvre. I considered the options quickly. I only saw one; kick him in the groin with all my might and run. I doubted that I would make the stairs. Before I could react he was on top of me, pawing me. He was close to me. I could smell his body, his breath. He smelt of sweat, not body lotion. His breath was a mixture of cigar and alcohol. Did I sense garlic? I couldn't be sure.

Even now I have limited memories of what happened next. At the time I was aware that he was all over me. His hands went straight to my skirt, pulling it upwards, over my hips. I raised Melissa's knee, catching him firmly in the groin. He stepped backwards, bent forward at the hips, holding his crutch. He looked at me. He was in pain, good job!

"You bitch, I'm going to have you, you're mine now."

The look in his eyes terrified me. They were cold and piercing.

"Where the fuck is Trevellian?" I thought as I ran, intending to reach the window, to signal him.

I had to pass Ramiro. As I did so he grabbed my arm, pulling me back. He secured me with his second hand and pushed me back over the desk. I was frantic. I knew what to expect. I feared the worst. My arms flayed. I reached at his face and with the long, developed nails of

Melissa's right hand, drew them down his cheek. Blood welled from the injury. He reached to his face with his hand and surveyed the blood. There was no further speech. He drew his right hand back and struck Melissa on the chin with his fist. My head snapped back. A misty haze crossed my eyes. I drifted into semi-consciousness.

I have worked hard to accept and acknowledge the events of the next few minutes. I felt myself being lifted onto the desk. I could smell and feel the man above me. I tried to fight him. I did not see him take the cocaine from his pocket. He tore it open with his teeth. I felt him compress the side of my jaw with one hand, forcing my mouth open. I tried to resist by moving my head from side to side. I felt the powder as it trickled onto my lips and my tongue. Eventually both went numb. I could not spit it out. I swallowed.

Slowly but surely the cocaine began to take effect. I had not experienced it before. Whilst still aware of the circumstances and surroundings, my will to resist began to fail me. A nausea overcame me that soon passed into a sense of relaxation and well-being. My co-ordination was lost. I knew I should fight, but I did not know how or whom. I lay my head back on the desk. The only words I could remember were:

"Help me."

I was aware that Ramiro had entered me. I was unable to stop him. He had torn apart the crutch of my knickers to remove that obstruction. He pulled my legs violently apart. He had already loosened his trousers. He pushed himself into me regardless of any damage he might cause. I remember feeling the pain of his entry. The cocaine was not sufficiently effective to cover it. It hurt me deeply. I remember opening my eyes.

Above me I could see the figure of the man as he forced intercourse. I could not prevent it. I tried to focus on him but could not. I looked at him. My past came forward to haunt me. I was in my thirteenth year. I was not in a warehouse in Rotherhithe. I was in my home. The man above me was not a stranger. I looked more closely, I should recognise him, but did not. Who was the man that abused me now? I focused further. The view of the second man drifted away, Ramiro re-appearing. The intercourse had finished. I had felt his action as he ejaculated. He had withdrawn from me. He stood above me, securing his trousers and coat. I heard his footsteps as he walked down the stairs.

Chapter Four

I could not move. I was aware that I had been raped. Initially I remained where I was, seeking composure. I struggled to clear my muddied brain. It took several minutes to focus my attentions and realise the true force of the occurrence. I pulled myself to my feet, pulling my skirt back into place. I put Melissa's hand to my jaw. It was painful and bruised.

I initially staggered around the room in no particular direction. Melissa was forgotten, this was me. The events of the evening, together with cocaine and alcohol, left me undecided and emotional. Tears fell down my cheeks as I sobbed uncontrollably. A mirror was affixed to the back of the door. As I moved, I saw my reflection. The care I had taken on Melissa's appearance was in ruin. My make-up was streaked and running. A large black bruise had grown on my chin. My jaw was swollen. I looked more closely. The inside of my mouth had obviously been cut when Ramiro had struck me. A trickle of blood existed at the side corner. I rocked towards the mirror in an effort to concentrate. My head fell against the glass and I rested there for a moment. It took all my effort to pull myself upright. I opened my mouth to look for the cut. My lips and tongue were swollen. I saw traces of white powder inside my mouth. I recognised it as cocaine.

With difficulty I tilted my head to look down my body at my clothing. My silk blouse had been torn open. The camisole top was also torn. My breasts were partially exposed. I pulled the top together with one hand. I continued to cry. I pulled my skirt back into place. It was badly creased and stained, but intact. I did not remove my damaged pants. My stockings were laddered and holed. I was a wreck.

I tried to straighten myself. I could not.

"Why am I here?" I asked the mirror image. It did not answer.

"Who am I? Melissa Grant. No, no I'm not, Katrina, Katrina Marshall, that's who I am."

I paused thoughtfully, fighting the effects of the drug. "Police officer. I'm a police officer, but what am I doing here?"

Further vital seconds passed. I remembered. "Ramiro, Carlo Ramiro. that bastard."

I continued to fight the debilitating effects of the cocaine. I walked to the blinds covering the window and opened them slightly. I looked down into the warehouse below.

I had failed to control Carlo Ramiro. He had tired of Melissa Grant. He had wanted, and expected, sex from her on the first night they met. I should have recognised the risk at that stage and called off the operation. Why else was Melissa at his party? He had liked her. He was aware that she had put him off but was prepared to accept that. She had made it clear that she would be willing next time. The next time had come, and she had rejected him. He could not accept her rejection twice. I didn't know whether he had enjoyed the enforced intercourse. It was Melissa's penalty, or the first of them. The price of her rejection would be absolute.

It was perhaps, unfortunate for me that the visitor had arrived. Carlo would not have noticed Melissa's avoidance of the cocaine. The truth of my tale had not worried him. But the visitor had arrived, and he had emphasised the doubt in Ramiro's mind. In this business there was no room for such doubt, there was too much at stake. The further success of the business depended upon it.

Carlo Ramiro was a callous and brutal man. In that few seconds he had reminded himself of his purpose for being in London. It was purely business, the importation and sale of cocaine. It was far more important than a mere street girl. I subsequently discovered that a consignment had been delivered that day. It had arrived in London in a container lorry from Europe. The passage between the Americas was becoming more difficult to arrange. Transportation was sometimes arranged through Africa, into Spain, by road to Amsterdam and by container to London. In this case the cocaine was contained within the framework of wooden pallets holding the legitimate load. The pallets had been carefully prepared, the wooden struts hollowed for the purpose. Eighty kilos of the drug, with a street value of two million pounds were imported in this way and more was to come.

I believe now that Ramiro's dissatisfaction with Melissa Grant caused him to seek solace with his wealth. He decided to check the importation to ensure its safety. The warehouse had been carefully designed to conceal the illicit consignment. The crates piled high upon each other were virtually impossible to move. They were the perfect cover. As Ramiro walked amongst them he took a remote control from his pocket. It looked like a standard television remote, but when fired at a specific location within the warehouse the intricacies of his trade were revealed.

Carlo Ramiro pushed the button and watched with some satisfaction as the electrically operated turntable whirred into action, swinging a huge alley of crates to one side. Beneath them, built into the floor of the warehouse was a large cavity which was exposed as the crates moved. Carlo looked down at the expanse of cocaine. There was over a metric ton of the white powder. One thousand kilos safely packed away. He admired the load. It cheered him. Ramiro had probably forgotten Melissa. She was in his past.

I looked down into the open warehouse. I saw the open 'grave' containing the cocaine. It was wrapped in cellophane, in individual kilos. I could not estimate how many. I saw Carlo Ramiro standing. I remembered his face and eyes. I graphically remembered the hurt he had caused me.

"The cocaine, he's with the cocaine. Trevellian, where the fuck are you?" I shouted sharply.

I remembered the reserve signal and ran to the office window. I opened the blind wide allowing the light to beam down into the road below. I stood in the light, without moving. I was clearly visible to anyone outside.

I subsequently read the official report of the operation and gleaned further information from Duncan Trevellian. He had been annoyed at their loss of the Mercedes in Southwark, even though it had only been temporary. He was, however, aware of the Rotherhithe warehouse and would have directed his team to that address had they not, again, found the car. This had proved unnecessary and the surveillance continued.

The knowledge had allowed Trevellian to make contingency plans in the event that I was taken to the warehouse. On arrival the team had designated positions and were able to take these up immediately and without direction. Trevellian carefully called each unit on the radio to ensure that they were in position. Whilst most points allowed vehicular access, to provide full cover some officers had to be on foot. Trevellian relied on their individual ingenuity to provide the best cover. Some would disappear into the darkness of a doorway; others would take tea with a local caretaker. One particular officer had been known to sit in a large, roadside dustbin for several hours, to preserve the ambience. Luckily on that occasion his car had been single manned.

The Detective Inspector was the only member of his team to know my true identity. They had all been introduced to Melissa Grant in an initial briefing. They had to recognise her during the operation. If any knew me from the past, as Katrina Marshall, then they did not acknowledge me, nor I, them. All were too professional. It was essential for the success of the operation and my safety, that there was no confusion as to my identity. I was Melissa Grant.

Trevellian had wanted Melissa wired for the operation. I had pointed out that the personal transmitter would be easily detected by Ramiro. It could only be located in the small of my back and taped in position. The microphone would have to be forward facing. I knew that Melissa's dress would not easily conceal the equipment. I did not expect to keep Ramiro totally at arm's length. The wire would put me at risk.

We had compromised. The technical department at Scotland Yard took Melissa's handbag for the day and inserted a false panel. Within that panel lay a transmitter. The microphone was concealed in the fabric of the bag itself, the aerial in the handles. It had been tested from the hotel. The wavelength linked it to a separate receiver retained by Trevellian. It had functioned correctly then. I had no receiver and therefore no way of checking it since.

We had discussed in some detail the back-up signal that I would use if the transmitter failed. It had to be clear, yet easy to adopt. I had to be visible to the team. We chose the simplest and most direct method. Merely for her to open the blind or curtain and stand still at a window. Sufficient time would be given to confirm my intention to signal; although such was my training that the safety net should not be necessary.

Trevellian had received a clear test signal from my hotel room. He had telephoned me to confirm it. His receiver was portable. He had listened to it closely since beginning the surveillance. He was uncertain as to its efficiency. The interference concerned him. The journey was not a good indication. He knew that Melissa would be silent within the car. It was unlikely that the driver would hold a conversation. My arrival at the warehouse did not assist his confidence in the equipment. He heard me directed up the stairs, but the steel framework of the building did nothing to improve reception. He tapped the receiver in an inane effort. He held it close to his ear and turned up the volume. The distortion merely became louder.

My appeal for support burst through Trevellian's receiver just seconds before Melissa was first spotted by Detective Sergeant Fergus Johnstone. Trevellian sat bolt upright as the words injected themselves into his mind. His finger was stopped in mid-tap. 'Where the fuck are you, Trevellian?' He knew it was time to move.

Johnstone had parked his Ford Escort in a small side road to the right of the warehouse. It was a pre-planned position. There was little for him to cover, the warehouse having few windows to the side. He was bored and becoming restless. The seat of the car was beginning to weld into the shape of his backside. He was wriggling in an attempt to regain some comfort when the blind of the first-floor window opened. The light was on in the room behind and Fergus watched carefully as Melissa Grant walked into that light. She stood without moving for several seconds. Her shape within the framework of the window, highlighted by the light from behind, caused the window to take on the effect of stained glass. It was churchlike, reminding him of the crucifixion. He gave her the opportunity to move before calling Trevellian.

"Duncan, standby. The blinds have opened and she's standing in the window on the first floor. I think it must be an office. She's not moving. It's definitely the signal."

Trevellian was not alone in his vehicle. The operation had incurred much pre-planning. Research into Carlo Ramiro showed him to be a violent man, not afraid to make use of specialised weapons and firearms. Liaison at an early stage had led to the employment of the Scotland Yard Blue Berets, an elite team of men, trained as one in the use of all guns. They were perfect for operations such as this. They operated much as commandos, absailing down buildings with sub-machine guns strapped over their backs. Whilst not required on this occasion, Trevellian had chosen to leave it to the professionals.

Inspector Henry Ramsbotham was to direct the police attack on the premises. His men were ready and waiting in a nearby van. He called them in.

"All units attack, attack, attack."

Chapter Five

Those inside the warehouse neither saw nor heard the approach of the forklift-truck towards the roller shutters of the main door. The forklift was not standard. It was large and heavy duty. Had they done so, they would probably have paid little attention. There were often vans and lorries loading and unloading in the area until late at night. Nothing was particularly unusual until a close study of the forklift showed a number of armed and uniformed men following close behind.

The lifting arms of the truck had been specially prepared for just this occasion. The ends had been ground to taper them flat. As the forklift neared the roller door it picked up speed. When it was within feet of the target, the police driver lowered the arms to the ground. As the truck hit the shutter the arms screeched along the tarmac, the impetus maintained as they forced under the door. With the forklift wedged in position the driver pulled on the lever. The door groaned and creaked as the arms pushed it upwards. The vehicle was tested to its limit but proved the stronger competitor. The door moved upwards. The light of the warehouse shone through as the gap enlarged.

The first of the Blue Berets rolled under the door at the first opportunity. They entered the warehouse quickly and efficiently, instantly assessing the location and running for cover as they regained their feet. Others followed. Several carried Heckler & Kosh sub-machine guns, those following just being armed with handguns. Henry Ramsbotham had, as his weapon, a megaphone.

“Armed police, stand still. Armed police!” His voice was amplified and echoed through the warehouse.

Ramiro's men were caught unawares. The first sign of the assault had been the teeth-grinding noise of the door as it was prised open. The man guarding Ramiro’s limousine had been the first to respond. He had drawn his holstered weapon and turned to the door as the invaders entered. As he raised his handgun to fire at one of the policemen, a short burst of automatic gunfire was heard. The guard’s weapon was thrown into the air as the bullets hit him in the chest. He was probably dead before he hit the ground. He lay for a second on the warehouse floor, his body twitching in the aftermath of death. It then stopped. He lay still and silent.

Carlo Ramiro was in the centre of the warehouse as the police entered. He was protected and hidden by the expanse of crates loaded around him. The initial burst of gunfire riveted his mind to the problem. For a few seconds he did not move as he assimilated his position. As the leading officers came into his line of sight he pulled the remote control from his pocket to reseal the vault.

Ramiro was lined by two of his own guards. They too possessed automatic weapons. The first had little or no time to react. As he raised his gun, to confront the approaching officers, their fire mowed him down. Ramiro and the second man retreated to take cover at the rear of the warehouse. There they would make their stand. Their action was to leave the drugs cache unattended. The moving turntable was acting to conceal the haul, but it responded slowly and had not completed its task. One of the Blue Berets, realising the importance of the find, picked a metal bar from the floor and wedged it against the sidewall and the turntable. The motor was designed to move the turntable but was not sufficiently powerful to remove the obstacle. Had it have been, there was the added safeguard of a safety switch, which stopped the table if any obstruction was sensed. The bar effectively stopped the attempted concealment of the drugs.

As Ramiro ran for cover, he passed the dead guard. The machine gun was still in his hand and Carlo bent to pick it up. He had no time for delicacy and could hear the man's fingers breaking as he pulled the weapon from the death grip. On reaching cover he turned to fight. It appeared that only he and the guard with him still had the ability to do so. He lay on the floor, his legs apart for stability. The gun was in the crook of his arm as he peered around the base of the protecting crate.

An officer ran into Carlo's line of fire. Ramiro had no hesitation in pulling the trigger. His fortress had been attacked and he was justified in protecting himself. It mattered not that the invaders were police officers and that it was he who was breaking the law. As far as he was concerned the Ramiro family had made their own law since he was a child and it was his entitlement to enforce it.

The bullets caught the officer in the upper thigh, taking his legs from under him. He was fortunate that Ramiro had not had time to consolidate his position before firing. His aim was rushed and accordingly too low. The policeman fell to the ground within feet of cover. He dragged himself forward on his arms. His legs hurt, and the movement took much effort. For a few seconds Carlo Ramiro had the opportunity of a second shot at the man. He hesitated. Whilst he was tempted to finish the job, the man was now no threat to him. In the seconds it took him to consider his action the man crawled to cover and safety.

More officers had now arrived at Ramiro's stronghold. There were evidently two guns facing them. The guard was kneeling to the other side of the protective shield. Unfortunately, in remaining on his knees he provided a greater target for the attack force. He looked around the edge of a box to aim as he fired. Only a few bullets had left his gun when the police bullet struck his head. It pierced his skull in an effective manner, spraying blood onto the wooden crate. The bullet lodged in the man's brain. He knew nothing of his death. The side of his head slid down the crate until it stopped on the floor of the warehouse.

The report recorded that Ramiro must have known that his position was untenable. There was no other sound of gunfire within the building. His other protectors had either been killed or arrested. The general workers within the warehouse were trusted men but were not armed nor expected to assist in situations like this. They would merely have surrendered immediately or thrown themselves to the floor in submission.

Carlo Ramiro must have ruminated upon his fate. To submit would most certainly mean a long term of imprisonment within a British prison cell. He could not expect less than ten years, probably more. Ramiro had always been a free spirit, not restricted by authority. His family wealth and strength had allowed this to be so. To rot in a prison cell was not for a Ramiro. His decision reached; Carlo Ramiro chose the path of glory. He lifted himself from the ground. His weapon was held at waist height and was firing as Ramiro rounded the crates at a run. He appeared to jump slightly as the first of the police bullets cut into his abdomen. He ran on still firing. His momentum was only slowed as more officers began firing on him. The bullets slammed into his torso, knocking him backwards. He attempted to fight against it but could not. As the life force drained from him his eyes appeared to open wide, looking upwards. His gun fell to the floor, clattering on the stone ground. His mouth moved but no sound was emitted. Ramiro fell to his knees first. His hands became clenched before him, as if praying. The firing had stopped as he fell gently forward onto his face, dead.

Duncan Trevellian only entered the warehouse once the shooting had ceased and the 'all clear' had been given by Ramsbotham. He walked through the roller door, ducking slightly as it had not been lifted to head height. As he walked through, those who had surrendered left the warehouse in handcuffs. All were workmen, easily distinguished in their overalls, apart from one suited Colombian. Trevellian would speak to him later, he thought.

Ambulances, which had been on standby, now arrived outside the premises. Fortunately, no police officers had died. Trevellian had no hesitation in crediting this to the efficiency of the planning and execution of the operation. Three officers had, however, suffered gunshot wounds; the most seriously injured being the officer fired upon by Carlo Ramiro. Several bullets had penetrated his legs and lower torso. He was wheeled through the warehouse on a stretcher, fluid replacement having already been catered for, the plastic pipes connected to bottles above.

As he watched the bodies of the opposition being covered, Duncan Trevellian felt a twinge of remorse. He had hoped that gunfire would be unnecessary, although recognised this as a forlorn hope. He knew that Ramiro would fight back when attacked. He accepted the consequences of this fight.

He walked further until coming to the cocaine 'grave'. It was still sufficiently open to recognise the contents within. He stood in much the same position and pose as that adopted by Ramiro some minutes earlier. The quantity of cocaine had a similar mesmerising effect on him.

"Was it all worth it?" He wondered.

An officer approached holding the remote control. He spoke to Trevellian:

"Ramiro dropped this when he ran, Sir. I think it opens the cover. The sensor's over there."

Trevellian followed the officer's indication and pointed the control accordingly. There were three buttons, coloured green, amber and red, following the traffic-light colours. Trevellian pushed the green button. The motor smoothly operated to draw the cover from the opening. As it came clear the metal bar, that had been inserted by the officer to jam the mechanism, fell to the floor. It landed silently, padded by the cocaine beneath it. Trevellian tried the red button out of curiosity. The door stopped moving. He found the amber button was effective in closing the door. He reverted to the green button to open it fully. He was intrigued by the efficiency of the concealment. The door supported crates piled high upon it. It was metal lined and sealed at the edges with rubber. Once closed the hideaway gave no indication of its existence. Even a give-away odour to the most highly trained police dog was suppressed by the engineering.

"Sir, I think you'd better come upstairs".

Trevellian was disturbed by Fergus Johnstone, who had first seen my signal. On his entry to the warehouse, following Trevellian, Johnstone had diverted to the side stairs. The offices had been cleared by the Blue Berets. They had found me alone. A uniformed, woman, officer remained with me until Johnstone's arrival. His assessment caused him to immediately require Trevellian's prompt attendance.

Duncan Trevellian asked no questions. Johnstone's sincere and firm request firmly indicated that all was not right. He feared the worst. He walked silently behind his sergeant. Trevellian's relief at finding me alive was short lived. He entered the office to find me sitting on the desk. My knees were drawn up to my chin. I rocked backwards and forwards. Although I had now stopped crying, my face was streaked with mascara, the dried tears showing their route clearly. The woman officer had found a blanket, which was wrapped around my shoulders. It fell loosely open. Melissa's damaged clothing was clearly visible. Trevellian knew that this was no time for the use of my pseudonym. Johnstone had remained at the door. The woman officer stepped back as he approached. He stood in front of the desk.

"Katrina, Kat can you hear me?" His voice was soft but firm. I don't remember him speaking to me. He received no response.

He reached forward, carefully with his right hand. As it touched my shoulder I pulled away, visibly rejecting his movement. He persevered. Using both hands he took my shoulders, protected by the blanket. I only know this now. It was not something I recollect.

"Katrina, you're safe now. This is me, Duncan Trevellian. I'm here to look after you. You're OK now."

Slowly I looked towards his face. I apparently focused Melissa's eyes on him. I'm told a wave of recognition swept over my face. I swiftly moved onto my knees. My expression changed to anger. I drew her hands into fists and beat Trevellian's chest.

"You bastard, Trevellian, you bastard. Where were you when I needed you? It's too fucking late now." I shouted into his face.

The tears were again flowing down my face as I responded to Trevellian's presence. My pounding apparently hurt his chest, but he did not flinch. I could have had no sympathy then and certainly have no sympathy now. He allowed me to vent my anger. I slowed. My beating was less forceful. My words changed to sobs and were slurred as I tried to clear the tears from my lips. My head fell forward onto Trevellian's chest. I continued to cry as he carefully put his arms around me to comfort me.

Duncan Trevellian stayed with me for several minutes before asking Johnstone to summon paramedics. It was apparent that I had suffered injury. I required treatment that could only be given in hospital. Trevellian accompanied me. My needs took priority over the clearing up procedure. He left this in the capable hands of Fergus Johnstone. I was subsequently pleased that he took this view. I would have hated him if he had not.

The cursory examination by the paramedics revealed that I had no life-threatening injuries. I might have disagreed with them had I been asked. I was walked slowly down the office stairs, to the waiting ambulance. Trevellian walked by my side. He held my hand to emphasise his presence and offer some comfort. I held it tightly. The damage to Melissa's clothing and nature of her injuries suggested some sexual interference. Trevellian did not know to what extent at that time. Nobody had yet asked me to detail the events and I had not offered any information.

We travelled together in the ambulance with me lying on a blanket-covered stretcher. Trevellian sat on the opposite side, facing me. The paramedic remained near to the door to allow me the feeling of privacy. Duncan Trevellian still held my hand.

"Can you tell me what happened, Katrina?" He asked gently.

I knew that the question had to be asked. It did not make it any easier to answer. The events of the day had heightened my emotions.

My injuries still hurt both physically and emotionally. I initially turned my head away from Trevellian as the tears again began to roll. I had no control over them.

"Come on Katrina, you're going to have to tell someone. It might just as well be me."

I turned to him. My second hand took hold of his one hand. Both hands gripped tightly. He was surprised at the strength of my grip. My eyes tended to squint as I peered at him through the watery haze.

"I was raped." I forced the words from my lips. They were almost impossible to say. They were the hardest words I had spoken.

This merely confirmed Trevellian's fears. He waited for a moment, allowing me to consolidate my first oral acknowledgement of the event.

"Ramiro?"

I pulled myself up unto one arm, leaning towards Trevellian. I became more intense merely having heard Ramiro's name. The tears had stopped flowing.

"Yes, Carlo Ramiro. Did you get him?"

In anticipation of Trevellian's answer my hand gripped his more tightly. I wanted to know.

Duncan Trevellian nodded. "Tell me more." He probed.

He could see the pain in my face as I recalled the event. The pain was real. "He drank Scotch. He had cocaine. He forced it into my mouth."

My statements were obviously disjointed. I wasn't thinking as clearly as I would have liked. My final sentence was filled with ambiguity. It had to be clarified.

"What, what did he force into your mouth Kat?"

"The cocaine, the cocaine of course." It was only at that stage that I realised the ambiguity. "No, nothing else, just the cocaine. That was enough."

He looked into my eyes. They were still camouflaged by Melissa Grant's contact lenses. They still therefore looked clear. Had he been able to see my eyes then the tell-tale vagaries of the drug would have been apparent.

"The man in the blue overcoat and hat. I don't know who he was. Did you get him?"

Duncan Trevellian thought. He was aware of all those persons either killed or captured. Nobody fitted my description.

"What man, Katrina?"

"English, in his fifties. He was in the warehouse. He sussed me, Trevellian. He was the reason that Ramiro turned on me. Did you get him?" He could see the pain in my face as I recalled the person. It was genuine pain. "He drank Scotch. "

"I don't know, Katrina. I'll find out. Leave it with me."

The ambulance pulled into the large and impersonal complex of Greenwich Hospital. This was a sixties conglomerate that had not weathered well over the many years of its existence. The back doors of the ambulance were opened to display the bland concrete walls surrounding the 'Emergency' entrance. Trevellian stayed with me as the stretcher was wheeled into a curtained cubicle.

"She's a police officer," the paramedic said to the staff nurse as we travelled through the magnolia corridor. The nurse nodded but continued reading the chart that she had in her hand. Once the curtain sealed the cubicle from the outside I spoke again.

"Duncan," I had recovered some of Melissa's composure. "I've got to get out of here. There's no way I'm staying."

"All right, calm down. Let's get you checked over then we'll move on. You've got be sure you're physically OK."

"I'm better." I tried to assure him. "I'm getting better all the time."

"Do you want to talk about it?" Trevellian tested.

"What do you want to know?" The effect of the drug was beginning to ease. I could think more clearly.

"This might be difficult; you might not want to tell me?" Trevellian was uncertain as to whether he should continue.

"Go on."

"The rape, the intercourse. Was it full intercourse?"

I nodded. My memory of the event made my face contort. Trevellian probed further.

"Was it only vaginal intercourse, or anything else?" He allowed his words to tale off, leaving the decision with me as to whether I would answer. I was silent for a moment. I found the question offensive.

"No, he didn't bugger me." I was unsure as to whether it was me, or Melissa, who answered. The voice was vicious. "He just fucked me."

I pulled away from him, again raising my knees to my chin. As if by micro-switch the tears flowed. Why I should respond like this I did not understand. I had no control over my emotions. Security could be found in the foetal position. It took some minutes before I again found some composure.

Both the nurse and the casualty doctor arrived at the cubicle together. The formally dressed nurse was short of humour that day. The long hours had passed slowly, and the department had been busy. Whilst she was sympathetic to her patient's injuries, she looked like she had a headache, was tired and wanted to go home. The doctor was a small, Asian, gentleman, possible of Indian origin. He was shorter than the nurse and walked behind her. He appeared dominated by her.

"Hello," the nurse acknowledged me. She ignored Trevellian. "I've got to fill in this form, then we'll find out what is wrong. Would you please leave us for a few minutes, Sir? There is a waiting room just outside."

"Duncan, don't go." I wanted him there. At that time even the nurse was a frightening sight.

"I've got to. You'll be all right with these people." He did not sound convincing. "I'll make arrangements for later on."

He pulled his hand from my grip and left the cubicle. He has since told me that as he walked along the corridor he heard the firm tones of the nurse.

"Now, tell us your name."

The sea of faces all appeared to focus on Trevellian as he entered the waiting room. They epitomised the casualty department of a large, urban, 'National Health' hospital. Many had waited for several hours for attention. Whilst their injuries were considered trivial by the hospital staff, they were of major importance to the patient. The faces showed the frustration many felt at the lack of treatment received. Trevellian approached the receptionist.

"Excuse me." She did not look up. "Excuse me."

The second attempt caused the middle-aged lady to look at Trevellian over her half-moon reading glasses.

"Yes?" She was abrupt.

He showed his warrant card. "I am a police officer. I wonder if I could borrow your phone?"

He was polite with the request.

"Do you not have a mobile?"

"Failed battery." He grimaced.

"Public phones are over there."

Trevellian was cast aside with a wave of the receptionist's hand. She looked back down at her paperwork. He recognised her absolute rejection of him. He turned and walked away controlling the abuse that he wished to deliver. He walked to the two public telephones. One was free.

Meanwhile, my resolve to leave the hospital was strengthened by the attitude of the nurse and support from Melissa. The questions were curt. I answered in a similar fashion. On completing the form with personal detail, she spun on her heel and left the cubicle.

"Over to you, Doctor." The throwaway comment allowed the small insignificant man to initiate his examination.

He awaited the departure of the nurse before speaking.

"Let's start at the top," his voice was heavily accented and difficult to understand. "Let's look at the injuries to your face first and then we'll have a look at the rest of you."

He moved towards me. His attitude was caring and thoughtful, a complete contrast to the nurse. I allowed his examination.

Trevellian took several minutes to complete his telephone call, making the necessary arrangements for my continued care. He did not wait to be invited back into the casualty. He walked through to the cubicle, with some purpose. He was not questioned. He stood at the curtain to my cubicle.

"Can I come in?" He called from outside.

The doctor's head appeared around the edge. "Ah, it's you. Yes, come in, we've just finished."

Trevellian walked back into the room. I was wrapping the red blanket back around both Melissa and myself. I was uncertain as to which identity I preferred at this time. It suffices to say that I had hated the doctor's examination no matter how important it was and who he was examining. Yet again I was defiled and interfered with. How many more times? I wondered.

The doctor sought my permission to disclose my injuries to Trevellian. I agreed.

"Now, she has no permanent injuries that I can see." The doctor told Trevellian. "Her face has severe bruising and a slight laceration. I have applied a temporary dressing."

Trevellian looked at the gauze and plaster on my cheek.

"There is major bruising to the inside of both her upper thighs. She has suffered some vaginal damage but everything else appears OK."

"Hey, hang on doctor, that's sufficient information for him." I thought but did not speak. Melissa said it for me. The doctor looked at me but continued regardless.

"I've taken no samples. For that I would suggest a female doctor."

"Thank-you doctor. I have made separate arrangements. Is your treatment complete?" Trevellian asked.

"Yes, there is little else we can do. But she should not be left alone."

With that I agreed inwardly. He turned to me. "You make sure that someone looks after you for the next few days."

He smiled at me in an attempt to offer some comfort. I gained none. I nodded my response.

The car arrived to collect us a few minutes later. Sue Page, a Detective Constable working for Trevellian had been withdrawn from the operation to assist. The Detective Inspector helped me to walk from the hospital to the car. I was relieved to leave the cold and sanitary premises. I had been allowed to continue my possession of the red, hospital blanket and this was firmly wrapped around me. Trevellian and I climbed into the back of the car. He introduced Sue Page.

"The nearest victim suite is at Kennington Police Station. I've arranged for it to be opened up for us. It's pretty secluded with its own entrance so nobody should see us. I've also arranged for a doctor to attend." Page told us.

"Well done." Trevellian appreciated her efficiency. He turned to me, "You know the formalities. We'll have to go through them for the evidence."

"Fuck the evidence." I thought. I was supported by Melissa.

Trevellian went on: "Carlo Ramiro must still be proved the perpetrator. His culpability will become relevant in the future. The evidence must be properly preserved."

He had seen the questioning look on my face despite me saying nothing.

I nodded. I could not argue. Duncan Trevellian was concerned that the trauma surrounding the events of the day had affected me more profoundly than was initially obvious. He was right. I had again become quiet. Whilst I nodded my replies I was not speaking. I had no desire to. The intensity with which I held Trevellian's hand worried both him and me.

Sue Page drove efficiently. It took us just over fifteen minutes to arrive at the police station, situated in Kennington Road. Whilst another sixties building it had been better preserved than Greenwich Hospital, and recently renovated. She parked the car in the rear yard and led me to the Rape Suite. These were innovations in the Metropolitan Police and were intended to offer a more caring attitude to rape victims. They provided a self-contained suite of rooms containing a comfortably furnished rest room, a doctor's examination room, toilet and showering facilities. For many years such victims had suffered in the standard station interview rooms, often to the detriment of the enquiry. The dedicated suites were certainly a step forward, although not for me.

The door shut behind Trevellian, effectively cocooning the three of us from the outside world. Duncan Trevellian sat me in an armchair provided. Sue sat in another. It was my first opportunity to relax. However, I did not do so.

"Katrina, Sue's arranged for a female doctor to attend to examine you. We need samples to safeguard us in the future. There's no use me being present. You don't want me there with the doctor, do you? Would you like me to go to your flat and get you some fresh clothes?"

I thought before speaking. Where were the keys to my flat? I remembered. "No, it's no good going to the flat. I left the keys in the hotel, in Melissa's room at the 'Aphelion'. My clothes are there as well."

The internal telephone in the suite rang. Sue Page answered it.

"The doctor has arrived." She told us.

I had met Doctor Angharad Stritch previously. She had been a police surgeon for thirty years. She was now in her sixties, and the Home Office remuneration was an excellent supplement to her Inner-City practice. She was no longer enthusiastic in examining rape victims. She tried to be sympathetic, but after so many similar examinations it now proved difficult. She was invariably called out in the middle of the night. After a full day's work, such nocturnal activities were a drain on her energies. She persevered, however. I dreaded her examination. I knew what was coming.

Duncan Trevellian welcomed her to the suite and introduced her to Sue Page and myself. He explained merely that he required a full rape examination. He did not detail events or my status as a police officer. It was unnecessary. I am still unsure as to whether I was recognised by Dr Stritch. I don't think she was interested in who I was. To her, my identity was irrelevant and at that time I felt like it certainly was.

"Katrina, I'm going to leave you in the capable hands of Dr Stritch whilst I go and get some more clothes for you. I won't be long OK."

I merely nodded. I was saying little at this time. Trevellian left the suite.

Dr Stritch was controlled by her messages on her mobile telephone and realised that it could go off at any time, notifying her of another examination. She had no time to waste. She walked into the examination room and prepared herself.

"Pop in here my love," she told me. "Take off your clothes and lie down on the couch."

I tentatively entered the examination room. Sue followed. Trevellian was probably driving the police car towards Piccadilly as the examination started. He did not see Dr Stritch donning her rubber gloves nor hear her say:

"Just raise your knees my dear and put your feet flat on the couch, apart. That's right, now this won't hurt a bit."

I expect that he was parking the police car close to the hotel as Dr Stritch turned to Sue Page, "Will you be collecting the exhibits?"

Detective Constable Page nodded.

"Upper vaginal swab," the doctor told her as she removed the probe.

"Not again," I thought. "How many more times?"

Trevellian told me afterwards what the hotel receptionist thought of me. I was not surprised. He presented himself formally at the Aphelion to obtain the key to Melissa's room without argument.

"I suppose you've arrested her," the receptionist said as she handed him the key. "I would have expected it. She looked the type."

Duncan Trevellian did not disillusion her. He walked to the lift without speaking. He assessed the contents of the room in one swift glance, upon entry. I had one holdall in which I carried my clothes, both for Melissa and myself. I had sufficient to provide a fresh change.

Trevellian chose the most sensible course and emptied the room of all my possessions. He found my keys and warrant card in the bedside table and carefully sealed them into the zipped pocket of my holdall. My makeup was placed into the adjacent cosmetic bag before being packed. Confident that he had missed nothing he left the room.

Dr Stritch handed the last exhibit to Sue Page.

"That's higher and lower vaginal swabs, pubic hair, finger-nail scrapings, blood and all the clothing. Is there anything else you think you need? How about saliva? Yes, we'd better be on the safe side."

She took a glass phial from her bag. "Just spit into this a few times, My Dear. Try to fill it up."

Angharad Stritch avoided calling any victims by their names. She used the term 'My Dear' to them all. It avoided familiarity and kept them at arm's length. In her earlier days she had allowed herself to be closer to individual victims. She found that this encouraged the story to be recounted, often resurrecting distress both in the victim and herself. She quickly decided that this was not her job; it belonged to the detective in charge. She was there to efficiently record the injuries and provide exhibits. From then on, she retained a certain remoteness.

Duncan Trevellian arrived back at the suite after the departure of Dr Stritch. He entered the rest area to find Sue Page sitting alone drinking coffee. I did not hear him return. His face subsequently revealed that he had been talking to Sue Page. I could imagine what was said. He would have said the same to me, in different circumstances.

"Where's Katrina?" His face expressed concern.

"It's OK, she's taking a shower. The doctor's finished and gone. I've got all the exhibits including all her clothes. They are bagged up separately. She should be finished soon." Sue Page looked at her watch.

Trevellian seated himself beside the officer. Personal contact was always good.

"How is she? Has she opened up to you yet?"

"No, not yet. I'm surprised really. Working undercover I thought she might be more resilient."

Duncan Trevellian would have nodded thoughtfully. That was the sort of thing he did. It was something about him that I grew to like.

"I could murder a cup of coffee as well." His face lightened as Sue catered for his request.

I had been abused by the rapist and then suffered further trauma at the hands of both the hospital staff and the police doctor. I had been required to remove my clothing, piece by piece. It was taken by the gloved doctor and handed to the gloved detective. Once naked I lay on a cold plastic couch whilst I was probed and swabbed. As I stood beneath the tumbling droplets of hot water, I finally appreciated the opportunity to recover my dignity and to be alone. I had removed Melissa's brunette wig and returned to my own natural blonde hair. I rinsed the shampoo from the fine strands with my fingers. As I soaped my body I was reminded of the evening as my hands passed over my injuries. My face was sore, my jaw beginning to stiffen. My thighs were bruised and painful. At last, however, I was beginning to feel clean. I was satisfied with the natural flow of water over my body. The heat of the water in the confined shower area emphasised my tiredness. It had been a long day.

I had made every effort to clear my mind of thought. I had to come to terms with the incident. I found the easiest way at that point was simply to eradicate all thought. Nobody had yet questioned me in depth and I appreciated that. I did not want to have to detail the incident at that time, perhaps tomorrow. I turned off the water, wrapping a large white towel around myself as I walked from the shower. I was not surprised to find Trevellian, ensconced with his coffee as I exited the shower area.

He looked up at me. "How are you feeling?" He smiled.

"All right." I attempted to return his smile. I failed.

"I've emptied your hotel room. I've got all your stuff here. Do you want to get dressed?"

"Yes."

I reached down for the holdall at Trevellian's side. I saw his eyes glance towards my body in the way that only men can. Maybe the soapy clean aroma of my skin touched his sense of smell. He could not avoid noticing my slender body through the towel as I picked up the bag. He couldn't see the bastard bruises though, could he?

"I won't be long." I told them as I left the room. I didn't mind him looking at me. Everybody else had. What was one more!

"What do you think?" Trevellian asked Sue, after I had left the room.

"I'm not sure. She seems far more composed now, but she hasn't spoken about it at all. It's late now. I think we should get her home and let her sleep it off. Speak to her again tomorrow."

"Yes, you're probably right. There's no rush after all."

Whilst there was a small face mirror fastened to the wall of the shower room, the suite had no full-length mirrors. The reasoning for this was simple. Many of the visitors had suffered quite horrendous injuries. A full-length mirror would allow them to reflect on these injuries in full and probably to their own detriment. I was therefore only able to see my facial injuries as I brushed out my hair. My cheek was swollen and yellowing. The pain added to my own tiredness and had given me a headache. I would be glad to get to my own flat.

I dressed in my own clothing. It was more practical and basic than Melissa's. I had returned my eyes to their natural colour. I pulled on a check shirt, tucking it into my blue denim jeans. I put my foot onto a chair to tie the laces of my trainers. It was only now that I felt intact again. I walked from the room. I pre-empted anything that Trevellian was about to say.

"I want to go home now." I told the officers.

"That's fine. You need some sleep. Let's go." Trevellian saw no point in delaying further.

The Detective Inspector drove the vehicle to my flat. He steered Sue Page into the back of the car with me. He hoped that this would give the opportunity for Sue Page to create a working relationship with me that would eventually extract the full story from me. I knew his strategy and had no time for it. I said absolutely nothing.

I lived alone in my flat on the west side of Clapham Common. It was only a short drive from Kennington. Trevellian stopped the car in front of the converted house. Many of the properties in this area had been sub-divided into flats. I owned the first floor of the terraced house. The small front garden led to a communal front door. The house had been built during the late nineteenth century, with the expansion and growing wealth of the capital. Trevellian got out of the car and opened the door for me.

He said to Sue Page, "You wait here. I'll see her up to the flat."

I gave him the key to open the front door. I simply did not have the energy or motivation to do it. He opened the door and we walked up the internal stairs to my flat. As we entered the flat itself, I switched on the central light. The wall colourings were soft and pastel. One wall supported the petite flowers indicative of Laura Ashley. The room was fully carpeted with a hint of primrose. The furniture was modern. It did not over clutter the room. Everything was spick and span, as could have been expected. I, at last, felt at home. Trevellian had been carrying my holdall. He put it down in the middle of the floor. He turned towards me.

"Will you be OK tonight?"

I nodded. He took a card from his pocket.

"Look, this has got my home telephone number on it. I'm not that far away. If you need to speak just ring me. It doesn't matter what time."

"What about your wife? I don't want to disturb her."

"I'm not married. I live alone, just like you. You'll only be disturbing me, so please don't worry." He smiled as he turned to leave the flat.

It was the early hours of the morning. There was little traffic on the road. I looked from the window as the police car drove away. I needed music in the flat.

"Alexa, play me some soul!"

Alexa did exactly as I instructed.

"The Bodyguard. That's exactly what I need, a bodyguard."

I walked into the bedroom. I threw myself onto the bed without changing. In only a few moments I was asleep. The music played on.

Chapter Six

Trevellian's night did not finish so quickly. I discovered that he was a divorced man who had lived alone in his Hammersmith Grove apartment for the past year. The financial burden of his divorce had not left him well off. His third floor, one bedroom, rented accommodation was not as luxurious as mine, nor so tidy. Duncan Trevellian spent the majority of his day at work. He needed the money and, since the separation from his wife, his working team had become his extended family. He sat in his one armchair and turned on the television. An old Christopher Lee movie lightened the screen. As the female vampire rushed at him through the screen, he picked up his mobile telephone. It had been re-charged.

He rapidly sent a message to Detective Sergeant Fergus Johnstone. His thumb hit the visible keys of his mobile phone. Johnstone would ring him on receipt of the message. He put down the telephone and sat for a moment, apparently watching the television but digesting none of the story. He only had to wait for a few minutes until the telephone rang.

"Guv'nor, it's Fergus. Some of us are still at work you know."

"I thought you would be. Tell me, how's it all going?"

"No problem. We recovered just over two hundred kilos. At a conservative estimate I reckon about ten million. Not bad, eh?"

"That's great." Trevellian tried to sound enthusiastic. "What about the death toll?"

"Ramiro and three of his thugs. We had two down. One only had superficial injuries. The other's a problem, looks like he might lose one of his legs. They're not sure at the moment. Tell me, how's the girl?"

"Not good. She was raped Fergus, by Ramiro."

"That's bad news, Duncan."

Trevellian changed the subject, so he told me.

"Fergus, what about the post-mortems, when are they?"

"Tomorrow afternoon, down at Blackheath. Henry Clayman's doing them, so you'd better be on time."

"I'll see you tomorrow morning then, and Fergus, thanks for your help tonight."

I slept fitfully. After only an hour I woke up, feeling uncomfortable in my clothing. I stripped off my jeans and shirt and returned to bed. This time I pulled the covers over myself before drifting off to sleep once more.

It was approaching 5am when the dreams began. My subsequent recollection of the dream was thanks to the great assistance of Emily Krystman, police psychologist. I believe this to be the only dream in my life that I now vividly remember and have grown to live with. Until the dream my efforts to blank my mind from the incident appeared to be working. The inky blackness of nothing slowly opened to reveal a distorted, floating view of the office at the warehouse. I was present in the office. I was alone. I was able to view the room from all sides. I was not restricted by my body. I looked from the window of the office down into the warehouse. Beneath me I saw the figure of Carlo Ramiro. He had his back to me, peering into the cocaine pit. I looked more closely. The individual kilos of cocaine were moving. They were changing. Each one appeared to take human form, dancing. They were individual mini-skeletons, each dancing within a mass grave. Suddenly Ramiro turned and looked up to face me. The classic South American features had gone. His face was red and fiery. He laughed, a deep guffaw penetrating the silence. His eyes were similarly red. There were two small horns protruding from his still black hair. He spoke to me.

"You're mine now; I can do what I want with you."

As I lay on the bed asleep my head must have rocked to one side as I felt his blow. It did not wake me up. I dreamed on, central in the nightmare.

"Help me, help me." I shouted unconsciously.

I imagined the cocaine being forced into my mouth. I was trying to cough it back. I saw my body arch as I relived the rape. I felt the pain of the enforced entry. I saw Ramiro above me as he penetrated me. I looked at his face again as the rape continued. I again saw the steely grey eyes of the intruder, but slowly they vanished, being replaced merely by darkness. Another figure appeared, continuing the man's actions. I focused on the second offender. It was a face that I knew from the past. The receding hairline, the brown, generally jovial eyes had hardened. The intercourse continued. The man spoke:

"You won't tell your mother will you Katrina? You won't tell her."

I knew that I should recognise the second figure that had abused me. I focused my dreaming mind on the task.

"I do know you." I shouted at the dream-figure as the intercourse continued.

I shot upwards on the bed, immediately departing from both dream and sleep as I identified the image. It was my stepfather. The man that had married my mother, after the death of my natural father. These were matters long since cast from my mind yet rekindled by the day's incident.

I was sweating profusely. My hands were shaking uncontrollably; my whole body shook. My hands went to my groin. I was again uncomfortable in that area, this time for a different reason. I felt the wetness of my pants. I had urinated in my sleep. I could not remember ever doing that before, even as a child. I was demeaned and frightened. I could not comprehend the effects of the trauma. My body racked with tears as the emotion poured from me. I remembered the year of abuse suffered at the hands of my stepfather, until I was strong enough to say no. I had not told my mother. Why not? I didn't know. Would I have been believed? I thought not. I cupped my head in my hands as I wept.

"What can I do?" I murmured through the tears.

My mind turned to the card, Duncan Trevellian's card. It was on the bedside table. I held back my tears as I looked for it. I picked up the telephone. I have no direct recollection of the call that I made.

Trevellian was sleeping soundly. His final conversation with Fergus Johnstone had satisfied him that there was nothing else that could be done that night. At that point he had realised his overwhelming tiredness and climbed into his bed. Seconds after touching the pillow, he was asleep. He was too tired to dream, and therefore took some moments to identify the ringing in his ears. At first his natural instincts took over and he reached out for the alarm clock. His hand fumbled on the bedside table as he tried to silence the instrument. It was electronic. One strike of the top button generally allowed nine minutes more uninterrupted sleep before repeating its interjection. Duncan Trevellian carefully opened one eye as he realised that the sound would not stop. He cajoled his brain into action, struggling to identify the interference.

"The telephone, it's the bloody telephone," he growled. He picked up the offending item. "Yes," he declared curtly into the handset.

"Duncan, is that you. Help me please, I need you."

Trevellian did not immediately recognise the voice.

"Who is it?" Before he had finished speaking his brain jerked into gear to aid the identification.

"Katrina, is that you? What's up?" He went on.

Moments passed before the voice spoke again. It was vague and distant. "I can't sleep; terrible dreams. I don't know what to do."

"I'll come over. I'll be about twenty minutes. Don't do anything. Just wait for me."

He could not see my response on the other end of the line. I nodded into the receiver without speaking and without knowing that the act of nodding could not be transmitted. Slowly I put down the telephone, terminating the call. In the past day I had gained some comfort from my attempts to return to the foetal position. Accordingly, I drew my knees up to my chin, my legs tight into my body. This position was difficult to hold when sitting on the mattress of the bed. As I lost my balance, I fell gently onto my side on the bed. I did not move. My hand slowly crept up to my mouth. I sucked my thumb.

Trevellian was worried. He dressed quickly, throwing on clothing from the night before that he had casually discarded onto the floor. He ran from his flat to his car. The drive to Clapham Common took less than fifteen minutes. He jumped three sets of red traffic lights. He was careful to ensure that no prowling policemen were nearby before he did so. On his arrival at my flat, however, he was met by a further frustration.

The Detective Inspector was aware of the early hour and considerate of the needs of neighbours. He assessed the situation before ringing my doorbell. He assumed that it was working, although the sound was not audible through the wooden front door. He initially gave one long ring and waited to be given entry. The door did not open. He rang again, longer this time. He paused for a moment and then repeated his action. He stood on the dark doorstep, cold and agitated. Again there was no reply. He stepped off the doorstep to look up at the first-floor windows. There were no visible lights.

"Katrina," he called softly. When this failed, he raised his voice. "Katrina, open the door."

I lay on my bed in a semi-catatonic stupor. I was aware that my doorbell was ringing. I was aware that I had called Trevellian and that he was due to attend. I wanted to get up and answer the door. For the first time that day, however, I felt comfortable and safe. I had recoiled from the event, returned to my childhood, locking out the present. To move would mean the necessary return to the current day and the trauma that accompanied it. The ringing doorbell was not sufficient incentive for me to move.

Through the window glass, I heard Trevellian's voice as he called from the garden. His voice became louder. He had called several times. In my distant, surreal world, his voice penetrated the restful, floating images that passed before me. I heard the neighbour's sash window as it was pulled upwards.

"Why don't you shut up," the old man shouted at Trevellian as his head poked through. "It's five o'clock in the morning and some of us are trying to sleep."

"Fuck off back to bed then." Trevellian's frustrations burst at this point. The old neighbour suffered his wrath.

The sound of this discourse rebounded soundly from my sense of responsibility. This nudged me from the rejection of the present, dragging me back to reality. My thumb left my mouth. My legs slowly uncurled. I rolled onto my back and thought for a moment. My hand reached out and turned on the bedside light. I left the bed and walked slowly to the door.

Duncan Trevellian was not proud of himself. The old man was right, of course. He was entitled to his sleep. Trevellian was employed as a 'peace officer' yet here was he, himself, breaking the peace. He quietened for a moment. He saw my light illuminate the darkness of my flat.

"At last." He moved back to the front door, immersing himself in the shadows of the doorstep.

I switched on the communal hall light before opening the front door. Although dragging myself from the bed to allow Trevellian entry to my flat, I had not returned to my senses. My actions were robotic. I had identified a task and moved to complete it. I had made no attempt to cover my state of undress or improve my demeanour in any way. To this day the thought that I answered the door to Trevellian, in this state, embarrasses me. Still, there is nothing I can do about it now.

The hall light created an eerie backdrop to the early morning mistiness as I opened the door. Trevellian stood ready to greet me, but the smile soon faded as he saw me. I stood, my hand remaining on the open door. My face was a deathly white; the whites of my blue eyes were now veined with red and appeared popping from my head. I had no make-up to disguise my pallid, clammy skin. The tears had run down my cheeks, dripped onto my chest and dried, leaving white, salty steaks. I stood before him purely in my underwear. My white bra had absorbed the sweat from my body. This had dried leaving salt stains. He cast his eye down to my once white pants. They were now urine stained and still damp. I had not washed myself. The yellow of the urine had blended with the bruising on my upper thighs. Whilst my blonde hair had only been washed a few hours previously, it was matted and twisted, reflecting my trauma throughout the night. Trevellian was appalled. The sight of me frightened him. He stepped up into the hallway. He put his hands on my shoulders, gently turning me.

"Let's go back up to your flat." He was calm and sensitive in his direction.

Duncan Trevellian had dealt with rape victims in the past and knew the sensitivity required. He had not, however, experienced such a profound effect on a woman. He was deeply concerned at my condition and now aware that significant drugs were involved. I could not be left alone for the rest of the night. He knew that. His first priority in the morning would be to ensure that I received the proper care. The huge resources of the Metropolitan Police could provide for that. Until that time, he would look after me.

Trevellian sat me on a dining chair and went to the bathroom. He put the plug into the bath and ran the water. He tested the temperature of the water with his fingers before returning to me. He took my hand.

"Up you get. It's time for a bath. You've got to get cleaned up again."

I obeyed his instructions. My mind had locked out its own capacity to control, as a safety measure. It still responded to the directions of others. I was aware of Duncan's presence although unable to properly react. Trevellian led me to the bathroom.

"Can you bathe yourself," he asked me with uncertainty.

I nodded at him but merely remained in the same upright position, making no attempt to move. Trevellian was flummoxed. He should have expected this total lack of reaction, but somehow had not. He had assumed that I would help. I did not.

"You need to clean up." He told me; still no reply.

Taking his career and life in his hands Trevellian made the only practical move. It was impetuous and dangerous. He went ahead anyway. He had no option. I can only thank him for that, to this day.

"Katrina, I'm going to have to wash you. You can't stay like this and I can't get anyone in to help, not now. Just don't blame me when you wake up, please." He smiled to himself nervously wondering just what he was doing.

Trevellian carefully walked behind me and undid my rear-fastening bra. He slipped it from my shoulders. I did not flinch. He took it from me dropping it into a wash basket in the corner of the room. My pants were more difficult. He eased them down my legs to the floor. He had to lift each of my feet in turn to release the clothing. They followed the bra into the wash basket. I stood before him unmoving, naked. He was acting in a clinical way, treating me as a patient. He took my hand and encouraged me into the bath.

For the second time in a few hours, my hair was washed. This time it was Trevellian's job. He found the shampoo in the cabinet. Fortunately, the mixer taps had a shower attachment that he could use. He thoroughly rinsed the shampoo from my hair. With soap he washed my body. He was confident when washing my back, uncertain when touching other parts of my anatomy. A decision had to be made. I had to be made clean. He finally closed his eyes and rubbed the soap into a lather on my body. At this time the privacies of my sex simply had to give way.

I knew what was happening. I had asked for Trevellian's help and was receiving it. Whilst my mind had blanked any possible response at that time, it retained its awareness. I appreciated his sensitivity and care. It comforted me. It allowed slight relaxation. My bath being completed, Trevellian lifted me into a standing position and began towelling me dry. I stood before him. I responded to him.

"Thank you, Duncan." I gently reached out with my right hand and touched his cheek.

My slight response enlivened Duncan's worried mind. At least I was still there. He led me back to the bedroom, the towel firmly wrapped around me. In the drawers he found a pair of pyjamas. He dressed me in them and put me into bed. I was half upright, resting on a pillow. My eyes were open. I smiled slightly at him.

"Don't worry. I'll make a couple of phone calls and we'll get you sorted out. You just need a bit of help, that's all."

He sat on the edge of the bed and picked up the telephone. He looked at his watch. It was six-thirty. His first call was to the switchboard at New Scotland Yard. Trevellian knew that the Police owned a nursing home, perhaps thirty miles to the west of London. It was available to provide care to ill or injured officers. This was certainly an appropriate case. He obtained the telephone number and dialled direct. He spoke to the nursing sister in charge. She introduced herself as Helen Tomkins. He explained my problem.

"Of course we can help. Can you bring her to us today? We'll get our doctor to have a look at her and she'll have constant attention. What time can we expect you, Inspector?"

"I'll have to make the arrangements and come back to you."

Trevellian's next call was to awaken Sue Page. She had left her mobile number. He had avoided waking her earlier. There was little she could do and no point in both of them losing sleep. She answered the telephone promptly. She had just got up. After an initial explanation Trevellian asked:

"Can you get her down there today?"

"Of course I can, Sir. I'll be with you at the flat in about an hour. Is that OK?"

Having addressed and solved the first problem, Trevellian went to my small kitchen and turned on the kettle. He brewed a cup of tea. He did not know whether I took sugar and was too tired to ask. He put a spoonful of sugar in each cup and poured from the teapot. He put the warm mug into my hands. His actions that night had some effect. I slowly raised the cup to my lips and sipped the hot liquid. I did not speak. Even so, Duncan Trevellian felt some satisfaction. I was surely in better condition than when he had first arrived.

Sue Page arrived on time. Her hair was slightly tousled, having also suffered a slight shortage of sleep. Trevellian assured himself that she could cope on her own before leaving her to the task. His day's work was only just beginning. He was tired but accepted that he would receive no rest. After leaving the two of us, he found time to return to his flat to change. The cleanliness of the previous day's clothing was now exhausted. He showered and dressed more formally. A cup of black coffee restored some of his energy. He telephoned Fergus Johnstone and arranged to meet him at the laboratory. He had two objectives. The first was to direct the examination of the drugs, secondly to submit my forensic samples for storage pending further developments.

Whilst I was en route to the nursing home with Sue Page, Trevellian went to the Metropolitan Police Laboratory. It was situated on the south bank of the River Thames at Lambeth. He met Fergus on the ground floor. They travelled up to the fifth floor in the lift.

"You look tired, boss. Have you been up all night?"

"Just about, Fergus, just about." Trevellian said no more.

As they left the lift he asked, "What about the prisoners. Are we going to get anything out of them?"

"No, I don't think so. I've got a couple of teams who will be interviewing them this morning. I'm sure the workmen didn't know anything anyway. Odds are that we'll have to release them. What's left aren't talking and never will."

"Tell me Fergus, did we capture a white man, in his fifties, blue overcoat and homburg hat?"

"No, nobody by that description. Why do you ask?"

Trevellian looked thoughtful. "It doesn't matter, Fergus, forget it."

The disposal of my forensic samples was a simple affair. A reception desk served those officers wishing to submit items. The foyer was not crowded. A detective in front of them submitted a sawn-off shotgun for examination. He was their only delay. On his completion it was their turn. The receiving officer accepted their submission.

"I'd like to see the drugs that we brought in last night, and the scientist dealing with them," the Detective Inspector asked him.

"Yes Sir, just hang on for a minute and I'll ring him."

According to the incident report, Dr John Holder had graduated in chemistry at Exeter University. He had worked for the Metropolitan Police for some years. He was experienced in the examination of controlled drugs. He had not seen so much cocaine, confiscated in one haul, before. The two detectives followed him along the laboratory corridors.

"Not a bad night's work, Inspector, there's a huge amount."

Trevellian smiled but said nothing. The scientists were entombed within the laboratory during their working day. The items were delivered to them cold, with little of the story surrounding their seizure. They hungered for more detail. It brought the submissions to life. It made the scientist a part of the job. On this occasion Trevellian wanted to give little away.

Dr Holder opened the door of a locked room.

"There it all is," he indicated within.

It was an impressive haul. It was stacked along the wall of the room. It rose up the wall several feet and was three packets deep.

"I've given a cursory examination to some of the packs", continued Holder. "The wrappings are polythene. They don't seem to have any individual markings. The stuff seems reasonably pure, probably uncut. I've got to check it more thoroughly. It will take a few weeks."

"I'd like some of the wrappings fingerprinted and a comparison of the various batches to establish that they're from the same source. You're right Doctor, not a bad night's work."

Trevellian and Johnstone had time for lunch before the post-mortems. They drove close to the mortuary at Blackheath before stopping. Two pints of draught Guinness weighed heavily on Duncan Trevellian's stomach. A turkey sandwich did nothing to lighten the load.

"Do you want another one? We've just got time," offered Fergus.

"No, two's enough for me. You have one if you want."

"I'm all right. We'd better be early rather than late. You know what Clayman is like. He won't let us in if we're late."

Dr Henry Clayman was a respected pathologist of many years standing. Despite enjoying unhealthy quantities of scotch, and having a penchant for the occasional large cigar, Clayman was always fit for work. He was cold and clinical in his dissection of the human body. The rougher jobs, he left to the mortuary assistant. The removal of the skull required an element of expertise with the small, electric, circular saw. Clayman simply did not wish to possess such an attribute.

Trevellian and Johnstone arrived at the mortuary with minutes to spare, the doctor already being dressed for the autopsies. The police officers were required to dress in a similar fashion. Trevellian did not mind the white apron that tied at the back, nor the green plastic overshoes. He objected to the material hat that reminded him of a J-cloth. A police photographer had also attended at Johnstone's request and Trevellian wondered if the protective clothing made his job any more difficult. Dr Clayman was smoking a large King Edward cigar.

"Let's go gentlemen. There are four in there to cut up and not much time to do it."

They followed the Doctor into the mortuary. The four cadavers were laid out on separate, white ceramic tables, next to each other. The mortuary assistant had already been at work. The face of each man had been carefully trimmed from the skull and folded forward, exposing the cranium. The top of the skull had then been severed with the aid of the electric drill and loosened ready for removal by the pathologist. The advantage of this system was that the face and hair remained intact and, when reinstated in its original position required remarkably few stitches to repair the damage. The cut was easily disguised by an efficient embalmer.

"Which one do you want to start with, Inspector?" Asked Doctor Clayman. "Have you got any preference?"

"Carlo Ramiro. He's the most important. Can you do him first?"

"Of course, but which one is he?"

The pathologist walked along the line of tables and flapped the faces temporarily back into position.

"This one?" He asked Trevellian at the first.

"No, that's not Ramiro."

They moved on, Trevellian having to study the face of each of the mortified bodies in turn. The dead faces were remarkably similar to each other. Whilst in life there would have been significant differences, the cruel act of death seemed to merge the likeness. He recognised Ramiro at the third attempt.

"That's him. Can we start with him?"

"Of course. Now is there anything particular that you want?"

"I'd like swabs of the hands, to prove his use of firearms before death, just in case anyone argues that we murdered him." The Detective Inspector answered the Doctor's quizzical look.

"We also believe that he snorted cocaine earlier in the evening. I'd like a nasal swab and the lungs tested for any traces of the drug. Also a blood test if that's all right. It's probable that he had sexual intercourse before death. Could you give me a penile swab and a pubic hair sample please?"

"Is that all you want? Can I get on with chopping him up after that?" Dr Clayman was getting bored. Trevellian smiled.

It took only a few minutes for the Doctor to provide the requisite samples. He handed each to Johnstone. It was agreed that he would care for the exhibits. Clayman then commenced his dissection of the body to establish cause of death. The chest cavity was initially examined. Clayman found that three bullets had penetrated. He used a chromed probe to establish the route of each before moving further. Carefully avoiding damage to those wounds, he opened the chest cavity. He cut between the rib cage and the Colombian and then down through the sternum. He individually severed the ribs to the left of the sternum to separate the cage. He prised it apart to gain entry to the cavity below. Again using the probe, he tracked the path of the bullets. He expected to find two in the heart. Deftly using his scalpel, he removed both the heart and the lungs as one. He placed them into a steel tray that his assistant held, for further examination. Two further bullets were tracked to the lower bowel.

"These wouldn't have killed him on their own. At least, it would have taken some time to die. I think we'll check the heart now. That's where the problem lies."

It transpired that Dr Clayman dissected the lungs before the heart. He showed the officers the tarred sections caused by smoking. He discovered that the third bullet had passed straight through the left lung.

"Strange, where did that one go?"

The Pathologist returned to the cadaver and rummaged in the chest cavity. The bullet was lodged, hidden, in the rear body muscles tucked up against the spine. He pulled it out in his forceps with some satisfaction.

"Here it is." He grinned as he held it up for examination.

His examination of the heart revealed the other two bullets.

"This is the cause of death. With these inside, the heart would have stopped almost immediately."

Dr Clayman's final act was to remove the brain for examination. It came out in one grey lump. It took seconds for his scalpel to slice through.

"Looks clean and healthy, not bad at all."

Trevellian had never been impressed by post-mortems. It was his duty to suffer them and accordingly he did so. He stood in the background throughout, saying little, merely ensuring that those required exhibits were obtained. Had anyone studied his complexion they would have seen it visibly fade. The photographer's camera clicked and whirred as he snapped from every angle. Duncan Trevellian often wondered why the police bothered with such morbid pictures. They were only ever viewed by the pathologist, when compiling his report, or at the training school by new recruits. The Courts avoided them at all costs.

The other autopsies were of less importance to the Detective Inspector. He stayed to keep Fergus Johnstone company. Johnstone had no option but to remain, as the Exhibits Officer. It was a repetitive operation that occurred each time. The officers could understand Dr Clayman's desire for alcoholic relief. It was approaching four-thirty when they were finally able to leave the mortuary.

On the drive back to Central London Johnstone asked, "What's next on the agenda then?"

"Are you all right sorting out the prisoners, Fergus? I don't expect anything useful from them."

"No problem at all. What are you going to do then?"

"I thought I'd drive down to the nursing home, to see how Katrina's getting on?"

"OK, I'll contact you if anything useful arises. Give her my best, I hope she comes out of it."

Johnstone dropped Trevellian at his flat. His car was parked nearby. Before embarking on the journey to the nursing home, Trevellian showered and changed. He felt better for it, washing the mortuary smell from his own body. It had permeated both his clothing and himself. It was the `formaldehyde' odour, although he understood the substance was little used now. They must have retained the smell in the new chemical, he thought.

It had been two long years since Duncan Trevellian's separation from his wife, Julie. His divorce had only become 'absolute' in recent months. Prior to their difficulties they had lived together in a detached house in the southern suburbs. They had changed the family car every two years for a new model. The long hours worked by Trevellian provided financial stability although finally proving to be the cause of the breakdown. Whilst his wife and small daughter were not wanting in material needs, emotionally they were starved of his affection. He generally left home in the early morning and did not return until late at night. He saw little of his daughter during her first, formative, years. He hardly knew her. Julie had suffered similarly. It should have been no surprise to Trevellian when, one day, she confronted him with the fact that she had met another man. He was, however, caught totally unawares.

"Do I know him?" He had asked naively.

"No, I met him at the club." She referred to the health club she had joined in her search for companionship.

Trevellian had agreed to leave the home soon afterwards. It had taken him a few days to find the flat, which he now occupied. A loyal man, he made every attempt to ensure that his wife and daughter enjoyed the comforts they had achieved previously. It was, however, impossible to support them all on his single wage and therefore their living standards dropped accordingly. He maintained mortgage payments and offered a regular subsistence payment in support. The inadequacy of his payments, however, soon proved to be the appropriate encouragement for Julie to seek employment. That was until her new compatriot moved in.

As Duncan Trevellian surveyed his meagre belongings, he remembered the galling feeling when she broke the news. He had telephoned her with the intention of visiting his child.

"Duncan, don't come now." Julie pleaded. "Look, I've got something to tell you. We're not alone anymore. Do you understand?" She paused awaiting a reply. None came.

"He's moved in with us, he's living with me now. It's going to be difficult for you to come here. You'll have to give us time."

Trevellian pulled on his casual, bomber, jacket and left the flat, pulling the door closed behind him. He walked into the street to his car. This vehicle was not two years old. It was almost seven. An old Ford, whose paintwork was fading. There was no rust, however, and the engine seemed to run on and on. He climbed inside. He turned the key. The engine started, and Duncan Trevellian headed in the direction of the M4 Motorway, west.

The journey was not long. He pulled into the forecourt of the nursing home just over an hour later. He had driven comfortably along the motorway from London. Sister Helen Tomkins was still on duty on his arrival. She had been present earlier in the day to admit me into the hospice. She was surprised at my poor state. She expressed her concern to Trevellian.

"She's sleeping at the moment. We've given her some tablets. I've asked the psychologist to have a chat with her tomorrow. Don't worry, she's more than efficient and should be able to help." She had responded to the Inspector's questioning look. "You can go in and see her, but only for five minutes or so. If you see her getting agitated at all then I want you out. Do you understand?"

"Yes, and thanks for your help this morning, Sister. I know it was short notice."

"It always is with you lot," the Sister chided him, smiling gently. "Katrina's room is third on the left down the corridor. Remember now, only a few minutes."

Duncan opened the door carefully. He did not want to disturb me unnecessarily. The room was not in darkness. A glass panel above the door allowed the light from the corridor to filter in, a design feature to ease the task of the nurses when checking their patients at night. The room was about ten feet square. It contained a wardrobe and chest of drawers. The bed was situated centrally against the wall, visible from the door. I lay beneath a single blanket, on my side facing him. He approached the bed and sat on its edge. He gently drew the blanket over my exposed shoulder. This slight action by him disturbed my sleep pattern and I rolled onto my back. My blonde hair fell from my face onto the pillow. I opened my eyes slightly, taking time to focus. A slight smile could just be detected on my lips.

"Duncan," I whispered. "Thanks for coming". I took his hand in mine as I slipped back into sleep.

Trevellian sat with me for over half an hour although I have little recollection. It was only then that Helen Tomkins reminded him that it was time to leave. I did not wake again during that time. He sat silently, looking at me. My face was now restful, adorned in innocence. A feeling of guilt racked him.

"What could I have done to prevent it happening?" He thought.

The Detective Inspector reviewed the operation in the silence of the hospice bedroom. Melissa Grant had to act alone, that was her job. It was dictated by the operation and encouraged by her training. The danger had been known to all. They had tried to cater for it. A personal transmitter might have been more efficient than the handbag version. He doubted it, he had used both before. Trevellian's lack of fault did nothing to quell his disappointment.

"Don't expect too much improvement for a few days," Sister Tomkins warned him as he left the Nursing Home. "But do come and visit her. She needs to know she has friends."

Chapter Seven

Juan Marco had difficulty in contacting Paulo Ramiro. Marco was fortunate that he had not been at the warehouse at the time of the police raid. The Lanthanum had been short staffed, and he considered that it required his attendance. Ramiro was fully conversant with the arrangements concerning the drug importation and storage. He did not need to be chaperoned. Juan Marco had passed a pleasant evening at the club, smoking large cigars and sipping champagne. He did not hear the news until the early hours of the following morning. It took several telephone calls to confirm the police raid.

Marco knew that his priority was to inform Paulo Ramiro of the death of his son. Although a still unconfirmed rumour at this stage, the father had to be contacted. The initial call took several hours to place. The Colombian telephone network was far from perfect. Paulo always appeared to take the bad news calmly and thoughtfully. He listened to Marco, saying nothing. A long silence followed as he digested the information. They spoke in their native, Spanish, tongue.

"Juan, are you sure?"

"As sure as I can be at this stage. I haven't spoken to an eye-witness, nor seen the body."

"I want you to get hold of our lawyer in England. What's his name; Herbie?"

"Herbie Bartlett," Marco interjected.

"Yes, that's right, Herbie. You get hold of him and get him to the police. You go with him and identify Carlo. Make sure it's him. Only when you're sure do you come back to me, you understand?"

"Yes, yes," Marco stammered nervously.

Marco did not sleep that night. He stayed at the club. It was to here that the information filtered. The family had their own informants on the street and in a short time the word was out. It was apparent that the police had conducted a fully equipped and professional raid. He was uncertain of the full death toll, but everything seemed to indicate that Carlo was one of the casualties. His other task, given by Paulo

Ramiro was to contact the lawyer Bartlett. He had to search the club for his home telephone number. It was scribbled on the back of his business card in a drawer in the office.

Whilst my knowledge of the Ramiro family and particularly Juan Marco grew continuously during these events, in recounting this version and for the sake of completeness I have had to make certain assumptions as to the activities of the opposition. I subsequently became aware of Herbert Bartlett and the nature of his business. Whilst I hope my account is true to life and doesn't defame him too much, do I care? I don't think so.

Herbert Bartlett had qualified in law in the late eighties. His route had been arduous, working as an articled clerk in a solicitor's office and gaining his academic qualifications through evening class. He was now in his late fifties, a small, rounded man with a balding head. His half-moon glasses barely managed to sit on his full nose. His suits were ready-made and shabby. He extracted full use from them. Bartlett had become involved with the Ramiro family some years previously. He had initially represented a courier, captured red-handed. He obtained an acquittal. It was then identified that he had much to offer. Having learned the hard way, he had become adept at the intricacies of criminal law. He was aware of the inadequacies of police evidence and how to exploit it. More importantly, he was happy to receive cash retainers for his expertise and had no moral compunction as to how it should be used.

Bartlett snored as he slept. His dumpy body took up much of the double bed and generally frustrated his wife's own sleep. She had lain awake for some hours, napping fitfully, when the telephone next to the bed sounded. She answered it promptly. Herbie did not stir.

"Yes," she asked firmly. She was not impressed at the disturbances either from Herbie or the telephone call.

"Mr Bartlett please. It's urgent." Marco tried to be polite.

"Herbert. Herbert, wake up. It's the phone, for you."

When he did not respond she prodded him in the back with the telephone receiver. He grunted as he rolled over.

"Herbert, answer this call at once, wake up," she demanded.

Juan Marco heard her demands at the other end of the line and reminded himself never to get married. Bartlett became rational and took the telephone from his wife:

"Hello."

"Mr Bartlett, Herbie, this is Juan Marco. You remember, I work for the Ramiro's." He gave Bartlett a few seconds to gain his thoughts.

"Mr Marco, yes. What do you want at this time? I hope it's important."

"Yes, it is. The police raided the warehouse last night. They were armed and there was a gunfight. Carlo was present. I believe he was either arrested or killed. I need you to find out."

"All right, Mr Marco. But there's nothing that can be done now. I'll meet you in the morning early, at eight o'clock. Where will you be?"

"At the club. I will stay here."

Bartlett handed the telephone receiver back to his wife. She said nothing as she took it from him. He pulled the covers back over his head and rolled back onto his side. After a few moments the snoring resumed.

It was after half past eight when Bartlett walked through the doors of the Lanthanum. Marco was sitting on a stool by the bar, drinking coffee. The bar was drab and brown, empty of people. During the day it had no atmosphere. It smelt of stale alcohol. Juan Marco looked tired. He had been awake all night. Bartlett wondered what stimulants had seen him through. He did not ask.

"You are late." Marco greeted him.

"I had to ring the office first."

Bartlett's excuse was merely that. The truth of the matter was that he had slept in. His first lie of the day did not worry him. There was no doubt that others would roll from his lips, whether in or out of court.

"Do I get coffee?" He asked Marco.

"Hold on, I'll get you some." Juan Marco left Bartlett and walked to the kitchen.

Herbie Bartlett pulled a mobile telephone from the pocket of his coat. It was a useful implement that allowed him to keep in touch. It also had too many functions, with which he had not yet come to terms. He rarely took photographs unless relevant to his work. He could, however, manage to dial a number. He rang his office. The telephone was answered by his secretary.

"Mavis, I'm going to be late. Can you hold the fort until I get there?"

"Yes Mr Bartlett, but don't forget you've got a ten o'clock. What do you want me to do about it?"

"Either deal with it yourself or rearrange the appointment. I'll be on the mobile for the rest of the morning. I'll get back when I can."

"OK Mr Bartlett. I will see you later."

Juan Marco returned with Bartlett's coffee. He had heard the tail end of the call.

"I thought you said that you had telephoned your office."

"So, I rang again. I like to keep in touch, you know. Time is money, after all." Bartlett smiled.

Herbert Bartlett ran a sole practice. He had split with his partner of some years after an argument that could not be repaired. He had little to offer another firm and therefore broke out alone. He operated from a small office in a side street off Earls Court Road, West London. His only employee and assistant was Mavis. The office was shabby and unkempt, much like its owner. He didn't worry. He could still afford the rent.

Bartlett examined Marco as to his knowledge of the incident. He was precise with his questioning, getting to the fact of the matter and eliminating peripheries efficiently. In a short time, he had extracted Marco's full knowledge.

"There's only one thing to do, Mr Marco. I will have to get hold of the officer in charge and examine the bodies. That's the only way to do it, otherwise we are just guessing. That way we might also get some other interesting tit-bits. I can't do it here. I am going back to the office. I will ring you when I get some news. I had better warn you, it might not be today."

Bartlett left Marco and hurried to the London Underground. He looked at his watch. If he hurried, he could still make the ten o'clock appointment.

Juan Marco stayed at the club. During the late morning he cat-napped in the office at the rear. Whilst not gaining true sleep, it refreshed him slightly. A little cocaine saw him through the rest of the day. It was not until the late afternoon that Bartlett telephoned him.

"It's been a hell of a day," he told Marco. "I couldn't get hold of the officer in charge, a guy named Trevellian. I won't get him until tomorrow now. I've spoken to one of his Sergeants, an officer called

Fergus Johnstone. He was involved in the raid."

"What did you get out him?" Asked Marco.

"Not much. He didn't want to talk. But there's no doubt about it. Carlo's dead. He was on the mortuary slab this afternoon. Him and, I think, two others. Johnstone wouldn't give me their names."

"I already know," confirmed Marco.

"You lost a load of gear, Juan. Around a couple of hundred kilos of coke they took."

"Yes."

"We cannot get the bodies released for a couple of days. We have to make application when they open the inquest. They won't release them before. I'll make sure it's done, but there's no guarantees even then."

"What do you mean?"

"I mean the police might not want to release them. They might want to hang onto them for some evidential reasons. I don't know what. All I know is that there's no guarantees, all right."

It was as a result of this telephone call that Marco again contacted Paulo Ramiro. Eventually the call was put through.

"Paulo. I'm sorry but it's true. The police have confirmed the story. Carlo's dead. We're going to get his body as soon as we can."

"You fly him home, Juan, you fly him home soon." Juan could not see the tears rolling down Paulo's cheeks although he knew they were there.

"I will Paulo. I will call you again."

Paulo Ramiro put down the telephone and walked from his whitewashed, hacienda style, home into the gardens of the ranch. He was devastated. Whilst he could have accepted the news from Miami, or here in Colombia, he had believed London to be a safe haven. Gunfights simply did not occur in London. Why did the police have guns? They were meant to be unarmed. The good old London 'Bobby', the publicity always read. He walked into the Colombian sunlight.

The Ramiro ranch was twenty miles from Bogota off the Tunja road. It was approached via its own long drive and was in an isolated location. The ranch was carefully fenced and alarmed. These facilities were supported by armed guards at regular intervals. This was not merely to protect the family against other rival drugs barons, but also from the genuine guerrilla problems that existed. There were many factions, each seeking supremacy. To achieve this, they needed money, and this could be obtained from robbery or kidnap. Whilst families such as the Ramiro's offered the most risk, they also offered the greatest rewards. Precautions were therefore a necessity.

The Ramiro family had firm roots in Colombia. It had been mooted that they dated back to the Conquistadors of the sixteenth century. The only support for this, however, was the Spanish background. The story remained no more than rumour. Paulo's father had developed the family business during the fifties. Following the war there had been an increased demand for restricted drugs. This demand had soared in the early sixties and continued growing. Initially the trade had been in marijuana, rather than cocaine. This had been heavily exploited by the American mafia in subsequent years. They moved into Colombia with great resources, setting up huge plantations. They did nothing for the Country, attempting to corrupt its fragile leadership. They became greedy and tainted their wares. They added impurities to improve profits. Buyers responded and this, coupled with the extra efforts of American authorities, caused the market to fail.

The Ramiro's had recognised the problems at an early stage and diversified their commodity. They chose cocaine, a move that was to see the business through the enforced recession. Their choice was natural, the drug emanating from the leaves of the coca plant that was easily cultivated within the region. The leaves of the plant had originally been chewed by the native Indians to improve performance and alertness. The extraction of the drug itself was only properly developed in the mid-nineteenth century. The Ramiro operation now had a highly sophisticated laboratory organisation for the production of cocaine hydrochloride, the white, water soluble, salt that had become so popular throughout the world. The business had gone from strength to strength.

Paulo Ramiro enjoyed his home. Whilst only a short distance north of the equator, it enjoyed a cool, pleasant climate, for it was also high above sea level. It was surrounded by the snow-capped peaks of the Andes Mountains. Paulo Ramiro remembered, in his youth, wrestling the lower climbs with his father. He looked with longing at the distant view.

In front of the house, by some thirty yards, was a fenced enclosure, securing Paulo's horses. It was not their only run, but the sight of the relaxed animals gave him pleasure, and he had developed his land accordingly. He walked to the white, wooden fencing and rested on it. He watched the horses. Only three were present. Two stood centrally in the paddock. They nuzzled each other. The third was a white stallion. It stayed apart from the others, feeding on the short grass. He called to the horse.

"Carlo, Carlo, come here boy."

Paulo Ramiro had named the animals after his family members. The horse walked slowly to him. As it approached, he reached into his pocket and took from it a cube of sugar. He held it out on the flat of his hand. The animal took the sugar in its mouth. It continued to walk forward, pushing its muzzle into Paulo's chest. It was strong and pushed him back. He stroked the head and petted the horse.

"Carlo, why you?" He asked, choking the tears from his eyes.

At about twelve noon the following day Trevellian was sitting in his office at New Scotland Yard. He had kept in constant touch with the nursing home and was aware that I was to be seen by the psychologist that day. Sister Tomkins had taken the number of his mobile telephone and promised to contact him with any developments. For the first time in several nights he had slept well, an uninterrupted sleep that had allowed him to recuperate and regain some of his energy. He had not rushed into work, arriving at just after ten-thirty. He sat behind his desk drinking coffee. On the opposite side of the desk was Fergus Johnstone, briefing him as to the developments since the raid. It transpired that very little had happened.

"Not one of them would say a word," continued Johnstone, having paused to sip his own coffee. "We were only left with the dregs. It might be that they knew nothing, or they were just too frightened to talk. It was probably the latter. They didn't say a word, not even their names. We haven't got the evidence to charge them with anything, not this lot. Those we might have charged are lying on the mortuary slab at the moment, I don't know what you think."

"No, you are right, there is no point wasting our time further. We've got the Ramiro drugs. That will cost them a small fortune. It will take them a long time to recover. Carlo Ramiro is dead, along with a couple of his henchmen. I don't think a court case can do much more damage."

"A couple of the workers are Colombian we think. They certainly look it. They haven't provided passports or anything. I've called in the immigration people to sort it out. It's likely that they'll just deport them back home. The others will have to be released."

Trevellian nodded. "Hang on to them as long as you can Fergus. No point in rushing."

"The only other thing was that I got a call from a sickly little brief. He calls himself Herbie Bartlett. Have you heard of him?"

Trevellian shook his head.

"Well, apparently he was acting for the Ramiro family. He wanted to confirm Carlo's death. He was asking about the inquest and when the body would be released."

"When is the inquest?" Trevellian interjected.

"It formally opens the day after tomorrow. They will adjourn it though, to allow time to prepare. I told him we would let him know then. He still wanted to speak to you though. I gave him this number and told him to ring."

Just at that moment the telephone rang. Trevellian raised his eyebrows, surprised at the coincidence. He picked up the receiver.

"Trevellian", he said into the mouthpiece.

"Ah, Mr Trevellian, I've been trying to contact you. I don't know if your sergeant told you. My name is Herbert Bartlett of Bartlett & Co. I am a solicitor acting on behalf of the Ramiro family. I understand that you are the officer in charge?"

"Yes Mr Bartlett, what can I do for you?"

"Can I confirm that you are in possession of the body of Carlo Ramiro, along with others?"

"Yes, that's right."

"Well, obviously the family would like his body released so that he might be given a proper funeral. When can that happen?"

"Certainly not before the inquest Mr Bartlett. I understand that Sergeant Johnstone had told you when that will be."

"So you will not object then, to the release of the bodies. You know that they are a good catholic family and want to give him a proper burial."

"Mr Bartlett, I cannot tell you whether I will object or not. We have not finished our enquiries at this time. You will have to make your application to the coroner on the day."

"Yes, yes, well thank-you Mr Trevellian. Now what about the warehouse, when can my client re-possess his property?"

"Just as soon as we have finished, Mr Bartlett." Trevellian was becoming agitated. It showed in his voice.

"And what about these drugs, Inspector, how did you know they were there?"

"Mr Bartlett, I am not prepared to discuss this with you further at this time. I will speak to you at the inquest. Thank you for calling." Trevellian put down the telephone.

"Bloody cheek the man's got." He told Johnstone.

In contrast, my days had been quiet. I had stayed in my room throughout, my only visitors being the nursing staff and Duncan Trevellian. I had said little to anybody. The nurses were aware of my trauma and merely passed the time of day with me. They did not pry. They allowed me time to recover. I welcomed this time alone. It allowed me to come to terms with the experience.

The physical effects of the rape had cleared quickly. Over the days the pain had faded, the bruising was now dark yellow and slowly disappearing. The nature of my employment as an undercover officer had caused me to always to expect the worst. I considered myself the eternal pessimist. I could accept that the rape was a business risk. It was not this one experience that had caused my disintegration. In company with the drugs and alcohol, the act had regenerated memories long since forgotten, put out of my mind many years ago. It was these recollections that terrorised me.

Emily Krystman had been a psychologist for many years. She had graduated from Edinburgh University in the late sixties, before expanding her academic and professional qualifications. She had been a consultant with the Metropolitan Police for seven years and this had rapidly become the mainstay of her practice. Police officers were not afraid to test her experience in a wide variety of fields, from personal matters to murders. She was a regular visitor to the nursing home and had assisted many officers in dealing with their problems. These were normally stress related and had a variety of effects from complete withdrawal to violence. She always ensured that the patients were aware that she was neither a medical doctor, nor a psychiatrist. She was not there to cure their illnesses or a particular disease of the mind.

Her job was to help them to address their fears or problems and bring them back into perspective. She hoped to do this with me.

It was early afternoon when she tentatively knocked on the door of my room. The initial reception by the patient was the thing she hated most. She could never predict how they would react, no matter who they were. On a previous occasion she had been attacked as she had entered the room. Often a patient would turn away, refusing to acknowledge her presence. Once the ice was broken, she knew that progress could be made. Those initial steps were, however, critical.

I was lying quietly on the bed within the sparsely furnished room. Since my admission I had been administered sedatives, I believed Valium. Whilst helping me sleep, they left me drowsy throughout the day. I did little, therefore, to pass the time. The drugs could not help stave off the boredom that was beginning to overwhelm me. I was aware that the psychologist was to visit. Whilst welcoming the break in routine, the intimacy of the visit worried me. I heard the knock on the door. As it began to open I swung my legs from the bed to sit upright. I faced Emily Krystman as she entered.

"Hi!" Emily tried to sound relaxed and confident as she entered. "Katrina isn't it?"

I said nothing although a slight smile recognised Miss Krystman's introduction. I looked at the woman as she stood just within the entrance of the door. Emily Krystman's training had taught her to avoid too great an intrusion in the initial stages. I saw a small woman, possibly in her fifties. She was under five feet three and this caused her figure to be rounded. No matter how much she dieted, she could not shift the excess weight on her hips. Her clothing was dull, a brown three-quarter length skirt and beige blouse. Her hair was curly and mousy in colour. She wore brown, plastic framed glasses. In her hand she carried a clipboard. I thought her non-descript. I don't now!

"Can I come in?" Emily persevered, having received little response.

I pulled out of my drug-induced vagueness. "Yes, yes, eh, sit down." I indicated a chair.

Emily Krystman made herself comfortable before opening the conversation. She started in an apparently relaxed mode although this did not reflect her true feelings.

"Katrina, I am Emily Krystman. I'm a psychologist working independently for the police force. I firstly want to make it clear that I answer to no-one, except to you and me. Nothing you tell me will go beyond these four walls. Do you accept that?"

This question caught me out. I had expected a "Do you understand?" To accept the word of the stranger, no matter how well recommended went against my natural instincts. I looked up at Miss Krystman and observed the woman. She looked trustworthy.

"We'll see." I replied.

Emily Krystman was not disappointed. She had not fallen at the first hurdle. My answer had not rejected her out of hand. It had left the door slightly open for progress to be made. She had to capitalise on her advantage.

"You know, no matter how many times I visit this place, I'm always impressed by the facilities: The television rooms, games facilities and even an indoor swimming pool. Have you tried them yet?"

I thought before answering. I had expected the Psychologist to launch into an analysis of my problem. In not doing this she had again caught me unawares. I realised that I had not left the room since arriving at the hospice and indeed was totally unaware of the facilities.

"No, no, I haven't. This place has got its own swimming pool?"

"Yes, indeed. It's down in the basement, for the use of the residents only. It's excellent for those people that have lost arms or legs. It allows them the privacy to come to terms with their disability. You know, they have awful problems accepting their fate."

This focused my mind on the problems of others. Several officers within the Force had suffered such injuries, particularly from terrorist explosives. In some ways it made my problems pale into insignificance. My physical existence might be damaged, but it was intact. I was silent for a moment before answering.

"Yes, I can imagine."

Emily Krystman was aware that my mind was elsewhere. Whilst she had broken the ice and gained access to her patient, she had to draw me out, to talk out what was troubling me. But I wasn't going to be drawn. Not at that time anyway. I remained on the edge of the bed. I was no longer looking at the Psychologist. I was sitting with my head bowed, staring into my lap. My hands were clasped in front of me. Emily rummaged in her abundant handbag. She found what she was looking for at the very bottom.

"Would you like a sweet?" She offered me, holding out two

coloured, boiled sweets.

"No thank-you." I looked up and smiled.

Emily unwrapped hers and put it into her mouth. She decided to hit the nail on the head.

"Can you talk about what happened, Katrina? Will you tell me about it?"

Again I was silent. I thought before answering.

"Yes, yes, I can. What do you want to know?"

"Tell me about the incident. Start from the beginning and don't hurry. I need to hear everything, no matter how trivial."

"But I can't."

"Shit," thought Emily, but said "Why not?"

"Because it's confidential, it's a confidential enquiry." I knew that I was talking rubbish, but it threw some of the owness back on the Psychologist.

Emily Krystman breathed a sigh of relief. "Its all right. I have to keep the confidence. I have complete clearance from Mr Trevellian. Nothing you tell me will go outside this room."

I studied the woman's face intently as she made this statement. I believed her. Not that it mattered anyway. It was too late. The operation was complete. I started the tale. It took some time. I detailed the operation and explained my role. There were certain matters that I did not tell. I did not trust the woman that much. I kept my alter-identity a secret. I changed locations and names. The rape, I was able to recount. I had thought about the incident during my enforced privacy. I had assimilated the physical trauma of the incident as being a business risk. This I could accept, as I would have with a more trivial assault that occurred during any arrest.

Emily Krystman listened to the story. Whilst she had been aware of the basic facts, I filled in much of the detail that was essential to her. As I spoke, Emily scribbled notes on her pad. Her writing was scrawny and virtually indecipherable, except to herself. She often used shorthand that only she could understand. Her notes would be typed and filed that evening.

As I spoke, Emily Krystman watched and listened, occasionally asking a question to clarify a point. There was something strange about my delivery, thought Emily. It took her some time to identify the fault. She could not put her finger on it straight away. It was as if I was recounting a soliloquy. I had learnt my lines and told them word-perfect. I made few mistakes.

"It's as if she's giving evidence in court," thought Emily Krystman as her concern grew. She was right, of course.

She gained little from this interaction, apart from the facts of the incident. I answered her questions with an "I can't remember", or a "yes, no". My expression was unchanging. As I coldly described the actual rape, the psychologist asked,

"What were you thinking? What did you feel when he was inside you, actually during the intercourse?"

I looked up. I focused on Emily for a second. My face registered apprehension and fear, but only for a short time. I saw her questions as inappropriate and unnecessary. But were they unnecessary? Where did she want to go with this? Her route obviously had an ulterior motive. I knew where it could go. Did I want it to go there? Emily Krystman watched as I fought to regain my detached control. My eyes returned to their glazed expression and I looked down to my lap.

"I can't remember?" I mumbled. I was lying.

Emily Krystman's writing became even more ragged. She had noted the reaction, not only mentally, but also on paper. She had written quickly, recording every blink of my eyes. On conclusion, she ringed the note with her pen. It was imperative that she remembered this item. As I reached the finale, I told of my treatment at the hands of the medical profession. I became agitated, aggressive and quite rightly so, I thought. They had truly pissed me off. What was more apparent to Miss Krystman was that I allowed myself to express these feelings. Her pen scribbled quickly again. The observation was worthy of another ring over her notes. I stopped talking. There was a short silence.

"Thank you, Katrina, for being so frank." Emily's face showed sincerity. "There were times, however, when I thought you might call me 'Your Worship'. I think we by-passed what is truly worrying you, didn't we?"

I feigned surprise as I looked at the other woman. "What do you mean? I've told you everything."

"Not quite, I think." She was a shrewd lady, I mused.

Emily Krystman looked at her watch, then back to her patient. She knew she had established an advantage and did not want to lose it.

Over an hour had passed.

"I'm going to leave you now, Katrina. I'll come back and see you again tomorrow, at about the same time. Today has been really useful, but if we're going to sort out your problem, you're going to have to trust me properly. You need to tell me everything, rather than just what you think I want to hear. I'll leave you to think on that one, OK?"

She smiled at me. A partial, nervous, smile was my response. She approached me and put her hands on my shoulders. I allowed her touch. Emily Krystman knew that she had broken another important barrier. I knew so to.

"I'll see you tomorrow, then." She walked from the room.

I watched as the Psychologist left the room. As the door swung shut, I physically relaxed and lay back down on the bed. I put my hands behind my neck and looked up at the ceiling. The discourse with Miss Krystman had cleared my mind. The concentration had driven the drugs from my consciousness and returned me to reality. I felt better. It was the first time that I had fully explained the incident. I now felt I had control of its effects.

That evening, for the first time, I chose to leave the room. Nurse Tomkins was on duty and had brought a meal to my room. I discussed the decision with her.

"You are looking better," said the Nurse. "If you feel up to it, after you've eaten, I'll show you around. There's actually not much to see. We've got the swimming pool. Hey, would you like a swim? I can get you a spare costume."

"Yes, that would be nice."

I ate much of the meal that had been served to me. I was hungry. I could not remember when I had eaten last. It had been several days ago. The food was of standard hospital production. The pork chop was over-cooked and tough. I managed a mouthful before pushing it to one side. The vegetables were similarly over-cooked to the point of softness. They were, however, edible, and I devoured them. The jam roly-poly and custard, for dessert, was good. It was possibly the best part of the meal. I enjoyed it. Helen Tomkins entered the room just as I had finished. In her hand she held a black, one-piece, swimming costume.

"I hope this fits." She looked at my empty plate. "It looks like you are feeling better. Carry on like this and we might have to let you go."

She gave me the costume. "I'll get rid of the tray and let you get changed. I'll be down the corridor at the desk. Come down when you're ready and don't forget your towel," she said as an afterthought.

I changed slowly. I chose to avoid nakedness by clothing myself in a dressing gown before removing my pyjama trousers. I knew that my injuries were healing but did not wish to be reminded of them at that time. I pulled on the costume. It was a tight fit but was comfortable. The cut was too high. The yellowing bruises on my inner thighs were visible. I ignored them and walked purposefully from the room.

Helen Tomkins greeted me as I walked towards her.

"Hi, you're ready. How does the costume fit?"

"It's OK thanks, perhaps a little tight."

"Don't worry, it will loosen off in the water. Follow me."

The nurse led me down a set of stairs into the basement area. I could feel the heat of the swimming pool as I entered. It was not a large pool, perhaps eight metres by four. The walls were tiled in blue, matching the cleanliness of the water. Nobody else was present.

"Enjoy yourself. You know your way out when you're finished?"

"Yes", I smiled. "Thank you." I turned towards her and briefly touched her hand.

The solemnity of the empty pool area was comforting and relaxing for me. I allowed the robe to slip to the ground and dropped the towel on top of it. My slippers were not needed on the clean poolside. I walked to the water and dipped in my foot to test the temperature. It was warmer than the average pool, more like a bath, I thought. I did not dive in. Although I was a competent swimmer, I had no desire to test my rate of recovery by over exertion. I tip-toed to a set of steps in one corner and slowly eased myself beneath the water line. I pushed myself away from the steps, on my back. The lightness of my body allowed me to float easily. My buoyancy was assisted by the water. The warmth permeated through my tired body. I gently kicked my legs creating some motion. I closed my eyes as I moved slowly along. My mind was blank. I thought of nothing.

For several minutes I drifted. I had benefited from my period with Emily Krystman. We had not addressed the issue that had troubled me. The essence of my resolution was that the true problem had been isolated and placed back into the depths of my sub-conscious, where it had been kept for so many years. It should never be resurrected.

I had been gently switching from my back to my front, in the water. A degree of confidence had been regained and this suddenly expressed itself in a desire to swim at pace. I stopped at one end of the pool and then readied myself for a sprint. I pushed off, little realising that whilst my injuries were curing, they still existed. My front crawl lasted for merely a few seconds before I carefully slowed. My thigh muscles cramped with pain as I sought speed. Even my arms, which I thought were un-injured, ached as I exerted myself. I swam to the side of the pool and used the ladder to aid my exit.

Helen Tomkins replaced the telephone receiver as I approached the desk.

"Did you enjoy that?" She asked.

"Yes, the water was lovely. My thighs hurt a bit though." I winced as I spoke.

"Too much, too soon, eh," the nurse laughed. "You're on the mend though. That is the important thing."

"I'll see you tomorrow." I walked back to my room.

Both the nurse and I knew that I had made progress that day. Helen Tomkins did not approach me with sleeping pills. I could ask if I wanted them. I did not ask. I went to bed and slept. It was a full night's sleep, undisturbed for the first time. I awoke the following morning relaxed and refreshed.

Emily Krystman arrived promptly at twelve noon. Her dress had changed little. She dressed formally but casually. She was not a dowdy person but recognised the needs of her patients. Again she knocked on the door before entering. I was alert and awaiting her arrival.

"Katrina, you look better today." Emily noticed the improvement immediately.

"I feel it." I began confidently. "I think our talk yesterday sorted out my problem, don't you?"

"Only you can answer that question." Emily gave a seriously quizzical look. "What was the problem that we sorted out?"

She sat in the chair without waiting to be invited and placed her writing pad on her lap.

"The rape!" I was direct in my answer wishing to be positive. "We talked about the attack. That was what was troubling me."

"Is that all?"

"I think so, don't you?"

I was unsure of Emily Krystman now. The uncertainty showed through as I twiddled my fingers in my lap. The Psychologist purposely did not answer my question. She was silent for a moment before speaking again. 'Tricky cow,' I thought.

"Katrina, I need some background information about you. I want to talk about your family. Do you mind?"

I had lost my initial confidence in her. I knew where she was going. I did not want to go there. What was in the past should stay in the past. I looked into my lap. I preferred to avoid eye contact.

"Why, what do you want to know?"

"It's just a formality. Yesterday we only talked about the incident. I really know nothing about you. It's only background information."

I knew that she was not telling the truth but was willing to show some cooperation.

"All right then. What do you want to know?"

"You were brought up in Devon, weren't you?"

"Yes, in Dawlish, outside Exeter."

"By the sea?" Emily smiled having been there for a holiday in her own childhood. "Do your parents still live there?"

"My mother does, yes."

"And your father?"

"He died when I was seven, in a car accident."

Miss Krystman looked at me. "I am sorry. I didn't know. So your mother, she is alone now?"

"No, she re-married. She lives with my step-father."

I was hesitant. We were drifting towards the areas that I wished to avoid.

"Do you have any brothers or sisters?"

Emily Krystman had noted my hesitancy and therefore stayed general.

"Only my brother Sam. He's five years older than me."

"He does not live at home?"

"No, he left when I was fourteen."

"So how about you, when did you leave?"

"When I was seventeen. I came to London to get a job. I was a secretary. I shared a flat with a friend for a couple of years before joining this job."

"OK, that's helpful. Now, I want to take you back a bit. What do you remember about your father?"

"Only good times. He was slightly older than my mother, self-employed, I don't know what as. He always looked after us. We were happy. Mum and dad were always there for us. There were no worries at all."

Emily Krystman watched me closely. I was relaxed as I spoke of my father. I went on to describe him and to itemise certain incidents that I remembered. They were pleasant, family memories.

"How did you all reconcile his death?"

"We were devastated. It took mum years to get over him. She still thinks of him now. I know I do."

"Yet she re-married?"

A mist crossed my face. I became agitated. "Yes, yes, she did."

"Tell me about your stepfather."

I looked fiercely at the psychologist. "Why do you need to know more? Have we not talked this through?"

Emily was firm in her reply. "I need to know, and I need you to tell me Katrina. When did your mother re-marry?"

"When I was ten. She had known him for a year or so. I don't know why she married him. Perhaps for security, I don't know."

"What is he like? What do you think of him?"

It was clear that Ms Krystman was not going to let this lie. I decided to stay with her.

"He was all right at first. The first couple of years were OK. But we didn't get on. He didn't like me. He was always having a go at me."

I was strangely calm as I replied. I did not feel calm. I was talking about something that I did not want to talk about. Emily Krystman was drawing from me things that I did not want to discuss. She was strangely compelling. I talked to her anyway. My eyes were transfixed to my lap. I did not want to look at her. My hands were clenched together. I did not want to show my feelings.

"Why did he have a go at you?"

"I was ill; at times I wasn't well."

"What do you mean?"

I slowly raised my head. "I don't know. I was losing weight."

"Katrina, do you mean you were anorexic?"

"I couldn't eat. I didn't want to eat."

"Why, Katrina. Why were you losing weight?"

"I can't tell you." I sobbed into my hands, shaking my head from side to side as I spoke. Crocodile tears, I don't think so. They were real. The Psychologist had hit the nerve.

Emily Krystman knew that she was reaching the crux of the problem. She could not stop now, or she would lose the initiative. However, she allowed a long silence. I benefited from that silence. I slowly regained my composure.

As she re-started Emily's voice was softer and less demanding. "Katrina, you've got to trust me. You need to talk about it. Whatever happened is what is causing this problem now. You know that and so do I. This is purely between you and me. Nobody else need know." Her voice trailed off.

An air of tension engulfed the room. The silence did not provide a relaxed atmosphere this time. The Psychologist was mentally willing me to speak to her. I wanted and needed to speak but something stopped me from doing so. My mind was in turmoil. Should I trust the woman sitting before me? She was a virtual stranger though she exhibited an empathy with me. But why should I speak?

I steeled myself and thought logically. The problem hidden for so many years had re-surfaced. It could no longer be placed under wraps. The time had come. My face hardened as I looked directly into Miss Krystman's eyes. The Psychologist held my gaze knowing the importance of the moment.

"He fucked me, that's why". My voice was loud and penetrating. The words burst forth. "For a year he fucked me. I couldn't tell my mother. I couldn't tell her that her husband was fucking her daughter. I had no-one to tell. I didn't know what to do. That's why I was losing weight. That's why I wasn't eating."

I was not crying. My eyes were staring as I remembered my fate. I had done with crying all those years ago. Emily reached forward and took my hand in sympathy.

"How did it start Katrina? Tell me what happened in the beginning."

I shook my head and thought back. "I think I was thirteen. My mother had gone out for the evening, I don't know where. My brother was out as well. I was on my own with him. Kenny, that was his name. That was what my mother used to call him. We were watching television; sitting in the lounge He went and got himself a drink. He brought it in and gave me a glass as well. I asked him what was in it.

He just told me to try it. He said I would like it. I think it was gin, gin and tonic. I drank it. I should have known, but I trusted him. He got me another. I wasn't used to it. I drank that as well. The next thing I remember was waking up on the sofa. He was on top of me. He was kissing my face. I still remember the smell of his breath. It was revolting. He had pulled off my pants and was trying to enter me. It hurt, but I couldn't stop him. I was drunk, and he was too strong. He forced his way in. He raped me."

Emily's hand tightened on mine as she relived the event with me. My eyes became more intense. "I was a virgin. This was my first experience. The bastard raping me was my first experience of sex."

"What happened then?" Emily did not want her to lose her track.

"It was all over in seconds. He came inside me and then it was over. He told me not to tell my mother. He told me that if I did, he would force her to choose between him and me. He would deny it ever happened. He would brand me a liar. I didn't tell anyone. I was too frightened."

"He carried on having sex with you?"

"Yes, there was nothing I could do about it. If my mother went out for an evening he was there, demanding it. I used to plead with her to take me with her, or not to go out, but she thought it was just me. I told her I hated Kenny. She assumed I was just rejecting him, as he wasn't my father. It even got to the point where he would come to my room in the middle of the night, whilst my mother was asleep. He used to get into bed with me. He threatened to leave her if I did anything. Eventually I just let him get on with it. There was nothing I could do."

"How long did it go on for?"

"It must have been a year or so, perhaps longer."

"And how did you stop it?"

"I was in a terrible state. I wasn't eating and was down to about forty kilos in weight. I stayed in my room all the time and wouldn't speak to anyone. They were all worried about me, especially him. He knew he was losing control over me, and that at anytime I might tell all. As he was on top of me, he used to plead with me not to tell her. He was getting nervous. Eventually I was at the end of my tether. There was nothing left to live for. One night I went to bed. I took a knife with me from the kitchen. I decided it was time to end it all, to commit suicide. Anyway, I didn't have the bottle. I tried cutting my wrists but couldn't pull the blade across. I fell asleep with the knife in my hands, under the blanket. He came in that night and shook me awake. He was in the bed beside me. He wanted sex. I rolled towards him remembering the knife. I held it to his throat and threatened to kill him. The knife was tight against his throat and cut him. He knew I was serious. I could have killed him there and then. I don't know why I didn't. He began to cry. He pleaded with me to let him go. I told him to get away from me and not to come back. It was that, that did it. He never troubled me again. I always took my knife to bed with me after that. In fact, I've still got it to this day, somewhere in my flat."

We talked further. The relationship was now far more relaxed. I had confided my innermost secret to Emily Krystman. I had never discussed it before and now had no option other than to trust her. We talked for another hour. Our conversation was not now merely confined to my problems although most of the conversation revolved around them. Emily knew that whilst I had finally spoken about my childhood assaults, the problems were not yet overcome. I would need continuing support and assistance throughout this crucial period. It was essential that I no longer thought of myself as being alone, of having to take the burden on my own shoulders. From that time onwards I did not.

"Is there anyone else who you could tell about this?" Emily asked as our session came to a conclusion.

"No, no-one. I don't think so."

"How about your boyfriend?"

"I haven't got one, not had one for ages. Work, I suppose."

"No close friends?"

"Not that I would trust." I stopped for a moment, my face showing that I was pondering.

Emily recognised the thoughtful look.

"Who?" She asked.

"Well, there is perhaps someone, maybe Duncan Trevellian. He has helped up to now, but I don't know if I should, or could."

"Would it help if I spoke to him, tested the water for you first. I could give him an idea of what's happened, but it's up to you."

Again I thought. "Possibly, but I have troubles even with him. He is a senior officer in the police. I am his subordinate. I did not declare my past problems when I applied to join and have hidden them since. He would have to detach himself from being my supervisor to simply being a friend. I don't know if he could do that. If not, it would prejudice my future and simply make things worse."

"I can make sure that will not happen."

"In that case, see what you can do. But please be careful. I do appreciate your help."

Emily had been putting on her coat as she spoke. "I'll try and get hold of him. I will get him to come and see you. Anyway, I will be back tomorrow. I'll see you then OK."

Chapter Eight

The inquest into the death of Carlo Ramiro and his henchmen opened at Southwark Coroners' Court before London's leading coroner Dr Felix Heimdall. Detective Inspector Trevellian arrived early. He knew this would be merely a formality, the inquest being adjourned until the conclusion of police enquiries. Even so, he wanted to be prepared. Henry Clayman, the pathologist had also arrived early. His briefcase was heavy with papers. A recently lit cigar burned between the fingers of his right hand.

"Good morning Inspector," he greeted Trevellian. "Not expecting any problems, I trust?"

"Good morning to you, Sir." Trevellian responded politely. "No, I hope not. However, it's always better to be safe in a case of this magnitude."

The two men chatted together for a few minutes. The court was quiet due to their early arrival. It was an imposing building being one of the older courts in London. It had originally been established to investigate dockside deaths when London had been a substantial and active port. With the demise of the Thames shipping industry the building had become under-used. It was a Victorian redbrick building. The courtroom itself was designed to place the coroner above those around him. He would sit in regal splendour in his carved wooden chair behind his raised bench. The legal representatives would face him from the lowered central well. A jury, if needed, would be to his left, at a height between himself and the counsel. The public were relegated to pews at the rear.

Herbert Bartlett and Juan Marco arrived at the courtroom a few minutes after Trevellian. He did not see them at first, being involved in conversation with Clayman. A small tea-bar had provided Trevellian with drinks for himself and Clayman. They sipped the warm liquid from plastic cups. Trevellian first registered the presence of the other two men as they approached the tea-bar. He did not know them, but realised from Marco's swarthy, South-American appearance that they would be on the other side. He had discussed Bartlett with Fergus Johnstone. The Detective Sergeant had, perhaps, been over zealous with his defamatory description of Bartlett. Trevellian had never seen him before although found many aspects of Johnstone's caricature were correct. He identified him accordingly.

Bartlett left Marco drinking the weak tea from the plastic cup whilst he approached Trevellian and Clayman.

"Inspector Trevellian, am I right?" He asked as he neared. "I am Herbert Bartlett representing the Ramiro family and particularly Paulo Ramiro, Carlo's father. Could I have a word with you?"

"Do excuse me." Dr Clayman picked up his briefcase and walked away from the pair.

"What can I do for you, Mr Bartlett?" Trevellian was polite, although he had no desire to be so.

"I intend to make application for the release of the bodies today, so that they can be returned home and have a proper funeral. Will you have any objections to that?"

"We have completed our autopsies, but the release will be up to the court."

"When do you expect the full inquest to take place?"

"Again, that is a matter for the court, but just as soon as our enquiries are complete".

"When will that be Inspector?"

"I can't say at this time Mr Bartlett. You will be fully aware that our agency will not be the only investigative agency involved. The Independent Police Complaints Commission has also been notified."

"Yes, Inspector. I am already aware of the involvement of the IPCC."

"Is there anything else Mr Bartlett?"

"How were you aware of the drugs, Inspector? Who was the informant?" Bartlett's easily answerable question did not wrong-foot Trevellian.

"You know better than to ask, Mr Bartlett. You know I would not answer that question one way or the other."

Bartlett asked no further questions of Trevellian. His slight huff as he walked away was audible. Her returned to Juan Marco and the couple whispered quietly together. Trevellian could see why he was not to be trusted.

The inquest started promptly at 10am. Dr Heimdall had dealt with most situations during his term of office and did not feel intimidated by the several deaths involved, nor of the serious implications caused by the involvements of drugs and police. His first action was to call Detective Inspector Trevellian into the witness box.

"Inspector Trevellian, I understand that police enquiries into this matter continue. Is that correct?"

"Yes Sir, it is".

"It would therefore be appropriate for this matter to be adjourned pending the completion of these enquiries. How long would you expect that to be Inspector?"

"About a month Sir."

"Well, if we adjourn for four weeks, then we can expect to proceed. Does anyone have any observations as to this course of action?"

Herbert Bartlett rose slowly to his feet before the coroner. "Herbert Bartlett, representing the family of Carlo Ramiro and the other men. Can I ask for the release of the bodies in order that the families will not be deprived of proper funerals and burials? They obviously intend to fly the men home to Colombia and preparations need to be made."

"What observations do you have Inspector?" Dr Heimdall asked.

"Whilst Dr Clayman has completed our examinations, Sir, the families have had no opportunity to question the findings or carry out their own post-mortems."

"I'm sure we will have no reason to question Dr Clayman," Bartlett was subservient. "Unless there is something surprising about their deaths."

Dr Heimdall looked around the courtroom, spotting Clayman sitting in the second row. "Dr Clayman, can Mr Bartlett expect any surprises?"

"I don't think so, Sir." Clayman began as he slowly climbed to his feet. "They all died from gunshot wounds. I suppose the only question might be; who fired the shots?" Clayman resumed his seat more quickly than he had risen.

"In that case I see no reason why the bodies cannot be released and so order accordingly. Is that all Mr Bartlett?"

"Just one other small matter, Sir. I would ask for the early release of any evidence, including details of any informants that the police might have used in this matter."

Dr Heimdall was too astute to be disturbed. "Mr Bartlett, any information as to police informants might be relevant in a criminal trial, but I doubt that it would be of relevance to the enquiry into their deaths. I suggest that you hold such applications at least until the inquest commences. Now, is there anything else before I adjourn these proceedings?"

"No, thank you," Bartlett sat as he spoke.

"This matter is adjourned accordingly." Dr Heimdall rose from his seat and left the room.

Duncan Trevellian arrived back at his office just after midday. He was aware that he had not visited me for some days. This weighed heavily on his conscience. He had simply been too busy. He had, however, telephoned and spoken to Nurse Tomkins on a day-to-day basis and was aware of my progress. The nurse had told him of the first visit of Emily Krystman and of my subsequent foray into the swimming pool. This tempered his worry somewhat, although he steeled himself to visit soon. Fergus Johnstone was at his desk on Trevellian's arrival.

"How did it go?" He asked Trevellian.

"Not bad Fergus. That little rat Bartlett was sniffing around. They are trying to ferret out whether or not we had a snout. I left him guessing. However, he did succeed in getting the bodies released. I suppose they will be flying them home soon."

Johnstone nodded. Neither was sad to see the departure of the deceased Ramiro. He began foraging through the papers on his desk.

"A woman rang for you by the way. A psychologist, to do with Katrina. Her name was," he paused for a moment. "It began with a K. Look; I've found it." He smiled as he held up a scrap of paper. "Krystman, that's it and here is her number."

"Thanks," Trevellian took the paper from him and walked to his own office. He shut the door, sat at his desk and then rang the number thoughtfully.

"Hello," answered Emily Krystman

"Hi, Duncan Trevellian, you rang me."

"Yes Duncan. I need to speak to you about Katrina Marshall. Is it possible we could meet today sometime?"

As a result of this conversation, at about four that afternoon, Trevellian drove west out of London. He had arranged to meet Emily Krystman in a roadside café just off the motorway. It was convenient to them both, he was driving west, and she was returning in the opposite direction. Trevellian was slightly delayed. He was fifteen minutes late. He approached the door to the café aware that the evening would soon close in. It was cold. A slight drizzle was in the air.

Trevellian entered the café, looking around as he did so. He instantly identified the figure of Emily Krystman. She was just as he had expected. Her seated position camouflaged her lack of height. The give-away was her brown coat covering her brown dress. She did not need to stand out. It was her patients that mattered. Trevellian walked to her table:

"Miss Krystman?" She nodded her confirmation. He held out his hand. "Duncan Trevellian. I'm sorry I'm late."

The Psychologist stood to shake Trevellian's hand. At that point he realised exactly how short she was. With a wave of the hand she invited him to sit. He did so. They ordered coffee from an attendant waitress.

"Thanks for coming Duncan. I know it was short notice, but I think it is important. It's about Katrina Marshall."

Emily Krystman initially spent some minutes assessing Trevellian as to whether he could depart from his role as a Police Inspector. She decided to take the risk. It was a worthy risk, as, at that time, I needed a friend. She went on to explain my trauma to Trevellian. She chose to reflect on the nature of my past history without revealing the specifics of my problems.

I accept a certain literacy freedom in reporting conversations about me, to which I was not a party. Even my best subsequent enquiries would not reveal the true detail of what was said.

Trevellian sat very quietly and intently, digesting every word. He did not interrupt.

"I haven't given you every detail, Duncan. I will leave Katrina herself to do that if she wants to. I have only told you this with her total agreement. The difficulty is that she has no-one else to tell. For some reason she trusts you sufficiently to share her most innermost secret."

Trevellian sat back in his chair. He picked up his cup and sipped his coffee. It was now warm rather than hot. Emily Krystman's tale had taken longer than expected.

"I'm amazed," he responded. "I had assumed that the rape itself had caused her reaction. I had no idea that she had any other problems."

"Nor had anybody else. She kept it to herself. She told no-one except me and now you. Tell me, are you prepared to help?"

"Of course I am. What do I need to do?"

"Firstly, forget you are a police officer and particularly her supervising officer. For these purposes you are her friend. Provide the support and comfort to help her get through this. I will be there as well, to help both of you. I don't expect you to do it all alone. You'll just have to take each day as it comes though."

"Yes, I understand," Trevellian began to stutter. His new found responsibilities were not him.

"Take my card. Ring me anytime, day or night. Anytime you need my help."

Trevellian has conceded that he continued the rest of the journey at a slow pace. His mind was elsewhere, on the subject of my plight. My recent rape had rekindled the abuse that I had suffered at the hands of my stepfather. A shiver passed down his spine as he considered the possible implications. He felt responsible. He had involved me in the operation. He mitigated the blame, as he could not have known. I had told no-one. Poor Trevellian, at times I felt that his suffering almost matched my own. He had no reason to feel any guilt at all.

Nurse Tomkins guarded the nursing home. She would not allow Trevellian access to my room without first introducing him. She was keen to ensure my privacy. I therefore had time to prepare myself for his entry. I sat demurely on the edge of the bed as he came through the door. The serious look on his face immediately told me that he had met with Emily Krystman. The butterflies in my stomach indicated my uncertainty as to his reaction.

"Hi Katrina," he said.

He walked straight to me with his hands forward. I tentatively responded with mine when he was close enough. He kissed my cheek.

"I had a meeting with your psychologist and she gave me an outline as to your past problems, Katrina. I'm so sorry I put you in the situation I did."

My emotion, yet again, overcame me. I burst into tears. My head fell forward into Trevellian's chest as I cried. He put his arms around me to comfort me. I had cried before, but this was different. These were tears of relief, almost of happiness. A weight had been taken from my shoulders. I now had some genuine support for my problems, problems that had been suppressed for too long.

It took me only a few minutes to recover my composure. I looked up at Trevellian, smiling through the tears. He took a handkerchief from his pocket and wiped them from my cheek. He sat beside me on the bed. We still held hands. We talked intensely for perhaps twenty minutes. I filled in the gaps with regard to my stepfather's abuse.

"You should have killed him when you had the chance." Trevellian interjected at one point, knowing that the comment was purely an emotional response.

"I sometimes wish I had. You know, he is still with my mother. I haven't seen her for ages because of it. I don't go to visit. I still don't trust him. Occasionally she comes to London and we meet and go shopping. Otherwise, I don't see my own mother. How's the job going by the way?"

The sudden change of subject caught Trevellian unawares. It was obvious that I was recovering rapidly. I was more alert and had purposely changed the subject.

"Eh, OK. The inquest has opened and has been adjourned. A creepy little lawyer called Herbert Bartlett is representing the family. He's been prying but got nowhere so far. We have released the bodies, so they will be flying back to Colombia soon. We haven't charged anyone. There didn't seem much point."

"It cost the family dearly though, didn't it? Not only the loss of the drugs, but the loss of Carlo and his boys. What was the final tally anyway?"

There was no doubt that I was feeling better. I had little or no sympathy for the Ramiro clan. They were drug dealers, killers and, more importantly, rapists. I blamed the whole family for my demise.

"There were four of them dead in total. We were only left with bit-players. We didn't lose anybody fortunately. We had a couple wounded, present company included of course," he added.

"Look Duncan, I am feeling a lot better." I paused purposely before continuing. "I'm ready to get out of here and get back to work. Will you help me?"

"Now slow down!" Trevellian was concerned at the apparent speed of my recovery. "You get out when the doctor's say you can. The first thing we'll do when that happens is to hit a pub and have a celebratory drink, OK?"

I nodded.

"I've got to go now, but I'll be back tomorrow evening. Let's see how you are then?"

Trevellian again kissed me on the cheek before leaving. On this occasion I responded slightly, returning the kiss. He left me to puzzle the direction and nature of our developing relationship if there was one. Melissa Grant would have hoisted him onto the bed at that point. I refrained from doing so, although I was tempted. After he had left, I lay back on the bed, my arms behind my neck supporting my head. I felt rested. For the first time recently, I did not dream that night.

Paulo Ramiro's own aircraft was dwarfed by the jumbo-jet, which carried the bodies of his son and their men from London to Miami International Airport. He had arrived early, ensuring that he was available to meet the plane and hoping to ease the administrative burden with his attendance. He had managed to do precisely that. Miami Airport, a large international complex, and identified as the lifeblood of the area, was set on the mainland, close to the Hialeah District. Such an environment created its own problematical administration. When a known Colombian drugs dealer faced the administration head on, the barriers could become impenetrable. Ramiro avoided this head-on collision. His only aim was to achieve the efficient transfer of the boxed bodies to his aircraft and then to take them home.

His first step was to approach the US Customs direct. This was not difficult. They were awaiting the arrival of his aircraft with suspicion. The thorough search revealed nothing. He approached the officer in charge. He introduced himself. The other man responded:

"Jessie Slyder. What can I do for you?"

The man chewed gum as he spoke in his natural southern drawl. His official cap was perched on the back of his head, a shock of curly brown hair bursting from under it. He held a clipboard in his hand. A holstered gun hung from his hip.

"Mr Slyder," Ramiro was polite. "My son and three colleagues were killed in an unfortunate accident in England. They are being flown here today and I wish to transfer the coffins onto this aircraft and take them straight back to Colombia. You will appreciate my sorrow. I ask for your assistance to make this as easy as possible for me."

Slyder was suspicious. "Why not fly them straight to Colombia, Mr Ramiro? Why trouble us?"

"It was merely the availability of flights. We wanted to get them home as soon as possible. There were no immediate direct flights that could accommodate us. That's why we are here."

"We will have to check the cargo before you are allowed to leave, Mr Ramiro."

Slyder was careful to refer to the cargo rather than, more intimately, the coffins.

"We will stay with you and await the arrival of the London aeroplane."

It was this that Ramiro had hoped to avoid. However, he knew of his reputation in the United States and appreciated that he would have to live with it. Whilst the Customs-officers would stay with him to protect their own, distrusting, interests it might serve his own purposes as well. Hopefully they would want him to leave the United States as soon as possible. That was his very intention. For once it would appear that both sides of the law were agreed.

Paulo Ramiro was supported by two of his henchmen, Jessie Slyder by two of his. The six men stood alongside each other as the jumbo jet taxied to a halt. The passenger walkway snaked towards the aircraft as it stopped, allowing disembarkation in comfort. It took only a couple of minutes for the loading gang to begin to remove the cargo.

The solid, sealed trunks had been loaded on two by two, on top of each other, during the flight. They had therefore taken the minimum amount of space. Even so they had barely fitted into the aircraft. They were removed with some decorum, although the workmen had little respect for their contents. They were placed on a trailer pulled by a small, tractor-style, truck.

Slyder had been speaking on his mobile telephone during the unloading.

"We will have to take them to the Customs-shed before they can be released Mr Ramiro. Have you got the paperwork for them?"

"Yes I have." Ramiro raised his hand and immediately a large brown envelope was placed into it. He handed the envelope to Slyder.

"This should correspond to the aircraft's inventory. I want to stay with them Mr Slyder. You'll appreciate that, as a father, won't you?"

Slyder thought for a moment. Indeed, he was a father. Did Ramiro know that already, or was he merely stabbing in the dark. Slyder took no chances. He had no reason to put himself at risk. He knew the Ramiro reputation.

"OK Mr Ramiro, but just you. The other two stay outside."

Ramiro nodded, and the group began to walk behind the slowly proceeding trailer. It was as if the funeral procession had already begun.

Juan Marco had travelled on the aircraft. He had been instructed by Ramiro to do so. This was partially to protect the cargo and ensure its safe passage. Secondly, Ramiro wished to speak to him, face-to-face, to establish what had happened. Marco travelled with trepidation. He had enjoyed his time in London. It was easy, and he wished it to continue. This incident would be attributed to him. It would be a mark on his career. It was possible that Ramiro might remove his status, demote him within the family. This was something he wished to avoid.

Marco was allowed access to the Customs-shed. He was accompanied by separate officer.

"Hello Mr Ramiro. My commiserations, Sir." He was subservient.

Ramiro did not reply. He was watching intently as Customs-officers unscrewed the securing catches of the coffins, one by one. They carefully opened each lid in turn and looked inside. Their faces painted the picture of what they saw. The two drugs-dogs remained silent by their side. Slowly and sombrely they replaced the lid and re-tightened the catches.

"All clear," one of them reported to Slyder.

Slyder walked slightly away from Ramiro and dialled a number on his cell-phone. He spoke quietly into it. On completion he returned to Ramiro.

"Mr Ramiro, you can leave the United States now, with your cargo."

Paulo Ramiro knew that Slyder was working to order. He would have liked to have been face-to-face with the person on the other end of Slyder's phone. He knew that was not to be.

"Thank you, Mr Slyder, for your assistance. Perhaps the coffins could be transported to my aircraft."

Slyder nodded in agreement. Ramiro noted that he was still chewing the same piece of gum. It was obviously his comforter. Slyder's expression barely changed as the envelope passed from

Ramiro into his palm.

"For your help, and for your family," Ramiro told him.

Ramiro's entourage made arrangements to depart from Miami International. Slyder only opened the envelope after the departure. The hundred-dollar bills were dispersed into his clothing as he walked away.

Once the aircraft was in flight, Paulo Ramiro addressed Juan Marco, who was seated beside him. They spoke in their native language.

"Juan, I want to know what happened. Tell me!"

Juan Marco recounted the facts, as he knew them. His information was hearsay, gained from his own investigations, as he had not been present at the scene. He had, however, made distinct efforts to verify every aspect through more than one source. He knew that he would have to account to Paulo and that his facts would have to be sound. He told the story as he knew it, missing out no detail.

"So, our assignment was on view to the police as they entered the warehouse. How was that, Juan?"

Paulo Ramiro had picked up a significant point. He referred to the drugs in various ways, on this occasion as the assignment. Conversations could always be recorded, and Paulo Ramiro was fully aware that, despite travelling on a private aircraft, the facilities available to various agencies had become more sophisticated.

"I don't know Paulo. Perhaps they had somebody on the inside. I don't know who, though."

"You had better find out then and find out quickly. If there was an inside informant, then he, or she, is to blame for Carlo's death. I want them found. What about the lawyer, Bartlett? Can't he find anything out? We pay him enough."

"He's been trying. The police have not told him anything yet."

"Find out Juan, find out."

I had been in the nursing home for ten days. I had made a solid recovery and expected to be released within a few days. Emily Krystman's visits had become less regular, although she still kept in contact. Duncan Trevellian was now a regular visitor, every evening if he could make it. On this particular evening, I was to be allowed to leave the hospice for the first time. This was for the long-awaited drinks-date with Trevellian. Some days ago, at my request, Trevellian had brought my clothes from my flat to the nursing home. I sorted through them, working out what to wear. It was to be an informal evening. Nowhere special he had told me. I stayed casual, selecting jeans and a green long-sleeved ribbed top. It was the first time that I had worn make-up since dressing as Melissa Grant. That now seemed a decade away. I was more demure than I would have been as Melissa Grant. My requirements were different to Melissa's. My lipstick merely complemented my skin colour rather than contrasting with it. Other make-up was used to enhance my own natural looks. I felt good, but apprehensive as Nurse Tomkins entered my room.

"He is here, Katrina. Are you ready?"

"Yes I am coming. Tell me Helen, do you think I should change these glasses for contact lenses?"

"No, I think you're fine just the way you are."

I picked up my jacket from the chair and swung it over my shoulder as I left the room. I nodded my appreciation of the nurse's comment. Duncan Trevellian waited for me in the corridor by the exit.

"You look lovely!" He said as I approached.

Nurse Tomkins smiled as she followed behind. She visibly noticed my steps lighten as he spoke. He took my hand and we walked from the home.

As we drove from the grounds, in Trevellian's somewhat battered car, he explained to me,

"I hope a Chinese is alright. I don't know this area at all and therefore asked the Nurse. She's recommended a Chinese restaurant in the town. It sounds all right."

"I'm sure it will be great". I was reassuring. "But I thought we were just having a drink."

I didn't care where we went. I was just looking forward to a night out with Trevellian. "If Helen Tomkins likes it, it will be OK."

I was right. The restaurant was not cheap. There was an over abundance of staff all ready and willing to serve. It was a large restaurant and appeared immaculately clean and well presented. The tables were well spaced, a revolving tray being centred on each. We chose a table in the window. We sat facing each other. After some discussion we ordered a set meal. It was safest and easiest. Trevellian drank lager. I drank mineral water.

"Thanks for bringing me here." I started after the waitress had left the table. "And thanks for looking after me."

"That's my pleasure. I'm enjoying it."

"I've remembered what I was like in my flat that first night. I feel really embarrassed about it. You had to bathe me and everything." My voice trailed off. It was the first time that this incident had been raised. I flushed slightly as I spoke.

"You've no reason to be embarrassed Katrina." Trevellian reached forward and took my hand. "I was expecting some reaction but nothing quite so heavy. Plus, the fact that it was the middle of the night, I think my natural instincts just took over. Still, at least we got you sorted out. Are you all right now?"

"I couldn't be better." My smile said it all.

The meal was excellent, the recommendation well justified. We started with crispy duck in pancakes. We used our fingers to roll the duck within the pancake and were grateful for the lemoned finger bowls provided by the waitress. We laughed as my pancake slipped from my fingers depositing the duck back onto the plate. The main courses included chicken with pineapple and beef with ginger. There was an assortment of stir-fried vegetables, noodles and rice. Despite every effort, we simply could not finish the meal.

I leaned across the cleared table holding my coffee cup in both hands. "You know a lot about me, Duncan, but what about you?"

"What do you want to know?"

"What happened to your marriage? I assume that you're on your own now, otherwise you wouldn't have been able to come down here so often."

Trevellian smiled. "You're right. It's been a couple of years now. It took ages for the divorce to be sorted out, but that's done."

"What caused it?"

"The job I suppose. I was working all the hours that God made. I was never home. She met another guy and they got it together. One day I went home, and she told me. That was that."

"And what about kids?"

"One, a girl. She's older now. I don't see her very often."

"Doesn't that upset you?"

"No, not now. What does upset me though is the money that she keeps demanding. I don't mind paying, but she's been living with him for over a year. She keeps wanting more from me. I'm still paying the mortgage for him to live in my house. That's why I'm so skint."

It was time to change the subject, but I was still curious. "What about girlfriends?"

The question revealed my own interest. Trevellian did not miss the point.

"No, there's no-one at the moment. No-one to take up my time, just you." He smiled.

I became silent. I was slightly embarrassed. I had been too obvious. I had liked Trevellian since meeting him. This had developed further with his attention to my plight. I had to clarify the situation. I had done so. Nothing more needed saying.

"I'll get the bill." Trevellian called the waitress to the table.

As we walked from the restaurant to the car, I slipped my hand into Duncan's. He responded, gripping it firmly. We drove back to the nursing home. Trevellian stopped outside the front door.

"I won't come in. It's getting late and I'd better get back."

"Thanks for a lovely evening. I enjoyed it." I leant towards him and kissed him on the lips. Before he could respond I had pulled back and opened the car door.

"When can you come again?" I asked as I left the car.

"As soon as I can get away, possibly tomorrow. I'll ring and get a message to you," he called after me as I ran to the door.

I turned and waved to him before entering. I looked, and was, confident and happy in the headlights of the car.

It transpired that Trevellian had no opportunity for a further visit. The following day he became entrenched at work and was unable to get away. I hoped that I had not been over obvious at the dinner table. The next morning at about midday he was sitting alone in his office, reading the Times newspaper when his telephone rang.

"Duncan, it's me, Katrina".

"Hi, how are you".

"OK. Look they're letting me out. Apparently I'm better. I've still got to keep in touch with Emily Krystman, but I can leave today."

"Do you want me to come and get you?"

"I hoped you'd say that, otherwise I'll have to get the train. What time do you think you can get away?"

"I'll be there at about five. I'll see you then."

Chapter Nine

Paulo Ramiro had arranged the funeral of his son. He would pay for the funerals of the other men, but his son was to be buried alone. It would be a private ceremony held in the small local Catholic Church towards Tunja. From there the procession would return to the Ramiro estate, which supported a small burial ground. This was in a secluded area, far from the house. Ramiro had buried his own parents there, and his wife's father. Maria's mother was still alive and occupied a room at the Ramiro home. Ramiro intended being laid to rest alongside them. He had not expected any of his sons to pre-decease him, albeit that he recognised the risks of his profession.

Carlo was to lay in-state on the morning of the funeral, allowing friends and relatives to pay their last respects. It was essential that he was properly prepared for the occasion. Carlo Ramiro was embalmed by the local Undertaker, Pedro Ipiales. It was not an easy job, following the intensive post-mortem of Dr Clayman. Ipiales had been provided with a suit, shirt and tie, with which to dress the body. This would cover the damaged torso but did little to disguise the marked head and face. The top of the skull, although removed, had been loosely replaced. At least this provided the appropriate shaping of the head. To bring some life into the face, after carefully re-establishing its integrity, he padded the cheeks and mouth with newspaper. This removed some of the gaunt lines. He left the mouth open slightly allowing Carlo's straight teeth to show in a slight smile. He had cleaned the teeth to provide the best appearance. His wife's make-up brought some colour back into the face. The Undertaker stood back to admire his handiwork. He nodded in satisfaction.

Paulo Ramiro examined the Undertaker's presentation. He would not be satisfied with second-best. The casket was rosewood, the handles brass. The lid was halved, in order that the top could be opened to display Carlo's face, the lower half of the body remaining concealed. He nodded in sad satisfaction. His head bowed slightly.

"Carlo, why you? It should have been me."

A proud man, this slight show of sensitivity lasted only a few moments. He straightened his shoulders, tightening the jacket of his beige, lightweight suit. He turned to the Undertaker, putting his arm across the man's shoulders.

"You have done a good job, my Friend. Carlo would have been pleased. You will bring him to the house tomorrow morning. OK?"

The man nodded. Paulo Ramiro pushed a roll of Peso notes into the man's shirt pocket. He continued to nod. He did not count the money.

Security for the funeral was tightened. Whilst it was protocol that funerals would not be disturbed by separate, competing, factions, cases had occurred where the opposition had taken advantage of a family's distress. Paulo ensured that this would not happen. Guards were reinforced, the perimeter fences close patrolled. Two of his most trusted men would man the gate. Only those with invitations would be allowed to enter. The supply of weapons seemed endless.

The initial reception was mid-morning, the church service scheduled at noon. The first of the family began to arrive at ten. Soon the drive was lined with black Mercedes, many of them stretched, and many bullet-proofed. They were parked in orderly fashion, one guard deputising as a car park attendant. Paulo Ramiro and his wife Maria greeted the guests as they entered the large reception room. Soft drinks, or coffee were served. There would be no alcohol until after the service.

Carlo's elder brother, Enrico, was one of the first to arrive. His wife Carla and their two children walked behind him. He approached his father. Their arms clamped around each other's shoulders.

"Papa, I'm so sorry. He was too young."

Enrico had not seen his father for almost a year. He concentrated on the American side of the business, particularly San Francisco. The Ramiro empire was thriving and required much attention. Enrico had developed beyond the supply of drugs into certain semi-legal businesses. He was kept busy and had little time to visit his home Country.

"It's good to see you again Enrico, and your lovely family. Carla, come here!" She responded and embraced her father-in-law, with respect.

Paulo's third son was simply known by his nickname 'Hotcho'. He, at twenty-four, had not been fully enveloped into the family business. Having academically benefited from the family money, he attended university in the United States. The opportunity to travel, following his qualification, was not to be missed and he was currently touring the East with his girlfriend Andrea, a young American. His respect for his mother and father, and his tie to the family, never allowed him to be out of touch. He had been easily traced to a Bangkok hotel. The two made immediate arrangements to fly home. They were collected from the airport. They had not had time to change and were still clad in jeans and T-shirts.

"Father, my commiserations, and I apologise for my dress. I must get changed."

"You must also cut your hair." Paulo tried some humour as he pulled Hotcho's long dark tresses. "What will your mother think?"

"I think for myself Paulo." Maria walked up behind them, pushing her husband to one side to welcome her son.

"Mother, father, let me introduce you to Andrea. She wanted to come, both to meet you and support me at this time."

They were more formal in greeting Andrea, but the warmth was apparent. It was the first opportunity they had to meet her. After kissing her cheek, Maria stood back.

"You must both come upstairs to change. Hotcho, your clothes are in your room. Andrea, we will find something to fit you." She marshalled the couple towards the stairs.

Paulo Ramiro was aware that over a hundred guests attended the funeral. How many over, he did not know. Carlo lay in state at the far end of the reception room. The casket was softly, if artificially, lighted. Too close an approach was prevented by a red-roped barrier in front. The stable-gate lid was half open. A white orchid had been placed between his cupped hands, contrasting against his dark suit. All the guests paraded before him. Some cried. Some were upright and firm. All were sad.

Promptly at eleven-thirty the hearse arrived at the front of the house. The coffin lid was battened down. Paulo and his two sons acted as pallbearers. Others had been nominated and did their jobs efficiently. Carlo was carried serenely to the hearse. The procession passed along the narrow Tunja road at slow speed. Its passage was corridored by armed guards, to the door of the church. The church, itself, had been searched and sealed earlier that morning. The hearse led the procession. Paulo and his immediate family travelled in the first of the Mercedes behind. Maria wept.

The service was brief. The Priest had known the family for many years. Whilst the Church did not condone the activities of the family, they provided valuable revenue and support. It turned a blind eye. The service concluded with a few words from Paulo. He ended:

"I know that Carlo would not have wanted sorrow to mourn his passing. He would have wanted joy and happiness. He always enjoyed himself and would have wanted us to do the same. I know that he would have appreciated all of you coming here today. I certainly do and thank you all. We will now take him back to his final resting place. After that I invite you to take wine with Maria and me. At that time, I hope we will all comply with Carlo's spirit. No more tears, just happiness."

Carlo's grave had been immaculately excavated. It was a perfect rectangle cut to the dimensions of the casket. The bare sides had been covered with green baize. As the priest said the words:

"Ashes to ashes and dust to dust," the coffin was smoothly lowered into the deep hole. As it disappeared, Carlo's mother Maria threw a cut flower onto it. Several other guests followed suit. The tear, that ran down her cheek as her son was buried, was clearly visible to all. Paulo stood stoically beside her, retaining his emotion. They stood for a few moments before turning their backs and walking to the house. The ceremonies over, they would properly entertain their guests.

The cut and thrust of drug dealing did not necessarily mean that all the competition was at war. A negotiated settlement was often cheaper and more satisfactory. Less harm to both the family and the business was caused. One guest at Carlo Ramiro's funeral was just such a competitor. Johnny Riccione was an American. His family had emigrated from Italy many years before. He was the linchpin of a syndicate based in Miami. Paulo presumed it to be Mafia based. Miami had proved to be a lucrative source of income for the dealers, both offering a reliable source of entry into the United States and providing a ready-made supply of customers. Whilst there was room for more than one major supplier, each was protective of his own foothold. This had initially been the case with the Ramiro's. Paulo's route into Miami had been carefully purchased through dishonest Government officials. The arrival of Riccione's operation caused great concern. Initially each party's reaction was to fight, pursuing the out-dated adage; 'the best man wins'. Carlo saw no benefit in this approach. Having lost several tried and trusted employees, he made contact with Riccione and substituted words for action. These negotiations formed a delicate, working, foundation, which had survived tentatively. Johnny Riccione and Carlo Ramiro had themselves developed a mutual respect. Paulo, aware of this relationship had invited Riccione to the funeral.

"Mr Ramiro, I was upset by the news of Carlo's death. I am grateful for the opportunity to pay my last respects. I offer my deepest sympathy to you and your family." Riccione was respectful throughout.

"Perhaps you might have a few minutes to discuss our future." The formalities completed; he got down to business.

"Yes indeed. The relationship between the Ramiro and Riccione families should continue, perhaps as an epitaph to Carlo. Come with me to the library. We can talk quietly there." Ramiro had expected this interlude.

Riccione walked side by side with Ramiro. He was a little taller, but with the same dark hair and Latin features. Riccione was in his forties but had worn badly. He wore dark trousers with a contrasting light jacket. His patterned tie did not reflect the sombre occasion. Behind the two men, followed their two bodyguards. Each was aware of their duties, although on this particular occasion no trouble was expected. It simply reminded each party that the other's trust was not complete.

The four men fitted comfortably in the expansive library. Ramiro gestured to Riccione to sit in a leathered chair in the centre of the room. Other similar chairs were set around an ornate coffee table. Ramiro walked to a drink's cabinet:

"What can I get you, Johnny? Can I call you Johnny?"

"Of course Paulo; Jack Daniel's please." The man replied.

The two bodyguards stood either side of the double doors to the room. They stood unobtrusively and said nothing. The two men continued as if they were not there. Ramiro sat opposite Riccione. He poured himself a similar drink.

"I liked Carlo. We spent much time together to organise a proper business relationship. Neither side, under our direction, has broken the truce, nor would I have expected them to do so. It concerns me, that without Carlo, our arrangements might flounder."

"I understand what you are saying, Johnny. I appreciate your attendance here today and your candid approach. I have no intention of spoiling anything. I think it has been profitable for both of us."

He paused as Riccione nodded in agreement.

"I understand your concern. You need direct contact in Miami. Somebody that has my full authority. The man, that I am thinking of, worked for Carlo in England. He was close to Carlo. Perhaps the change of scenery would do him good. Carlo trusted him and so do I. Juan Marco; he is here today. I will tell him and then introduce him to you."

The two men stood and shook hands. "Paulo, I now recognise from where Carlo got his wisdom."

"Thank you, Johnny. Let us always talk rather than fight."

Sir Matt Stephens, Commissioner of Police of the Metropolis, held his annual cocktail party several months after the Ramiro raid. He was unsure whether he enjoyed such formalities. They had, however, become an established part of the rank. It would take a brave man to depart from establishment. Stephens was not that man.

He had not expected to rise to the exulted rank of Commissioner when he joined the service. He had done nothing special. He had simply been in the right place at the right time. In his mid-fifties, he was not the youngest Commissioner ever, although, he liked to think, one of the best. He had not rushed to make changes. He had seen that too often in the past. Each Commissioner had to be seen to make his mark. Change occurred for change sake. Stephens had selected another route. He firmly believed that London's method of policing had evolved with time, that the systems in place were effective and efficient. He avoided change and sought a period of stability. He found this encouraged those beneath him but more importantly, made his life a lot easier. Unfortunately, the position required long hours. Today was no exception.

The Commissioner's cocktail party was held in the large hall on the fifth floor of Scotland Yard. The hall was originally designed as a lecture theatre but doubled nicely for such festive occasions. Stephens's advisers had told him that the cocktail party was essential. It would allow him to entertain those politicians and socialites vital to the well-being of his position. It would stave off criticism by allowing frank discussion in a suitable social climate. Stephens had attended the cocktail parties of his predecessors. He was uncertain that there was foundation to the advice given but went along with it anyway.

Matt Stephens had much support. Most senior officers working at the Yard, and many from adjacent stations, attended. It was a time and opportunity to be seen. All but few drank soft drinks. It was not for them to be seen tipsy. The internal caterers had watched this trait develop, over a period of years, and had designed their own lemonade mix, accordingly. The drink was decanted into individual glasses. Each waiter carried the glasses of the prepared drink alongside a bottle of wine.

It was the first time that Rupert Veneer had experienced a commissioner's cocktail party. Michael Farrar MP, the Home Secretary, had suffered them in previous years but continued his duty steadfastly. This year he had refused to attend alone and insisted that his understudy keep him company.

"You will enjoy it." He instructed Veneer when forwarding the invitation.

For Rupert Veneer the evening had not yet become tedious. The party had started at seven, although the guests had only started to arrive just before eight. Veneer and Farrar arrived at eight-fifteen. They were to stay until nine-thirty, not long enough to become bored. Veneer admired the formal dress of the uniformed officers. He had not realised that police officers had their own, evening, apparel. The jackets were sort and cut to the body. The silver buttons stood against the dark blue material. The individual ranks were distinguished by lapel badges.

Veneer pushed his glasses back onto his bulbous nose as he admired the slender figure of the woman Superintendent. The waisted jacket suited her. The skirt fell below her knee but had been individually tailored to her body. She seemed young to have reached the rank. She was side on to him, across the room. Her profile was attractive. He watched in admiration.

"Home Secretary, welcome."

"Thank you, Commissioner." Protocol demanded a proper address in public. "May I introduce you to my Under- Secretary of State, Rupert Veneer."

"Mr Veneer, you are welcome."

Veneer's attention was drawn back by the direct address. He took the outstretched hand of Sir Matt Stephens and shook it warmly.

"A pleasure, Commissioner. Thank you."

"Well, Matt. How are things going?"

The formalities over, Michael Farrar relaxed the conversation to practicalities.

"OK, Michael, nothing too problematical at the moment. As you know, we are getting over the recent press assault on corruption."

"Yes, that old chestnut will raise its ugly head regularly. You dealt with it well, though. Something better comes along for the media, and they just drift away."

"Shame about the crisis in the city, but it did me a favour, I can tell you. I was almost at the point where I would have to make a statement and we both know how badly wrong they can go, don't we?"

The knowing laughs of both men passed straight over the head of Rupert Veneer. His attention was drawn back to the Superintendent. He watched her move to another small group to continue her social commitments. She was graceful, yet purposeful. Her jaw jutted slightly as she interjected and drew the attention of the group. He could imagine her breasts firm against the tailored material concealing them. He glanced around. There were several groups to delay her arrival at his. He sighed. Her conversation must be more stimulating than that of Farrar and Stephens.

"Are you tired, Rupert?" Farrar chastised him obliquely having noticed his reaction.

"No, Michael, I was just thinking how upsetting it must be for all those honest men and woman out there, when they are subject to such a press tirade. It must affect them all. It must adversely affect morale within the Police Service. So unnecessary, I was thinking."

Veneer knew his response was appropriate. His ability to think on his feet was one of his assets. He said what he knew the Commissioner wanted to hear, a sympathetic voice for his problems. As Michael Farrar nodded his assent, Veneer knew that he had been forgiven for his mishap.

Sir Matt Stephens had warmed to Veneer.

"Tell me about your initiative, Rupert." Veneer noticed that he now called him by his first name. "A Commons Committee into juvenile crime. How's it coming along? Any progress yet?"

"This is a long project, Commissioner. We don't expect any early, startling, results, but things augur well for the future. We are currently looking at the effects of drug misuse. We have accepted written submissions from several Police Forces, including your own, Commissioner. All very useful, but tell me, your own battle against drugs must, at times, be soul destroying?"

Veneer had instantly drifted into politician-speak. He had failed to answer the question poised, choosing instead to divert the subject with his own question in response.

"It is difficult", the Commissioner admitted, not being a politician. "Our seizures this year have been at record levels. We have arrested more major league dealers than ever before. It seems impossible to stem the tide, however. Just too many easy profits are being made."

"So, what is the answer then, the way forward."

"To hit the men at the top; those arranging the initial importation and sale, to stop it at source. As you know, we put an enormous amount of resources into this, with appropriately good results."

"Yes, I read of a raid a couple of months ago; big seizure of cocaine, a Colombian family. You took out the main man, now what was his name?"

"Ramiro, Carlo Ramiro. He was shot dead in the raid. Unfortunate, but a hazard of the trade, I would suggest."

"A good result for you your drugs squad, though. It must have devastated the family. I bet they will re-think their operation in this Country."

"Yes." Sir Matt Stephens was thoughtful. "It had its downside for us as well."

"And what is that?" The Secretary of State was interested and inquisitive.

Stephens did not answer directly. "Our undercover officer was raped by Ramiro, now pregnant by him; not a good result for her or us. Still enough said."

"Indeed, Commissioner, a dangerous job. I have always thought your undercover officers to be a brave group of people. Tell me, is the girl all right? How has it affected her?"

"She's OK now, as I understand, although it affected her badly in the beginning. Still one of the risks of the job."

"Quite so, Commissioner." Rupert Veneer's attention had waned. "Would you excuse me for a moment?"

"Of course."

The Commissioner turned back to Michael Farrar and within seconds they were engrossed in deep conversation. It seemed that neither would miss Rupert Veneer.

"If Mohammed won't come to the mountain," thought Veneer as he turned in the direction of the woman Superintendent.

"How do you do, Under-Secretary?"

The man stood before him as he turned, blocking his way. He had his hand outstretched. As Veneer took it, he tried to peer over his shoulder to identify his potential prey. He could not see the Superintendent through the obstruction. He turned his attention to the fifty-year-old, greying man. He wore a grey, pinstriped, suit that had seen better days. No evening attire for this officer, thought Veneer. There was something piercing about his eyes, however. Veneer was concerned that the full glass of scotch, held by the man, might spill.

"Jack Knight, Mr Veneer. Detective Superintendent Jack Knight."

Rupert Veneer realised his loss as he watched the long legs of the woman Superintendent carry her towards the exit of the hall. He resigned himself to his present company.

"And what can I do for you, Mr Knight?"

Unfortunately, I had no idea of the Commissioner's indiscretion or the likely repercussions that I would suffer. At the time of the cocktail party I was engulfed in the unwanted pregnancy, following the act of Carlo Ramiro.

The trauma of the incident had materially affected me and absorbed all those treating me. None of us gave thought to a morning-after pill. The first period missed was during my recovery and I put that down to the intense anxiety. I had missed periods before. I thought nothing of it and mentioned it to no-one. The second was more than just coincidence. I waited an additional week before thinking the worst. A simple test purchased from the local pharmacist proved positive. My pregnancy was confirmed by my doctor.

In the weeks following the incident my life had taken an uphill turn. My secret shared with Dr Krystman and Trevellian was no longer a secret. A weight had been lifted from my shoulders, only now for a heavier weight to be placed upon them. For two weeks I pondered the situation. My doctor offered an instant abortion. There would be no delay. The second opinion would be a formality. I was initially tempted to terminate the pregnancy immediately but was also aware that I need not rush. The decision had to be made within the first twenty-four weeks. I had ample time to make a balanced decision.

I telephoned Trevellian, now my trusted friend. Little did he realise that he was about to share another innermost secret. I asked him to my flat for drinks one evening.

"Trevellian, I'm pregnant." I threw at him as he sipped his drink.

"Good for you, who's the lucky dad," he smiled benignly knowing that it could not be him.

Trevellian had wanted our relationship to develop beyond friendship. He had hoped that we would become lovers but veered away from it, to prevent damaging our valuable friendship. He knew that I needed his support more than his love at this moment. He would do nothing to threaten that support. He believed that I felt the same. I did nothing to change his mind. He concealed his hurt at my pronouncement. Whilst he had remained my friend, he believed that I had taken a lover.

"Not good for me, Duncan. Not good for me at all. The lucky dad's dead. It was Carlo Ramiro."

Trevellian jolted forward. His glass fell from his hand in shock. The liquid content lifted from the glass, as if in slow motion, and deposited itself on the arm of my settee. The glass fell to the carpeted floor, fortunately not breaking. It rolled slightly before coming to a rest.

"I'm sorry, Katrina." Trevellian picked up the glass from the floor and put it carefully on the table." I need a towel or something."

I returned in seconds, placing a cloth across the fouled arm. I pushed Trevellian over slightly as I squeezed next to him. I took his hand.

"I just don't know what to do, Duncan. I am in another quandary. I need your help." My smile belied my true feelings.

"Katrina, I'm not sure that I'm the one to help with this one. Your decision will affect your whole life. You'll be tied to the child, no matter who the father was. You'll have to give it your full commitment. No, you need better than me." He thought for a moment. "I know, how about Emily Krystman. She told you to ring at any time. Let's go and see her."

Emily Krystman had, indeed, told me to ring at any time and was pleased to receive my telephone call.

"Of course I can see you, today at 3 o'clock. You know my address, don't you?"

Emily Krystman worked from home. Her employment by the Metropolitan Police so dominated her career that she was now employed predominantly by that organisation. She retained some private clients. Those within the police force would generally only be seen by appointment at police headquarters. There were a few exceptions. I was one of those exceptions.

Miss Krystman found an instant empathy with me. She did not know why. I had so many problems it was difficult to establish which specifically caught her attention. It was, perhaps, the overall innocence of a person so badly treated during her childhood and who now held such a position of experience and maturity. Emily Krystman foresaw that within my apparently fragile exterior, there was inner strength. Had she met Melissa Grant she might recognise the materialisation of that inner strength.

The Psychologist's Pimlico flat was still owned by an established trust although property developers had registered their interest. Her lease was safe and established. She awaited a realistic offer of purchase. She would not hesitate to go elsewhere. The stairs to her flat were outside. There were no lifts. The double-glazing was ill fitting and draughty in winter. She had central heating although the gas fires in each room provided adequate warmth and were possibly more efficient.

Trevellian went with me. I had insisted that it be so. I felt some trepidation as we walked up the stairs. Trevellian led the way. I reached forward and took his hand in my own for support.

"Come in, come in, my Dears," Miss Krystman welcomed us. "The kettle is on. I'll make a nice cup of tea."

We followed her into her cluttered study. The bookcase was overflowing. Academic scripts were now spread over the floor. We were left alone for only a few minutes until Miss Krystman's triumphant return with tea,

"And bourbon biscuits," she smiled.

"So, you're pregnant, are you?" She reiterated my statement of fact. "And it is Ramiro's child. Firstly, Katrina, are you sure. Do you need a DNA test?"

"No, I am sure. There was nobody else. It had to be him." I thought for a moment. "A DNA test might be a sensible option in due course. We have a sample of Carlo Ramiro's DNA don't we, Duncan?"

I turned towards Trevellian. He nodded his confirmation.

"Tell me Katrina. How do you feel about the pregnancy?"

I sipped my tea and carefully put the china cup back in its saucer.

"I've come to terms with the fact that Ramiro raped me, and with your help I've seen off the other skeletons in my cupboard. But this is something completely different. I am in two minds and I don't know which way to go. A child should be born out of the love between two people. This one would not be. His father is dead. His conception was by such a violent act that I will never forget it. Will I resent the child to such an extent that I grow to hate him?" I had no idea of the potential sex of the child.

"You're calling it 'him' Katrina. Why do you think that is?"

"I don't know. I don't know if it would make any difference if it were a girl. Would a boy remind me more of his father? Would I hate him for that reason alone?"

"Just for a moment, forget completely who the father is and the fact that you were raped. Are you ready for a child, Katrina? Do you want the responsibilities that go with it? Your single life would be over in a flash. To be a single parent is no joy ride. Most important is the child. If you cannot love it, then get rid of it now: No second thoughts. But these are decisions that only you can make, because, at the end of the day, you are on your own. As you quite rightly say, the father is dead, it will be just you and the child."

Emily Krystman had made nothing easy for me. As I left the flat with Trevellian I was no further forward. A decision had not been made for me. The ball was firmly back in my court. It was later that evening, in the solitude of my own flat, that I sought solace from my other companion.

"Melissa, what would you do?" I talked to the bathroom mirror. The reflection changed to my alter-ego. I had not seen her since the incident with Ramiro.

"You've got to take control of your own life Katrina. You've been dominated by others for too long now. Remember that this child is half yours. After nine months of pregnancy, it will be all yours. Ramiro cannot interfere. He is out of the way. You have the good fortune that your job will be held open, even if you only want to work part-time. You know you want this child, otherwise you wouldn't be thinking twice about an abortion. Get on with it and enjoy it."

Melissa Grant was at her most persuasive and I listened to her. She was right, deep down, I did want the child. I wanted something of my own, to love and care for and that nobody else could spoil. My decision was made that evening. The idea of abortion was cast from my mind.

I worked until my seventh month. My pregnancy was not uncomfortable. A slight increase in my own bodyweight was considered healthy. Some said I blossomed as I approached motherhood. They were lying. I did not believe them. The sensitive balance between toppling forward and avoiding the inevitable back strain became more difficult. My evening sickness passed at three months. I had expected morning- sickness, but it had not materialised. My sickness during the late evening was unexpected and uncomfortable. Still, it did not last long.

It was during my thirty-fourth week that I was admitted to the maternity ward with high blood pressure. For several days previously I had suffered headaches and giddiness. My doctor recognised the problem before he pumped up the band tied tight around my right arm.

"It's time you went in," he told me as he telephoned the hospital.

My labour was induced. On this occasion my treatment at the hands of the National Health Service was caring and thoughtful. Whether this was due to the removal of the stress attached to emergency work, I didn't know.

The pain of the later stages of labour and delivery was intense. I had experienced nothing like it before. The rape paled into insignificance in comparison. Had cocaine been available to reduce the agony I might well have accepted it. I had resisted the offer of an epidural, wishing the birth to be natural. I gasped at the gas and air to ward off the intermittent, but constant, body seizures.

I was alone at the birth, with just medical staff to support me. They had not asked where the father was, they were too discrete. I had considered asking Trevellian to be present. He had been my consistent visitor throughout. I wanted his support but knew that I must suffer this one trial alone.

"Push, Katrina, one long push. I can see the head," the midwife instructed.

I pushed. I would never remember quite how I pushed. I had been told to push through the pelvis as the uterus contracted. I presumed that I did so as the midwife did not complain. I could feel Danny being pulled from my body,

"It's a boy," the midwife exclaimed with pleasure. "It's a boy, Katrina. Just wait until I clean him up and then he's yours."

I heard the faint cough as the mucus was removed from the baby's mouth. I heard the slap as the midwife shocked him into life. I vividly remembered his first broken cry as he claimed his independence. He was wrapped in a white blanket when he was placed on my chest. My eight hours of labour had tired me, but I felt intense pleasure as he lay upon me. I took him in my arms. We lay together for the first time. This was my child. This was Danny, Danny Marshall. Any link with Carlo Ramiro ceased from that time on.

I was sitting at my desk in the CID office at Kingston Police Station. The transfer had been arranged for me. Kingston was a busy suburban town. It had a newly developed shopping centre, the envy of other authorities and was generally a wealthy area. The Police Station was busy, although nobody was honestly overworked. I found the place surprisingly peaceful after my previous Central London postings and forays into the fantasy world of undercover policing.

The sun was bright. My desk was situated by a window overlooking the street. I sucked the top of my pen dumbly as I gazed out into the brightness of the day. I was relaxed and satisfied. My life had improved a thousand-fold. I was finally at peace.

Eighteen months had now passed since the incident at the warehouse. My son, Danny was ten months old. He was born a month prematurely, his early birth initiated by my worry. He was the product of the incident at the warehouse. He was Carlo Ramiro's son. He did not know and might never know. That's something I'll decide in the future.

I returned to work six months after his birth. The Metropolitan Police was a flexible employer and would have accepted a longer absence. However, I was organised and settled and, if honest, I needed adult company once again.

Danny had not initially been difficult. I had breast-fed him at birth but changed to a bottle at four months. The problems were mine, not

Danny's. He was a hungry child who devoured his nourishment. In later stages I realised that I simply did not naturally provide enough milk to satisfy him. The change was a natural progression that benefited both of us. It allowed me to plan my return to work and his care during the day.

I had kept my Clapham flat. There was no need to move at the time. I liked the flat and was now established into the local area. Danny was too small to make any difference. My journey to work had been lengthened by a detour to the child- minder. She was a local woman with a youngster of her own. Three children of working mothers made up the group. They were all just beginning to crawl. Danny was the youngest but adored by the rest. Winifred Peters originated from Jamaica. She was a qualified nurse as well as a registered child minder. Her own baby's father was a carpenter. He lived with them although they were not married.

"I will never marry him, the bastard." She told me at an early stage. She did not explain the problem further and I did not ask. I was, however, suitably impressed with Winifred's determination and independence.

I initially worked six hours a day, leaving Danny with Winifred between 9.30am and 4.30pm. The police accepted these hours without question and paid me proportionately. Nobody within the organisation seemed to care one-way or the other. Danny still woke up early in the morning, at about 6am. This allowed me the vital first few hours of the day with him. The morning chaos, as I rushed to ready both of us, passed by him.

Winifred always had the baby ready for collection. He was cleaned and changed, although this task was simplified by the continuing supply of disposable nappies. Danny was generally content after a day with Winifred. He slept during the short car journey home, but then was ready for play. I loved this time of day. I could relax with him; the pressures of work having evaporated. I stripped off my work clothes and lay naked on the bed with my child. He lay upon me and I felt the touch of his skin on mine. He would lay quietly in my crooked arm as he sucked the milk from his bottle. He would lay across me as I winded him, occasionally throwing the milk back up, onto me.

Trevellian was still my favoured visitor. We were close friends and would now remain as such. I would have taken him as a lover earlier, but the time for that had now passed. I trusted him and relied on him as a friend. I did not wish to jeopardise that friendship. I would watch as Trevellian bounced Danny on his knee. The child was older, and stronger in the back. He could now support his head comfortably, although Trevellian supported him carefully. Danny smiled and gurgled gleefully with each bounce. I wished Trevellian had been the father. He was what Danny would need as a father. I dreaded the day that I would have to explain to Danny. Still, that day was still a long way off.

"Has anyone seen the Detective Chief Inspector?"

I was facing away from the door. My desk was in the large general office, which all the detectives occupied. Each had their own desk. Mine was halfway down the office close to the window. The words cut into my thoughts.

I recognised the voice. The sound of it sent a shiver down my spine. Even so, initially I could not place it. Detective Chief Inspector Roy Hines was present in the office. He had his back to the door but turned when he heard himself mentioned.

"Hello Sir," he greeted the man. "I didn't know that you were here."

"I understand that you've got something for me, Roy?"

These words jolted my memory. I had heard similar spoken to Carlo Ramiro in the warehouse on the day he died. I searched my memory for clarity. It was the voice of the man who had identified my deception. It was the man who had taken the money from Ramiro. I looked at my hands. My pen had slipped from them. They were shaking uncontrollably.

"Come to my office." Roy Hines led the visitor out.

I carefully turned my head to glance towards the doorway. I recognised the same homburg hat, the same blue overcoat. I was careful not to stare, in case I was noticed. His face had not changed. It was still the face of a worn, fifty-something, man. His eyes looked clearer, however and the facial lines less ingrained. On the last occasion I had seen him he had been full of drink and drugs. This time he did not appear so.

Jeremy Martin was a young detective on his first posting at Kingston. He was twenty-three years old but looked younger. He sat opposite me, his desk facing mine. I leaned towards him and asked quietly:

"Do you know the man that's just asked for the DCI? He's leaving the office now."

Martin looked towards the door as the two men walked out. He thought for a moment. "Yes, he's the new Detective Superintendent, covering this Area."

"What's his name?" I probed.

"Knight, Jack Knight. He's only just transferred out here. He was working on a central squad somewhere. Rumour has it that he turned into a drunk, either drink or drugs I don't know which. Apparently, he spent the last few months drying out. They've put him out to pasture, his last posting."

Jeremy Martin was pleased to supply the little information he knew. It made him feel important and knowledgeable.

"Thanks."

I tried not to simply discard him, although in using just that one word I knew that I had done so. Jeremy's smile left his face. He grunted as he looked back down to his paperwork.

My mind was in turmoil. The episode in my life that had caused so much heartache and physical pain was suddenly resurrected. I thought that I would never see nor hear of the man again. He had faded from my thoughts as the incident had faded. Yet here he was, and even worse, he too was a serving police officer. What would I do? More importantly, what could I do? My face darkened as I meditated on my position. I realised that my recognition had been by the shortest of glances. Whilst the voice had penetrated my mind, I knew that I would have to have a closer look to verify my belief. I stood up at my desk.

"Where are you going?" Asked Jeremy innocently.

"To the toilet." I gave an automatic answer.

I walked from the office. Roy Hines had his own office, just down the corridor. As I walked towards it, I could hear the voices of the two men. The sound of Knight's voice cut through me like a knife. I was sure it was him. The visitor sat just within the doorway, in an easy chair. He was facing Hines, at his desk. As I passed the door, my movement made him glance towards me. It was a reflex action. He did not look at me, merely noting my movement. It did, however, give me the opportunity to identify him, face on.

"It's him, I know it's him." I thought as I carried on past the office door.

I made it to the toilet, but only just. I was fortunate that the room was unoccupied. I needed a few moments to regain my composure. I could not initially understand why his presence should have such a dramatic effect on me. I thought for a moment and soon realised the reason. This was the man who had betrayed me. Without him, Carlo Ramiro would have accepted that I, too, had taken the cocaine. There would have been no deception. I would not have been raped. I put two fingers down my throat and threw-up into the whiteness of the porcelain toilet. It was an unnecessary reaction. It relieved the tension.

I stood at a sink and splashed water on my face. I wiped it clean with the hand towel before looking at myself closely in the mirror. I felt that I had aged instantly. With the support of Duncan Trevellian, I had put this incident behind me, yet now it was back to haunt me. Again I re-lived it, although in brief. I pulled myself together. I had to. I walked from the toilets. As I again passed Hines's office, I noted that the man was no longer present. He had left. I walked back to my desk and sat quietly.

For half an hour I sat at my desk doing nothing. I did not move. I did not speak. The top of my pen was held to my mouth with my right hand. I sucked it as if sucking my thumb. Jeremy Martin continued working. He had not noticed my predicament. He was busy with his paperwork. At last he stopped working and took his jacket from the back of his chair.

"I've got to go out, just into the centre to take a statement. Do you want to come for a walk?" He asked me.

"No, no I won't," I looked at him blankly.

"OK, I'll see you later."

My thoughts, for the remainder of the day, were dictated by the events that had occurred. I was not troubled by my past experiences. I had finally put those behind me. As the day passed, however, an urgent need for revenge built inside me. My initial reaction fell on the side of justice.

"I'll put the bastard behind bars", I thought as I drove to collect Danny.

Chapter Ten

I learned much about Jack Knight in the ensuing period, following my discovery, and even more later. He had served as a police officer for twenty-seven years. His 'Geordie' accent had faded over the years spent in London. He was the son of a coal-miner, born in a village outside Newcastle. His mother had been a dedicated housewife. He had recognised at an early age that the demise of the pits would lead to unemployment within the area. The streets of London were still paved with gold and therefore he travelled South. His police career had commenced soon after his arrival. It was a solid job in those days and offered the security that he sought. He had married his wife Margaret some three years later. She was a southern girl enticed by his rugged northern looks and attitude. They were still married to this day, although she wondered how.

Knight's only resentment, as to his emigration South, was the premature death of his father. For many years he had suffered from lung fibrosis caused by the coal dust. It was this that finally killed him. Whilst Knight attended the funeral, there was little else that he could do to support his mother, except to ensure that she was financially secure. His missed his father and wished that they had more time to spend together. His mother's subsequent death had severed his only other direct connection with the North.

Knight had two children, both girls. They were grown up, in their twenties. Both were married with children of their own. They had secure family lives. He enjoyed their company, but now they were not reliant on him. He found the solitude of his own and his wife's company unnerving. When the girls were living with them, they had little time for each other. It made their relationship easier to contain. The lack of distraction now emphasised each of their faults. It made Knight feel vulnerable. It did not help them to get along together.

For many years Knight had found himself becoming more and more sceptical. For a young man, the police force was a fine profession. It gave total support. The pay was acceptable to a man in his twenties. Knight had progressed slowly through the ranks, spending his time within the Criminal Investigation Department. He had not worn a uniform since his second year of service. Although he had made, what others would consider, good progress, he had become dissatisfied with his lot. Why, he was unsure. It was possibly due to the moral change of society, or the lack of support from the courts. He felt the main reason was internal, within the job, although he could never put his finger on the exact cause. He knew he should have left years ago.

Jack Knight had been drinking heavily for a long time. In early days this was a working tradition that rapidly became ingrained into his personality. Detectives seemed to believe that they were impervious to harm. Whilst the attitude of his contemporaries had changed in this respect, Knight's had not.

Jack Knight's moral values had been set by his own standards. He made no excuse that he and his family came first. The public and the police force were a poor second. He had never been against accepting the odd gratuity. In early years a small cash payment could make his memory slip. It might be enough to secure bail for a petty criminal. However, as Knight's family expenses increased his salary did not seem to match. He therefore found himself supplementing this by demand. Rather than the villain setting the price, it became Knight himself who did so.

The salary mismatch became more problematical when his wife decided that the two girls should be privately educated. The state system was not for them. Margaret herself did not work. The responsibility for meeting the bills lay with Knight. He met the challenge valiantly. He worked harder to meet and arrest the villains. The villains worked harder to keep him off their backs. The mutually beneficial arrangement worked to the advantage of everyone. His daughters were well educated.

Knight's posting to Scotland Yard's serious crimes branch had put him in an ideal position to touch the higher echelon of certain criminal syndicates in London. A year or so previously he had penetrated the fringes of Carlo Ramiro's, British, operation. The arrest of two drivers transporting cocaine led Knight to delve into the family. The police force held intelligence on Ramiro. Knight had access to this intelligence. His approach was direct. He went straight to the heart of the matter, the Lanthanum club. There, after some persuasive talk as to his abilities, he had been introduced to Juan Marco and then to Carlo Ramiro. The relationship had flourished. All were businessmen. Knight had a service to sell; Ramiro had the money to make the purchase.

Knight had dealt in this way in the past. He was used to selling a lack of service, rather than anything requiring positive action. The villains simply paid him to leave them alone. This did not satisfy Ramiro. He required something finite for his money and was sufficiently devious to develop the situation to his advantage.

Jack Knight was not a difficult target for Ramiro. Ramiro ballooned Knight's ego by pretending to be subservient. He paid Knight as requested and rarely argued the cost. Knight became more confident. He enjoyed the facilities at the Lanthanum and began to use it more frequently. He failed to recognise Ramiro's ulterior motives. Free drinks lowered his inhibitions. Pretty girls lowered them further. It was not long before the girls, who themselves were employed by Ramiro, had led Knight onto the perpetual cocaine roller-coaster. The power base had significantly changed. Knight had now become reliant on Ramiro. Carlo Ramiro tapped the worth of the relationship. In no time Knight was providing positive information. He had access to files and computer records. He had knowledge of operations that might affect the Ramiro empire. He provided Carlo Ramiro with this information.

Knight was leaving the warehouse as the police raid began. He was yards from the side, pedestrian, door as he heard the main gate being forced. He had been on sufficient similar operations throughout his career to immediately and instinctively recognise what was happening. His mind kicked back a gear and raced to regain control. The pedestrian walkway was protected from view by the large wooden crates. He stood against one whilst he took stock of the situation. He knew there was only one way out.

As the sound of gunfire passed further into the warehouse Knight knew that adrenaline would be pumping into the police officers, allowing mistakes to be made. This would be a large operation with many officers, not all knowing each other. Jack Knight took off his distinctive hat and rolled it into his pocket. He took out his warrant card and displayed it on his coat. He left the seclusion of his hideaway and walked boldly to the door.

Chaos reigned around him as he walked. On the floor were the bodies of men, presumably suffering gunshot wounds. Several others were handcuffed and grouped together, under the supervision of armed officers. Only two uniformed and armed officers guarded the open entrance. Knight headed towards it.

"Give us a hand here mate."

Knight's attention was drawn to an officer struggling to handcuff a prisoner. Both were standing, the policeman holding the man against the wall. The officer was trying to force his arm behind his back to link his two arms together. The man was resisting. He was too strong for the lone policeman. Knight had to make an instant decision as to his action. It was a two-way street. Either he could help, or he could continue. Each course could draw the suspicions of the officer and the attention of others. His sense of self-preservation took over. No definite decision was made. Jack Knight walked up to the two struggling men and forced the arms of the prisoner together. The grateful officer snapped the handcuffs into place. Once secured the man stopped fighting.

"Thanks mate," said the policeman as Knight resumed his long walk to the door.

The officers guarding the door paid little or no attention to Knight. They had been within view and witnessed him subduing the prisoner. They could see his warrant card displayed prominently. They assumed he was a part of the task force. He walked past them, raising a finger in acknowledgement as he did so. Jack Knight disappeared into the darkness.

Knight's first return to the 'Lanthanum' club had occurred soon after the death of Carlo Ramiro. His past history, within the club, was a past that he had enjoyed, albeit a little out of control. Moderation was the key, he thought, as he entered the club again. Juan Marco had recently returned from the Colombian funeral ceremony, albeit on a temporary basis. He welcomed Knight into the club. They talked at the bar:

"Why did you not warn us of the raid, Jack? Did we not pay you enough?"

"I did not know. It must have been the best kept secret this year, perhaps the only kept secret. I just did not know."

"Who conducted the raid then, which department?" Juan was

quizzical.

"The drugs squad."

"But I thought you were in charge of the drugs squad?"

"Not this one. I cannot be in charge of everyone, Juan, not everyone."

"But that's why we paid you, Jack." Marco's voice trailed off purposely.

Another scotch and water was served by the barman to Jack Knight. He raised the tumbler to his lips. Despite the cooling effect of the ice, his lips were dry. He ran his tongue across them as he replaced his glass onto the bar. Marco was not drinking.

"Paulo Ramiro is not happy Jack. He wants to know how this happened. We were set up; we must have been. We want to know who by, Jack, I want you to find out for me, for the sake of Carlo Ramiro. It is up to you Jack."

Knight nodded. Marco had not mentioned his visit to the warehouse that night. He obviously did not know. The only surviving soldier did not know that Knight was present. He was relieved. His secret appeared safe. He knew that he could have told Marco of his presence, but to do so would have left too many unanswered questions. If he was not a part of the police operation, why was he allowed to leave? How did he leave without being noticed? Why had he not assisted Carlo Ramiro to escape? Jack Knight did not want to answer these questions. The answers would not convince Juan Marco or Paulo Ramiro. It would place him at risk when that risk could be simply avoided by saying nothing.

His visit to the Lanthanum had paved the way for the future. The trips to the London club became bi-weekly, a Tuesday and Thursday excursion. He contained his consumption of whisky and cocaine. When using the former he hoped a liberal sluice of mouthwash would disguise his misdemeanour. The drug was not difficult to conceal. For all outward appearances, Jack Knight remained the rehabilitated policeman. For the eighteen months since the raid he had lived his double life.

I stood in the dark doorway, opposite the Lanthanum club. I was cold and bored. My dedication to the task remained my priority, however, and I persevered.

"Got a light, Luv", the prostitute held her cigarette in front of my face to reinforce her brazen words.

I shook my head. I looked at the girl as she walked away. Despite the weather her red skirt barely covered her overt stocking-tops. Her breasts were amply displayed for potential customers. Her hips swayed erratically as her stilettoed heels found the gaps in the paving stones.

"I've had enough" I thought, as I viewed the typical Soho street.

I walked from the doorway and away from the club. I looked at my watch as I did so. It was eight-thirty. Winifred had agreed to look after Danny for the evening. I had explained that an urgent job had come up. The baby-sitter was only too happy to help.

I had followed Jack Knight for several days. He had been easy to locate. He spent the majority of his day at his office, or in the 'Horse and Hounds' close to it. My early departure was explained by the sudden virus that Danny suffered. Nobody questioned me as to my short day, nobody honestly cared.

This was the second time during my short period of surveillance that Knight had visited the Lanthanum. My fears were confirmed that he was still in bed with the Ramiro family. He was a bent policeman who had caused my rape and almost cost my sanity. He was the worst type of policeman, one that had to be stopped. I pondered how that could be achieved as I walked away from the club.

Duncan Trevellian had not expected the visit from me. He opened the door to his flat to find me holding Danny in my arms. The folding pushchair, resting against my left hip, did not fare well on the turning staircase. Accordingly, I had carried my son up the final steps.

"Come in, come in," Trevellian welcomed me, taking the pushchair from me and swinging it into his confined hallway.

"I wasn't expecting anyone," as he tucked his sloppy sweatshirt into his jeans as he spoke.

"I can see," I smiled.

We knew each other sufficiently well by now, not to worry about appearances. This did not help Trevellian, however, as he self-consciously slipped his feet into his shoes to hide the holes in his socks.

"Tea?"

He left me with Danny in the lounge as he slipped out to the kitchen to plug in the kettle. It took him a few minutes before returning with two mugs of tea.

"Anything for Danny?" He asked me.

"No, I've got it all in here." I replied.

I indicated the large holdall that I now carried everywhere. It was brightly patterned and shoulder-slung for ease of carrying. Danny was sitting on my knee facing me. I bounced him gently. He gurgled in time. Trevellian could see the smile on his face. I smiled back, coaxing him on. The tie between us was obvious.

"Well, it's nice to see you, Katrina, but I wasn't expecting you. Is there a reason for the visit or is it just social?'

"You remember I mentioned to you about the man in the homburg hat and blue overcoat, the man who came in when I was with Carlo Ramiro, who spotted my trick with the cocaine?"

Trevellian remembered the man. They had not traced him. Nobody remembered seeing him apart from me.

"Yes, I do, but we did not identify him though, did we?"

"I have now, Duncan. I have now, and you wouldn't believe me if I told you." My eyes opened wide as I spoke.

"Go on then, try me."

"Jack Knight, Detective Superintendent of the Metropolitan Police. It was him, Duncan. He is on the Ramiro payroll."

"How do you know, Kat, how did you identify him?"

"He works at Kingston Police Station. He has been put out to grass. I saw him in the CID office the other day. I recognised him. I couldn't fail to do so, could I?"

"You could be mistaken, Katrina. That was a traumatic night. Think about what happened to you. It would be a simple mistake to make."

"I am not mistaken, Trevellian." My voice emphasised the point. "Why don't you, of all people, believe me? I followed him and guess where he led me."

I looked Trevellian in the eye, the anger in my face showing. I had stopped bouncing Danny. He had stopped smiling.

"To the Lanthanum club, to Ramiro's club. Now why would he want to go there, Trevellian, if it wasn't to collect his wages?"

Danny was bored. I had stopped bouncing him. He was looking around but could not turn easily as I had hold of his waist, supporting him. His arms balanced him as he tried to turn. Eventually he gave up, turning back to me. I was no longer smiling. He could sense that I was upset. If I was upset, then he was upset. He cried. It was not noisy at first. He rapidly corrected that.

As Danny cried, I pulled him into my chest to comfort him. I patted his back, his head resting on my shoulder. The noise of his cry battered my eardrum. It probably did not help Duncan Trevellian.

"There, there, Danny. Come on now, don't cry." That was me, not Trevellian.

Trevellian touched my shoulder. I looked askew at him while continuing with Danny.

"I'm sorry, Kat. I was wrong to doubt you. Of course I believe you and now, believe me, we will do something about Jack Knight. He will be sorted."

I was unsure whether I accepted Duncan Trevellian's statement. He was a Detective Inspector, prospectively competing against a Detective Superintendent. I doubted that the formal, internal, procedures within the Metropolitan Police would suffice.

In days following I was driving my newish Ford through the streets of south London towards my home. The South Circular was crowded, the roads made even narrower by parked cars. The power steering was invaluable in manoeuvring the small car, which was agile in traffic. I would turn further south into Trinity Road, towards Balham. There I would collect Danny from Winifred Peters. I looked forward to seeing my son again. A day at work was becoming too long for us to be apart.

Danny had not inherited my looks. He had dark hair, his skin buffed with a slight tan. He had the looks of his father. I could recognise it, in him, already. His startling blue eyes contrasted against this. I was pleased he had something of mine but was uncertain how long they would last before the brown pigment overtook the blue. I loved the child. It was a shame that I had not loved the father.

I was slightly late in arriving at Winifred Peters' address. I was regularly a few minutes late. I always blamed it on the traffic. I would do so again today. I had difficulty in parking my car. I left it on a yellow line, hoping that the Council parking attendants were not in full flood. I reached the door of Winifred's Victorian terrace and rang the bell.

"Winifred, I'm sorry I am late. The traffic on the South Circular again." I pre-empted any enquiry as the baby-sitter opened the door.

"What do you mean, Miss?" Winifred appeared bemused. Her face suddenly cracked as the grand, Jamaican, guffaw passed through her open mouth. Her eyes lighted with the humour.

"You've forgotten that you phoned me, haven't you? You've come all this way for nothing. You're working just too hard for your own good, you know. It wasn't allowed, back in my time. You had the baby and you had to look after it. You couldn't rely on the baby-father you know."

"I didn't ring you today, Winifred. I'm here to collect Danny. Is he ready?"

"You don't understand, Missy. You rang me earlier and told me that your friends would pick him up. Well, they did so." She looked at her watch. "More than half an hour gone, by now."

"What are you talking about, Winifred? What friends? where is Danny? Please get him for me now."

"But he's not here any longer. Your friends took him."

I pushed past Winifred Peters as she spoke. I entered the narrow hallway and ran to the rear room. This was used by the baby-sitter during the day and doubled as a playroom for the children. I threw open the door. The solitary child looked up at me as I entered. It was not Danny. Another working mother late for collection, the small girl was uncertain whether to laugh or cry. Eventually she did neither and simply turned away to carry on playing with the toys.

"He's not here, I told you. They came and collected him earlier."

I was frantic. I controlled my urge to shake Winifred violently.

"Who collected him? What did they look like?"

"They said they were your friends, a man and a woman. You had telephoned me earlier and told me they would be coming. Friends from America, you said. They were American. They sounded like it."

Winifred Peters was becoming confused. She remembered the telephone call allegedly from me. She knew what she had been told and believed it. She could not understand why I could not remember the telephone call.

"But I didn't ring you." I repeated, taking the woman's shoulders in my hands to reinforce the point.

"Sure sounded like you."

"But it wasn't me." I shook her as I spoke.

Duncan Trevellian was still in his office at New Scotland Yard when

I telephoned. Fergus Johnstone had just laid a fresh mug of tea onto Trevellian's desk. The Detective Inspector looked forward to drinking it. It had been a long day. He was drawing the mug to his lips as the telephone rang. The mug never did reach his lips.

"Come on Fergus. We've got to go, another emergency. I'll tell you in the car.".

It took the two men ten minutes to escape the underground car park at the Yard and another fifteen to negotiate their way to Winifred Peters' address. Trevellian had not known what to expect. It transpired that I was steely eyed and determined. It caught him unawares.

"Winifred Peters, my child minder." I introduced Winifred with a wave of the hand before continuing, "She received a telephone call at about 3pm today on her home number. She believed me to be the caller, although obviously she was mistaken. I apparently told her that I was delayed at work but that I had two American friends who were staying with me. I told her that these friends would pick up Danny for me. She believes that I mentioned their names, but she cannot remember them at the moment. I've left her thinking about that one. Anyway, these so-called friends arrived at about 5pm, possibly half an hour before my normal arrival time. She thought nothing unusual and handed Danny over to them. Her description is vague, a man and a woman, both strong American accents, possibly in their forties, casually but expensively dressed. She thought the woman wore jeans under a three-quarter length Mac. They were both white, possibly had a black cab waiting outside."

"And, of course, you hadn't telephoned, nor did you have friends visiting from America."

"Astute, Trevellian. Now, your job is to find my child and I want it done quickly. We need some uniformed officers out here to carry out house-to-house enquiries and I want any local, open, land searched. I also want you to check local hospitals, a long shot, but you never know."

"Sounds like we're redundant," Fergus Johnstone mumbled. Trevellian nudged him to quieten him, but I had already picked up on the comment.

"No so, Sergeant, though I seem to remember you were so, at my son's conception." My tongue was cutting, a side that Duncan Trevellian had not yet experienced. He was quiet, assessing my reaction. I was curt and clipped, an emphasis through formality, he thought.

"Fergus, I want you to track down the taxicab, if it existed. Try the central radio system, and if not local radio. Let's get this thing moving. Talk to the baby-sitter and go through it again." Trevellian told his sergeant.

Johnstone nodded and walked to the car. It would become their centre of operations; the mobile telephone battery being charged from the car. The police radio also connected directly to the central control room.

"How are you holding up, Kat," Duncan Trevellian asked me once Fergus Johnstone had left.

"I'm all right, Trevellian. I'm not going to fall apart again if that's what you're worried about. Just find my son for me, will you?"

"I'll do that, but first I'll make a cup of tea. We've got a few minutes before reinforcements arrive and you look like you need one."

Trevellian looked towards Winifred Peters. She was sitting on the settee within the children's' play area with a large handkerchief to her nose and eyes. The sobs were gulping and noisy. At regular intervals she blew her nose with a trumpeting sound. She had been like this since realising that Danny had been taken.

"I'm sorry Missy, I'm sorry," she kept muttering to herself.

I had, long since, given up comforting her. I should have done, I know.

It seemed like an age before two large white police vans arrived, spewing out its, testosterone-laden, crew of uniformed policemen onto the footway.

"House to house enquiries please chaps." I heard Trevellian's approaching words as he walked out to greet them.

I allowed him to begin his briefing before walking around the group to Trevellian's plain car.

"I'm sorry if I was a bit terse, Fergus, not a good time." I spoke quietly through the open window of the vehicle.

"My fault, Kat. I said the wrong thing."

"How's it going, any luck yet?"

"Not a thing. We've got the hospitals being checked. The troops have arrived for house-to-house enquiries and we've tried the radio cabs. Nothing yet I'm afraid, I will also get the local traffic cameras checked to see if they can help us. Don't worry, Kat, we'll find him." He looked up at me as he spoke. His eyes reflected the sincerity in his voice.

"I wish I was so sure." I walked back towards the house.

The kettle was still boiling as I walked into the kitchen. Trevellian had turned it on but never finished the job. Typical man, I thought. I knew that they could all use refreshment and found tea bags in a cupboard. I made several cups, taking the first to Winifred Peters. The child minder was no longer crying. She was settled in a seat by the window watching the activity outside.

"Drink this. there's sugar in it. I don't know if you take it or not."

"That's fine, thank you Missy. Have they found him yet?"

"Not yet, but they will"

"I hope so, I hope so."

Winifred's hope did not materialise into reality that night. The house-to-house enquiries revealed nothing. One couple in the house opposite thought they saw a cab pull away earlier, but to them it looked like any other cab. Other residents had seen or heard nothing. Trevellian was not happy.

"We'll carry on in the morning, Kat. Someone must have seen something."

"I don't think so," I answered. "There was nothing to see, just a couple picking up a child from the child-minder. Nothing unusual about that is there?"

It was late when the search teams gave up for the night. Realistically they should have given up hours ago but, for a fellow colleague, they kept on looking. They found nothing.

"It's time to go home, Kat. Do you want me to drive you?"

"You can if you like".

Trevellian left Johnstone to take the police car back to Scotland Yard. He drove my car back to my flat. It was a short journey and we said little on route. Trevellian walked me to the flat.

"Do you want me to stay with you?"

"You can, yes, but just for the company Trevellian." My look needed no interpretation.

Trevellian and I slept together that night. The sex was a side-line, but I allowed it to happen. It took little to seduce Trevellian. It was a pleasant event although not essential. His company was important. I had lost my son. I needed Trevellian's company.

I leaned against Duncan Trevellian as we talked together. He put his arm around me.

"Do you know what Danny has given me, Trevellian?" I did not wait for him to answer. "He's given me a life outside the police force. For the first time since I've lived here, I've walked regularly on the Common. I'll admit it's not a great common, but the first time I discovered it was when I walked Danny across it. I always imagined it to be dangerous, full of muggers and rapists. I was wrong. A jogger ran past us just the other day. He stopped and walked towards us. A young black lad in his twenties, bobble hat, goatee beard, the lot. I thought he was after my bag, police training I suppose. Anyway, he walked up to Danny in his pushchair and pulled a lollipop from his pocket. He looked at me and asked if he could give it to him. My first reaction was no, but I agreed. He turned and ran on. Just a friendly gesture from a friendly guy. He waved as he ran off. Not everybody's bad, you know, Trevellian."

Duncan Trevellian nodded. He said nothing. There was nothing for him to say. I was talking to myself, not to him. He was the comforter, perhaps the lollypop.

"Its incredible Trevellian. he gives me someone to love, someone who I know will love me in return. He wants nothing from me that I can't give. If I feed him, he smiles. If I play with him, he laughs. He gives me the stability that I've never had, always wanted but never had."

As I talked, I fell more heavily onto Trevellian's shoulder. He knew that I was tired but had under-estimated just how so. He only realised that I was sleeping as he heard my breathing deepen. He was not going to move me. He was not uncomfortable. He allowed his own eyes to close. He slept till morning only opening his eyes as the daylight crossed his face. He looked at his watch. It was 7.30am. He was outstretched on the double bed. He looked around for me. Only seconds passed before I walked into the room carrying two cups.

"A nice cup of tea in the morning, just to start the day off right."

I tried to sound jolly, but Trevellian could see from the dark lines under my eyes that I had not slept well.

"Thanks, Kat," he took the cup. "I just hope that the day does start off right."

"We will see. We can't ring Fergus Johnstone yet. He won't be in the office."

"I know he wanted to get some publicity out on the morning radio. Odds are that he will be in the office early, but we'd better give it another half hour."

"I'm worried that we won't find Danny, Trevellian. You want to know why?"

"Go on."

"Two Americans, Winifred said. Don't you think that's strange. Why should two Americans take my kid, and more to the point, why should they go to so much trouble to get him. If they wanted to steal a child they could have gone to a hospital, a park, anywhere. But no, they targeted my kid. They knew who I was, which baby-sitter I used. They rang her up pretending to be me. Now why should they go to all that trouble?"

"Ramiro, Paulo Ramiro."

"You've got it in one. Just imagine what Paulo Ramiro would be thinking if he knew he had a grandson, Carlo's child. Do you think he'd sit back and do nothing? I don't think so."

"But how would he know about Danny?"

"Jack Knight, Trevellian, that's how. You don't think this is just coincidence do you. Everything's fine until I identify Jack Knight as the man at the warehouse. I then tell you about it. Just think, Trevellian, who have you told?"

Trevellian racked his brain. He had initiated an enquiry, but that enquiry was meant to be confidential.

"That's right, you know what the Police Service is like. A secret is no longer a secret once it is told. I bet he found out about Danny and told Ramiro. Danny will already be with his grandfather, or close to it. We won't find him in London, Trevellian."

The Detective Inspector considered my words closely. The same fears had not passed him by. My pregnancy had been a closely guarded secret, but I was right, a secret shared with one other was no longer a secret. Our concerns were not helped by the telephone call from Fergus Johnstone at just after eight.

"Guv'nor, first lead so far. We've had a response to the morning radio news. Did you hear it?"

"No I didn't Fergus but do go on."

"We've had a call from the cabby. He picked up two yanks and a child. He took them to Heathrow. He dropped them off at Terminal Five last evening. I've got someone going out to the airport at the moment. With a bit of luck, we might find their flight."

"I, somehow, don't think so. Thanks Fergus. Thanks for calling. Come back to me if anything else comes up."

"No problem. Tell me, Trevellian, are you coming in today or do you want me to cover?"

"Play it by ear, Fergus, I might be a bit late."

Duncan Trevellian put down the receiver and slowly but surely broke the news to me. I did not cry; I had a tenacious look. It surprised Trevellian.

"As I said, we won't find Danny, not in this Country at least. It seems I'm going to have to go further afield."

Melissa Grant emerged from the Aphelion hotel. In eighteen months nothing had changed. She used the same room, probably for good luck, although the last occasion had brought her none. I had preserved my own security by refusing to allow Melissa to change at my address. Familiarity had made the Aphelion comfortable.

I had recently shortened my own blonde hair. This assisted in fitting Melissa's tightly covering hairstyle. Melissa's green contact lenses disguised my eyes but irritated slightly. I hadn't needed to wear them for a long time. They were an essential part of the disguise. Tradition insisted that I check her appearance in the mirror before leaving the room.

"Long time, no see," I welcomed the return of my alter ego. Even viewing Melissa in the mirror made me feel empowered. I had a job to do. I had decided that Melissa was the right person to assist me.

"Get on with it, girl. We've got work to do." Melissa spoke to me.

Melissa hailed a taxi from the Soho footway. It was a black London cab and stopped immediately.

"Where to, lady?" The driver asked.

"The Lanthanum Club, do you know it?" Melissa asked.

"Everybody knows it." The taxi driver raised his eyebrows knowingly as he spoke.

I shut the door and he accelerated away.

Melissa Grant was not recognised by the doorman as she

approached. He allowed her to pass, however, without question. It was early evening and the club was not crowded. There were no particular personalities to protect. He had given the girl a casual glance. He assessed that she would not give him a problem that evening.

I recognised nobody within the club. Although much time had passed since my last attendance, that concerned me. Melissa ordered a drink, scotch and water, over ice. The barman was a young South American, I thought. His hair was brown and bushy. His eyes clear and brown. He had an engaging and hypnotising smile as he served Melissa's drink.

"Is that all?" He asked.

"Yes, for the moment." Melissa returned his smile.

I walked from the bar and pulled a seat to a circular wooden table. I looked around. There were few people within the club. Whilst it was not late, those present had obviously been there for some time. An older man, dark-suited and with loosened tie, slouched over the bar, the smoke of his vape shrouding his face. He should have been smoking a normal cigarette, but the rules prevented it. There was an open-air smoking area at the rear of the club. I absent-mindedly took a 'John Player Special' from Melissa's bag and allowed the filtered end to touch her lips. My need for a cigarette had been triggered. I walked to the smoking area. It was empty of people. Perhaps a minute passed before I flipped open Melissa's lighter and flamed the end. I smoked slowly before returning to the interior of the club.

Nobody was on the dance floor. Merely background music played over the loudspeakers. The Latin temperament of the club was, however, evident. Two pairs sat at separate tables, engulfed in their own conversation and well-being. They had no time for outsiders. In between whispered words the lips of the dark haired, woman touched those of the man opposite her. The other pair were both men. They appeared intimate, but their lips were apart.

Melissa Grant sipped at the drink. I did not rush. There was little atmosphere. The barman lazily wiped a clean glass with a cloth. He had wiped the same glass for some minutes. He had little else to do. I was aware that he had noticed Melissa. He had made some attempt to pretend that he was otherwise engaged. This pretence was fading, the length of her black-stockinged legs captivating him. I did not pull at Melissa's short skirt nor did I swing my legs under the table to conceal them, there was no necessity. I recognised my legs as a formidable asset and used them accordingly. They remained crossed, however, although in the young man's line of sight.

The barman watched as I uncurled my legs and stood up from the table. There was nothing else to watch. The man at the bar had long since bored him. The effects of strong drink had now made him incomprehensible. The couple at the table were engrossed with each other and had not moved for some time. The businessmen were entrenched in negotiation, although occasionally pausing for service. Melissa Grant was a breath of fresh air.

"Another?" He asked as she approached.

"Yes please?"

Melissa sat on a stool at the bar. Her skirt covered little. His interest was obvious. He pulled himself to the optics and refilled the glass. I opened her bag in search of money.

"Don't bother, it's on the house." His smile contrasted the brightness of his straight teeth against his dark complexion.

"Thanks," Melissa smiled in return.

"I haven't seen you here before."

"No, I've been here once or twice, but not recently. When did you start working here?"

"Only a couple of weeks ago. I came over from the States."

"Maybe you can't help me then, I'm looking for someone. He doesn't seem to be here anymore.".

"Who's that? Maybe I can find out."

"Juan Marco, he was working for Carlo, before." I allowed Melissa's voice to trail off.

The barman's smile disappeared sharply. He became serious. His look was quizzical.

"Juan's not here. He's returned to the States. He is in Miami now." He noticed my restlessness as he spoke.

"Why do you want him? Perhaps I could contact him for you."

"I need to speak to him. It's confidential. I need to speak to someone close to him." My eyes told him that his position as barman did not instil confidence.

"I am Juan's nephew, Cris. They named me after the explorer." He explained to me. "What you say to me you say to Juan."

He held out his hand to reinforce his introduction. I took it.

"And who are you?" His broad smile returned.

"I'm Melissa, Melissa Grant." I paused for a moment. "I met your uncle at Carlo's last birthday party. I don't know if he'll remember me. Tell him, I've information about Carlo's death, about who set him up. But I will only tell him." I answered his querying look.

"OK Melissa, but I can't contact him now. Come back and see me tomorrow, at about the same time, and I'll have an answer for you. Tell me though, why do you want to help us? The Ramiro's that is. What have we done for you?"

The answer was slow to arrive. "You just don't know what the Ramiros have done for me. It would take too long for me to tell."

Cris looked at Melissa quizzically.

"I'll see you tomorrow then." Melissa's smile, as we left the club, said nothing.

My decision to use Melissa Grant as my agent took careful consideration. My first impulse was to fly to Colombia, find Paulo Ramiro and demand the return of my son. I knew this would not work. I would not get close to Ramiro, he would be too well protected, and, more importantly, I did not know where he was. I analysed the options. I did not know for certain that Paulo Ramiro had Danny. If I was wrong, Ramiro might still be unaware of the existence of his grandson. I would like to keep it that way.

Chapter Eleven

Melissa Grant returned to the Lanthanum the following evening. Cris was again behind the bar. His smile had not lessened. He greeted us as a long-lost friend. He left his post, walking to the other side of the bar. He held out his hands and kissed me on each cheek. It was unexpected but pleasant. Melissa smiled in response.

"Melissa, I welcome you back, and I have good news, but wait, let me get you a drink."

Cris returned to his role and poured a single scotch from the optic. He placed it in front of me. I picked up a water jug, liberally diluting the spirit. He leaned on the wooden bar as he spoke.

"I spoke to Juan on the telephone last night. He remembers you and would like to meet you."

"Good, when will he be here?" I was pleased at the news.

"You must go to him. Here, I have the instructions." Cris took a white envelope from his jacket pocket and handed it to Melissa across the bar.

"Where is he?" I asked as Melissa took the envelope.

"Miami."

The reply was given naturally but caused my heart to skip a beat. I opened the envelope carefully and partially removed the contents. The aeroplane ticket showed London Heathrow/ Miami International. It was a return ticket with British Airways. The date of departure was the following morning.

"It's too soon." I murmured uncertainly.

"Juan wants to see you as soon as possible. He said it was important. I only told him what you told me, Melissa. You must go. The ticket is paid for. I've written further directions for when you arrive."

I thought and decided instantly. "I will go."

The smile returned to Cris's face. Melissa Grant had one more drink and left the club.

Angelo's was a small hardware shop in the back streets of the Hialeah district of Miami. The shop was old and traditional with a large storage area to the rear and a jumble of oddments within the shop itself. It was not a serve-yourself store, the customer having to ask for his required product. The rear area was cluttered, yet organised. The numerous, and closely packed, shelving containing a myriad of hardware needs. Only the proprietor, aptly named Angelo, knew of the whereabouts of all the items. To the outsider, the shop seemed remarkably busy. A constant stream of customers passed through its wooden, chimed, door throughout opening hours. It was surprising that the occupants of this area should be do-it-yourself enthusiasts.

The Hialeah district, in which the shop was situated, was not an affluent area. The population consisted mainly of Hispanic or Cuban immigrants. Angelo suited the area well. He was a second-generation shopkeeper, his father running the store before him. Now in his mid-thirties, Angelo had long since recognised that his own prosperity required diversification of trade. His father had created a traditional store that had developed with the area. Unfortunately, the area had developed at a greater pace than the store, leaving it behind. The risk of bankruptcy had forced Angelo to seek other trading products. His discovery of white snow had seen the business prosper wholeheartedly.

Angelo's initial approach to the Ramiros had been treated warily by both sides. Whilst street dealers were vital to the drug distribution net, too many were merely addicts themselves, just supporting their habit. Angelo was beyond this, being a businessman although in a lesser vein than the Ramiros. In a short time, Carlo Ramiro had recognised his worth and Angelo became an established middleman. His custom had increased as his reputation grew. He now regularly purchased up to ten kilos a week from the family, channelling this onwards to the lower tier dealers. The likes of Angelo were vital to the continuance of the Ramiro empire.

Angelo recognised the dangers of dealing in drugs. He rarely kept large quantities at the premises, although as his trade increased this became more difficult. He remained loyal to the Ramiro family, despite approaches from other organisations. He found the family reliable, the quality of their product beyond reproach, and their support acceptable. Although a muscular and capable man, Angelo's protection was supplemented by a variety of weapons throughout the store. He rarely had to resort to them, trouble only ever coming from minor delinquents at a level beneath him. These he could easily handle. He was aware that the Ramiros exercised an uneasy truce at the level above.

The chimes sounded as the door brushed passed them on opening. Angelo was in the rear of the store. He walked slowly forward to the counter. He recognised one of the two men who had entered.

"What do you want, Chuck?" He asked the man.

"Mr Riccione is not happy, Angelo. He does not understand why you will not deal with him. He told me to come and talk to you."

The two intruders looked much alike. Both were dressed in shabby grey suits, both hatted. Whilst still strong and able, their bodies were suffering the abuse of age. Their faces were tanned and craggy. They looked liked walnuts, he thought, although far more difficult to crack.

Angelo knew Chuck from the past. He had worked for Johnny Riccione for many years and was the mainstay in encouraging such tradesmen to change sides. His presence was imposing and had persuaded others accordingly. Angelo was not to be swayed. Both Chuck and Riccione knew that. Whilst regular visits encouraged him, Angelo was protected by the strength of the Ramiro family. The pressure for him to change suppliers had never escalated into violence. Even so Angelo was apprehensive at such visits. His hand invisibly checked beneath the counter to ensure the presence of the baseball bat.

"Chuck, you know there's nothing to talk about. You know who I do business with and that is not your boss."

"Angelo,"

Chuck was now leaning on the counter. His grin showed the gaps in his teeth from previous encounters. As a younger man he had replaced those lost with porcelain copies. These proved even easier to lose. For many years he had stopped trying.

"Angelo, Mr Riccione insists that we do business." Chuck's smile continued.

Angelo had similar conversations with Chuck in the past. This, however, did nothing to stop the butterflies fluttering in his belly. He was nervous. He had reason to be. His attention had been engulfed by Chuck. He had failed to notice the second man, who had edged around the counter. As Angelo's hand tightened around the baseball bat, he felt the pressure of the small revolver in his temple and the man's hand as it clasped his wrist.

"I don't think so!" It was the first time that the second man had spoken. "Chuck's lost too many teeth already. Now let's put both your hands on the counter, where we can see them, shall we."

Angelo had no option but to comply. He loosened his grip on the bat and allowed his hands to come into view. He placed them flat on the counter facing Chuck. The pressure in his temple remained.

"Now do you want to deal with Mr Riccione?" Chuck continued.

"You know the Ramiros will not allow this Chuck. Surely Riccione doesn't want trouble with them."

"Mr Riccione doesn't care about them. Mr Riccione's bigger than them."

Chuck's smile had broadened. His large hand engulfed the right wrist of Angelo. From his left pocket Chuck took a pair of pliers. The pressure of the gun in his temple increased.

"What are you going to do?" Angelo's voice trembled as he appreciated the danger he now faced.

"Your first warning, Angelo, your fingers are in the wrong pie and you know what happens when they are in the wrong pie?"

Angelo screamed as his right forefinger broke under the pressure of the metal pliers. It now had three joints, three knuckles. The pain shot into his arm. He tried to pull his hand away. He was restrained by Chuck.

"Your fingers or your life," the second man chuckled.

The second finger hurt less. It cracked as it broke, blood trickling down his hand as the sharp bone broke the skin.

"You bastard," Angelo hissed at Chuck as he progressed onwards.

The third and fourth fingers broke easily under the pressure of the pincers.

"Now remember, you deal with Mr Riccione in the future. Its time your contract with the Ramiro's was broken, or else."

Chuck flexed his own right fingers at Angelo, as if to state the further consequences of non-compliance. He released Angelo's wrist and returned the pliers to his pocket. The two men backed to the door; the gun still levelled at Angelo's bulky frame.

"We will be back to take your first order." Chuck let the door swing shut behind him. The chimes were barely audible to Angelo. The pain had now numbed his brain. He looked at his misshapen hand. It was swollen and bloody. He left it on the counter as he reached for the telephone.

The journey to Heathrow Airport from my flat in Clapham was not easy.

I intended taking a bus over the river to Chelsea and the Piccadilly Line underground train from there. My small, dark green case was heavy. I had packed much into it. Whilst the attached wheels allowed me to tow it, it caught on the uneven flagstones of the footway. I had no hesitation in flagging down an empty black cab as it passed.

"Where to lady?" the cabby demanded as I opened the door.

All cabbies sounded the same in London. He made no effort to assist me with my luggage. I pulled it into the passenger compartment with me, knowing that I would incur an extra fare otherwise. I put it on the bench seat. Bugger him and his cab.

"Harrods." I stated. The underground line passed close to the store.

I sat back in the cab as it glided through the traffic. The cabby was chatting. I was not listening to him. That did not worry him. He continued regardless. I checked Melissa's handbag to make sure I had not forgotten anything. I pulled out a passport and opened it. The picture showed Melissa Grant. It was a genuine passport, which had been properly supplied by the Passport Office on my application.

I had not chanced leaving my flat dressed as Melissa. I had always avoided such obvious risks and continued to do so. I would change at the airport, probably in the ladies' toilets.

The underground train left Knightsbridge station at regular intervals. I only had to wait a few minutes. Whilst the train was crowded I found a vacant seat close to the sliding door. The particular train was painted in airline colours. I preferred it to the usual drab grey. The seat was uncomfortable. The man, next to me, was overweight and encroached into my area. My case was close to me. I did not want to lose it. I had not bought a magazine. I would do so at the airport, I thought.

As the train neared Heathrow, the commuters alighted leaving just the airline passengers. They were young and old alike. The youngsters slung rucksacks over their shoulders. The older passengers carried more conventional luggage. I was concerned that I was ageing prematurely.

I thought back to my last conversation with Duncan Trevellian. I hoped that I had not been too obtuse. I liked him, but I had other priorities at this time. He had telephoned me the previous evening.

"How are things going? I was concerned that I hadn't heard from you."

"OK. Tell me Duncan, have you any more news from the airline? Have you identified the Americans yet, or their destination?"

"No, I'm sorry Katrina, nothing yet. But we're still trying hard. I've got a full squad on it, don't worry."

"What do you mean don't worry, Trevellian. Of course I'll worry!"

"I'm sorry, Katrina. Wrong words at the wrong time." His voice showed genuine regret. "Look, are you in tonight? I thought I'd come round."

"Not tonight Trevellian, if you don't mind. I'm off on a journey tomorrow, starting early."

"Off on a journey." Trevellian's voice was quizzical. "Where to?"

"Miami, I'm going to find Danny."

The short silence allowed Trevellian the opportunity to think.

"Do you think that's a good idea? We need to talk about it and maybe arrange things properly."

"I've done enough talking and look where that's got me. No Trevellian, I'm off tomorrow. I'm going to find my son and bring him home. I'll see you when I get back."

I had cut the conversation short. I had purposely decided my course of action but knew equally well that I could be persuaded otherwise. I knew I would put both myself and Danny at risk. The easy option would be to run with the police investigation, knowing it would lead nowhere. This was my son, my problem, I knew what I had to do. I still dwelled on the conversation as the train pulled into Heathrow.

"Heathrow, Terminal Five," came over the loudspeaker reminding me of the arrival. Other passengers had already left the train. I jumped to my feet and pulled my case from the carriage as the doors began to close. I followed the growing crowd towards the departure lounge. The walk from the underground station to the Terminal building was assisted by moving walkways. The flat escalator design worked efficiently, particularly when heavy luggage had to be moved as well. I allowed those in a hurry to overtake me. I relaxed my grip on my case and stood beside it as it travelled with me. I looked at my watch, I was in no rush, and I had ample time to book in.

Juan Marco was a loyal employee of the Ramiro empire, as was his father, and his father before him. Marco knew no other life. As a young boy he remembered his initial years in the Bogota apartment. His father had travelled regularly, the needs of the business drawing him abroad. Marco had clear recollections of his mother, a beautiful, house-proud woman. She had cared for him in the absence of her husband. In his father's presence they cared for him together.

Marco's upbringing had been enclosed. The apartment was comfortable, if not luxurious. His parents drove an imported Mercedes-Benz. His lifestyle was beyond the poverty with which he was surrounded. He had little contact with other children of his own age.

The exception to this was Carlo Ramiro. Juan's mother spent much time at the Ramiro ranch. His parents were not merely employees, but respected friends of the Ramiro family. Juan loved the freedom of the hacienda. With Carlo, he explored the land, searching for uncovered mysteries. They were often turned back by the accepted boundary guards, when their exploration threatened to go beyond the perimeter of the estate.

Juan's mother had died prior to his teenage years. The cancer that racked her body had not been properly diagnosed due to the deficiencies of the Colombian medical system. Her death was painful and full of sorrow for both Juan and his father. He remembered the time well. They did not recover from the trauma easily. His father was a changed man thereafter, until his own death within the year. This death was unexplained, an accepted occurrence within the business. It was only years after, as an adult, that Marco learned the truth of his father's passing.

On his parents' deaths, Juan Marco had been totally accepted by the Ramiro family and moved into the family ranch. He was brought up as one of their own, as a brother to Carlo. His education continued within the confines of the house. His upbringing became even more secluded.

It was natural, therefore, that in more recent year's Juan Marco should support Carlo Ramiro. He had travelled with him to Miami,

London and other destinations. An endearing factor of Marco was that he always recognised his place, despite his privileged treatment by the family. Whilst treated as an equal, he knew that he was not. Carlo was a friend, but also his employer. Juan Marco was able to draw the fine distinction between the two and act accordingly.

Juan Marco had been shocked, and permanently wounded, at the death of Carlo Ramiro. He knew it as a risk of the trade. Indeed, his own father had suffered a similar fate, albeit not at the hands of law enforcement officers. It did not however, make the news any more palatable. He loved Carlo as a brother yet respected him as an employer. He would always miss him.

The proposal from Paulo Ramiro that he should now run the Miami operation was a great complement to Juan Marco. Miami was the mainstay of the business. In early days, much of the illicit trade was conducted through Miami, from business negotiations to routing of exports. Whilst tightening controls had necessitated the development of other routes, Miami remained a focal point. In that City the Ramiro empire flourished.

The news of Angelo's mistreatment reached Juan Marco in his office above the Godolphin Club, on Miami's Golden Beach. Above the offices were the opulent rooms of the multi-storey hotel of the same name, all part of the Ramiro, Miami, assets. Paulo Ramiro had named the club from his love of the Arabian horse. The Godolphin Barb was an originator of the modern Arab breed. Evidence suggested they had crossed with the Spanish conquistadors, in the sixteenth century, and had been forerunners of the South American horse. Whether or not the story was true was irrelevant to Paulo Ramiro. It had some romance, some history. He also liked the name and used it accordingly.

"It seems like the Ricciones are trying to muscle in."

Alby, the 'White Rhino' was, to the Ramiro family, as Chuck was to the Ricciones. He stood before Juan Marco's desk, his hat held in his hand, in deference to the man in charge. Alby had said enough. He had recounted the problem and injuries to Angelo. His final comment conveyed all. Juan Marco was aware that he was being tested. The truce arranged between Carlo Ramiro and Johnny Riccione was always subject to re-arrangement, dependant upon the relative strengths of the two parties. Despite Riccione's pledge to Paulo Ramiro, at Carlo's funeral, the test was now in place. Juan Marco's reaction would be closely monitored, both by the Ricciones, and by his own employees. His response would determine the continuance, or otherwise, of the Ramiro dominance in Miami. He sat for a few minutes in thought. Alby remained, unmoving.

Juan Marco had expected the challenge to come earlier. Despite being Paulo Ramiro's loyal lieutenant, his rise to such a prominent position allowed scope for a hostile take-over. To achieve such a take-over required strength, however, and it had taken time for the Ricciones to develop that strength. The challenge had now been laid. His reaction would be closely monitored. Juan Marco initially considered telephoning Paulo Ramiro, to seek his advice and direction. He rapidly dismissed this idea. Paulo had put him in charge, it was his decision to make. To seek reassurance would merely reveal his own weakness, would diminish his standing in Paulo's eyes.

"Where is Angelo now?" Marco asked the Rhino.

"Back at the store. They've released him from hospital. He's back to work, Boss."

"We will go and see him, Alby," Juan Marco looked directly at the man and smiled laconically.

"Get the car ready. I'll be down in five," he directed.

"Yes, Boss." the white Rhino turned and left the room without question.

The Mercedes-Benz had smoothly crossed the bridge from Miami Beach to the mainland. The driver had chosen the N. Miami Boulevard, a direct route to Hialeah. All the glass in the car was armoured and tinted. Whilst Juan Marco could observe the activities of those outside, they could not see in. Such was the nature of the vehicle itself that many watched as it passed, wondering which celebrity was inside. Alby sat in the rear of the car with Juan Marco. He was satisfied with this protection. The Rhino was a heavyweight, a bodyguard to be respected. If he were to be put down then the driver would respond, also suitably armed and able to protect. If both were lost, then Juan Marco knew that he would be in trouble. He patted the .38 revolver seated in the shoulder holster under his left arm. This would be his final protection.

The car approached Angelo's store in the run-down district of Hialeah. Juan Marco had been to this area before, with both Paulo and

Carlo Ramiro. They had, however, avoided the less affluent areas to follow Paulo's love of racing at Hialeah Park. It was a regular excursion on his rare visits to the city. Marco had met Angelo, but it was always Angelo who travelled to see him. This occasion was an exception to the rule and Angelo would know it to be so.

The street was narrow for the normal run of American highways. Cars were parked either side, often on the sidewalks. The buildings were drab, in need of painting. The effect was to enclose the area further. The car stopped in the road, double-parked, outside Angelo's store. There was not enough room for another vehicle to pass. The traffic would have to be patient. The Mercedes would not move whilst Juan Marco was in the store. Alby opened the door for his boss. He stood in the opening and glanced up and down the street. When satisfied he stood to one side allowing Juan Marco to exit. They walked from the car.

The formality of protection was one thing that Juan Marco had not missed during his stay in London. Juan Marco had enjoyed the informality of the Lanthanum club. The club could not similarly exist in Miami. Entry to the Godolphin was strictly vetted. Only those who were known to the management, or their guests were allowed through the door. The bouncers were not merely unarmed strong-men, but highly trained employees whose sole aim was to prevent trouble. Now back in the rigours of Miami, Juan Marco accepted the protective regime that surrounded him.

The wooden door opened allowing the tinkling bells to signify their presence. Whilst Alby was the first to open the door, he was the last to enter, having again checked both inside and outside the premises. Juan Marco admired this ability to be everywhere at once. He approached the counter, noticing the array of yesterday's pots and pans littering the shop. Angelo walked from the rear of the premises. His hand was heavily bandaged. His fingers were individually braced and stuck out like a garden fork. A sling supported his arm to prevent unnecessary movement.

"How are you, Angelo?" Juan Marco was sympathetic.

"I am not pleased, Mr Marco. I am not pleased at all. I have been treated badly by that bastard Riccione, but for why? This is not my fight; it is between the two of you."

"I know that, Angelo. Make no mistake, Riccione will be punished.

This will not happen again. Now tell me Angelo, how is your hand?"

Angelo had not smiled. At this point his creased brow lightened slightly. "It could be worse. They say that the fingers will mend themselves. They will work again. The sooner the better." At last he smiled.

"I am pleased that it is not permanent, Angelo, now tell me how are your wife and family?"

Juan Marco had knowledge of Angelo, but before the visit had been updated. It was essential that he portrayed an appropriate caring image. Angelo, similarly, knew of Juan Marco's position since the demise of Carlo Ramiro, and treated the man with the due deference he deserved.

"They are well, thank you Mr Marco."

"Now tell me Angelo, are your medical bills settled? Is there anything we can do to assist?" Angelo shook his head.

"You will be informed, Angelo, of the retribution, and when it has occurred. Before I leave, I assume our business arrangements are unaffected by this unhappy incident?" Marco's tone was not threatening, but firm.

"Most certainly Mr Marco," Angelo was quick to respond. "But I'd rather this did not happen again. I have only got this hand left."

The two men smiled as Angelo offered his left, un-damaged, hand to Juan Marco. They shook hands firmly and sincerely. As Marco turned, he knew that his visit had been successful. The personal touch always helped. Alby checked the roadway before allowing Marco to leave. They walked quickly to the car.

Alby, the White Rhino, was not South American. Born and brought up in New York, the poverty of his formative years, coupled with his orphaning at an early age, caused him to turn to petty crime. He eventually recognised the need to depart from his home town for safer climes. He remained an East Coast, American, boy, tracking his way through Maryland, Norfolk, Virginia and the two Carolinas before finally arriving in Miami. Now in his mid-thirties, he had worked for the Ramiros for several years, initially as a driver. His loyalty had allowed him to progress.

Alby was a big man whose nickname fitted him aptly. His shoulders engulfed his neck and appeared to emanate from his ears. These were firmly attached to the side of his head, a little too small and a little too fat. His nose had been broken several times over the years and had roughly reset itself. His brown hair was flat and receding, there being only any length in the short ponytail, at the back of his head. His eighteen stone frame caused difficulty in buying clothes. His few suits were well worn, although not shabby.

"Well, Alby, it looks like you have a job to do." Juan Marco addressed him as the car began moving back to Miami Beach.

"What do you want me to do, Boss?"

Juan Marco paused for a moment, thinking. The retribution had to be clear and appropriate, without escalating the problem.

"I need a hand!" Juan Marco smiled ruefully. He turned to Alby. "I need Chuck's hand, Alby. It will be presented to Angelo in return for the damage to his fingers. But I do mean just his hand, Alby, not his head."

The White Rhino nodded without turning his head. "I understand, Boss."

Chapter Twelve

Chuck had enjoyed his evening off. Several days had passed since he had spoken to Angelo. He had forgotten the incident. It was just another day's work, upon the instructions of his employer Johnny Riccione. Chuck did not think too much on the implications of his actions. To do so might cause him to morally reflect. He was unsure whether he was able to understand this concept. It had been mentioned to him some years ago by a friend and colleague. He had not understood it then and did not understand it now. It was easier not to think. His friend and colleague was now dead, his forehead penetrated by a lead-shot. Perhaps he thought too much!

Chuck's companion wore little. Her skirt was too short and her top too low. She would have looked better had she have worn something less revealing. She looked good to Chuck, however. It was rare that any female found him attractive. He was flattered by her compliments.

The club was not owned by Riccione but was controlled by him. It was on the mainland, in downtown Miami. Chuck felt safe here. He was relaxed. The woman had bumped against him as she passed. She had dropped her handbag. Her cigarettes and lighter spilled out onto the floor.

"Let me help?" Chuck grunted his offer of assistance.

The two met together as they reached to the floor. The woman's dress rode up her thigh. Chuck was impressed.

"Can I buy you a drink to make up for my clumsiness?" He offered.

To his surprise the woman agreed. She seemed impressed by him. They talked together. They drank together. They were a little drunk when she suggested that they should leave the club for a quieter atmosphere. She led Chuck from the premises by the hand. He followed in a lambish manner, his testosterone bubbling. The alleyway at the side of the club was dark and silent. Two large bins concealed them from the lighted main street. She leant against the high wall of the building and drew him into her. They kissed. It was sometime since he had kissed a woman. He relished the renewed experience.

Chuck initially thought the pressure in the rear of his neck was from the woman's hand. It was only when Alby's voice broke the silence that he appreciated his problem.

"Chuck, it's time we left," Alby tweaked the handgun to remind Chuck of its presence. The man responded and separated from the woman.

"You, go now. before you get hurt," Alby waved his spare hand at the woman in a threatening manner.

She hurried from the alley. As she reached the main street, she slipped her hand into her bag to check the presence of the two, hundred dollar-bills that Alby had given her earlier.

"An easy night's work!" She told herself, as she walked back to her usual street corner.

Chuck knew that his problems had just started as he climbed into the back of the car. He did not doubt Alby's professionalism. He knew him by reputation. He did not dislike the man. He knew that he was merely obeying instructions as he, himself, would have done. Chuck waited for the second when Alby's attention would be elsewhere. That time did not come. His last chance was as he entered the car. He took hold of the doorframe and launched himself backwards, intending the full weight of his body to catch Alby unawares. Chuck did not discover the outcome of his spontaneous action until much later. The butt of Alby's gun made contact with Chuck's head as his arm muscles tensed. The hammer-like steel struck Chuck with the full force of Alby's right arm. A black veil immediately crossed Chuck's eyes and his legs separated from his body. He tumbled to the floor, half in and half out of the vehicle. The driver had to help Alby bundle him into the car before speeding off.

Angelo's own hand was feeling a little better as he cut the cocaine into one-ounce bags in the back of his shop. The task was made more difficult with one hand. He spilled some of the expensive powder onto the floor.

"Damn!" He cursed and flexed his right hand within the sling, hoping for some sign of improvement. The sharp pain through to his upper arm was the only response.

"Damn!" He cursed again.

The front door of the store was always closed whilst Angelo

prepared his day's goods for sale. The door was strong, the locks secure. He had never been raided by the police. He was satisfied that the Ramiros' support would prevent this happening, although he could never be certain. He had virtually finished his task when the doorbell rang. He returned the drug to its concealed cabinet before walking to the front of the store. He lifted the net curtain covering the door and peered through. The large frame of Alby blocked out the natural daylight. Angelo slowly unlocked the three security devices before opening the door.

"Come in." Alby followed him to the counter.

"Mr Marco sends his compliments, Angelo. He hopes that this will lessen your pain."

Alby placed the shoebox that he was carrying on the counter. Angelo was intrigued. With his good hand he took the lid from the box and looked inside. What he saw repulsed him, but he did not show it. The hand was hewn from the wrist and lay serenely in the box. The fingers were bent downwards, supporting the limb as if in life. At any time, Angelo expected it to jump from the box. The flesh was white, drained of blood. It looked cold. Angelo did not touch it to find out. The centre finger sported a gold, half-dollar ring. He recognised it as Chuck's. He returned the lid to the box.

"Would you thank Mr Marco?" He was polite. "I would be grateful if you would dispose of this for me. Honour is satisfied."

Alby nodded at him and picked up the box from the counter, nothing else needed saying. Nothing else was said. Alby left the shop. He was unsure whether any sharks presently fed in Biscayne Bay. If so, one might enjoy the snack. He did not remove the ring. The big fish would simply have to digest it, he thought as he hurled the hand into the sea.

I felt very alone as the aeroplane flew over the Atlantic Ocean. Whilst dressed as Melissa Grant, I thought as Katrina Marshall. My thoughts were depressing. Too much solitude, and too little to do, caused me to relive the experiences and traumas of the past. Not only the immediate past, my childhood had been reopened by the events and I mulled on that too.

"Was it my fault?" I thought as I dozed fitfully through the journey.

"Could I have stopped it?"

"Would you like a drink? Coffee, tea, or something stronger?" The serene, female, voice interrupted my nauseous thoughts.

I opened my eyes. The hostess hovered over me, awaiting a reply.

"Yes, thank-you. Coffee would be nice."

"Just drop down your tray and I'll pour it." The woman turned to the chromed trolley beside her and pulled it forward. She reached for the stainless-steel pot of coffee.

I eased down the small table as directed. I was concerned that my reply to the hostess was mine and not Melissa Grant's. My training and expertise had taught me that, once in character, I became that character. One mistake could be my last. I considered the problem. It had rarely been necessary for me to become another character for more than a few hours, a day at the most. Now I was Melissa Grant and would remain so for the foreseeable future. I steeled myself to exorcise Katrina Marshall. I sat upright in my seat as I did so. The hostess served my coffee.

"Thank-you. I'm sorry, I wanted black coffee. and a scotch and water, with ice if you have it."

The slight Liverpudlian dialect grew stronger as Melissa spoke, but not so strong as to be easily identifiable.

"No problem." The hostess turned back to her trolley.

I picked up Melissa's capacious shoulder bag and rummaged within it. I emerged holding a small mirror. I stood the mirror on the aircraft table and, with both hands, swept Melissa's auburn hair back into a satisfactory condition. The hostess disturbed me with her drinks.

"Excuse me. one black coffee, and one scotch and water, with ice."

If the hostess had noticed that the auburn tresses were false, she did not show it. The trolley moved on to the next row of seats.

I refreshed Melissa's makeup, again searching within her handbag for the appropriate items. I felt better, my confidence had returned. I wriggled in the seat to become more comfortable. The flight was long. I would rather it was over. From the corner of my eye, I noticed my neighbouring passenger, a middle-aged businessman, examining my legs. Why did they always do it? My short skirt had ridden up. I carefully pulled it back to a suitable length with both hands. I was in no mood for conversation. I isolated myself with headphones and watched the in-flight movie as I sipped the drinks, alternately.

Phil Shanks was equally concerned when Duncan Trevellian told him of my unexpected trip. They sat in Shanks's office at New Scotland Yard.

"What's going on Duncan?" He asked.

"She's gone to find her kid, Phil. That's what's going on. What concerns me is that she won't be thinking straight. tunnelled vision and get herself in more trouble."

"But why the States, and why Miami?"

"I don't know. The people who took Danny are described as Americans and were last seen at Heathrow. Katrina's got it into her mind that Paulo Ramiro has come to collect his grandson. As you know, his firm also has a Miami base. Maybe she's just trying her luck."

"More importantly. Who has she gone there as?"

"We had better find out." Trevellian said earnestly.

It took few telephone calls to establish the flight and the person travelling thereon. Melissa Grant was listed as a prior reservation on the passenger list. The British Airways, business class, flight had been purchased in London. The ticket had been paid for in cash. There were no details of the purchaser. The flight had left Heathrow and was en-route to Miami.

"Have we got any friends in Miami?" Trevellian asked.

Shanks shook his head. "Not at this short notice. We could try a cold phone call, but I'd be concerned at giving too much information away."

It was not easy to make the contact between London and Miami. Shanks chose to approach Miami Airport Customs direct. He considered the local City Police, but realised their difficulty in deploying officers at short notice. He found the number for Miami Airport through the Internet and telephoned direct. He had to wait for several minutes while the switchboard operator tracked down the appropriate extension.

It was now just after midday, London time, or before 7am in Miami. Jessie Slyder had just arrived at work. He was not looking forward to the day ahead. A late night and too much bourbon had provided him with a residual headache. On his way in he had stopped at a small delicatessen he regularly used and picked up a pair of bagels, filled with cream cheese. The first had just entered his mouth as the telephone rang.

"Shit!" He mumbled through the heavy dough. He let it ring but was forced to hurry his first mouthful. He swilled the remnants down his throat with the cup of black coffee that he had poured on his arrival. He picked up the handset.

"Slyder!" He barked into the speaker.

"Hi, my name's Phil Shanks, I'm calling from Scotland Yard in London. I'm looking for someone in Airport security who could do me a favour later on."

Slyder was bemused. It was the first time he had direct contact with another Country's police force. He put his bagel carefully onto the bag on his desk. He would finish it after the call.

"Well, Phil, you've found your man, Jessie Slyder. What can I do for you?" He drawled.

"Mr Slyder, great."

"Jessie," Slyder interrupted.

"Jessie." Slyder could not see Shanks smiling at the other end of the line. "Jessie, thanks for your help. There's a lady that's flying from London Heathrow to Miami right now. We have an interest in her. I can't tell you why, but I wonder if you could spot her on arrival and see what information you can find out."

"Of course Phil. What do you want to know?"

"Where she is going Jessie. but anything you can find out will help. But I would be grateful if you don't make it obvious. We don't want to raise her suspicions. and of course this is a confidential enquiry."

"OK Phil, just give me her name and flight number and I'll do what I can. Oh," he said as an afterthought, "you had better give me your number as well."

The relevant information having been provided, Slyder replaced the handset and picked up his bagel. At least today might be more interesting, he thought as he took a large bite.

The flight had arrived on time. As the passengers got ready to disembark many stretched or flexed their muscles to disperse the cramp from their bodies. It had been a long flight, some eight hours. Most passengers were tired, not from energy expended, but from the boredom of the journey. I was no exception. I straightened Melissa's short skirt with some dissatisfaction. I didn't like wearing it, even less when it was badly creased. As I pulled it taught, I cursed that I had not dressed more sensibly for the journey.

"Still, too late for that now", I thought as I walked towards the exit of the aircraft.

Another half an hour passed before Melissa recovered our suitcase in the terminal building. I was pleased that it was intact, or even there at all. Melissa picked up the case. Passport in hand I headed for the check-in. I did not notice the overweight, fifty-year-old man, in his airport uniform. He noticed Melissa though. He replaced the usual passport controller as I reached the end of the queue.

"Your passport please." He drawled as Melissa arrived before him.

I handed over the passport. I expected no problems. The passport was genuine, if in a false name. The visa inside was similarly genuine, although arranged by Shanks through his contacts at the US Embassy. Slyder studied the document closely. He could find no fault.

"Are you here on business or pleasure Miss Grant?"

His southern drawl caused me to look at him.

"Pleasure." Melissa responded.

"Are you visiting anything or anyone special whilst you're here?"

"No, just sightseeing."

"Where are you staying?"

"I haven't booked a hotel. I was going to find one once I arrived."

I wondered why this man was asking so many questions. I had not heard other passengers being interrogated to such a degree. I looked at him quizzically. Slyder noticed my querying glance.

"Thanks very much." He cut short. "You have a good time in Miami, but be careful won't you?" He gave me back the passport. I took it and walked on without comment.

As I walked through the main concourse, the abundance of new and strange faces relieved me. I was tired after the journey and the underlying strain of disembarkation and check-in had tested me further. I saw the sign for the 'ladies' as I passed it and spontaneously turned and walked in. I did not notice the small, Colombian, man walking quickly towards Melissa. As I passed through the door his pace slowed. He came to a stop and waited impatiently. He knew he should have spotted Melissa as she left the Passport and Customs control.

I refreshed myself and repaired my worn make-up. I watched my face in the mirror as I brushed Melissa's auburn hair. There was not the same satisfaction as brushing one's own hair. I looked less strained than I had on entry, although I knew the anxiety was merely hidden. I would not relax until I had returned to London. I again straightened Melissa's skirt. I took the case by the handle and pulled it from the powder room. I was pleased with the small in-built wheels that saved me lifting the luggage,

The man stopped Melissa as the door swung shut behind me.

"Miss Grant?" He ventured uncertainly. I nodded.

"I have a car for you, from Mr Marco." His South American accent was unmistakable.

"OK, thank-you." Melissa replied without smiling.

"Here," he smiled having finally identified his prey. "Let me take that for you."

The chauffeur took the case from me and lifted it easily. He walked beside me, leading Melissa to the street and the large black Mercedes parked close by. Neither of us, nor the chauffeur, noticed the uniformed man watching us as we drove off.

Jessie Slyder did not need to leave the terminal building. The car was easily visible to him. It was a car that he had seen before. He had seen many like it, but he knew this vehicle. It belonged to the Ramiros; it was a part of their Miami fleet. The driver was not new to him either. He had seen him several times before. Slyder knew him as just a driver. The man was at the bottom of the pecking order. He rarely left the sanctity of the driving compartment. Melissa Grant was suddenly more interesting. He returned to his office and telephoned London.

"Phil, it's Jessie Slyder. from Miami."

"Jessie, thanks for ringing back so promptly." Shanks sat in his office alone. "What can you tell me?"

"Your girl's well connected, Phil. She was picked up at the airport by a car belonging to the Ramiro family. You must have heard of them. Didn't your boys take out Carlo Ramiro recently?"

Shanks sat upright in his chair at the first mention of the name.

"Jessie, indeed we did. Tell me, did she look as though she was welcome?"

"She certainly did. The car was waiting for her. A big black one, chauffeur driven. She was an important guest."

"Thank you, Jessie. We appreciate your help."

"Before you go," Jessie's drawl created an unnatural pause. "Why are you interested in the girl."

Another long pause occurred whilst Shanks considered his reply. To give Slyder nothing would only increase his interest, possibly to compromise Melissa's position. He obviously could not tell him the truth, however.

"Grant's involved in drugs, Jessie. We've suspected her of climbing up the ladder for some time. It seems like we were right. We'll be looking at her more closely when she comes back."

"Has she been convicted then?"

"Nothing yet but we're keeping an eye on her, that's all."

"That's strange", Jessie Slyder inadvertently scratched his head as he spoke. "Her visa was OK. They obviously didn't know of your interest."

Shanks did not tell him how it was obtained. "I don't know. Still, thanks for your help, Jessie. Keep in touch if anything else comes to light."

The conversation concluded, the Detective Chief Inspector in charge of undercover operations sat fixedly at his desk for a few minutes considering the options. I was glad that I did not know of his activities at this time. Had I been there with him I might have given him an option of my own. My file was before him. He read it thoroughly. There was no doubt that my experience was insufficient to ensure my safety.

"What is she up to?" He sighed.

Shanks leaned forward and again picked up the telephone handset. He would soon be standing before the Commissioner, explaining the actions of his rogue officer. He sighed again.

The Mercedes barely touched the back streets of Miami. The freeway swept me past the squalor and poverty to the relative comfort of Miami Beach. The bridge across the bay appeared the obvious physical barrier between the two. Minor traffic jams allowed me a limited view through the darkened windows of the vehicle. A view largely obscured by the myriad of yellow cabs surrounding us. Once on the move, I could have been in any other city. The buildings were the same, the claustrophobia rarely changed.

The car finally halted at the entrance to the Godolphin Hotel and nightclub. The driver mumbled something to the doorman who had opened the car door, standing to one side allowing Melissa room to get out. He took my case from the car trunk.

"Follow me, Miss."

He appeared a pleasant, older man. I followed him towards the foyer. The entrance to the building was crescent shaped, sweeping up large, curved steps towards the circulating doors. To the far side of the Mercedes, in the centre of the crescent, was a cultivated, flowered area. A large fountain, at its heart, threw the water into a high arc. The water was a virtual mist before returning to the pool for recirculation.

I was impressed by the frontage. As Melissa walked up the wide steps and approached the glassed doors, the crystal lit interior sparkled out to greet us. Being the middle of the day, the foyer was quiet. As Melissa strode through the thick carpet I commented on the relaxed atmosphere.

"It gets real busy later, when the club opens. You'll be surprised." The doorman stopped in the centre of the foyer and turned to Melissa.

"If you take the elevator to the first floor, you'll find Mr Marco expecting you. I'll look after your case. Don't worry about it." He answered my question in advance.

Melissa walked to the lifts with her created air of confidence. It was essential that I ensure that she retain that air. She was positive in her step. She did not hesitate to demand the first floor as she entered the elevator. On our arrival she was greeted by a receptionist.

"Miss Grant," the woman smiled. "We have been awaiting your arrival. At least the flight was on time." She spoke as she walked towards a large, light, wooden door. Melissa continued in her step, just behind the receptionist. I wondered where we were going. Melissa did not ask.

"Mr Marco's expecting you. You can go straight in." She opened the door, gesturing that Melissa should continue.

Juan Marco was concluding a telephone call as we entered. It allowed me a vital few moments to consolidate myself with Melissa's surroundings. Marco sat in regal splendour behind a large, light oak desk, trimmed in green leather. A single white orchid be-splendored a slim, simple, glass vase placed centrally on the desk. His dark suit was carefully cut. His clean-shaven, tanned skin had lost none of its appeal.

The office was large, perhaps seven metres square. The decor reflected the general ambience of the hotel. It was bright, yet heavily furnished. I tested the thick pile of the carpet, unobtrusively, with my foot.

"I wish I had one like this at home." I thought.

His telephone call concluded, Juan Marco walked around the desk and approached me as I stood within the centre of the room.

"Melissa, it is good to see you again." He took my shoulders in his hands and kissed me on each cheek. Melissa responded. I realised why I had preferred him on our first meeting. He had a grace of bearing, an attractive man.

"Hello Juan. So much has happened since we last met." Melissa looked at him sincerely as she spoke. She was not over-powered by either the surroundings or the man before her, albeit that I was.

"Indeed it has, Melissa. You will know that I was deeply upset by Carlo's death, as was his father, Paulo. I'm sure you were as well?"

Melissa nodded serenely.

"Still, enough of that for the moment." He smiled again. "I remember our dance, before Carlo intervened. Perhaps during your visit, we might repeat the occasion?"

"I am already looking forward to it."

"I know that we have some serious talking to do. but we are not going to do that today. We have prepared a room for you, and you have the rest of the afternoon to relax. I, unfortunately, have work to do this afternoon, but this evening I shall entertain you. We will dine together, yes?"

"Yes."

"Then I will see you in the bar at, what shall we say?" He looked at his watch, "eight o'clock. I'll see you then. Meanwhile Sandy will sort out your room."

It was apparent that Sandy was the receptionist. Juan Marco waved his hand to Melissa as we re-entered Sandy's office and shut the door. Sandy held a plastic card. I took it.

"What's this?" I asked.

"A security key, they're more reliable than ordinary keys and more easy to re-programme. Don't you have them in England?" She seemed surprised.

"Probably." I was sure they did, albeit not in the Aphelion Hotel that Melissa Grant preferred.

"Room 711. Take the elevator to the seventh. It's all ready for you. Your suitcase will be in the room."

As I opened the door to our comfortable hotel room, Juan Marco spoke on the internal telephone to the doorman who had assisted me.

"Was anything in her luggage?"

"No, Sir, nothing special at all. At least, nothing you should be interested in." He smiled at his innuendo.

"It was replaced exactly as it was. No locks were broken. nothing disturbed?"

"Certainly not. It's in her room already. She'll never know that we looked inside."

"Good. Well done and thank you?"

I was impressed by my reception. Juan Marco had lost none of his in-built charm. I liked him but reminded myself that this was a business visit. My room was more than comfortable. I looked out of the large, sealed window, across the Biscayne Bay to the City beyond. I turned to my suitcase laying open on the capacious bed. I pulled from it a short black evening dress. I looked to the mirrored wardrobe door before sliding it open. I placed the dress on a hanger provided. I brushed it straight before placing it in the wardrobe.

I walked to the bathroom. I opened the door and looked inside. This was a typical hotel bathroom, sporting a bath that doubled as a shower, and a toilet and washbowl. The fitments were not typical, however. The taps were gold, not painted gold but properly plated. Each white towel and bathmat had the hotel logo etched in gold on a corner. The floor was similarly, luxuriously, carpeted. My unpacking could wait, a shower could not. I unzipped Melissa's short skirt and allowed it to drop to the floor. I shut the bathroom door behind me and locked it, through habit.

Juan Marco was not expecting the call from Jessie Slyder. He had met the man just the once, when the body of Carlo Ramiro was transferred through the Airport. He was aware that Slyder had assisted the organisation and would continue to do so. He did not like the man. He liked nobody without loyalty and Slyder had no loyalty. Still, that made him useful.

"Put him through," he told Sandy.

"Mr Marco, it's Jessie Slyder, from the Airport."

"Mr Slyder, what can I do for you?" Marco had difficulty hiding his distaste.

"I understand that you have a visitor, an English girl, Melissa Grant?"

"What if I have, Mr Slyder? What's that got to do with you?"

"Just trying to help, Mr Marco. I thought you might like to know that the London police have been asking after her."

"Why was that?"

"They suspect her of dealing in drugs, Mr Marco. I can't think why." His voice reflected his sarcasm. "Apparently she's a known dealer in London. At least, that's what they told me."

"And what did you tell them, Mr Slyder?"

"Nothing, Mr Marco. Not a damn thing. You know me."

"Yes I do. Now tell me, who was the officer making the enquiry?"

"A Detective Chief Inspector. Phil Shanks. from Scotland Yard."

"Thanks for the information, Mr Slyder. Your expenses will be reimbursed, obviously."

Herbert Bartlett had finished early at court. The case had collapsed, not through his expert defence but through the simple incompetence of the prosecuting authority. Bartlett was pleased for the defendant, if not for himself. He had planned a three-day trial and appropriate refunding from the Legal Aid Agency. He would now have to find other ways to replenish his lost revenue. He mumbled to himself as he rummaged through the filing cabinet in his outer office.

Mavis Brown sat at her desk in silence. She knew when Bartlett was having a bad day. It was a regular occurrence. She just let him get on with it. She often wondered why she stayed with him. The office was dowdy and small. More often than not she covered it alone. She had little company throughout the day. Bartlett's downmarket clientele could not be considered company. At least, when Bartlett was in residence, he could be pleasant. He was not pleasant this day. She again ruminated on her future. The telephone rang. She answered it curtly.

"Bartlett's."

"Herbie Bartlett, please. I have Mr Marco calling from Miami."

Sandy's voice was clear and friendly.

Mavis covered the handset. "Herbie, you've got a call from Miami. Come and take it."

Bartlett moved quickly for him, recognising an unexpected source of added income.

"Bartlett." He introduced himself.

"Herbie. Juan Marco. how are you?" He did not wait for a reply. "I have a small job for you."

"What is it Mr Marco?"

"I want to find out about a girl who is over here, an English girl. Melissa Grant. Scotland Yard have already made some enquiries. I want to know more. Get Knight on to it. He must be able to help."

"Let me get a pen." Mavis had pre-empted his thought and held out her ballpoint. "Right, tell me about her."

The conversation continued for a few minutes more. Marco told Bartlett all he knew about the elusive Melissa Grant. He realised as he spoke that he knew very little. She had an endearing quality of young girl lost. It allowed her to say little about herself. Marco resolved to correct the situation.

Chapter Thirteen

Phil Shanks and Duncan Trevellian sat next door to each other, in silence, outside the office of the Metropolitan Police Commissioner. It was late evening, London time. Shanks and Trevellian felt like naughty schoolboys, waiting to be punished by the headmaster. There was no reason for either of these senior police officers to feel like that. Perhaps it was the ambience of the fifth floor of New Scotland Yard. The floor that housed the top man was serene, quiet, unlike the bustle of those surrounding it. Nobody visited unless they had to; a place to be avoided.

It did not help that the Commissioner's secretary was, by tradition, the final bastion for the protection of the vulnerable. Trudy Simms was no exception. Older than the Commissioner, her maternal instincts were to the forefront. She knew that intruders could potentially upset her ward. She was determined that this would not happen. Trudy's trim, but stern visage, belied her true nature. Her horn-rimmed, half glasses, intimidated. Her permed, grey hair was part of the barrier. She purposely did not colour it. She glared over her glasses at the visitors if they dared to break the silence.

One man that Trudy Simms could not intimidate was the Assistant Commissioner Cecil Parkes. He was a buoyant, bubbly, personality, fully confident of his own abilities. The atmosphere lightened as Trevellian and Shanks heard him approach.

"Trudy, my old duchess, how are you today? Still guarding the gate, I see. Lovely to see you again."

He turned to the two policemen. "Phil, Duncan, good to see you both too. Looks like we've got a problem or two to sort out, eh?"

He smiled as he shook hands with each man in turn.

"Shall we go in then Trudy. or are you going to keep us waiting all night?"

Trudy Simms grunted her disapproval. Secretly she enjoyed the attention paid by Parkes. She would, however, never show it.

"Wait, while I check," she ordered as she flicked the switch on the internal intercom. "Sir, your visitors are all here now."

"Send them in." The sound of Stephens's voice boomed down the communicator.

Sir Matt Stephens walked around his desk as the three men entered. He gestured for them to sit around a pre-laid coffee table. The chromed vacuum flask was standard issue throughout the Force. It was effective in retaining the temperature of any beverage. The plate of biscuits contained chocolate bourbons, Parkes's favourites. He did not wait to be asked before the first biscuit slipped into his mouth.

"Shall I pour, Commissioner?" He smiled.

The Commissioner nodded, initially offering the more serious front required of his rank.

"Well, Mr Shanks." Sir Matt Stephens addressed him formally. "Best you explain how our young officer has gone off the rails."

"Yes, Sir." Shanks relayed the account from the outset, ensuring that all relevant detail was included.

Whilst Shanks recognised Matt Stephens as Commissioner, he saw him more as a football manager. His approach was direct. His aim was to win, to achieve the best. He was not a politician, more a man's man. Stephens had lost weight since accepting the position. He had aged considerably throughout his two-year reign. His face was noticeably lined, his fair hair beginning to grey. Whilst in public he was always politically correct, in the privacy of his office he allowed himself more flexibility.

"So, we don't know for sure what she is up to, except that she's in company with the Ramiros, one of the most successful drugs families, on both sides of the Atlantic."

"That's right, Sir." Shanks was more relaxed having finished his soliloquy.

"Now, what about Jack Knight, Cecil? He's more your department, isn't he?"

"Yes, Sir, he is. Although it's fair to say that Phil and I have been working together on this one. There is no doubt that he is involved but we haven't had the manpower to keep a permanent surveillance on him."

"OK, Cecil, but what definite links are there between Knight and the Ramiros?"

"He's been seen to go to their club. the Lanthanum. in Soho and of course, if what Katrina Marshall has told us is to be believed, he has been copping payoffs from the Ramiros."

"That's not good." Matt Stephens rubbed his chin with his hand as he thought. "If the Ramiro's have the girl's son, could it be that Jack Knight was the informant? Did he tell Paulo Ramiro of the existence of the boy? I can think of nothing worse."

The other officers had clearly all considered the possibility.

"There is nothing worse, Commissioner." Cecil Parkes confirmed the view of them all.

"Is there anything we can do to stop him, Cecil?"

"Nothing direct, Sir. To do so would put the girl at risk."

"OK, but I want a team on him more regularly. Use Trevellian's men if you have to. There's nothing worse than a bent copper. He's got to be stopped. Now what about the girl, Katrina Marshall? What are we going to do about her? We don't even know what she's up to."

"As I see it, we've got two choices; either we deny any involvement, declare her officially rogue and let her stand or fall alone." Cecil Parkes started.

"Yes." It was plain the Commissioner did not like that idea.

"Or we re-adopt her. Take the operation on as our own and take control as best we can. Just think. how many operations do we let run when we haven't got a clue what the undercover officer is doing?"

"But they're generally in this Country. This girl is in the States. Even worse, in Miami, and involved with bad people."

Cecil Parkes was not to be discouraged. "I'll give the DEA a bell. I'm sure they will help. We have done them one or two favours in the past. I'll sort that side out. If it all goes wrong, we can always withdraw and declare her rogue at any time. All we were trying to do was to infiltrate a criminal organisation. There's nothing special in that is there?"

"OK." Stephens was almost convinced, "but we've got nobody in Miami. no liaison with the Americans. What do you suggest Cecil?"

"We've got no choice. We've got to keep this in-house. There's only one man for the job." He smiled broadly as he turned to Shanks. "That's you Phil. How quickly can you pack?"

Shanks knew it was coming. He bowed his head and shook it slowly from side to side as Parkes turned to him. As his name was mentioned, he looked directly at the Assistant Commissioner. His face lightened. The apparent distress was feigned.

"You know I'm always packed and ready to go, Guv. Is tomorrow morning OK, or do you want me out there tonight?"

"Tomorrow morning." Cecil Parkes now turned to Duncan Trevellian:

"Duncan, we'll have to put a permanent eye on Jack Knight."

"No problem. I'll sort that out in the morning."

"That settles it then." Matt Stephens was pleased with the result of the meeting. He walked to the cabinet at the rear of his desk. He returned with a bottle of Johnny Walker and four glasses.

As he poured the drink he commented:

"The final act of diplomacy lies with me, Gentlemen. I think, tomorrow morning, I shall have to apprise the Home Secretary of our action. That is, we have an official joint operation with the American authorities. I hope for all our sakes that nothing goes wrong."

I had checked the bathroom thoroughly. I had been trained to be careful, and in my current situation intended to be so. No hidden cameras, or listening devices were apparent in the bathroom. I searched hard. I knew what I was looking for having used them myself on numerous occasions. A tiny hole in the crevice of tile grouting was sufficient. I could find no fault. I was concerned at the mirror above the basin. It was affixed to a wall adjoining the corridor. It should not be a problem. I studied the chamfered edges. Whilst satisfied that it was nothing more than just a mirror, I covered it with a towel. It was only then that I allowed herself the luxury of removing Melissa's false hair, in order that I could wash my own.

With the thumb and middle finger of my left hand I held my left eyelids apart and allowed the green contact lens to drop into my right palm. I repeated the exercise with the other eye. The full-size lenses were placed next to the sink ready for re-use. I looked at my face in the hand mirror from my vanity bag. Katrina Marshall looked tired.

The hot shower enlivened me. The opportunity to relax was essential. This was possibly the only place that I could do so and only then, if careful. I made the most of my short time alone. I finally towelled myself vigorously with the thick, but firm, bath-sheet. I fully dried my hair before pinning it closely to my head. I carefully brushed and tidied Melissa's auburn tresses before fitting the wig to my own head. I rinsed the green lenses before returning them to my eyes.

"See you, Katrina." Melissa's firm touch of Liverpudlian returned.

Melissa Grant pulled the towel from the mirror. She stood before it naked. She did not care whether she was seen naked or not. If they had never seen a naked woman before then this would be their first. It was, however, essential to preserve Melissa's own identity. I used the mirror to replace Melissa's traditionally heavy makeup. Only then did I pull a towel around myself and leave the sanctity of the bathroom to complete my unpacking.

Juan Marco looked at his Rolex watch. It was eight-fifteen. Melissa Grant was late, but then, so were most women. He would give her a few minutes more. His Bacardi had been poured into a large glass, over ice. Coca Cola had been added until the mix was one inch from the rim. The spirit was therefore adequately diluted, but still strong enough to taste. Marco stayed with this drink throughout his working night. Many guests wanted to buy the Boss a drink, he had discovered. This drink was sufficiently flexible to leave him with a clear head the following morning.

Marco did not have to look at his watch a second time. Melissa Grant entered the room with no fanfare. She was only noticed by her prospective escort. Juan rapidly concluded the short conversation with an admiring husband and wife team. He excused himself, breaking from their overpowering chat. They walked towards each other.

I had been impressed with Juan Marco when we first met at the Lanthanum club. I was equally impressed now. His tuxedo was tailored to his slim torso. The white shirt heightened the tanned face. His hair was brushed backwards and probably sprayed to keep it in place, I thought. His eyes had the familiar glint of a man enjoying himself. His broad smile was not engineered. He again kissed Melissa on both cheeks as we met.

"I thought you were not coming. You are late." He chided Melissa playfully.

"I'm sorry Juan," Melissa feigned sorrow in reply. "I simply couldn't decide what to wear."

He pushed me gently from him and looked at Melissa carefully. Her short evening dress was patterned with sequins, though not overbearingly so. It was sleeveless, enhancing the vulnerability of my small, fair-skinned shoulders. The silver, filigree, chain around my neck supported a small locket for Melissa.

"I hope my photograph is in there." Marco indicated the locket to Melissa.

"It could be." She responded.

"You look beautiful. you were worth waiting for." Marco appeared sincere.

"Thank you, Juan." I smiled as Melissa reached up with both hands to straighten his slightly crooked bow tie. "There, that's better."

"Shall we eat now, or would you prefer an aperitif?"

"Let's eat. I can drink at the table." Melissa was firm.

We walked beside Marco towards the open plan restaurant. He carried his drink in his right hand. I carried Melissa's small evening bag in my left. Our adjacent hands were free. I felt him tentatively touch my fingers with his. Melissa responded and took his hand. I recognised a flow of energy between us. It concerned me. I was tempted to immediately let go of him. Melissa would not have done and therefore I could not.

The Godolphin was busy that night. This was not merely a hotel, but also a nightclub. I could here the music from the far side of the room, through double doors, which were ajar. The door was guarded by an evening-dressed attendant. He was a large swarthy, South American. Several others were placed strategically throughout the floor area. Beyond the doors, the lighting was dimmed. Marco saw Melissa looking therein.

"The dance-floor. perhaps we could try it later? I seem to remember that our last efforts were interrupted."

"They were."

"Would you like a drink now?"

"Scotch and water, thanks, but go easy on the water."

Melissa would stay with that throughout the evening, just as Juan Marco would stay with his Bacardi.

The gazpacho, served cold, was sufficiently, but not over spiced. Melissa sipped it from her spoon. I had finished her first scotch. She did not have to re-order. The waiter paid special attention to Juan Marco and his guest. Her glass was replenished.

The restaurant was limited in its menu. The dishes were mainly steak-based. I chose fillet for Melissa. She would like it. Marco told her that the meat was Argentinian. Although ordered medium-rare, it was served well cooked. As I did not mind, Melissa could not. She enjoyed the meal.

Whilst eating, the conversation was light and relaxed. Only on its conclusion did Juan Marco lean across the table.

"So, Melissa Grant. tell me about yourself. What do you do in England?"

I returned to my practised and rehearsed cover story.

"I work for an advertising group, mainly in tele-sales. I work in an office a lot of the time although I do get out to meet clients."

Juan Marco asked the name of the company. I was able to reply. If he checked her story, he would find it to be correct.

"And how did you come to be at the Lanthanum Club on poor Carlo's birthday?"

I could see Marco's genuine hurt in remembering Carlo Ramiro. I recognised his sensitivity and liked it, even if I did not share it. I was careful not to appear bland.

"A friend of mine was invited. I don't know by whom. I was to meet her there, but she didn't turn up. Then I met you. and you introduced me to Carlo. You know the rest."

"But do I? So what have you come here to tell me?"

I paused before speaking. Juan Marco had given no indication that he believed me to be other than Melissa Grant. If he had seized Danny, he must surely know of my double identity. If so, he was playing a convincing bluff. Only time would reveal the truth. I realised that Melissa's own story must be equally as convincing. I wanted it to stand alone and carry the correct emphasis.

"I was with Carlo, at the warehouse, when it was raided. I was in the office above. I watched as it happened. I saw Carlo shot, Juan."

Marco sensed my pain. He reached across the table and took my hand in his. "Go on," he urged.

I pulled my hand back from his to wipe a tear from my eye.

"It was horrible. The door barely creaked as they forced it up. They were through and swarming into the warehouse before anybody knew what had happened. Carlo had opened the cache. the drugs were on show for all to see. He must have been set up."

"We know that, but by whom. Do you know who set him up?"

I looked Marco directly in the eye. Melissa's eyes glistened with emotion. He found her sincere, and attractive.

"There was another man there, Juan. Carlo knew him. He came to the office while we were there. Carlo gave him money. He paid him off. They left me and went down to the warehouse. Carlo was showing him the drugs when the police broke in."

"What did this man look like, Melissa?" Juan Marco was sceptical, although the girl was particularly convincing.

"He was in his fifties. drank too much. used too much cocaine." I smiled at Melissa's description. Marco was nodding, registering the detail. "He wore a dark homburg hat and overcoat. His eyes were cruel. He was an Englishman, Juan, a white Englishman."

"And his name, did you find out his name?"

"I found out his name. and what he does for a living. He is a policeman. his name is Knight, Jack Knight."

Juan Marco leant forward. His face showed how seriously he had received this information.

"Are you sure?" He asked Melissa.

"Yes, I am sure. I've seen him since. I know it was him."

"But how do you know he set Carlo up?"

"He was there. He was there when Carlo opened the safe. It was the only time the drugs were on show."

"But how can you be sure?"

"Oh, I am sure, Juan, I am sure." Melissa was emphatic. I did not elaborate; I did not have to.

Juan Marco sat back in his chair and sipped his thick, espresso, coffee. He needed to digest, not only his dinner, but also the information that he had just received. He thought it over slowly. It was believable. He had seen Knight a few times. He had not liked the man at all. He had no time for a man who had no loyalty. He liked Knight less than he liked Slyder. Loyalty was vital within the Ramiro family. Without loyalty a man would die. He would be killed.

The family had to make use of these people, however, to ply their trade. They were useful to oil the mechanism, to bypass bureaucracy. Indeed, both Jack Knight and Jessie Slyder had been developed in that very way. They were useful aids to the Ramiro empire, but never to be trusted. Juan Marco knew that Knight had been susceptible to money and cocaine. He had proved reliable in the past and as a Detective Superintendent within the Metropolitan Police, Marco expected him to prove reliable in the future. He had access to most information. The warehouse had been raided before. They had always been warned by

Knight. The drugs had been moved; the mechanism locked. The police found nothing.

Marco had found it strange that Knight had known nothing about this last raid. He had accepted his explanation that the secret operation had been kept secure. However, if what Melissa Grant had just told him was true, then Knight had lied to them. He had denied that he was present at the warehouse. It added credence to the girl's story. Marco looked at his watch. He considered the time difference between London and Miami. It was too late to call Herbie Bartlett, he thought. Early the following morning, it would be his first priority.

Juan Marco replaced his coffee cup in the saucer and again took Melissa's hand in his. His actions were smooth, yet sympathetic. He was confident and relaxed.

"We will speak again of this, Melissa, but not tonight. For the rest of the evening, we will enjoy ourselves. We will dance. I remember, you like to dance."

I nodded Melissa's agreement. I saw the sincerity in Juan's face. He did not disbelieve me. I knew he would check further. I relaxed slightly, the first hurdle was over, I thought. Juan Marco stood from the table. Melissa followed suit.

"One last question, Melissa." He paused melodramatically. "Was Knight arrested by the police?"

"I don't know. I did not see him during the raid or afterwards. I don't know."

"And you, what about you?"

I recognised this as a judgement call. Such a simple matter had not been properly prepared. I had overlooked it, yet it was a vital point of my cover. My moment of thought was indecipherable.

"Yes. They took me away. I was questioned and then released. I think they realised that I had nothing to do with it." I bluffed. I hoped I was convincing.

Juan Marco took Melissa's hand and led her towards the darkness of the dance-floor.

Jack Knight walked through the Underground Station at Earls Court. This was one of the busier crossroads of the London Underground system, with many passengers passing through the concourse each day. The District and Circle lines passed over-ground through the Station, whilst a lift, into the depths, found the Piccadilly line.

The Station had deteriorated through the years, thought Knight as he walked. A flower seller was within the entrance, her display set up on a market stall. It brightened the otherwise dull surroundings. She appeared to be doing little trade. The newspaper stand was outside the Station, in front of the entrance. Although the footway had been widened at this point, the stand caused some obstruction. The footway chicaned due to its presence. The heavy pedestrian traffic in and out of the Station was congested. It was not helped by the ne'er-do-wells who loitered at the entrance. They were generally grubby, dirty, middle-aged men or women who had lost their way. They tended to swill their beer from the can, their martini from the bottle. At least he kept his own misdemeanours private, thought Knight.

Knight had not expected the telephone call. He was even less impressed that he had received it at home. His unsettled life needed no further disruptions. Fortunately, he had answered the call.

"Mr Knight, I'm sorry to disturb you at home. I'm Herbert Bartlett, Bartlett & Co, solicitors. I've been asked by the Ramiro family to contact you, to see if you can assist with a certain matter. I wonder if we could meet, Mr Knight?"

"How did you get my home telephone number?" Exclaimed Knight.

"That doesn't matter, Mr Knight. We need to meet. Will you come and see me?"

Herbie Bartlett had little sympathy for the Superintendent. A bent policeman was the worse kind to deal with, never to be trusted. He could afford to put pressure on this man. He had purposely telephoned him at his home. It was the first use of that pressure.

"Yes, yes. Where and when?" Knight knew he could not refuse.

"My office, I'll give you the address. Tomorrow at mid-day." Bartlett was at his most forceful. He enjoyed exercising a position of authority.

"I'll be there. But Bartlett, let me tell you, don't ever ring me at home again." The roles were temporarily reversed.

Knight therefore continued to walk along the Earls Court Road. Bartlett & Co was situated in a side street just off the main thoroughfare. Knight crossed the road at the junction. In a corner doorway sat another of the Earls Court underworld. The man wore trainers without laces. His heavy brown overcoat showed stains. It did not matter. He pulled it tight around him to keep warm. His hat was knitted, grey in colour and covered the tops of his ears. He was unshaven, his beard showing the remnants of his previous meal. A can of 'Fosters' sat by his right hand. He held out his left as Knight passed.

"Spare some silver, Guv'nor," he begged.

Knight waved the man away, pre-occupied with the forthcoming meeting.

"Bastard!" The tramp called after him.

As Knight walked through the outer door of Bartlett & Co, he did not see the tramp apparently talking into his sleeve.

"He's into offices, all units standby. I'll walk past and find out the exact location."

The tramp shuffled to his feet, not forgetting his can of beer. He put the can to his mouth as he walked along the side street. He was unnoticeable, fitting into the ambience of the area. He slowly returned to the junction, re-establishing his position in the doorway.

"He's gone into a solicitor's office, Bartlett & Co. I have control of the exit. I'll let you know when he comes out."

Duncan Trevellian was grateful to Fergus Johnstone for taking the role of the tramp. His, ever loyal, Sergeant had not hesitated to volunteer. Johnstone was experienced and competent in the art of surveillance. A man of many characters, he carried most of them in the back of his car. Once he realised that they were approaching Earls Court, Johnstone had made his quick change and positioned himself within sight of the entrance, able to control Knight when he left the Station. This had allowed Trevellian to call off the foot officers who had travelled with Knight on the train. This prevented over exposure and, more importantly, the risk of the operation being blown.

Trevellian's concerns as to Knight's involvement were shared by Phil Shanks and Cecil Parkes. Trevellian's heart missed a beat when Johnstone informed them that Knight had entered Bartlett's firm. He knew Bartlett from the inquest, knew that he was a representative of the Ramiro's. This information linked Knight even more firmly to the family.

Jack Knight entered Bartlett's office to be confronted by his right-hand woman, Mavis Brown. She was as dowdy as she sounded, with the personality of a terrier.

"What do you want?" She demanded, peering at the man. Knight felt like an interloper. He was taken aback by the woman.

"I've got a midday appointment with Mr Bartlett. Is he in?"

The woman made no further acknowledgement, nor needed any further action. Herbie Bartlett wondered from a rear room, a small smile on his face as he held out his hand to Jack Knight. The Detective Superintendent took it gingerly.

"Follow me, Mr Knight." He led Knight into the rear office. Bartlett shut the door.

"We can speak privately in here. You will have to excuse Mavis, she's a bit curt sometimes. but she keeps away those people that I don't want to see, and believe me Mr Knight, in this line of business there are plenty."

Knight nodded as he squeezed into a chair in the small room. The two men were separated by a large desk that took up much of the available space. There was just room for two chairs either side of the desk. It was no easy task to sit in either of them.

"Mavis will make us coffee in a minute. You do take coffee Mr Knight, with milk and sugar?"

Again Knight nodded his approval.

"Ah good. well let's get on with it. You know why I asked you here don't you?"

"No I don't. You told me on the phone that it had to do with the Ramiro family. I don't know why you think I can help with the Ramiros."

"Oh, come along Mr Knight, let's not be coy. I've spoken to Juan Marco. It was he who told me to contact you. He explained to me that you were. how shall I put it, a friend?"

"How do I know that this conversation is not being recorded, Mr Bartlett?"

"I act for the Ramiro family, Mr Knight and, I understand, on occasion, so do you. I have no need to record anything."

"So, if I can help, what do you want? What do the Ramiros want of me?"

"Jack," Bartlett feigned friendliness. "Mr Marco has an English visitor that he needs to know more about. and he needs to know urgently. Her name is Melissa Grant. She is offering information about Carlo Ramiro's death, about how it happened. She says she knows who set Carlo up."

This was a set back for Jack Knight and the look on his face showed it.

"It wasn't you, was it Jack?" Herbie Bartlett had noticed the colour drain from his face.

Knight feigned laughter. "No, it's too hot in this little rabbit hutch. Get on with it Bartlett, before I finally pass out through lack of air."

The reference to the rabbit hutch cut Bartlett to the quick. It was a small office and he recognised that. It was, however, all he had and all he could afford. He resented the man's insult. In all, he resented the man.

"You were meant to have provided this information long ago, Mr Knight. The Ramiro's expected you to be able to tell them why Carlo was not warned of the raid and why he was killed. They have heard nothing from you."

"I could not tell them what I did not know. I wasn't present, and nothing was forthcoming. It was the best-kept secret in the Metropolitan Police, that raid. Nobody knew about it."

"Well, it seems that someone knows more than you, Jack, and now we need to know more about her. Best you get on with it, eh."

"I'll come back to you, Mr Bartlett."

Knight was barely able to extricate himself from behind the desk to leave the offices. He was aware that Mavis Brown had not left her desk, nor made for the kettle, since his arrival. He would not have enjoyed the coffee, had he have received it. He left the offices, pleased to be back in the fresh air of the Earls Court Road.

As he returned to the Underground Station, he considered Bartlett's direction. Whilst it was not an order, it was certainly more than a request. He was concerned to protect his own integrity. He had now denied his presence at the warehouse on two occasions, once to Juan Marco and now to Herbie Bartlett. He should be safe. There was nobody to contradict him.

"Except the girl!" His train of thought continued as he walked back to the Underground.

Brad Baker had been a Drugs Enforcement agent for five years. For four of them he had been based in Miami. He did not like the city. It contrasted badly with his Boston upbringing. He was a young man with a young wife and two small children. Whilst they lived in a better part of the city suburbs he would have preferred to have been elsewhere. Brad had been recruited to the DEA at college. He had been approached and was impressed by what he had heard. He had not realised that the tales of excitement had been over-exaggerated. The job was certainly more mundane than he had expected. He was overburdened with paperwork and formality.

The Federal building, on 1st Avenue and 3rd Street, was formally a post office. The thirties building was built on the site of one of the early Miami schools. The 'Stars & Stripes' flew listlessly from the white flagpole outside. The building itself was large and shabby, in need of a new coat of paint. The irregular rendering was beginning to show through the faded whiteness of the previous coating. The building had suffered the ravages of public spending cuts, that the current administration felt necessary to protect their budgetary forecasts.

The call from Washington had been unexpected. It was rare that the office was contacted from the Centre. Perhaps something interesting would happen, Baker thought, optimistically, as he listened to the voice on the telephone.

"Baker, you are aware of the Ramiro family?"

"Yes, Sir," Brad was respectful to those in the Centre.

"When did we last work on them?"

He cast his mind back. It was some time since they had worked on anyone. " I'd have to check the records."

"No time for that now Baker. We've had a call from the Brits, London police. They've got an operation running at their end. One of their undercover operatives, a girl, has infiltrated the Miami end of Paulo Ramiro's drugs empire. They want us to provide immediate cover. Their man is flying over in the morning; Detective Phil Shanks. You have got to collect him from the Airport and get it all together. We don't want anything going wrong."

"What sort of cover do they want, Sir. Shall I wait until this guy Shanks arrives?"

"No. set it up now, a surveillance team with full equipment. Get them together and put them on the hotel. what's it called? The Godolphin: I want it up and running within the hour."

The telephone call caused a flurry of excitement for Brad Baker and his few colleagues. Whilst trained in surveillance, as part of their initial training, most of their work was now routine, mundane enquiries emanating from the Centre. They occasionally trained together to retain some expertise. The single telephone line was overworked as Baker called in his team.

The facilities were not available, nor in use within the hour. The radio batteries would not be charged within that time. Two men busied themselves in cleaning the old blue Dodge, observation van. It had not been swept since its last use. The used hamburger boxes should have been removed. The smell was unpleasant. Other vehicles had been used by agents on an individual basis. They had rapidly replaced the family cars in usage. The officers were recalled and the vehicles re-deployed.

Baker accepted that they would not be operational until the morning. He used the rest of the day to properly research their adversary. They had worked on the Ramiro's in the past and should have been working on them now. He did not know why they were not. He read the files in brief. He was suitably impressed by the opposition.

Sir Matt Stephens had visited Michael Farrar at his offices before. The Home Secretary enjoyed a standard of office life that matched Stephens' own. The Commissioner fared well in his work comforts. He wanted for little. The Home Secretary was similarly comfortable.

"Commissioner, come in." The Home Secretary welcomed him personally. "You have met Rupert Veneer, haven't you?"

"Yes I have. How are you Mr Veneer."

"I am well, thank you, Commissioner." The Under-Secretary pushed his glasses back onto his bulbous nose as the Commissioner shook his hand.

"What can we do for you Matt? An extra-ordinary visit I believe, is something up?"

"Nothing too serious Michael, but something quite confidential." He glanced at Veneer.

"I'm sure we can trust Rupert, Matt. After all, he has access to all the records anyway."

The Commissioner was hesitant. "All right Michael, but no records, at all, on this one, OK?"

"Of course, now what's up?"

"We have an officer in the States at the moment, in Miami. She's working undercover."

"Nothing unusual about that Matt, go on."

"I've mentioned to you about the officer, who was raped by Carlo Ramiro, before his place was raided last year."

"Yes."

"And became pregnant by him and had his child."

"Yes, I remember."

"Have you read in the papers about the child that was kidnapped in Balham recently?"

"Yes I have, bad matter eh."

"It was her child, wasn't it?" The Under-Secretary was ahead of his mentor.

"Yes it was, and she's gone out, to Miami, to find him."

The three men paused as coffee was brought into the office on a silver tray. They waited for Farrar's personal assistant to leave before continuing.

"Sugar, Matt?" The Commissioner nodded.

"Why did you send her out there. Surely it would have been better to send another officer, not personally connected with it all."

"That's why I'm here, Michael. We didn't send her out. She went on her own. We've now got the problem that she's running loose in the States. We couldn't have that, so I've decided to formalise the situation. I've sent out a back-up. He's liaising with the American authorities to, at least, give some protection. We've got no contact with her at the moment and no control over her actions. It could all go horribly bent on us."

"Best you see that it doesn't Matt. I suppose she believes the Ramiro family were involved in the kidnap, then."

"That's right. She's gone out there to get the child back."

"Risky business, so you've now turned this into one of your joint operations, have you?"

"Yes, I thought it would be for the best."

"Not necessarily for the best, Commissioner," Rupert Veneer interjected.

Both men paused to listen.

"I would advise you to heed my old mother's warning, Commissioner. Ride a two-legged horse and you will be sorry. An ass with four legs is more agile than a two-legged horse. It seems that you're about to ride a horse with two legs."

"So, have you got any better ideas, Mr Veneer?"

"I have not, Commissioner, unless you cut her adrift. You have made it plain that you do not intend to do that."

Matt Stephens slowly shook his head from side to side.

"In that case, I toast the two-legged horse."

I woke late the following morning. The thick curtains in my room effectively blocked out the light and allowed my sleep to continue. Whilst I would argue that I was overcoming the symptoms of jet lag, the fact that I had danced into the early hours must also have affected me.

On waking, I pulled the curtains apart and allowed the daylight to flood the room. I looked out onto the panacea of the seascape. The sun was already high in the sky, its light reflecting from the small waves. I turned back within the room. It was light and restful. The double bed was covered with a white duvet. It had proved comfortable. I walked back to the bed and threw myself across it. I turned and lay on my back.

Juan Marco had been the perfect host. We had danced together within the small club, the darkness of the dance-floor giving us privacy. Juan had a sense of rhythm and an easy ear for music. His body was fit. He moved in unison with the beat. Both Melissa and I similarly enjoyed dancing and responded to his style. As I remembered the evening, I thanked the dance studio, in London's Chelsea, for my further lessons, as well as my mother, for instigating the ballet lessons. I had realised the importance, to my under-cover role, of being multi-skilled. The benefits of dance could never be under-estimated. I had attended on a regular basis for several months. I was proficient and comfortable on any dance-floor. Melissa benefitted from my training.

Juan Marco had responded to Melissa Grant. Juan led Melissa through the South American jive. I did not pull away as the music slowed. Both our bodies and our lips had touched during the evening. The tantalising touch, as our mouths closed together, was disturbed by a slight change in rhythm. I was touched by Juan's breath as we pulled apart. The dancing continued.

Juan had walked Melissa to our room. As we travelled upwards in the elevator, his hands reached to my waist. He did not pull me into him. I was glad that I did not have to resist.

"You are a beautiful woman, Melissa. The evening had been wonderful. But be careful, you tread on dangerous ground."

He kissed Melissa goodnight. For the first time that evening, the sensual moment was allowed to continue. Marco made no effort to follow Melissa into our room.

"I have much business to do tomorrow, Melissa. I shall be engaged for most of the day. I will meet you in the evening, you will meet Paulo Ramiro, Carlo's father. Until then, the day is yours. Perhaps you will see the finer parts of Miami?" He raised a quizzical eyebrow.

As I lay on the bed reconsidering the evening before, I hoped that I had not gone too far. Had the priority of finding my son not overridden the situation? I might have found Juan Marco unacceptably attractive. I recognised that I needed him on my side if I had any chance of finding Danny. I was not convinced that he did not know where Danny was, that he was not involved in the kidnap. His actions the previous night left me uncertain, however. Could he have covered his knowledge so persuasively? I thought. Or was it that he actually did not know? Would Paulo Ramiro have arranged the kidnap without involving Juan Marco? I thought not. If the Ramiros did not have Danny, then who did? I was worried.

"Danny, Danny, where are you?" I banged my head into my pillow in frustration. Where was my son?

I dressed slowly. The day was mine, as Juan Marco had pointed out. I would achieve nothing further that day in my quest. To mope at the hotel was pointless. I would sightsee and shop. I dressed practically in 'Levi's' and a grey jumper. I was careful to preserve Melissa's bold makeup. Melissa and Katrina could not be allowed to merge. I breakfasted late, but that did not matter. The service was immaculate and willing. Whilst accepting the offer of a cooked breakfast, I finally admitted defeat and pushed the hash browns to the side of the plate before sipping my coffee from the large cup. It was milky and sweet. I enjoyed it.

"Have you finished? Too much for you, Madam?" the waiter reached for my plate.

"Yes, thank you. It was fine." Melissa did not smile in response.

"OK, have a nice day," as he walked away.

I sought the advice of the receptionist before leaving the hotel. I was then armed with a guidebook to Miami and tips as to suitable venues to visit. The Hall Porter summoned a waiting, yellow cab for me. As it took Melissa from the hotel towards the mainland bridge, I did not see the large black Mercedes cruise from the back of the hotel.

Juan Marco had not allowed a lack of sleep to inhibit his working day. He was at his desk at ten, albeit a little tired. He had found Melissa's company stimulating. Under different circumstances, he would have flowed with the tide. There was no doubt that he would have tested her resolve to refuse him. As it was, he pulled away at the last minute. After all, this was business, most serious business concerning the death of his good friend Carlo Ramiro.

Marco again disturbed Herbert Bartlett from his work. Mavis switched the telephone to hold:

"It's that American again, Herbie. What's his name? Marco."

"Shit!" Bartlett realised that he had not heard again from Knight nor contacted him further. In fact, he had forgotten all about it.

"Have you told him I'm in, Mavis?"

"Yes, come on, you'll have to take it."

"Herbie, have you contacted Jack Knight yet?" Marco forewent the formalities of introduction.

"I have spoken to him, Mr Marco. He came here, to my offices, but I have not heard from him further. It seems strange that he has not come back to me. I'm sorry, I will chase him up."

Bartlett feigned sorrow. He would add it to Marco's final bill, he thought. He had no hesitation in blaming Jack Knight for his own forgetfulness, the man deserved it.

"Herbie, I don't want you to contact Jack Knight again. Do you understand me? No contact!" He emphasised.

"Why's that?" Bartlett was surprised.

"When you spoke to Knight, he denied to you that he was at the warehouse when Carlo was killed. Is that right?"

"Yes, that's right Mr Marco."

Marco was thoughtful. "He did the same to me Herbie, when I saw him in the Lanthanum, after the raid."

He continued. "Herbie, I want you to find out if the girl, Melissa Grant, was arrested by police after the raid. Was she present at the warehouse? If so, why? Secondly, I want you to find out if Knight was present. Do your best and do it urgently, OK?"

Herbert Bartlett wiped his brow at the conclusion of the telephone call. Mavis Brown stood up and plugged in the electric kettle. An unusual gesture, but on this occasion she recognised his need.

Alby 'The White Rhino' opened the door of the Mercedes limousine to allow Juan Marco access. It was a standard gesture, perhaps unnecessary at the entrance of the family hotel, but maintained nonetheless. The car pulled away soon after Melissa Grant's taxi had reached the bridge.

"Have you got the camera?" Marco asked Alby.

"Yes, Boss." Alby picked up the Canon camera from the back seat. It was not the type of camera that he was used to. He preferred a 38. He held it to his eye. His fat fingers fumbled with the mechanism. Eventually the zoom lens moved in and out with some efficiency.

"Are you sure that you're going to be able to work that, Alby? If not just use your cell."

"Yes, Boss." Alby's conversation was limited.

The Mercedes swept them towards the Miami centre.

The Orange Bowl Stadium had proved a convenient meeting place in the past. The large car parks were open and easily accessible. The stadium had been based in central Miami since the early thirties. It had grown considerably due to the continuing popularity of American football. It was regularly full of enthusiastic spectators. Today was not one of those days. The car parks were little occupied.

The brown Ford was already at the meeting place. The engine was turned off and cooling. It had been there for some minutes. The black Mercedes dwarfed the smaller car. The driver left a suitable distance between the two vehicles. Through the darkened windows, Marco watched as the door of the Ford opened. Jessie Slyder walked nervously towards the limousine. Marco left the Mercedes himself. Unusually 'The Rhino' stayed in his seat. Marco met Slyder some ten yards from the Mercedes, between the two cars.

"Jessie Slyder, thank you for coming to see me," Juan Marco purposely held out his hand. Slyder took the offer and shook vigorously. Marco was glad when the clammy grip was released.

"Jessie, I appreciate the telephone call. It was very useful. You have given valuable assistance to us since assisting Mr Ramiro in clearing his son's coffin for collection. You appreciated the traumatic situation and acted very properly. We have much confidence in you, Jessie and would like to see your responsibilities grow, and, of course, your rewards."

Slyder was surprised by the complimentary attitude of Marco. He had not expected it.

"It is my pleasure, Mr Marco," he blustered.

"I would like to give you a little something for your assistance." Marco took a money clip from the pocket of his suit and carefully counted out two thousand dollars in large bills. He handed them to Slyder. He did not release them immediately, prolonging the time when both men were holding the money.

"I hope you will accept this, Jessie, that you won't find it offensive."

Jessie Slyder did not hear the click of the camera as the aperture opened and closed. Alby took several pictures of the meeting. It would provide a permanent record of the meeting, frame by frame.

Neither Jessie Slyder, nor Juan Marco heard the similar camera sounds from the Blue Dodge van that had pulled into the car park some way behind the Mercedes. It had parked some distance away from the two vehicles and had not been noticed. The two federal agents within the vehicle had scrambled for their recording equipment.

"It sounds like we've hit lucky straight off." Brad Baker turned to Phil Shanks. "Your operative must be a good omen for us," he smiled.

Baker had collected Shanks from the Airport that morning. They had not met before but responded well to each other from the outset. Shanks was impressed that Baker was up and running with the surveillance operation. Baker was impressed when Shanks urged him back to work.

"The hotel can wait. I'll find one later, when we finish," Shanks told him.

So it was that the two men sat in Baker's car just outside the Orange Bowl. They were out of sight in a side street but in contact through the radio. Shanks was formally suited and booted, having prepared for a formal greeting at the conclusion of his flight. Baker was more informally dressed. They had thrown Shank's luggage into the boot of the car. It would travel with him throughout the day.

"It sounds like a pay-off." Baker explained. "Juan Marco is Paulo

Ramiro's right-hand man in Miami, since the death of Carlo Ramiro. He was pulled in specially, from London. But I suppose that you know that already."

Shanks nodded but said little. He appreciated the explanation.

"Marco appears to be paying someone off. We have photographs and a boom mike recording the conversation. We think it's a customs officer. The car is registered to a guy called Slyder. We'll check on that later."

The name rang a bell in the back of Shanks's memory. The length of the journey had tired him, however. He missed the connection.

All the electrical recording equipment was based in the Dodge van. Whilst the camera, even with its large telephoto lens, was easy to conceal, the directional microphone was more difficult. Whilst particularly sensitive, it had still to be directed at the parties involved, preferably through unobstructed space. This had been achieved through the open front window of the van, the driver remaining in position to direct the microphone. He held it in his hand. It was not stable. Any slight movement caused distortion on the recording.

"Keep it still," the agent in the back of the van whispered as he re-adjusted the fine-tuning to achieve the best recording. He returned to his primary task of photographing the meet.

"Thank you, Mr Marco, if there's anything else I can do for you?" Slyder folded the notes with one hand and pushed them into his trouser pocket. He was anxious now to get away.

"Indeed there is." Marco was not going to allow him to escape easily. "Your role is important to us; we will be calling upon you very soon."

Slyder nodded. He listened intently. "What's that for, Mr Marco?"

"We were impressed in the way you cleared Carlo Ramiro, and our other friends, through the Airport. It minimised the grief of all the families and particularly that of Paulo Ramiro."

"It was nothing."

"The decision appeared yours, Jessie. Is that always the case when a body has to be transported between countries?"

"It is at Miami. We try to be sympathetic to the family, to cut out any distress. If the papers are correct, the formalities complete."

"Oh, they will be Jessie; they will be. So, a sealed coffin through the airport, properly documented, could be checked out by you. You would have the authority to do that?"

"I'd have to check it thoroughly Mr Marco, before I could let it through."

"Of course you would, Jessie. But for us, you'd clear it out of the US?"

"I could do that. Yes, Mr Marco, I could do that, but I'd be taking a great risk. I don't know if I should take that risk."

"You will be well looked after Jessie. I'm sure you will not suffer."

Slyder gave a wry smile. They were talking the same language. He had been suitably impressed with his recompense so far. Such a further gesture could cause the replacement of his old Ford with a newer model.

He held out his hand to Marco. "I'd be pleased to help, Mr Marco. Contact me when you need me." His confidence restored, his hand was no longer clammy. His handshake was firm.

"Indeed we will. Goodbye Jessie." Marco returned to his vehicle.

"Goodbye Mr Marco." Jessie talked to his back. He watched as the Mercedes moved off. His step bounced as he walked back to his own car. He could foresee a further, more beneficial, relationship.

"That was good," Baker told Shanks when they later heard the tape of the meeting in the sanctity of Baker's office.

"Slyder's a customs officer at the Airport. He's obviously on the Ramiro payroll. From the conversation it sounds like the Ramiros will try an exportation through the Airport, with Slyder clearing their cargo. We'll be close behind."

"We took a large amount of cocaine from the Ramiros, at their warehouse in London," Shanks explained. "That was some time ago now and they will have had time to rebuild, but they won't like too many losses, particularly big ones." Shanks's memory suddenly jolted. Jessie Slyder, he remembered the name. He thought for a moment. He chose to say nothing to the American. He hid his concern.

"Now tell me Brad, have you seen our girl yet?" He asked.

"No, not yet, but it's early days yet."

Chapter Fourteen

I had enjoyed my uncluttered and uncomplicated day alone. It had allowed me time to relax, to concentrate on the natural activities as a tourist. My life had been directed by events. I had followed that direction, shielded by my alter-self, Melissa Grant. Although still outwardly appearing as Melissa, I allowed my own personality to filter through. My long-strapped shoulder-bag was slung over my shoulder.

I thought of Danny as I toured Miami. I remembered his gurgling smile as I bounced him on my knee. I remembered the delight at watching him push the chiming-ball across the floor of my flat. I remembered the soreness of my breast when I had tried to feed him naturally. I remembered the unforgettable odour of his spoiled nappies. My nose turned up as I thought, blocking out the imaginary smell. I knew that I could do nothing to assist him today.

The cab took me through the city to the south. A visit to Coral Gables had been highly recommended by the receptionist. I was suitably impressed by the recommendation. The area was a delight. Buildings constructed in the rock of its name. I visited the old fire station. I imagined the original depth of colour, created by layer upon layer of encrustation, now faded by the strength of the Miami sunlight and thoroughly washed by the weather. I marvelled at the skills of the stone-masons who had worked the material and particularly with the hatted gargoyles that decorated its frontage.

I was taken to the exotic Venetian Pool, close to the historic Biltmore Hotel. The clarity of the spring water tempted me to strip off and dive in right there and then. I refrained from doing so. Again, the coral was predominant at the waters edge, the contrasting colours of the palms and the backset of larger trees completing the picture. I learned that the semi-tropical climate encouraged the fast growth of such foliage and despite some disastrous storms, the flowers regenerated and bloomed again, overnight.

My day would not have been complete without a visit to the shops. I was taken to a most picturesque mall. It was set on three stories with ornate steps leading to the central plaza. A tiled walkway led through a myriad of small shops. I paused for coffee under the blue umbrellas overlooking the plaza before venturing through the displays. I appreciated the value. I did not refuse a new pair of Levi's at knockdown value. I looked long at competitively priced electrical-wares. A Hispanic shopkeeper, whose encouragement to buy led to a further reduction in price, secured my attention. I had no camera. In my haste to leave London, it had not been packed. The Olympus was a third cheaper here. He would throw in a case and films. It was automatic and virtually worked itself. I did not buy it. My I-Phone was sufficient for my needs.

I returned to the Godolphin in late afternoon. The sun was dropping in the sky and the tall buildings created dark but intermittent shadow. I rested my head against the back seat of the taxi as it approached.

"You mind if I drop you off just around the corner, Lady?" the booming drawl of the taxi driver disturbed me. "It's just that the front's filled with big limos. I'll never get out again."

"No, that's OK."

I looked to the front and recognised his concern. The front drive of the Godolphin was blocked. The problem had been caused by one abandoned vehicle. I could see the driver, cap on head, dragging the luggage of his passenger, towards the main door. The other cars sat patiently. The drivers did not sound their horns. Each one of them had been in his position. They were sympathetic. They were in no rush. Their rich employers could wait for a few moments.

The taxi driver was a different individual. He was paid by the minute and wanted to get back on the road again. We turned down a small road by the side of the hotel. Even that road was partially blocked by a breakdown vehicle that was double-parked. The driver stopped in the middle of the road.

"That'll be twenty dollars, Lady."

I gave him twenty-five. He grunted his thanks as he drove off.

I was left standing in the centre of the street. Another car sounded its horn for me to move. I received no sympathy whatsoever. I looked at the truck that was double-parked. It was plain white. There was no sign writing to identify the company. The mechanic was working on an adjacent car. The hood was up; he was bent towards the engine. His white overalls matched his truck. At the sound of the car horn, he looked up. He glanced towards me and I towards him. There was something unusual about him. It was not immediately apparent to me.

"Mercedes 500SL," I smiled as I thought. "Not as reliable as they're made out to be. I didn't think they broke down."

I admired the car, nonetheless. It was a vehicle that I had dreamed of, that one day I would own. A sharp red in colour, the convertible roof was down, exposing the plush, cream leather upholstery.

"I'll have it, broken down or not." I thought as I turned towards the entrance of the hotel.

Duncan Trevellian accepted the telephone call from Herbie Bartlett, although not prepared for the questions put. Bartlett was his usual, untrustworthy, self.

"A couple of questions, Mr Trevellian. As you know, I act for the Ramiro family. We met some time ago, at the inquest. There are just a couple of points I wanted to clarify."

"Go on."

"I understand that a girl was present at the warehouse on the day of the raid, that she was arrested by your officers; a Melissa Grant. Can you confirm this please, Inspector?"

Trevellian was caught off-guard. This was not something that he had discussed. He thought of Katrina in Miami. The question would not have emanated solely from Bartlett. He paused too long.

"Inspector," Bartlett reminded him of his presence.

"I'm checking, Mr Bartlett, if you'll just hang on."

"Now, what would Katrina have told them?" He thought.

He could not second-guess. Her presence was too easy to establish. There were still witnesses who could have identified her.

"Yes, Mr Bartlett, she was there, but was released once we had established that she was not involved."

"And a Detective Superintendent Knight? I understand that he was in charge of the operation and present at the warehouse?"

"No, he was not in charge," the insult was shown in Trevellian's voice.

"And present?" Bartlett persisted.

"He was not there either."

"Well thank you, Mr Trevellian." Bartlett knew when he had gone too far.

The call concluded Trevellian wondered if he had answered correctly. He hoped so. He had little time to ponder further. Fergus Johnstone called him.

"He's on the move, Duncan. If you don't get a move on, we'll lose the team".

Trevellian pulled on his jacket as he ran from the office. He registered his intention to inform those above him of the most recent call, particularly Phil Shanks in Miami. It might be relevant to him. He dropped from the fifth floor to the basement. For once the lift worked efficiently. Fergus Johnstone was awaiting his arrival.

"Get in, we've got to get moving. For once he's in his car."

Knight knew his way. Having served across the Metropolis of London for many years, it was only natural that he should. He was, however, travelling in his own, private, car. He therefore stayed on the major routes. He drove slowly. He was in no rush. He knew his destination.

Trevellian logged the movements of Jack Knight. The only significant issue occurred late into the evening in a small side road, off the Finchley Road, in north London. The surveillance team had stayed close to Knight throughout the day and were tiring. Trevellian realised the greater chance of mistake through tiredness and was ready to suspend their activities. The loss of information would be less dangerous than the increased chance of discovery by Knight.

"The car's slowing, it's parking up," came from the observing vehicle.

"Let's get up close to him, on foot, and see where he goes," Trevellian instructed.

Jack Knight was watched as he deliberately locked his car. On this occasion his homburg remained on the rear parcel shelf. He had chosen not to put it on. He left the car and walked to the front door of a terraced, three-storey, Victorian house. He rang the bell.

Trevellian was not familiar with the house and had no time to check the occupants on the electoral register. The description of the bug-eyed man answering the door did not initially assist Trevellian to establish the relevance of this visit. It was unfortunate that the eyeball could not get close enough to hear the conversation.

"They're quite heated, Guv," came over the radio. "Knight's poking the guy in the chest with his finger, nothing too violent, but he's making his point."

Trevellian instructed another of his team to register the vehicles parked close to the address. The Porsche stood out amongst them.

"The occupant's responding, he is arguing back. Hold on, his hands are spread, it's obvious Knight's got control, the other guy looks worried."

"Get in closer and see if you can hear the conversation."

"I don't know that I can, Guv. I am only two-doors down, at the front door. Stand-by, I'll try."

The radio was quiet for some time. It seemed to Trevellian an eternity.

"It's no good, Guv. They finished just as I got close. The front door's closed, Knight's on the move again."

Trevellian terminated the surveillance operation when it was clear that Knight was returning to his suburban home.

"Check that address out, Fergus, when you can. We need to know the occupant," he instructed his Sergeant.

Juan Marco telephoned me soon after my return to the hotel. I lay on the bed in my room, to receive the call. I could imagine him there beside me. His voice was soft and rhythmic.

"Did you have a good day, Melissa?" He asked. I was pissed off that he was not speaking to me.

"Yes, Juan, I did. I'll tell you about it later though."

"Indeed you will. Tonight you have an appointment to see Paulo Ramiro, Carlo's father. He has come to Miami especially to see you. I trust that you will not let him down."

"Of course I won't. What time, Juan."

"At ten o'clock. We will leave the hotel at nine-thirty. Shall I collect you from your room?"

"I'll look forward to it. A little earlier if you can make it." Melissa flirted with Marco, I hoped that she had not gone too far.

Marco was not early, a fact that slightly disappointed me. I had hoped that he might respond to my obsequious offer. It was apparent that he divorced business from pleasure. I must do the same. Melissa had dressed somewhat formally that evening. She retained her sharply contrasting make-up. Her auburn hair bounced as ever. I had lengthened her black skirt. It was just above the knee, perhaps two to three inches longer than usual. Her tights were darker and of a heavier denier, slightly less revealing and slightly more severe. Her black cardigan properly covered her shoulders and disguised her figure. I looked at her in the mirror.

"Appropriate." I thought.

Juan Marco was obviously of the same opinion. He looked Melissa up and down as I opened the door.

"Very formal and very suitable." He nodded and smiled. "Shall we go?"

Melissa took his arm as they walked from the hotel. He did not reject her loose grip. They walked through the front doors, the attendant opening the glassed door for us. He raised his forefinger to his cap.

"Good evening, Mr Marco. Shall I get you a car, Sir?"

"No, I'll take mine tonight."

"OK, Sir. Have a nice night."

We walked down the stepped frontage. The fountain before us twinkled in the false lighting of the hotel. The night was beginning to close in. Marco led me to our left.

"Where's your car?" Melissa asked as we turned into the street beside the hotel.

"Just there, across the road."

He took a remote control from his pocket and pointed it. He pushed the button. Melissa Grant watched as the car lights of the red Mercedes 500SL flashed in response to its signal.

"Once, twice," she counted.

Before the car flashed for the third and final time, I responded. I did not know why. My arm tightened on Marco's. I initially pulled. He resisted. His face showed astonishment. I adjusted my efforts and pushed him sharply. I caught him off balance and he fell to the footway. I fell on top of him, Melissa's hair covering his face. I held him to the floor in a protective manner. We were shielded from the Mercedes by the front of another, parked vehicle. I held him there for several seconds. My grip eased slightly as I realised that nothing had happened. He pushed me up slightly by the shoulders. He was still prostrate on the footway.

"Melissa, what are you doing?" He tried to keep a straight face but could not. He laughed as he spoke, spurned on by Melissa's dishevelled state.

"I thought," I did not finish the sentence.

The blinding flash and deep boom of the explosion were inseparable. I threw myself back across him. We did not see the hood of the Mercedes gently rise from the car, as if in slow motion, as the explosive took effect. Despite the weight of the metal used in the car, it continued to rise to the vertical, then fell across the car windscreen. The glass shattered. The driver's seat had already left the car and was circling majestically overhead before falling to the centre of the road with some force. The back folded into the base as it landed. The whole car had lifted several inches from the ground and landed heavily. The tyres had deflated, either by the force of the explosion or by flying metal.

The brightness of the secondary explosion, as the petrol tank ruptured, lit the evening sky. The force tended upwards, spraying burning debris across the whole street. The cars either side were themselves seriously damaged. The burning spirit ran beneath them, threatening further explosions. The Mercedes was, by now, effectively gutted.

Melissa lifted herself from Juan Marco as the main force subsided. Sitting, still, on the footway, she turned her back to him.

"Brush me down," she told him frantically. "Before I catch fire as well."

Juan Marco could see the burning fragments that had landed on me, singeing the wool of Melissa's cardigan. He pulled off his jacket and used that to protect his hands as he swept them from me. He put the jacket around my shoulders and peered around the front of the protective car. He could see the charred wreck of his vehicle. The roadway was strewn with burning debris. The flames were slowly dying down.

Both guests and employees were now running from the hotel. The doorman reached us first.

"Mr Marco, Madam, are you both all right?" He helped us to our feet.

Marco brushed himself down. I checked Melissa's hair. It was still intact. I straightened it with my fingers and her nails.

"Stand up straight," Marco told Melissa. We did as we were told.

He walked around me and tidied Melissa's dress carefully. He took his jacket from my shoulders and brushed the back before putting it on.

"Are you all right to carry on?" Melissa nodded her agreement. I would carry on regardless. I had a job to do, to find my son, Danny.

"You'd better get me that car, now." Marco told the doorman. "And make sure the mess is cleared away after the firemen have finished."

"Yes, Sir."

Marco said little until we were secure in the back of one of the limousines. Alby was now driving. He had been released for the evening. He had not left the hotel. His recall to duty was of his own volition.

"How did you know?" Juan Marco asked Melissa.

"When I came back this afternoon there was a mechanic working on the car. The taxi dropped me off close to it." I explained in response to his look.

"I thought it was unusual for a Mercedes to be worked on in the street, or even to break down at all. When you unlocked the car, it was obvious that you knew nothing about the mechanic, or you would have said something. There was something else as well", I thought for a moment, searching my memory. "Mechanics don't wear shiny black shoes and this one did."

"Clever girl, you saved my life. But had you thought a bit sooner, you might have saved my car as well." Marco sensitively stroked the back of my hand. He had held it throughout the explanation.

"And mine too." Melissa smiled.

Brad Baker turned to Phil Shanks as the explosion lit the sky. Even in their position they heard the disturbance. The radio burst into life with those agents in view.

"What shall we do Brad?" The nearest shouted into his set.

"Nothing, I repeat nothing," Brad was directive. "Keep your positions and observe. We've got a specific job to do. Let's not give it away."

"Shall I call the fire service?" Baker asked Shanks uncertainly.

"You could do, but they might ask questions. They might drag us into it. Plenty of calls will have gone into them already. Leave the locals to sort it out. It's important that we stay with them, to find out where they're going."

They did so. Both Marco and I were unaware of their company as we travelled in the black Mercedes.

Paulo Ramiro considered Miami merely a transit point in his extensive business empire. It allowed him access to the large and vulnerable market of North America along with suitable European connections. He did not like the city and had no need to. On each visit he longed for his return to Bogota. As he aged, the longing became greater.

Ramiro could stand Americans. He could stand Italian Americans. He liked South Americans. He had, however, little time for Cuban Americans, of which there were an abundance in Miami. He found them unimaginative and dull. He generally found Miami much the same.

Paulo Ramiro had not bought a house in Miami. That signified some sort of permanence. He had settled for an apartment, in a condominium towards Coconut Grove, overlooking the Atlantic Ocean. He had chosen the top of the building. His apartment varied somewhat from others in the condominium in that it occupied the whole top floor. He had chosen it that way. He preferred the privacy and security.

Ramiro patiently awaited the arrival of his right-hand in Miami. He was apprehensive. He was keen to hear the news that had been promised. He reminded himself that an English rose never came without an accompanying thorn, that caution was the key word. The telephone rang. He walked positively to it and paused for a second before picking up the receiver.

The Mercedes swept into the underground garage of the apartment block. Little had been said during the journey, perhaps through the delayed shock of events. Alby had driven smoothly. Once in the back of the car I had removed Melissa's woollen jumper and made attempts to rejuvenate the fabric. I was uncertain as to my success. Juan Marco left his jacket untouched. It would be discarded and replaced at the end of this evening. Having completed my task to the best of my ability I settled into the comfort of the vehicle. I opened Melissa's handbag and took from it her cigarettes. I offered one to Marco. He shook his head. I flipped the Zippo lighter and drew heavily against the flame.

Alby ensured the garage was secure before opening the car door for us. Paulo Ramiro's security staff travelled with him. They were known to Alby. He aspired to reach their position one day. He treated them with deference. He nodded slowly to the guard at the elevator entrance. The man's head barely moved in reply. He was, and would remain, alert. Alby remained with the car. He knew his position in the hierarchy.

The elevator climbed smoothly through the floors. I could barely feel the movement until it slowed rapidly as we approached our destination. The doors opened. The second security man, at the door to the apartment, was similarly alert, his right hand seated comfortably within his overcut jacket. He had been warned of our impending arrival through the short-wave radio which nestled in his jacket pocket and which was connected to his ear through an unobtrusive earpiece. He nodded us past.

Juan Marco knocked on the door of the apartment. He did not wait for an answer but pushed open the double doors. His direct entry had been authorised by the security guard. No further delay was necessary.

The overwhelming feeling of size and opulence within the apartment initially stunned me. A sea of beige carpet faced me. I was aware of the quality of the material. To the centre of the main room, the carpet was boldly patterned, a symmetrical shape in bright colour. It was positioned perfectly, perhaps made for the room.

I saw Paulo Ramiro as he replaced the telephone receiver. He initially had his back to us as he looked through the windows towards the ocean. He turned and walked towards us.

"Juan Marco."

A small smile creased his ageing face. I could see the older face of Carlo Ramiro.

He took Marco's hand. They embraced as father to son. Ramiro turned to me.

"And you must be Miss Grant." It was not a question.

He held out his hand to me. I took his hand in mine. His grip was firm, his brown eyes piecing. I retained eye contact until it was politic to look away.

"Come in and sit down," he told us. "I understand that your journey was explosive." His face showed no humour. His statement needed no answer. It was clear that he knew of the events that had occurred.

Ramiro directed us to three chairs surrounding a coffee table and overlooking the sea. The chairs were upright and leathered. I found little comfort as I took my seat. The enforced, upright position, however, preserved the formality of the occasion.

"I was not impressed," I heard Juan Marco saying as I unobtrusively wriggled my backside into the firm leather.

"We have had some difficulties with Riccione of late, Paulo. I thought they were settled, but obviously not."

"Then we shall have to settle them, Juan, but enough talk of this. We are here at the request of Miss Grant, is that not so?"

Ramiro raised his right hand to shoulder height and clicked his thumb and forefinger. A prompt response was received from a guard, doubling as a butler. He arrived carrying a tray of drinks.

"Scotch and water, over ice. Is that right Miss Grant?"

I nodded for Melissa. I was aware that Ramiro was establishing his authority with his show of knowledge. He took a cigarette packet from the tray.

"And I understand you smoke, Miss Grant. Am I correct?"

Again, Melissa nodded as I took the offered cigarette. At least it was not our favourite brand. I picked up her handbag from the floor to search for the lighter. Before I could open it, a flame danced into life before my eyes. I lit Melissa's cigarette. If Ramiro had intended to worry me, he had succeeded. He knew too much about Melissa Grant, but did he know about Danny?

Both Paulo Ramiro and Juan Marco took their glasses from the tray. Marco's, I recognised from the cola, drowning the spirit. I was unsure of Ramiro's beverage.

"So tell us about Mr Knight, Miss Grant?"

Ramiro was direct in imposing his lead. I started hesitantly. "I'm not sure where to begin." I faltered.

"Let me assist you. Tell us why you were at the warehouse at the time it was raided, Miss Grant, and let me caution you, I can cope with the truth, but I cannot stand deceit."

"I was there at Carlo's invitation. We met at his party. He wanted to see me again. He invited me to the warehouse. He sent a car for me."

"And what were your motives, Miss Grant. Why did you want to see the warehouse? Was it Carlo you wanted, or perhaps our imported goods?"

"A little of each." Melissa had regained any composure that I had lost. I reminded myself of my raison d'être. Melissa looked Ramiro straight in the eye.

"You will be aware Mr Ramiro, if you have done your homework, and I'm sure that you have, that I do have an interest in cocaine. It excites me, and I don't deny it. I also had an interest in your son. He excited me as well. I possibly had a dual motive for visiting the warehouse, but both were lost by the turn of events."

My direct approach took Ramiro off-guard. I identified an advantage and determined to keep it. I wanted to rush up to Ramiro, grab him by the lapels and shake him.

"Where is my son, you Bastard?" I would have shouted at him.

I knew I could not do that. Until I could establish his involvement in Danny's taking, I could not reveal the truth of my visit.

"Mr Ramiro, I liked your son. He invited me to the warehouse on the day of the raid. I was with him when Knight arrived. Carlo paid him off just minutes before the raid began. Knight would have been there during the raid, but mysteriously disappeared without trace. Strange that could happen, eh?" I took a long draw on Melissa's cigarette as I allowed time to emphasise the point.

"And so, Miss Grant, why should we believe that Knight set Carlo up? He has been in our employ for some time. He was always a useful source of information, for which I must say we paid. Why should I believe what you are saying?"

"Two questions you must ask yourself, Mr Ramiro. Firstly, how were the police able to raid your warehouse without Knight warning you? And secondly, how did Knight manage to escape when nobody else did?"

Ramiro was silent.

"Let me assist with the answers. On this occasion Knight did not warn you of the raid. That was because he was in charge of it, the senior police officer involved. You wonder how I know this Mr Ramiro, because after he left the office, I watched both him and the raid through the office window. I watched him approach the officers, shake hands on a job well done and walk back through the door with them."

Ramiro glanced towards Marco. "Knight has stated to both me and Bartlett, the lawyer in England, that he was not at the warehouse that night. Either he's lying or."

"Or I am," Melissa Grant took up the challenge. "How would I know about Knight if I had not have seen him at the warehouse? He was not at your son's birthday party, or, at least, I don't remember him there."

Ramiro again looked at Marco, who slowly shook his head.

I went on. "Carlo would not have told me of his informant, not after such a short relationship. There is no other explanation."

"And why would you tell us, Miss Grant."

"Revenge, Mr Ramiro. I want revenge, just like you. That's why I'm telling you." Melissa looked sincere as I spoke.

"And why should I believe you?"

"Just check the records Mr Ramiro. You surely can do that. Carlo left us alone in the office at the warehouse while he went to check his consignment. Knight wanted to have his way with me. I had to fight him off, Mr Ramiro, but before I could do so he had forced cocaine into my mouth and tried to force himself into my body. I OD'd on the drug. When the police found me, they initially thought I was just Carlo's tart, hysterical at his loss. It was only later that they realised the truth. I could have died with Carlo, and Jack Knight wouldn't have given a toss, just as he did not give a toss about Carlo."

Paulo Ramiro's facial expression remained static. He did not smile; he did not grimace. He simply looked at Melissa as she told her tale. If he had taken Danny, seized his grandson, then he would know Melissa had avoided the truth. If so, he did not reveal it. Again she had gained nothing. She steeled herself for a long trawl.

"And, if having verified your story, Miss Grant, what do you want us to do for you?"

"I merely want the same as you, Mr Ramiro. I want Jack Knight rubbed out, erased, eliminated from the face of the earth". Melissa Grant was convincingly passionate. She expressed my true desire for Knight.

Paulo Ramiro was silenced, and rarely so. His desire for revenge was intense, although his feelings were professionally hidden.

"And now, Miss Grant, I thank you for your candour. But let me warn you, we have a way of dealing with those who are not totally honest with us. It is a way that would not give you pleasure, Miss Grant."

Paulo Ramiro stood up from his chair and walked slowly towards me. His face was stern. He continued.

"First we cut the throat, from here to here." He leaned towards me and with his right hand traced the line across my own throat. The shiver down my spine was so emphatic that I was sure he must have felt it. "Then we reach in and pull the tongue through. It hangs down like a tie, a Colombian tie."

He paused. I wanted to throw-up. Even Melissa was intimidated. "Such people do not lie twice, Miss Grant. Do you understand?"

Paulo Ramiro returned to his seat. He had made his point. I nodded inanely. Melissa did not steer me in a different direction.

"You will speak further of this to Juan Marco, you will share further detail with him. I now have to speak to him about other matters, matters that do not concern you. Perhaps you wish to refresh yourself after your eventful day."

I recognised the rebuff and slowly began to rise from my seat. It was time for me to get out of there. I had said enough. My bottle was about to go. Melissa's was no more intact. I stood straight. As I did so my chair was swept back, Ramiro's assistant vacating my position.

"Another second and I would have been on the floor." I thought.

I followed my attendant to the far side of the apartment. I spotted Ramiro and Marco reflected in a large mirror, adorning the wall that I was approaching. They were huddled together in deep conversation. The door to the bathroom was opened for me. I walked through without a backward glance.

I released an indecipherable sigh of relief as I entered the sanctity of the room. I retained my guard, however, revealing nothing to prying eyes. I scanned the room quickly. Another room, another mirror. I approached this one directly and peered into it, apparently studying Melissa's reflection in a confident and assured manner. I carefully adjusted Melissa's hair, shaking it free in attempt to remove the insidious particles of Mercedes-Benz. I picked further pieces from her singed jumper, finally combing the strands of wool clean. I tested her nails for damage. I found one broken. I cursed gently as I took a file from her purse. I looked around for somewhere to sit. There was only one place. I perched on the toilet seat as I tidied Melissa Grant's damaged talon. I crossed my legs. Melissa's skirt exposed my thigh. I did nothing to prevent it. I did not witness the discussion between Paulo Ramiro and Juan Marco.

"The Riccione's must be given a firm lesson, Juan Marco. I trust that you have something in mind?" Paulo was inquisitive.

"I have, Paulo. Leave it with me if you will. I will not displease you. I hope my response will show a certain finesse. They have damaged my property and I will see to it that I damage theirs."

"You must be absolute, Juan. You must prove your position. Do not under-estimate the opposition, or even those on your own side. Loyalty comes from respect Juan Marco, and that respect must be earned."

"I understand Paulo, have confidence."

Paulo Ramiro sat back in his chair and drew long and hard on his Cuban cigar. He was thinking. Some seconds passed before he spoke again.

"Take the girl with you. Show her how you treat those that cross you, Juan Marco. It will be a salutary lesson for her as well. She will learn our ways rapidly."

The short knock on the toilet door signified that now was an appropriate time for Melissa Grant to return to the company of the two men. Several minutes had passed since my incarceration. I had waited patiently, retaining my composure. I stood and re-adjusted Melissa's clothing. I walked from the room and approached Juan Marco. I stopped slightly behind him, using his body to shield me from Paulo Ramiro. I had been schooled in discretion during my undercover training.

"Miss Grant, it has been interesting." Paulo Ramiro held his hand out to me. As he did so Juan Marco stood to one side. I took Ramiro's hand. I wanted to rip it off his arm.

"It is probable that we will not meet again, so I wish you well."

I was unsure as to whether there was anything menacing in his voice. I hoped not. I followed Juan Marco as we left the apartment.

Paulo Ramiro turned and walked to the window and looked out again over the ocean. He remained so as the man entered the room.

"Well," he asked.

"Nothing, boss, not a sign. She sat on the john and filed her nails. She showed no sign of nerves, in fact, no sign of anything."

"Thank you." Paulo Ramiro showed no emotion. He digested the information for future consideration. It proved nothing.

Chapter Fifteen

Inspector Phil Shanks peered into his third bottle of Budweiser about the time that I pulled the covers over my exhausted body. My day had been long and eventful. I was too tired to consider the consequences. Within minutes I was asleep. I slept deeply.

Shanks, himself was tired. Jet lag had set in. He had not properly rested since his arrival, straight from aircraft to surveillance vehicle. He was pleased when Baker pulled to a stop outside the small bar, on the outskirts of Miami. The American sat on the stool next to him. They both leaned heavily on the bar.

This was a roadside house that Baker had discovered soon after his arrival in Miami. It was on his way home and allowed him to relax, after the tension, or boredom, of the day. The bar was small, but clean, and appeared to have been in position prior to the development of the city. The interior was of dark wood. The walls were similarly lined, enclosing the area within. They were stained with years of use and many layers of varnish. The wood beneath could not be specifically distinguished. The swing-door, with a small, glassed window, camouflaged the interior. The majority passed the small hostelry without a second glance. The few who found it used it regularly as a refuge.

"So what's she up to?" Baker asked the English Detective.

Shanks was aware of the necessity to prevent the integrity of the imaginary operation.

"She was sent in to infiltrate the Ramiro empire. She was given a free hand. She's there to gain intelligence." Shanks did not look up from his beer bottle.

"But what about her last contact. What did she have to report? When was it?"

Shanks paused. On deciding what he should say he looked up:

"We haven't heard from her for some time, Brad." He was sincere. "We were worried about her and you can understand why, can't you?"

Baker nodded slowly. He lifted his own bottle of Budweiser to his lips and drank deeply. The beer was warm but quenched his thirst.

"She's certainly infiltrated the organisation. A meeting with Paulo Ramiro is an honour indeed and she's running around with his right-hand man. Marco has taken charge of the Miami arm and has established himself. She is in important company. Is she up to it?"

The final question concerned Shanks. He knew of my training. I had been involved in several successful enterprises and was ready to progress. The rape by Carlo Ramiro had been a reminder to Shanks of the risks involved. I had been removed from the list of undercover operatives.

"I hope so." He replied to Baker's question. "I do hope so."

The two men emptied their bottles. Baker looked at his watch.

"We had better go. We will have to microwave dinner as it is."

They walked to the door. The beers were paid for. Baker waved to the barman as they left.

Shanks was honoured at the reception given by Baker. On his arrival in Miami, it was apparent that the two would get along. In the first hours Shanks had become involved in the surveillance and had no time to find a hotel. Baker had pre-empted a late-night search.

"You'll stay with us." He had insisted.

Brad Baker lived out of town with his wife, Amy and their two small girls. Whilst they were within easy travelling distance of the city, they were far enough distant to be safe. They lived on the Fort Lauderdale road, in a relatively new, but small housing estate. The houses were single storied, the roads wide. For Shanks this was in stark contrast to his own upbringing on the outskirts of London. There, everything was crowded.

Amy accepted Shanks without question. She too was originally from Boston and wished she was back there. She was a protected girl from the north-east. She did not find herself easily accepted in the extroverted area in which she now resided. Even the cosmopolitan air did not help. The attractions of Disneyland were no substitute for the quiet refinement of her hometown. Amy found Shanks a refreshing novelty, refreshing due to his reserved nature. She instantly liked him.

Amy was light on her feet and welcomed Brad with a faint kiss to the cheek.

"The kids are in bed, but won't sleep until you say goodnight," she told him.

Baker needed no second telling. He loved the two girls. He saw little enough of them as it was. He did not hesitate in walking to their room.

"Busy day, Phil?" Amy asked.

Shanks nodded. She could see his mind was elsewhere. She knew better than to question him further. Brad returned to them.

"They're both asleep. They didn't stay up for me," he sounded disappointed.

"Coffee, Phil?" He asked Shanks.

Again the English Policeman nodded. He followed Baker to the spacious kitchen. As the American filled the kettle with water, Shanks spoke:

"I must ring home tomorrow, to update them with what's happening. I will do it in the morning." He looked at his watch, registering the time difference.

"Is it all right to phone from your office."

It was the American's turn to nod. The kettle boiled. Baker poured the coffee.

It was 12 noon British time, and 7am on a clear day in Miami. Assistant Commissioner Cecil Parkes had worked a full half day already. His lunch was at his desk. On this day he was busy. He had asked his secretary to hold his calls. He was therefore surprised when the telephone rang.

"It's Detective Chief Inspector Shanks phoning from America, Sir," his secretary told him.

"Put him through."

Both Shanks and Baker were up early. Baker knew that Shanks had prioritised the phone call and needed to get that over and done with. The team had been briefed to be in position by eight. It was rare for there to be movement prior to this time. Marco preferred late nights and late mornings.

"How is the operation? Update me!" Cecil Parkes asked when he heard the connection made.

"I'm not sure, Sir. I must say I'm a little concerned." Shanks went on to brief Parkes, fully, as to events to date.

"She's either completely in control and working wonders for us, or she's lost it completely and working for the other side," Parkes summarised after hearing the facts. "What do you think Phil?"

"She is working purely for herself, that's what I think. Her one aim is to get her son back and that's what she is going for. The trouble is, it makes her dangerous. She is not working within the standard rules and she's outside our control. I don't like it one little bit."

"Thank you for updating me, Phil. Stay with it and bring her back in, if you can."

The conversation finished, Shanks did not see Cecil Parkes push back his chair and walk purposely from his desk. Parkes knew that the Commissioner was in his office and would wish to be appraised of events. It would upset him if he were not. It would upset him even more if the Home Secretary asked questions for which he was not prepared. Parkes strode towards his office. The wrath of his secretary, Trudy Simms, would be brushed aside on this particular day.

Juan Marco and Melissa Grant breakfasted together. Marco formulated her itinerary. I followed on accordingly. We sat facing each other, across the table, in the restaurant. Marco perused the menu. I rarely ate breakfast. I would settle for strong coffee.

"Do you mind if I smoke?" I asked Juan Marco politely.

"Not in here," Marco commented. "There are too many people around and you know the rules."

I appreciated that Melissa was now a member of a rare breed, a smoker. Smoking had been banned from public areas in the UK and the US was no different. I closed Melissa's handbag shutting the cigarettes and lighter therein.

Marco looked up from his menu, "You look good Melissa, especially in the morning." I returned his suggestive smile. "But today you look tired. Have you been sleeping OK?"

"Yes, Juan, but the events, of yesterday, have caught up on me."

I knew what he was saying. I had studied my own face, and that of Melissa Grant. I had noticed the tell-tale crows' feet from the corner of each eye. The dark smudges under my eyes signified my lack of sleep. It took the elaborate application of make-up to disguise the signs. I had obviously been somewhat unsuccessful.

I had acted instinctively in setting up Jack Knight. I did not like a bent copper and Knight deserved the consequences of his actions. My priority over-rode any need to protect Knight, if that need existed. I knew it did not. I did not want to declare the true reason for my visit at this early stage. I had found nothing to support my belief that the Ramiros had kidnapped Danny. If I was wrong, I would unnecessarily inform Paulo Ramiro of the existence of his grandchild. The time might come, however, when that declaration might be my only other option. Once my own efforts had expired, the safety of my son, Danny, might force me to enrol Ramiro's help more formally. That time had not yet come.

Juan Marco ate a full cooked breakfast. He was hungry that morning and enjoyed the meal. I sipped my coffee and watched him. He was as methodical in eating as he was in life. He ate cleanly and delicately. Whilst clearing his plate, he retained etiquette. On completion he dabbed his still clean napkin across his lips.

"I needed that, Melissa. Are you all right? You haven't eaten anything at all."

"I rarely eat in the mornings." Melissa told him firmly.

He put the napkin to the side of the empty plate. Within seconds both had been cleared by the ever-attentive waiter.

"You wished to see a part of our business Melissa Grant. That is why you were with Carlo, at the warehouse, that night. You are an inquisitive girl. Today you will see a part of our business. We have an important meeting to attend, and tomorrow, perhaps another meeting. You will see how busy I am and why I also look tired."

"What have you got to do today?" I asked, aware of my increasing involvement.

Marco simply smiled. "You wait and see. We will leave at midday. Do you ever wear anything more practical Melissa, perhaps trousers?"

I thought for a moment. Melissa Grant never wore trousers, although I did. She would have to borrow mine.

"I have jeans with me." Melissa told him, but clearly showed her distaste.

"They will do fine. I am sure you look equally as good in them."

It took Melissa Grant some time to change into my clothing. I was loath to do it, recognising that part of Melissa's identity might suffer. As I pulled the denim over my hips I frowned at my reflection in the mirror. It was not like Melissa to wear such casual clothing. Determined to compensate for this intrusion into her being, I selected a bottle green silk blouse. I left several buttons tantalisingly undone. The colour of the blouse contrasted heavily with her auburn hair. I rolled the sleeves just one turn, to release her forearms. I capped the blouse with a short mohair cardigan, the borders of which ran smoothly into the waistline. I hunted for a large, buckled belt. Melissa would have brought one with her. I did not. I settled for my more subdued version.

The Orange Bowl car park was now a familiar place for Jessie Slyder. Since his last visit his bank account had received an unexpected bonus. He had not contacted his bank manager to complain about the misplaced credit. He had not attempted to trace the cash deposit. He chose not to check his bank statement. That way it was purely an honest mistake.

He had expected the telephone call, although not so soon after the last meeting. He was nervous. He had committed himself to a course of action that could cost his job, or his family, or both. He did not like it. On the positive side, however, he had worked for many years as a dedicated Government man. He had given himself to the benefit of society but received little in return. His family took his wages. There was nothing left for him. Why should he feel corrupt? All those honest, elected officials, were far more corrupt than he could ever be. Despite his excuses, the daily import of cream-cheesed bagels weighed heavily on his stomach this day. He set off early, he did not want to be late for the meeting.

Melissa Grant climbed into the back of the limousine and moved to the offside before sitting. Juan Marco followed her in. Alby, The White Rhino, was driving. The car pulled away smoothly. They travelled slowly away from the hotel. Juan Marco handed me a camera.

"You've dressed me in the wrong clothing if you want pictures." Melissa quipped.

Marco smiled. "Perhaps later. This time Alby will be taking pictures of the two of us."

He handed me a folder containing the previously down-loaded pictures, taken by Alby. I looked at each carefully. I had been trained to be observant but usually missed every clue. However, I immediately recognised the fat and untidy frame of Slyder. It was he who had initially questioned me at the Airport.

"What has this to do with me, Juan?" Melissa's voice showed some apprehension.

"Nothing, nothing at all. You asked for our help, we just need a little help from you in return. You merely have to show your commitment to us. To assist me in this difficult meeting." Marco smiled obtusely.

Baker kicked his car into action as the black limousine pulled away from the hotel. Shanks had listened intently to the radio as the occupants climbed into the vehicle.

"It's definitely her," he told Baker. "Let's get after them."

The team had been waiting for two hours. Their bodies were imprinted onto the car seats. Paper mugs that once contained coffee were scattered on the floor-pans. As the vehicles pulled away, the remnants dripped onto the worn carpets. The Dodge van was, perhaps, the slowest and most uncomfortable. It pulled out last, at the back of the team. It would not be used in the mobile surveillance. It was too easily spotted.

"Which direction are we going?" Shanks asked his host.

"Towards the centre of town. I'm not sure yet, you'll have to wait and see."

Shanks settled back into the seat of the motor-car realising that there was little he could do.

The black Mercedes travelled slowly. Today the traffic into Miami centre was heavier than usual. It did not worry Juan Marco. It was his prerogative to be late. He took the photographs back from Melissa. He placed the album in the inside pocket of his jacket. His suit was clean cut, possibly of Italian design. It was charcoal grey in colour, with a fine pin stripe. The material was silky to the touch. I liked it. It enhanced the man who wore it. My hand brushed his jacket accidentally. He responded by taking my hand in his.

"There is nothing to worry about, Melissa. I expect nothing special from you. This is a friend with whom we are dealing and developing. It perhaps emphasises how thorough we are with those who we do not know."

I took the hint. The point was made for my purpose. I was treading a dangerous path. Now, the full danger of my escapade was being made clear to me. The limousine pulled into the car-park of the Orange Bowl. The Dodge van had arrived before us. It did not stand out amongst the few other parked vehicles.

Brad Baker was proficient at surveillance, if a little rusty. His natural, instinctive, ability had returned with the few days of practice. He had recognised the probable destination quickly and despatched the Dodge van to cover it. Far better that the vehicle was in location prior to the arrival of the target. His second sense had paid off. The van was in position, and in control, as the Mercedes-Benz pulled into the car park. The boom microphone and zoom-lens were both operational.

Those manning the van had been warned in advance with regard to Slyder's vehicle. The second use of the same venue indicated a possible meeting with the same person. This also proved to be the case. The, brown, Ford was easily identifiable. It cruised into the car park just minutes after the arrival of the Dodge. Slyder sat, fat, behind the wheel. He had not changed from his airport uniform, merely stripping off the easily identifiable jacket and tie. The epaulettes on his white shirt easily gave him away. The team in the Dodge were fortunate. He parked not far from them. They did not have to move.

Alby parked the, stretched, vehicle a suitable distance from the brown Ford. He left the car to check the area for his employer. His scan took in the blue Dodge, but it was sufficiently covert to reveal no particular danger. He returned to the driver's seat.

"OK, Boss," he confirmed, to Marco, that his exit was safe.

"Come along Melissa, let's see how he responds to you."

Marco picked up the port-folio of his last meeting and slipped them into the inside pocket of his jacket. He left the vehicle. I followed by the same door, sliding across the seat to facilitate my exit. I walked slightly behind Marco, allowing him to obscure me from view.

Slyder left his car and walked towards us.

"What's she doing here?" He demanded as he neared Marco. His face showed genuine concern.

"She is with me, Mr Slyder. Does that cause you a problem?"

"No, Mr Marco, but she's the English girl, the one that Scotland Yard enquired about."

His drawl became more specific as he began to wail. He chewed as he spoke. It annoyed Juan Marco. It was unnecessary.

"I'm sure that enquiries are often made of me when I arrive in a different country, Mr Slyder, but does that make me a bad person?" Marco responded.

"Of course not, Mr Marco," Slyder was subservient. "But can we trust her?"

"She is with me," Marco waved his hand in conclusion. "Enough has been said Mr Slyder. Now, to business: Let me introduce you to Miss Melissa Grant, although I understand that you have already met, when she passed through customs at the airport."

I nodded Melissa's agreement having learned more, through this short conversation, than I had expected. I had been unaware that quite so much interest had been shown in my arrival. I was concerned to learn that my own police-force had contacted the United States. That could only be Trevellian, I thought. He was the only one who knew that I was travelling.

The two men continued talking. Marco was leading the conversation.

"You still want to help us, Jessie, do you not?"

Slyder wriggled on the hook. "Well, Mr Marco, I'm not sure I can. I have a family, my job."

Marco reached to the inside pocket of his jacket. Slyder stopped his waffling and stepped back, in genuine fear of what was to appear in Marco's hand. I watched carefully. I was equally concerned. Juan Marco simply produced the photographs and handed them to Slyder.

"Do you think you'd still have a job, or even a family, if these were to get into the wrong hands. I don't think so, Jessie. Now are you on our side or against us?"

Slyder shuffled quickly through the photographs, his fat fingers sticking on the shiny surface. His recognised his burly frame in each shot. He saw the last pay-off in his greedy hands. He returned the envelope.

"Of course, I'm on your side," he smiled weakly. "Now what can I do for you, Mr Marco?"

"Good." Marco patted Slyder's shoulder as he smiled. "Now our friend, Melissa, has a problem in Miami and needs our assistance. She has suffered a bereavement whilst out here. A close relative of hers: Your cousin wasn't it, Melissa?"

I returned my lower jaw to a normal position as he turned towards me. He had not seen it drop in surprise as he spoke. I had no idea what Juan Marco was talking about but presumed that I would find out later. I knew that I was as tied as Slyder. Was I in too deep? Probably, as usual, I thought. I looked suitably morose. I nodded. There was no need for a reply.

"Poor Melissa wants to take her cousin back to England." Marco had turned back to Slyder. "We were impressed by the way you handled Carlo Ramiro's return to the United States. We want you to do the same for Melissa's cousin, to smooth the way, to arrange the paperwork and to personally supervise his loading onto the aircraft. We will, of course, have ensured that he is properly prepared. We will spare no expenses on his coffin. We must rely on you for a smooth exit from the US, and, of course, Melissa will similarly arrange his arrival in England."

My heart jumped as he spoke. I instantly realised that I was now being drawn into the Ramiro pocket. I knew that there would be nothing for nothing in this outfit but had not envisaged them moving so quickly. I remained quiet. I resolved that I would never go undercover again. I wasn't good at it.

Marco held out the banknotes clearly before tucking them into Slyder's shirt pocket.

"A little more on account."

Alby's photographs would form a permanent record of the occasion. Suitable to ensure Slyder's continued assistance. Baker's record was equally as permanent and more complete. He also held the recording of the meeting. It would prove invaluable in the future.

Melissa was initially silent as the limousine pulled away from the meeting place. I was thinking. A few minutes passed before Melissa spoke.

"Juan, I'm not sure I can help you. I'm not sure I'm prepared to."

Marco turned to her, taking her hand between his. He gently stroked the back of her hand.

"But you came to us, Melissa. You have asked for our help to assuage your need for revenge. There was no hesitation in your voice yesterday, when you spoke to the father of my good friend, Carlo Ramiro. Surely one good turn deserves another?"

He could feel my hand within his. Melissa held it firm. I would have trembled uncontrollably.

"I offered information in return for that assistance, Juan." Melissa's voice was firm. "You know that Paulo Ramiro wants to avenge his son's death. You need nothing further from me."

Marco's right hand moved swiftly to my jaw. His grip was firm but not painful. He turned my head so that our eyes were in direct contact. I could see his change in look. His face had steeled. His eyes had lost their depth.

"We do, Melissa Grant, and you will do what we ask of you!"

The words were fired through gritted teeth. It terrified me. His face was inches from mine, our eyes in direct contact. I saw the warmth return to them as his lips drew closer to mine. He touched me gently, the sensitivity of our mouths responded to each other. The passing threat relieved removed my resolve. I knew that I should not be doing this. I knew also that I would not, could not stop. My hand reached to the back of his head, pulling him to me. I ran my fingers through his dark hair. I was uncertain as to whether it was Melissa, or me, who had responded to him.

Alby, The White Rhino, was a discreet man. He turned on the radio in the front of the car as he heard our initial encounter. A push of a further button raised the screen between the front and rear of the car. We were given our privacy.

Baker was pleased with the progress of the day. He had managed his team well, with excellent results. He deserved a pat on the back and would give himself one. Shanks seemed less elated.

"We need to listen properly to the tape." He told Baker. "And we need to do it soon. I must hear, first hand, what went on."

"You know what went on." Baker was on a high. "They've set up a deal involving Slyder. We're going to get a good result from this operation. I can feel it."

"But what about our girl?" Shanks was less convinced. "How involved is she?"

"Stop worrying, Phil. We can safeguard her. We'll sort it out."

Baker had not convinced the English Detective. "I need to listen to the recording, Brad. I need to hear the full implications of it. Can you call the van for a meet?"

"OK Phil, but that'll mean we can't cover them properly whilst we're out of it."

He glanced at Shanks and realised his true concern. Both their car, and the Dodge van, pulled away from the limousine before them. Shanks would have been even more concerned had he known what was happening in the back of the Mercedes.

The, Scotland Yard, DCI was even less pleased after hearing the recording of the meeting. He and Baker sat together in the office at the Federal Building. The microphone was sensitive and had worked well. There was little surrounding interference and the voices were clear. On occasion, there was some fade, which made it difficult to pick up exact words. The meaning was clear, however.

"We've got major problems with this one Brad. If our girl is involved in exporting the gear, at this end, you'll lose any case that you put forward. You know how tight your laws are. The defence would simply allege that she was the instigator of the deal, the major purchaser. We'd call her an agent provocateur. Do you use the same term out here?"

"We sure do, and the courts are very strict about it. Any allegation of entrapment could cause us serious problems. What do you suggest, Phil?"

"We've got to be really careful. She must avoid any connection with the drugs at this end. We can take them out before they reach England. But anything too overt could put her in danger." Shanks thought for a moment. "I'll have to see her. I'll have to tell her."

He looked at Baker as he spoke. Both knew the risk of approaching Melissa Grant.

I sat in my room during the late afternoon and evening. Juan Marco had yet more business to transact. I was not invited and did not want to get involved in it. I had to assimilate my feelings, my actions. I had under-estimated the true implications of approaching the Ramiro family. But was it too late?

I wished I was as hard as I had intended my alter-ego to be. It never seemed to work out. My sensitivities showed through. I knew that I should have declined the offer of undercover work, although in my wildest dreams, I had never imagined such consequences. I was on the edge of my bed, leaning forward, my head in my hands. I could feel the slight shake of my fingers, the dampness of my palms. I wanted to sob but could not. I opened my eyes. I still wore my jeans. They were tight and their disturbance in the rear of the Mercedes did not show. My blouse was, however, creased and looked untidy. I thought of the intercourse with Juan Marco. Why had I allowed it to happen? What had it achieved?

"You did it because you wanted to." The broader Liverpudlian dialect of Melissa Grant cut into the silence. "Don't say you didn't enjoy it because you did. Now stop having a touch of the seconds, light me up a cigarette and get me out of these damn jeans."

The flip-top of the Zippo lighter clanged shut in the silence of the room. I knew that I should not smoke in the room, but I needed to. Melissa Grant took a long draw on the JPS Superking. I took the smoke into my lungs and held it there. I felt no buzz, as I had done in her early days of smoking. Perhaps it was time for both of us to give it up.

"I think not," I spoke out loud, responding to Melissa. I tried to take control of my surroundings. I knew that I was lying, and Melissa was right.

I discarded my jeans and the creased green shirt. I padded around my room in bra and pants. I felt more comfortable. I checked the wardrobe to find clothes more in keeping with Melissa's style. I had only changed at the request of Juan Marco.

"Fuck him!" Melissa was outspoken. I remembered his gentle touch as we made love.

I showered, allowing the falling water to rinse away my experience. I had lost the detached attitude required of an undercover officer. I was here on business and must remember that. I was in no hurry to restore my appearance. The evening was mine. I would dress, eat and drink at the bar. Melissa Grant would have no qualms about drinking alone. She had done it many times before. I was Melissa Grant.

Phil Shanks had not easily convinced Brad Baker that to approach me was his best course of action.

"These are dangerous people, Phil. One step out of line and you could put both you and her at risk. Do you want to take that chance?"

The two men and their team were taking time out from surveillance. The success of the day, in observing the meeting, between Marco and Slyder, should have encouraged an early shutdown. Both recognised that there were insufficient facilities for twenty-four-hour cover. They knew that certain activities would be missed. So far, they had been lucky. Baker would normally have dismissed the team for the day. Shanks had asked him not to. They took time out to discuss it. They sat in a bar, a short walk from the

Federal building. They drank their Budweiser's from the bottle.

"I've got to speak to her, Brad. I know it's risky, but I'm sure it'll be riskier not to." He wished he could confide the truth. He could not.

"It's apparent that she's in deep, possibly too deep," he continued. "At the moment she does not even know that I am here. She believes herself to be alone. She has got to know that I'm working for her, on the outside. We need to steer her in the direction that we want her to go."

"So what do you propose?"

"If we have a man who is comfortable in the hotel, we'll work this evening and put him in to the hotel. If he identifies a time that is safe, he can call me in. I'll approach her. She knows me. It might faze her a little, but not as much as a stranger approaching. I'll only need a short time. I'll be out as quickly as I entered."

Baker did not miss the analogy.

"That quick, eh," he smiled. The smile faded as his mind returned to work. "We do have a man that will be comfortable in the hotel. OK Phil, if that's what you want, that's what we'll go for. You'd better be careful though."

The team slotted back into formation with little fuss. They were familiar with their targets and with their deployment. They had said little to each other while waiting a decision from Baker and Shanks. A couple had paperwork to catch up on and sat at their desks achieving some progress. The others drank coffee and caught up on the day's news. Any surveillance operation was tiring, and no matter the success, drained the individual. This was no exception.

On return to the Godolphin Hotel, they re-deployed with minimum disruption to the surroundings. A single officer, within the confines of the hotel, was sufficient to identify the target. The other units did not therefore encroach, but remained at a safe, covert, distance. Shanks would be called in at the appropriate time. The others were there to cover the unexpected, merely as a reactive force should events not go to plan.

Simpson Ojorgi had worked with Brad Baker since his arrival in the Town. Simpson was an older man, coming to the end of his service. His looks belied his age, however. He remained tall, although he felt his height was diminishing with age. He was dark and debonair. He dressed smartly, but casually. He was at home in the comfortable surroundings of a hotel foyer. He preferred it to the front seat of an old Pontiac, littered with empty Burger King boxes.

Simpson had infiltrated the hotel at an early stage. He had recognised his preference and made efforts to achieve it. He was the spotter, the man at the front line who first identified the target. Simpson made himself indispensable in this position. His easy gait and comfortable appearance had gained him access without question. The staff simply accepted him as another guest. He sat within the foyer, reading a newspaper or sipping a coffee. His true raison d'être was never guessed.

Melissa Grant had now regained her confidence and used her purposeful approach to re-establish her position. In some ways I was sick of her. I knew that I had insufficient strength of character to do what she did. I forever re-lived my immediate past experiences, rather than accepting them and moving forward. I had developed Melissa Grant as a different, more forceful, confident, character. The two of us did not always get on.

I had spent some time in the hotel room. I had removed any trace of Melissa's dishevelled state and tidied her appropriately. Although removing the physical evidence of Melissa's activities with Juan Marco, I had not wanted to wipe my memory clean. I had enjoyed his attention, his gentle touch. I had encouraged him, wanted him and therefore caused Melissa to take him.

Juan Marco was a careful, sensitive, man. Whilst the rear of his limousine might not have been the most appropriate place for our first sexual encounter, the propriety of time had led us both forward. His initial, rough approach had been tempered with Melissa's response. Our mutual attraction had existed since our first meeting at the Lanthanum Club in London. It flowered within the restrictive confines of the Mercedes-Benz.

Melissa Grant would not spend the evening confined to a hotel room. That suited neither her personality nor my desire. Juan Marco might not be available to accompany me. That did not matter. I would entertain myself. I stood away from the mirror and straightened Melissa's short skirt. Trousers were not for her. Her make-up was, as usual, bold. It was not outlandish. I slipped my stockinged feet into her shoes. The heels added, perhaps, three inches to my height and made my legs appear longer. I was satisfied with the effect. I walked from the room with confidence and took the lift to the bar. A drink would stimulate and relax me, and Melissa more so.

Simpson Ojorgi was relaxed but alert. He did not react to my arrival in the hotel lobby. He had instantly registered Melissa, although his sight of the lifts was limited to the corner of one eye. He purposely avoided a direct line of sight. It was simply too obvious. To the passer-by Simpson merely looked like another hotel occupant. The newspaper held before him shaded his gaze from others. His lightly tinted glasses similarly disguised his eyes. The microphone in the lapel of his jacket caused him to lean slightly as he spoke quietly into it.

"Brad, standby, the Target's in sight."

"OK, Simpson, keep me updated. Phil will be ready for you."

Some minutes passed before Simpson Ojorgi spoke again.

"She's in the bar, alone. She's just ordered a drink. She's all alone, sitting at the bar on a stool. Now, looks good, Brad."

"We'll give it a few more minutes to make sure, then Phil will come in. Keep your eyes open Simpson."

Baker turned to Shanks. "Get yourself ready Phil. It's almost time to go."

Shanks wore a white, herringbone, jacket that he had purchased in London prior to the trip. He thought it suitable for the, expected, sunshine. He would wear it rarely, in London, and never to work. His bright, crimson, tie was equally as loud. Only his sombre grey trousers dulled the picture.

"Pick up a cab Phil and hold it for a while until I give you the OK. Then take it up to the front door and walk right in."

As Shanks climbed from the passenger door, Baker waved his hand in a semi-salute. It was either a mark of respect, or Baker was saying goodbye, Shanks thought.

A few minutes passed before Ojorgi gave the go ahead. The cab-driver would have been happy to wait forever. The meter had been ticking from the start.

"The Godolphin!" Shanks started hesitantly.

Then with more confidence and in a rapidly developing, if unconvincing, South American drawl.

"The Godolphin Hotel please, Driver."

The journey took minutes. Baker was sufficiently distant to remain covert, yet near enough to remain in control. Shanks had barely relaxed in the back seat when the yellow cab pulled up at the hotel. Shanks paid the driver before leaving the vehicle. He walked boldly up the entrance steps. The Doorman nodded as he approached.

"Evening Sir, I hope you have a good one."

Shanks said nothing in reply but smiled as he passed. He had walked into dangerous situation in the past, but somehow, he had never been so nervous. The planning was usually his. This was not the case today.

The English Detective was aware of the interior of the hotel. In the debriefings Simpson Ojorgi had adequately described it. He had under emphasised the opulence, however. Shanks was suitably impressed as he strode towards the bar. His confidence was increasing with every step. He did not seen Simpson, nor did he hear his simple words,

"He's in."

Shanks was single minded in his task. He was observant and spotted Melissa Grant immediately. I was seated on a barstool at the bar. I had a drink before me and sipped stoically. I looked across the bar. My gaze did not waver. I had not expected him nor seen him approach.

"Bourbon on the rocks!"

The barman picked up the ten-dollar bill after serving the drink. He thought the man's accent strange, possibly because he had already been drinking. He was boisterous, his dress sense terrible. The barman put his change on the bar. He did not speak to him. The customer picked up his glass and sidled along the bar. The barman could see me, just feet away. He knew me to be a friend of the Boss. He watched as the man approached me. He walked to the end of the bar and pushed an unseen button.

"Can I buy you a drink?" The broad South American was not pretty to my ears. I did not look round.

"Piss off!" I commented through clenched teeth. I was in no mood to talk. I did not look at Shanks, nor recognise his voice. In hindsight, I should have done. Nobody could naturally have had such an appalling American accent.

"Do you always talk to your Boss that way?" The man's voice had altered. The familiar London accent jolted my memory. I looked at him in surprise.

"Phil, Phil Shanks, it's so good to see you." I leaned towards him.

"Careful, Girl. Be careful."

I held back realising my current position. I glanced around hoping nobody had noticed. I regained my posture and again looked straight across the bar.

"Now listen, I haven't got long. I'm here with you. We've got a team behind you and know what's going down. We know about the meeting with Jessie Slyder. You must be careful not to get too involved. Don't go near any drugs, not with Slyder anyway. Do you understand?"

I nodded but continued the facade.

"Why don't you piss off!" I said loudly enough for others to hear.

"Any trace of Danny?"

"No, not yet, but I'm still looking," I hissed through my lips as if continuing the rebuke.

The barman kept a close eye on the couple. I had initially reacted as if surprised. He could understand it. I had not expected the approach. I had been keeping myself to myself. The man was intruding.

Alby, The White Rhino, responded promptly to the warning button. The barman was pleased to see him.

"The guy could cause problems Alby. I think he's drunk and coming on to the lady."

"Time he left," Alby grunted as he walked along the bar.

He took Shanks's arm without hesitation.

"Are you all right, Miss?" He asked me.

"I'm OK, Alby. This pain in the butt's just leaving."

"Indeed I am," Shanks allowed the drawl to return. He had looked at the bull-neck of the man and felt his steely grasp. "I'm sorry if I troubled you, Ma'am." He feigned slight intoxication. "I'm going now."

Phil Shanks walked from the bar; his task achieved. He knew that the large aggressor was merely a few steps behind. He would not confront the man. There was no point. He just wanted to leave the hotel.

"He's out." Simpson Ojorgi spoke into his lapel as the door closed behind Shanks. Ojorgi stood slowly and placed his newspaper on the seat. He followed Shanks down the steps to the street.

"Who was he?" Alby asked me as Shanks walked away from us.

"Just some uninvited drunk. Thanks for getting rid of him."

Melissa Grant had answered enough questions. I resumed my line of sight across the bar, effectively dismissing the minder. Alby followed Shanks slowly from the hotel. He thought little more of the incident.

The visit of Phil Shanks lightened my spirits. At least now I had support on the outside. That support brought its own difficulties, however. I had not had long enough to speak to Shanks. It was apparent that he was aware of Jessie Slyder but was he aware of my involvement. He had warned me off. But would my lack of involvement satisfy Juan Marco? I thought not.

Chapter Sixteen

Fergus Johnstone told Duncan Trevellian who occupied the Finchley Road address, that Jack Knight had visited. Trevellian was surprised.

"Rupert Veneer, no less, the Honourable Under-Secretary of the Home Office."

"So what's Knight got on him?" Trevellian mused.

"Whatever it is, it gave Knight the power to poke a politician in the chest. Not many of us would want to chance that, would we?"

Trevellian smiled, remembering the fate of a colleague who had done just that at a House of Commons function.

"Trouble was," he told Johnstone, "The Member of Parliament was one rather large lady minister with a penchant for her own sex. Harry, the Horse, was a bottom pincher who pinched the wrong bottom on that particular day. It cost him his job, forced to resign. Hung on to his pension though, I think."

"Why did they call him Harry the Horse, Duncan?"

"I don't know, Fergus, I just don't know", Trevellian smiled as he spoke.

"Anyway, back to the task in hand. Best we go and have a word with Veneer, don't you think? It might be interesting."

Duncan Trevellian had much difficulty in arranging an appointment with Rupert Veneer. His secretary at the House of Commons was difficult to contact. Fergus Johnstone finally gave up on the telephone and resorted to the written word. It was his letter, written on behalf of, and signed by Trevellian, that finally gained some response.

"Mr Veneer would not wish you to come to the House of Commons," his secretary finally telephoned. "He would be grateful if you could attend his home address."

So it was that Duncan Trevellian and Fergus Johnstone again tested the traffic of North London before finally pressing the doorbell of Veneer's fine Victorian residence. Rupert Veneer answered the door himself.

"Inspector Trevellian, do come in." He offered his hand to the policeman.

"Detective Sergeant Fergus Johnstone!" Trevellian introduced his colleague.

"Do come into the drawing room."

The two policemen followed Veneer through the wooden doorway. The room was lined with books and centrally decorated with a fine wooden desk. It was, as he looked beyond the desk, that Trevellian received a jolt as to his expectancy of co-operation.

"Detective Inspector Trevellian, good to meet you again." Herbie Bartlett enforced his advantage.

"Ah yes, Inspector, might I introduce my solicitor, Mr Bartlett of Bartlett & Co. I think that you have already met. Is that right?"

Trevellian nodded but did not approach Bartlett further. The Lawyer had known better than to offer his hand in greeting. It would be rejected. The pause stilted the atmosphere as the Detective Inspector re-assessed briefly.

"Bugger it, let's worry him anyway," he thought. Fergus Johnstone knew better than to speak. His silence was absolute.

"Well Inspector," Herbie Bartlett broke the silence. "Mr Veneer would wish to know why you want to interview him."

"Shall we sit down, Gentlemen," Veneer offered.

The two policemen sat in upright chairs close to each other. Bartlett remained with the desk between them, taking the desk-chair after they were seated. Veneer remained standing for a moment.

"Can I get anyone a drink?" He ventured.

His offer declined, he, too, sat down.

The interlude had given Trevellian the opportunity to gather his thoughts. The presence of Herbie Bartlett had added a sinister aspect to the enquiry. It was another link in the chain incriminating Veneer. The Detective Inspector had just two options, walk out or stay and test the water. If he walked out, he would gain nothing. He chose the latter.

"I understand that you know a police officer, Detective Superintendent Jack Knight. I'd like to know of your relationship with him."

"I've advised my client to answer none of your questions, Inspector." Bartlett interjected.

"Might I ask why, Mr Bartlett. Does your client have something to hide?"

Bartlett gave a wry smile in reply.

"Mr Veneer, we were involved in the raid of the warehouse in Rotherhithe about eighteen months ago. Perhaps you read about it in the newspapers, or" Trevellian deliberately left the sentence unfinished.

Rupert Veneer glanced nervously towards his solicitor.

"I think Mr Veneer is aware." Bartlett was leaving nothing to chance.

"A girl was raped just before the raid, Mr Veneer. We believe that Jack Knight knew something about it. What about you, Mr Veneer, do you know anything about it?"

Trevellian's voice hardened in the final words. His stared at Veneer, his piercing eyes appearing to squint slightly. Fergus Johnstone sat forward in his chair towards the politician, adding to the pressure. They had played these parts many times before, with varying success.

Duncan Trevellian saw the beads of sweat appear on the upper lip of Veneer. As he moved his eyes from Trevellian his glasses slipped slightly from his nose. He pushed them back with a shaking hand. He remembered the Home Secretary's words,

"First give-away of a poor politician!"

"I'm afraid Mr Veneer seems unable to help you, Inspector." Herbert Bartlett had noticed the signs and knew that Trevellian had too.

The Detective Inspector threw in his final play. "Mr Veneer, we believe that Jack Knight was involved, with somebody else, in the rape of this young lady. If you're withholding information you will be guilty as an accessory after the fact. Think of it, Mr Veneer, possible imprisonment, but certainly no more career."

"Inspector, I think you've said enough. Let me see the two of you out." Bartlett led the two policemen to the door. Rupert Veneer did not move. He was firmly implanted in his seat.

"Don't think you went a bit too far, Duncan?" Fergus Johnstone ventured as they walked to the car.

"I hope not, Fergus. I think maybe he knows more than we realised."

Rupert Veneer wiped the beads of sweat from his forehead as the officers walked away from his home. He had enjoyed the evening with Jack Knight but regretted the consequences of it. The Commissioner's cocktail party had been a stolid affair. Once the woman Superintendent, with the lithe and slender body, had left Veneer had little else to hold his interest. Jack Knight easily drew his attention as he told his tales of the Metropolitan Police. All were much exaggerated, but all held Veneer's waning interest.

"Do you want to get away and have a proper pint somewhere?" Knight asked the Under-Secretary before an hour had passed.

"I don't think I can, Jack, much as I'd like to. I'm tied in with the Home Secretary and it doesn't look like he's ready to get away yet."

"Leave it with me, my Friend," Knight was at his friendliest as he walked to the Commissioner's group.

"Commissioner, I am sorry to disturb you!" He turned to Michael Farrar. "Just to let you know, Sir, that I am taking Mr Veneer on a guided tour of the Yard. I understand that this is his first visit and he hasn't had the opportunity to look around."

"That's very good of you, Superintendent," the Home Secretary responded. "Let him know that I won't be staying much longer. I will probably have gone by the time you get back."

Knight nodded as he returned to Veneer.

"Easy Rupert, now grab your coat and let's move on, shall we?"

The two men were a strange mix. Jack Knight was, perhaps, fifteen years older than Veneer, but that age difference was barely noticed. The ageing Superintendent had more panache than the bug-eyed politician. His knowledge of central London gained him access to establishments that Rupert Veneer did not know existed. Veneer followed his lead and gratefully received the free drinks as they were delivered. Knight drank double scotch to each of Veneer's lagers. Regardless, Rupert Veneer believed that he was the first to feel the effects of the drink.

"Not another, Jack," he pleaded as they stood at the bar of the third club.

The discotheque drowned his voice. He took the pint glass when it was delivered. He had obviously not been heard. He placed it on the bar in front of him and peered into the depths of the frothy, amber, liquid. The club was full, and Veneer was sure that he could see the dancers reflected through his drink. He looked more closely.

Etta Van-de-Hooran was a, monied, South-African. She displayed her elegance and breeding overtly. Her voice sung in her clipped South

African accent. It offended or delighted those she met. Any offence was quickly overcome by the charm of her personality, by the attention she paid to her prey. Etta was not a lady for the ladies. Men's company she enjoyed, and they enjoyed her extrovert, though sometimes intense, character.

Etta Van-de-Hooran was not startlingly pretty. Her angular features belied her true good looks. Her bearing was upright and trained. She moved gracefully and with confidence. Her coat was despatched as she stopped fleetingly at the cloakroom. She did not wait for a ticket. She would expect the attendant to remember. Her long, black evening dress was cut high at the front, but dipped at the back to show the tantalising curvature of her spine. It enhanced the slender lines of her body. Its, slight, over-length even covering her feet to accentuate the gliding motion of her movement. She swept to the bar.

"A gin and tonic in a large glass." She turned to the man beside her. "And what are you doing here, My Lovely?"

Rupert Veneer was enjoying his night out with Jack Knight. He had drunk plenty but paid for nothing. He was now being addressed by a beautiful woman. Etta leaned slightly towards him. She picked up her drink, not turning away from Veneer.

Stevie Thomas had not been surprised to hear from Jack Knight again. He had worked regularly for him in the past. Thomas had been employed by the Metropolitan Police for five years. Prior to this he had been a self-employed electrician. The recession had hit him hard. The job had been advertised in a daily newspaper. He had read it in his van, as he sat in a too familiar traffic jam. The pay was not good, but it would be regular. A bit more security would do him no harm.

Thomas proved his worth rapidly. He was a young man who was not afraid of work. He was introverted, enjoying his own company, especially when at work. He was able to keep confidences. His first foray into the field of undercover operations came after about a year. His department was suffering a bout of heavy sickness from a rampant flu epidemic. Stevie was one of the few not affected.

"I've got an urgent job for you," his Boss had said. "But you've got to keep your mouth shut. This one is confidential, OK." Stevie had nodded as he received the instructions.

Thomas was a personable young man who was instantly liked. He found that trust, once earned, in undercover work, rapidly became absolute. The officers working in such roles tended towards insecurity and therefore relied heavily upon those they trusted. Once this relationship was established, it remained, the officers demanding the support from their particular allies. Jack Knight had controlled such operations.

Thomas had met Knight at the hotel.

"This one is absolutely secret," he was told when they met. "Any word of it, even afterwards, could put me in real danger, and I mean real danger." He emphasised his words.

Thomas said little. He rarely said much, until his expertise and advice were required. Even then he kept it to a bare minimum. Most of his clients did not need to know, nor understand, the technical equipment. They just needed it to work to their specifications. Knight told him what he needed.

"That's not a problem, but I'll need the room a couple of days in advance. Let me know when you're ready".

Thomas had been given short notice. He had received the final telephone call the previous evening. It was not difficult to re-arrange his workload. The Metropolitan Police was a flexible employer. In his role the flexibility was of his own making. His drill bit into the wall as he secured the small camera. He expected no disturbance unless a resident complained. Knight had acquired the requisite permission from the hotel management to install his equipment. He had not asked how; it did not matter to him.

The camera would be activated by a simple switched mechanism attached to the door. It would be operative whilst the room was occupied. It had a silence override, whereby it would shut down if nothing was heard for two minutes, resurrecting itself when sounds recommenced. It was carefully installed in the top cupboard of the fitted wardrobes, hidden from view. It focused through a small hole in the door. Thomas had drilled this close to a junction of decorative trims. He closed the doors and studied it closely from a distance of a few feet. It was barely noticeable. He nodded in satisfaction.

The recording equipment was compact. Its separation from the camera allowed the eye to be smaller and easier to conceal. The signal was transmitted to the computerised recorder by a miniaturised device that was easy to conceal.

The installation had taken less time than Stevie Thomas had expected. He double checked his work before leaving the room. He handed back the key to the room as he left the hotel. As he reached the street he stopped. He took a cigarette from his packet of Benson & Hedges. He cupped his hands as he lit it, to protect it from the faint breeze. He drew on the cigarette as he walked back to his van.

Rupert Veneer interested Etta Van-de-Hooran. Why, he did not know. It did not particularly bother him. He had taken several glasses of beer. He was relaxed and rested. He enjoyed her company. He saw her as an insecure socialite, hiding behind a facade of bravado. Why else was she so overt, so direct.

"Let me buy you this one. We've had two of yours already. I must stand a least one round, you know."

Etta took a twenty-pound note from her small bag and handed it to the barman as another two drinks appeared before them. Rupert Veneer had not intended to stay so long, or drink so much when he left the Commissioner's party. Her company was, however, appealing. He had little reason to leave. He looked for Jack Knight. He could not see him. He had obviously slipped out while Veneer was distracted.

Etta Van-de-Hooran touched the ends of her short, dark brown, hair as she talked. It was a tailored cut, short into the neck and parted, in boyish style, on the left. It was gelled and set. Her eyes were obscured by heavily tinted, gold-framed spectacles. Her makeup paled her skin, at contrast with the tanned look expected of South Africans.

"So what do you do?" The woman asked him, sipping her drink at the end of her question.

"I'm in politics." Veneer told her. It was obvious that she had not recognised him. "I work behind the scenes, one of the back-room boys."

"And are you successful? I like successful men." Etta allowed her voice to tail off.

"I like to think so. Yes, I am, but what about you?"

"I'm fortunate that I don't have to work anymore. I was married, a lovely man, a little older than me. I was distraught when he died. I was left all alone. He was so lovely." She did not sound convincing.

"He left me everything, a house, money, a car, everything. Wasn't that so sweet of him? I did love him." She smiled broadly as she recounted the tail.

"So, what do you do with yourself?"

"I enjoy myself, Rupert Veneer, and tonight I am enjoying myself with you." She leant slowly forward and gently kissed his lips. As she drew back, she knew that the idea had been firmly implanted into his mind. He would not be going home early.

"Let's have another drink."

Veneer rummaged in his pocket for his money, allowing himself vital seconds to disperse the rising temperature he felt in his face. He had never been picked up in a bar. It was pleasant, if somewhat disturbing. He could feel the adrenaline rising within him, or was it testosterone? Either way, it was enjoyable.

His stomach had been filled with beer some time ago. He was now onto shorts. The scotch barely touched the sides. He ordered another.

"Double this time," he instructed the barman.

"Why haven't I seen you here before?" He asked Etta.

"It's because I haven't been here before." She laughed and paused before continuing. "But that's my loss. I presume that you are a regular."

"A couple of times a week." He lied. "It suits my needs. I enjoy it here."

"And so you should. You work hard, you need to relax."

As she spoke, Etta's hand reached to Rupert's tie and loosened it around his neck. She reached to the top button of his shirt and flipped it open.

"There, that's better. You looked so formal. You look better already. Stay here, I'm just popping off to powder my nose."

Knight watched as the elegant woman swayed her way, across the dance floor, to the toilet. He continued to watch as the door swung shut behind her.

"Do you want another drink", Veneer asked on her return. "I've just got myself one."

Etta looked at his replenished glass on the bar.

"No thanks, Rupert. I think I've had enough."

She moved closer to him, leaning gently on his shoulder and speaking quietly into his ear, allowing her breath to tickle his eardrum.

"Isn't it time we moved on from here? Think what fun we could have elsewhere, somewhere more private, perhaps."

Rupert Veneer grunted in agreement. The words stuck in his throat with anticipation. His glasses had slipped down his bulbous nose. He pushed them back. He felt the temperature rise again. He knew he was out for the night. He threw a five-pound note on the bar as they left. It was unusual for him to tip. He was feeling generous tonight. He followed Etta like a small dog. She led him by the hand to the door. Her coat was handed to her as she reached the cloakroom. Etta was not somebody to be forgotten easily.

A London taxi arrived as if by premonition. Veneer did not query the venue. He did not need to know. They sat side by side in the rear of the taxi-cab. Etta slipped her arm through his and moved close to him.

"I'm cold," she whispered quietly. He put his arm around her shoulders drawing her closer to him.

Etta's hand moved to the front of his jacket, resting above the pocket as she turned to him.

"It's only a short journey, then we'll make the evening ours, My Lovely," she crooned.

Her hand played nervously with the top pocket of his jacket. She reached inside in a playful manner.

"What's in here then?" she joked, as she pretended to pull the small polythene packet from his pocket. She cupped it in her hand to shield it from the driver's view, as the politician noticed the white powder inside.

"Shall we try this later?" She whispered to Veneer as she tucked it into his pocket.

"We might just do that." He tried to disguise his drunkenness.

Rupert Veneer was relaxed and restful. He had enjoyed the evening, so far, and intended to make the best of the rest of it. He was aware that he now had cocaine in his top jacket pocket. He was too drunk to care. The girl had palmed it efficiently, before producing it from his pocket. He was pleased with her response to him. If that response needed cocaine, so be it. He would share the occasion. It would enliven the rest of their night together.

Their arrival at the hotel went largely unnoticed. The Night Porter sat, barely sighted, reading his newspaper. He was not an over-enthusiastic worker and preferred the guests to approach him. Etta led Rupert Veneer, by the hand, through the foyer to the lifts. She took the key to the room from her handbag. She had retained it purposely.

Etta slowly unlocked and opened the door to the room. She obstructed Rupert Veneer's view and thus his hearing, to prevent him hearing any sound as the camera activated. She pushed the door open and walked to the bed. Etta switched on the bedside light to retain the ambience. This was a room she knew well. She had no difficulty finding the switch in the dark.

"Come in, Rupert, and make yourself comfortable." Her accent emphasised each syllable of the final word.

Veneer walked into her lair, with the drink induced confidence that also blinded him to her motives.

Etta threw her coat onto the bed.

"Another drink Rupert?"

He looked towards the display of bottles on the dark-wooded chest of drawers by the window. Etta drew the heavy, patterned, curtains as she approached, blocking out the London lights. She did not wait for Veneer to answer before picking up the scotch bottle. She poured him a liberal helping in a large glass. She kept her back to him as she allowed the diazepam powder to trickle into the glass from the unfolded wrap of paper in her palm. She picked up the glass and swirled the liquid around to help conceal the drug. Before giving the glass to Veneer, she poured a gin and tonic for herself, minimising the gin. As she turned towards him, a glass in either hand, the scotch was again disturbed. She could see no trace of the white powder.

"Cheers, Rupert, down the hatch," she emptied her glass into her mouth, encouraging him to do the same. He followed suit, either the slight bitterness of the drug, or the strength of the scotch, catching his throat. He coughed.

"Do you want another, to wash that cough away?"

He paused. "No, I've got a better idea." He reached into his top pocket pulling from it the small plastic bag of cocaine.

Whilst not entirely unexpected, his desire to further his intake concerned Etta. It had seemed entirely fitting that the diazepam should have been administered to him. Very soon he should be drifting into a deep sleep. The intake of more cocaine could be dangerous. She invisibly shrugged her shoulders.

"Who cares?" She thought.

She cleared a space on the polished surface of the cabinet and Veneer set to work with his credit-card, organising the soldier-straight lines of cocaine. He had used the drug just once before, but watched it prepared on several occasions. They inhaled the drug together, Etta placing a large pinch on the back of her hand and taking it like snuff. The deterioration of Veneer was rapidly becoming evident. He was barely able to complete his line before retiring to the bed. Etta Van-de-Hooran was aware that the camera was still running and played to it. She walked to the bed. The thin shoulder straps of her dress slipped over her shoulders, seductively. It fell to the floor.

"Rupert my love, I want you," she commented as she walked, semi-naked, towards the bed.

Rupert Veneer's dream was erotic, nauseous, and often incomprehensible. Etta Van-de-Hooran seduced him. They kissed deeply as she removed his clothes. She was naked as she sat astride him, taking the effort from him. He focused his eyes on the wondrous curves of her body as the dream continued into blackness. The inky darkness engulfed him until the dancing figures of the angelic hallucinations filled his being. Each was faced by Etta's haunting looks. His eyes opened, and he awakened abruptly.

Rupert Veneer assessed his surroundings. He lay on a strange hotel bed. He was naked, his clothes strewn around the room. There was nobody else present. He lifted his head from the pillow. A searing pain prevented him from moving far. He lay back. He slowly used his hands to test his environment and himself. His arms explored the double bed but found nothing other than himself. His body appeared intact, although as he reached his chest area, he felt encrusted and matted. Similarly, he found the effect on the pillow and bed. He risked raising his head again to verify his thought. It was, indeed as he had expected, vomit. He had thrown up during his sleep, all over himself.

"Shit," he said loudly as he pulled his tired body from the bed.

The effect of standing was to return the feeling of nausea to Veneer's fragile body. As he felt the contents of his stomach climbing to his mouth, he strode quickly towards the toilet, his hand preventing a further, premature, discharge. His conversation with the porcelain bowl was limited. He finally felt able to stand, without vomiting. He did so.

Above the sink was a small mirror. He looked into it. He did not like what he saw. His white, drained, exterior confronted him. He was unshaven, even his hair looked congealed. He looked no further. He climbed into the bath, turning on the shower above. The water instantly struck his body, draining from it into the tub, slowly disintegrating the distasteful coating and washing it away. He stood for several minutes without moving, allowing the water to wash over him. He found shampoo and soap and washed thoroughly. The warmth of the water returned his circulation and returned colour to his skin. He left the bathroom, walking slowly back into the bedroom.

Veneer found his clothing and was pleased that it had not suffered the same deposits. He dressed slowly. As he did so he searched his memories of the previous night. He found few. He remembered the club. He remembered Etta Van-de-Hooran. He remembered the taxi ride to the hotel. He remembered his intake of cocaine. He checked the cabinet as if to verify his memory. Slight traces of the white dust remained. He slowly cleaned the side with his handkerchief.

Rupert Veneer could remember little else. He had a vague recollection of having sex with the woman but was uncertain as to whether this had actually happened. He checked the room for some trace of her. None existed. As he strapped his watch to his wrist, he looked at the face. Both hands pointed to the top of the dial.

"Twelve o'clock, noon, oh shit," commented Veneer as realisation struck him. It was now the following day. Worse, it was halfway through that day. He hurried from the room. He was engrossed in his thoughts as he left the hotel. He noticed neither the name of the hotel, nor its location, as he hurried away, searching for an underground station.

Veneer did not see the girl sitting in the foyer of the hotel. She was partially hidden by a newspaper and looked nothing like Etta Van-de-Hooran.

"Make sure he wakes up." Jack Knight had told her as he took the Flash Drive from her. "Ring me when he leaves, and I'll make sure the room is properly cleaned up."

Etta was one of her many false names. She was a prostitute by trade and had been so for many years. She had known Jack Knight for several of those years and worked for him previously to avoid her own arrest. He now paid her for her efforts, although only a meagre sum. She could have earned the two hundred pounds in one hour on the street, she thought, as she counted the twenty-pound notes.

"We need a politician in our pockets, Jack," he had been told. "There's a lot in it for you, Jack. You will make a lot of money and your reputation within the organisation will soar."

Jack Knight was not worried about his reputation within the organisation. It was the money that persuaded him. It was not difficult to find a target. He carefully scanned the guest list of the cocktail party. Few politicians were invited, and Rupert Veneer's name jumped at him. Knight's plan was not easy to execute. To rig the hotel room was simple, to get Veneer to the room more difficult. He was pleased that it came off. He had relied heavily on Etta and she had performed well. He had considered giving her a little extra, then chided himself for being silly.

Jack Knight looked at the recording, having plugged the Flash Drive into his computer. He had viewed it the day after it was taken. He was impressed. Rupert Veneer must accede to his demands. The man could not say no. The release of the recording would finish his career. Knight would develop Veneer himself. Better to retain control of his pet politician. He would relinquish it only when the time was right.

Maximillian Pfieling, or just Max, was the son of a German immigrant. His grand-father had been a staunch Nazi supporter, who had run from Germany during the final stages of the war. He had settled in the United States having followed a difficult and nefarious route through South America. Fortunately, his activities were on the periphery of the Party. No war crimes had been alleged against him.

Max was now fifty, the result of a relaxed cohabitation within the new fatherland. His father had died some years ago, the rigours of his past life having caught up with him. Max senior was an innovative man, however, and had established his small family business to fill an unrequited need. Miami had seen a resurge in organised crime. The gangs did not always get on together resulting in regular and torrid bloodbaths. There was a need for negotiation. Max senior offered the independent facilities for that negotiation.

Initially times had been hard. Criminal overlords would use his facilities on the pretence of a negotiated settlement, merely to trap their prey and centralise the slaughter. His father was no junior player and rapidly established his own support staff to prevent such trickery. His premises were now secure. No weapons were brought in from the outside. His record was respected, having taken over the business on the death of his father.

The first Pfieling premises were located in the Hialeah District, close to Angelo's small shop. Max Senior had prospered rapidly. The independent and assured service attracted business. Max would now acknowledge that his father's business grew on the back of organised crime. His father would have contended that he merely dealt with shrewd businessmen. It was certainly now true that the facilities were used by honest and dishonest alike. It was ideal for a negotiated settlement whether to avoid the court or the knife.

The original premises were no more, the Pfieling's having developed as they grew. Max now occupied a conference centre in North Miami, towards the beach. The building was double-storied and set within secluded grounds. Max Senior had purchased the land before the heavy development of Miami, allowing his son to develop it when the time was right. The conference centre had been purpose built. The Pfieling expertise had ensured that it was fit for the purpose.

The gates, securing entry, were electronically opened and steel backed. They were guarded both physically and by camera. The drive was open and bordered by lawns. These were carefully mown and stretched around the central core, the conference centre. This allowed easy protection against uninvited guests. Certain undisclosed surprises would ensure that any unauthorised approach was further hampered. The centre was now in use daily. During the occurrence of a conference, security was complete and obvious. At less sensitive times the guards melted back into oblivion, electrical surveillance and minimum cover sufficing.

On this particular day the security was extensive. I watched from the smoked window of the Mercedes as it swept along the drive to the centre. I had not chosen to attend, but had been told by Marco, over breakfast, of a business appointment that day. I was in the first of two cars, more for effect than purpose. Those negotiating would be Juan Marco and his counterpart Johnny Riccione. Few would be allowed within the negotiating chamber. Even fewer would actually speak. I travelled with Juan Marco in the first car. The White Rhino sat in the front of the car next to the driver. Alby was quick to leave his seat as the car stopped at the entrance. Juan Marco had no need to open his door, Alby already had control of it.

Marco waited for Melissa Grant to follow him from the vehicle. He watched as my legs exited first. He had commented on Melissa's short skirts. He enjoyed the relaxed glimpse of my upper thigh. But this was business. He turned and walked to the entrance. Melissa followed closely behind him.

Max Pfieling was at the door. His more important guests warranted his greeting. Juan Marco received his personal attention.

"Mr Marco, welcome." Pfieling shook his guest's hand warmly.

The pure wool of Marco's suit was soft to the touch. It contrasted harshly with the rough corduroy of Pfieling's jacket. Max was not a great dresser. He had never found the necessity for fine clothes. It was not the money; he could easily afford them. He had no need for status, and to him fine clothes were merely a status symbol. He liked to be comfortable. His denim jeans and corduroy jacket provided that comfort.

Max Pfieling had not aged well. Like his father before him, his hair had greyed prematurely. He was now white, although still carrying a full head of hair. The dishevelled beard and moustache belied his years and made him considerably older. He was a tall man whose height had falsely created a slight stoop. He was bi-lingual; his father's guttural German being spoken during his formative years. He had preferred to retain a slight Germanic accent to accentuate his background.

Max led Juan Marco to a large, framed gate.

"I'm afraid even you must past through this, Mr Marco." He explained, referring to the metal detector.

Entrance to the complex was closely supervised. All visitors underwent a thorough search, including examination by metal detectors, both fixed and hand held. Pfieling had just one problem since their introduction. Plastic explosive carried through, by a revenging renegade, did not activate the detectors and caused some damage when ignited. Since then, he had also installed a visual X-ray unit. He had no troubles since.

All guests were welcome to carry small arms to the building, but the rules required these to be left at reception. They were tendered to the receptionist who locked them securely in individual safes. They were returned at the conclusion of proceedings.

Juan Marco had used the facilities on several occasions. He was aware of the protocol. He was comfortable with it and respected

Pfieling's professionalism. The facilities were second to none. Each conference room was secure. Recording equipment and closed-circuit television were standard. The conference table was circular and of solid beech wood. The matching chairs, bound and furnished in leather, were evenly spaced around the table. Negotiations should have no sides nor partitions.

Alby was the first to enter the room. Despite the security arrangements he still preferred to satisfy himself in advance of Marco's entry. Juan Marco entered on his signal. Melissa was honoured to follow close behind. I was more uncertain. Marco approached a trolley in one corner. The thermos flasks were provided by Pfieling's staff. They would be safe.

"Coffee, Melissa? Let me pour," he smiled as I approached him briskly.

I slowed. "Yes please." Melissa answered.

He recognised some uncertainty in Melissa. It was, in fact, my uncertainty.

"Sit down, Melissa." He pulled a chair from the table, having placed Melissa's coffee before her. "Sit down and relax."

Shanks and Baker had followed the entourage, at the rear of the surveillance team. Baker pulled to the gates, a safe time after Marco had passed through, to give Shanks a closer look. He pulled the hood of his car on the pretence that the vehicle was overheating. Shanks only questioned him after they had regained a safe distance.

"Well, Brad, what is that place then?"

"Max Pfieling's conference centre. A place where the top men can get together and sort out their problems in safety."

As he spoke a second motorcade passed their position. The vehicles were all black, although this time native of America. Their length and flat-sidedness were thus emphasised.

"And here comes the opposition; Riccione and family."

Juan Marco stood close to Melissa as the door swung open allowing Johnny Riccione to sweep into the room. His dark jacket hung from his shoulders, exposing the matching waistcoat beneath it. In his right hand he carried a large cigar. In ignoring protocol, he was emphasising his own importance. The cigar glowed gently as the air passed over it. On reaching Riccione's lips, it reddened and then died again. Riccione inhaled some of the smoke, though not all. He blew it from his lungs before speaking.

"Juan Marco, shall we get on with this. It might be good to know why I am here."

He seated himself at the far side of the table, directly opposite Juan Marco. Riccione's compatriots sat around him. Marco's men remained standing. The reason soon became apparent. Paulo Ramiro needed no introduction as he entered the room.

The Bell Huey Cobra helicopter was a remnant from the Iraq war. Whilst respected by those who flew it, and particularly by those who languished on the ground awaiting its arrival, at the conclusion of the conflict it had fallen into disuse. Paulo Ramiro felt his purchase of the aircraft to be a bargain. It had required some modernisation and servicing. It now rested proudly, within a hangar at the Ramiro ranch, in Bogota.

Ramiro's influence with the bureaucracy of Colombia could have prevented registration of the aircraft. This was not necessary. There was no secret as to his possession. The helicopter was proudly used to entertain selected friends, or for a fishing trip high into the Andes Mountains. The craft was not simply used for pleasure activities but had certain business advantages, particularly when the identifying transfers were removed from its body.

The aircraft had set off the day previously. Its cargo being mercenary fighters, employed by Ramiro. They were occasionally necessary to fulfil a specific task, and this was one of those occasions. The men were mainly European, two British, two Irish and a Frenchman. The one Brazilian had been picked up in a recent skirmish in South America. They were fully equipped to fight. The short machine pistols were Russian by manufacture, supplied through Cuba. Their arsenal was cosmopolitan.

Names were unnecessary when working. They rejected more regular military titles in favour of numbers. There was no doubt who was Number One. The English, ex-SAS, captain stood out by height and bearing. Each operation was coloured, and the colour prefixed the number. Today's operation was White. It had been taken from the colour of the produce paying their bill. White One was in the belly of the helicopter with his team. White Four flew the aircraft.

They had flown low over land before crossing the Caribbean Sea. They had skirted Jamaica to avoid conventional, scheduled aircraft. Their speed of 200 mph was slow but not laborious. White Two threw the but-ends of his untipped cigarettes into the ocean, through the open door. White One reminded himself to impose a no-smoking rule on their next escapade.

The unauthorised landing on a small airstrip to the east of Havana, Cuba, allowed them to rest for the night. They did not leave the aircraft. Its safety was of paramount importance. The American dollars had only turned the eyes of the authorities away from the landing. No security was offered or expected. It was an effective purchase, however. No attention was paid to the helicopter or its crew during its short stay in the country.

The convenient stopover left them an achievable hop to Miami. The last step of the journey was, however, the most dangerous. The Americans were ever vigilant, particularly with regard to approaching craft from Cuba, whether by sea or air. To fly low might defeat the radar, but not the visual sighting. The route would therefore be detoured, through the smaller islands of the Bahamas, thus approaching the mainland through the back door.

Johnny Riccione was fortunate to own several houses throughout the United States, much due to his involvement in the sale of drugs. Despite this international business, Riccione had not ventured beyond America. His Miami base was at Fort Lauderdale. The house was set above the sea line, overlooking the Atlantic Ocean, to the north of the Town and possible forty miles from Miami. Riccione was happy with the arrangement. His family were distanced from his business. The roads were wide and the cars similarly. He was chauffeured during his daily travel and, speed limits apart, the journey would rarely take more than an hour.

His family were content in their home. His wife, an Italian-American, originating from a separate family, felt secure. Their two young children were unworried. They were protected by high walls and electrically sealed gates. Whilst the seaward side was open, the drop to the sea was sheer. Riccione's henchmen patrolled the grounds at regular intervals.

Riccione had not been surprised by the invitation to negotiate. He had expected it. Juan Marco was of a different ilk to the Ramiros. Johnny Riccione was confident of winning a larger share of the Miami market. The exploding Mercedes motorcar had been an initial indication that his power base was strong. He left his residence, for the journey to Max Pfieling's, in buoyant mood.

The helicopter passed unnoticed on its inward passage. It travelled low across the ocean, the crests of the waves visible to the occupants through the open door. The sinister dark grey colouring allowed it to blend with the surroundings. Whilst noisy within the machine, the open expanse of the Atlantic Ocean dissipated the sound rapidly. It was difficult to establish from where the sound was coming.

It was a bright morning, the sun climbing in the morning sky. The guard had completed a circuit of the grounds. There was nothing to trouble him. He was unworried. He walked towards the ocean view, lighting a cigarette. The sun was on his back. He was in restful mood, his gun slung loosely over his shoulder. His lungs filled with smoke. He held it in for a moment, feeling that would boost the nicotine intake into his blood. He blew the smoke from between his pursed lips, slowly.

The American football hit the guard on the back on the legs. There was not great force to it. The ball bounced back and stopped, on the grass, behind him. He turned and reached down to pick it up. He threw it back at the small boy running towards him.

"Be more careful, Johnny, or you'll lose it into the sea."

The boy stopped abruptly and was staring through the guard.

"Don't worry Johnny, you haven't done anything wrong."

It was only then that the guard realised that the boy was looking beyond him. He had failed to register the sound of the helicopter blades against the waves of the sea hitting the land below. He could only now distinctly differentiate them as the aircraft raised above the cliff-line to be visible. The guard swung towards the helicopter, as if in slow motion, un-slinging his weapon from his shoulder as he did so. He was too late. The dart hit him in his upper thigh immediately impregnating him with the drug that would send him to sleep for several hours. It was almost instantaneous. As his hand reached the trigger guard of his gun he was already dropping to the ground. No shots were fired.

The invading force left the helicopter before it had landed. Each man nimbly jumped the six-foot gap as it hovered. They ran towards the house, separating in a fanning motion as they travelled. Their automatics were shouldered at this time. They had been instructed that death was to be avoided. Each man was separately armed with a dart pistol that had been so effective on the first guard. White One believed the drug to be a derivative of curare, the South American arrow poison. It proved similarly effective on the other guards.

Johnny Riccione was not surprised at the arrival of Paulo Ramiro. He had expected Juan Marco to conduct negotiations alone. Paulo Ramiro obviously created a more serious element, one that could not be avoided, however. Riccione stood for the older man. He was welcoming.

"Paulo Ramiro, I did not expect you. Is there a need for you to be here? Is this not a matter raised by Juan Marco that can be settled with Juan Marco?" He probed.

"I was in town, Johnny. I had nothing else to do. I thought I would listen in." The man smiled enjoying Riccione's uncertainty. "Sit down Johnny. There's no need to stand for me. I'll just take a seat next to Juan Marco."

Riccione twisted the large cigar between his lips. He wanted to moisten the end, but his mouth was dry. He took it between his thumb and forefinger and removed it to speak.

"So why are we here Juan Marco. What do you want of me?"

Paulo Ramiro sipped the black coffee that had been immediately placed before him. He did not have to ask for it. It was hot and sweet. He remained silent, leaving Juan Marco to do the talking.

I was nervous. My senses were aware of the heat emanating from the body of Juan Marco, sitting beside me. I saw the slight beads of sweat upon the brow of Riccione. The bodyguards from each side were alert, despite their weapons having been removed. I foresaw trouble. I did not know what to expect. Whatever it was, I was in the firing line. I shifted Melissa's chair slightly away from Juan Marco. My own body temperature was rising. Perhaps it was the heat of the room. I looked for a reason.

At last Juan Marco spoke. The silence seemed interminable.

"Johnny, we seem to have reached an impasse, a stalemate. I appreciate that our dealings might sometimes overlap, but there is room for the two of us. It would seem that you are now unhappy with your share of the Miami cake. You want more, and want to take it from us, the Ramiros." Marco waved his hand to encompass the family.

"I believe that you thought I would be the easy touch, following the death of Carlo Ramiro, God rest his soul!" The Ramiro party crossed themselves, Paulo looking sincerely hurt.

"You felt that now was the time to move in, that I wasn't man enough for the job. Unfortunately, you were wrong."

Riccione was shaking his head, looking down towards the table. The cigar in his hand needed re-lighting. "That's not true Juan Marco. How can you think that?"

"I think that, Johnny Riccione, because it is true. First there was Angelo, a simple and small customer who hurt no one. His fingers were broken for no good reason. What good did that do you? I will tell you. it merely resulted in your man losing his hand."

Chuck was standing behind Johnny Riccione. He kept the stump of his wrist in his coat pocket. He was able with one hand. He had always accepted the penalty of his career. However, on this occasion, as Marco spoke, he felt the stump tingle as if the hand remained, a feeling he had not experienced before.

"Your response was to fill my car with explosive, to take my life and remove me from the scene. I was only saved by good fortune and the powers of observation of my friend, Melissa Grant. Had she not been with me, I would not be here today."

I found the compliment disconcerting. In other circumstances I would have enjoyed the praise. On this occasion I would rather have remained anonymous. I remained still, making no eye contact with the opposition. I took a short opportunity to glance upward towards the face of Johnny Riccione. He did not smile but looked relaxed. He was obviously more comfortable with Paulo Ramiro having taken a back seat. He felt he could cope with Juan Marco. He was no competition.

"Get to the point, Juan Marco. Whilst I enjoy sitting here, drinking your coffee, I have a busy day ahead of me. Nothing you mention was to do with me. I am innocent." He opened his hands to Juan Marco as if to prove his statement.

"Johnny, we are tired of your games. We do not wish you to leave us, for somebody else would merely try to fill your place. We are happy to accept your presence, but you must accept us. You must pledge that these incidents will stop."

"I could pledge that now Juan Marco. But if I had no intention of keeping the pledge, it would be worthless, and what would you do about it?" Riccione had regained his full confidence. He stared menacingly at Marco. The cigar was back in his mouth. He lit it as he spoke. The smoke engulfed him. That, which he had inhaled, he blew towards his opposite number.

"This is a response that I had not wished for, Johnny." Paulo Ramiro had remained silent but now intervened.

The American turned his attention to the older man. "Paulo Ramiro, you know I have respect for you and your family. When your son Carlo ran the Miami side of your operation there was no trouble. Times change, Mr Ramiro. Juan Marco has not been a true successor, he is not a part of your family, and you, Paulo, have relinquished control of your empire. You spend too much time with your horses now. You do not know what is going on."

"I know exactly what is going on, Johnny. You have stretched yourself too far. You cannot afford a war and yet that is the way that you are heading."

"I don't think so, Paulo. You are getting old. You come here with your young pretender. But I hold the ace here today. I have your grandson, Paulo."

He paused, watching the face of the Colombian intensely. There was no change of expression, "You did not know of your grandson then, Paulo. Here, look at his pictures, he's a handsome little chap."

Riccione held up his right hand to receive a folder of photographs from Chuck. He pushed them across the table to Ramiro. Paulo Ramiro slowly reached forward and picked up the photographs from the table. He paused for a moment, leaving them in their concealing envelope. He took the photographs and studied the first carefully. It showed a young child on the knee of Johnny Riccione.

"You choose to sit with his mother, I choose to sit with her son, Paulo. You must ask her if I am right."

I am sure that Melissa did not visibly slide down in the chair, but I felt as if I had done so. My position had been instantly declared by the stranger sitting opposite me, my life venomously imperilled. Anger engulfed me, overcoming my terror. I felt Melissa's hand shake, but she said nothing.

Paulo Ramiro slowly took other photographs from the envelope and spread them on the table so that I could see them. I studied each picture carefully. They were all based on the same theme, probably taken at the same time. Each photograph showed my son, Danny, with Riccione. In certain photographs, the armed guard could also be seen, whether for effect or by accident, I was uncertain. I felt a pain in the pit of my stomach as I examined the pictures of my son. I wanted to kill Riccione and all those connected with him. I knew I could not.

Paulo Ramiro allowed me ample time to study the pictures. The one word he uttered was whispered sharply to me,

"Well."

Melissa nodded confirmation without speaking.

"So now you know, Paulo. Carlo's only son, his only successor and I have him. It seems that I have something you want, Paulo, and you have something I want. Perhaps it is time that we traded."

"How did you find him, who told you of him?" Ramiro's voice was steady.

Riccione was full of confidence.

"It seems we both have our informants, Paulo. The English police-force is a cheese full of holes."

He laughed aloud at his analogy. The rest of the room was silent. His confidence became boastful.

"You do not realise your waning influence, either at home or abroad, Paulo Ramiro. We also have policemen and politicians. It is time for you to be more careful, Paulo. Those that are loyal only for money are easily made disloyal."

Each word had been seized and carefully stored by Juan Marco. He had no doubt that Paulo Ramiro had done the same.

"You think you hold the winning hand, Johnny, but you are wrong. A full house wins this hand, and I hold that full house."

Marco now re-entered the conversation. He clicked together his finger and thumb, signalling Alby to release the television monitor from the wooden housing.

"I would like you to watch a short transmission, Johnny. You might recognise the location. I should tell you that you are watching live television, Mr Riccione. This is no recording, no staged event."

Marco's voice had hardened. I could feel the tension in the room as the sides thrust and parried. The bodyguards had tightened the outer circle. Alby pulled open the polished, wooden, cabinet doors to reveal the large television screen. A smaller cabinet held a camera on a balanced telescopic stand. Alby angled it as best he could to cover those seated at the table. He pointed the control at the appliances and pushed the buttons. The television burst into life and the small red light on the camera showed it to be transmitting. I leaned slightly forward, almost looking over Marco's shoulder.

"You can't see." He pulled his chair slightly back giving Melissa a better view. I was not sure that I wanted it.

The television picture initially showed the sea. Riccione should have recognised it as the view from his back garden but did not.

"Well, what am I looking at? Don't waste my time, Marco." He was becoming angered.

"I'm surprised that you don't know. Pan around now please."

Marco's final remark was to the camera operator at the Riccione household. He watched as the picture moved inland. I heard Riccione's breathing grow deeper as realisation dawned upon him. The picture rested upon his family, his wife and children standing in the garden. Riccione had already seen his bodyguards laid out upon the floor, hands behind their necks. He recognised the Kalashnikov rifles of the Ramiro mercenaries. He saw the helicopter silent on his lawns, the blades having now stopped rotating.

"Are they all right?" He hissed through clenched teeth at Marco. "If anything happens to them, I will kill you."

Juan Marco was not fazed by the standard response. He had heard it many times. It was generally the good guy who used the lines. He did not consider Riccione the good guy. Riccione's henchmen had stepped forward in a more menacing manner. They were amply covered by his own men. Without weapons they were no problem.

"Johnny, of course they are all right. Ask them, the camera works both ways you know."

Riccione's first words were Italian.

"English, my friend," Marco interrupted, "or at least Spanish so that I can understand."

It was, however, apparent that the moment was lost. Riccione turned back to Marco.

"What do you want? Let's settle this thing so we can both get out of here."

"Johnny, I want you to realise that a war between us would be of no benefit to you. You would eventually lose, be wiped out. It would also cause me much difficulty. I cannot accept, however, your recent behaviour and wish it to stop. If it does not stop, the next time we will not use tranquilliser darts. Their weapons would cause much damage to your family. I do not wish it so. The choice is yours."

"OK, Marco, you've made your point."

Riccione was re-gathering his composure. He lit his cigar. He sucked on it heavily. I noticed that the nicotine had stained his fingers heavily.

"I'm afraid to make my point is no longer sufficient, Riccione. I now need something more."

"And what's that going to be?" The beads of perspiration had returned to Riccione's forehead. He was worried for his family. He disguised it well.

"It seems that Miss Grant, sitting beside me, has unfortunately lost, not only her son, but also her cousin. He was travelling in this country when she heard that he had died. She has unfortunately been unable to locate his body. She asks your help, Johnny Riccione, don't you Melissa?"

I was concerned. I wanted Danny back and would do anything to get him. I knew that I was in Marco's hands, in his control, my only chance being to play along. I nodded.

"I was fortunate that she was returning to the hotel when your man, poorly disguised as a mechanic, rigged my Mercedes to explode. She was convinced it was her cousin, he looked so similar. Wasn't that the case Melissa?" I nodded again.

"And so, Johnny, all I want to do is provide my dear friend, Melissa Grant, with the body of her cousin so that she might return to England. Will you help her?"

Riccione had grasped the nub. "Boxed or unboxed?"

"Boxed."

"He will be delivered immediately. If Chuck might leave for a short time, he will make the necessary arrangements."

"Of course. Alby assist Chuck with regard to delivery and Chuck," the one-handed man turned to Marco, "nothing foolish please. Mr Riccione has his family to think of."

Marco turned back to Riccione, "and, of course, her son. The family would not be complete without her son, just as yours would not be complete without your son. Let it be so!"

Johnny Riccione nodded reluctantly to Chuck as he left the room.

The hour passed slowly before Alby returned to the conference room. The talking had been done. Riccione had nothing more to say. He knew he could not leave until the deliveries had been made. It would be a simple matter. The man was local. Chuck knew him well. The silenced .22 would pass straight into his brain and kill him within seconds. He would be delivered, still warm to the touch. That would satisfy the requirements of the Ramiro family and, hopefully, save his own. It was a minor price to pay. The man should have been more careful. He had failed in his task.

Danny was not at the Riccione home, but within a short distance of the Pfieling centre. Chuck would arrange his collection. Both would be delivered at the same time, one living, one dead.

On his return, Alby walked straight to Juan Marco and whispered in his ear. He backed off.

"It would appear that honour has been satisfied on this occasion, Johnny. We will leave now. One hour after our departure your family will be released to enjoy the rest of the day. I wish you well, Johnny Riccione."

Juan Marco followed Paulo Ramiro from the room. They travelled away from the building together, in Paulo Ramiro's car. Melissa followed behind in Juan Marco's, driven by Alby. I could not hear their conversation but imagined their satisfaction. I wished I felt equally at ease.

The lead car turned left from the main gates and stopped only one hundred yards from them, by a parked van. I recognised several of Marco's men standing around it. I remained in the car but watched as Juan Marco walked to the back of the van. The doors were opened for him. I could not see within but imagined the content. After briefly surveying the interior, Juan Marco walked back to my car. He opened the door. He got into the car and sat beside me.

"Your son has been delivered to us, Melissa, along with the man who blew up my Mercedes-Benz. You must identify them both. I warn you, Melissa Grant, you are not in favour with Paulo Ramiro, and yet your son is with his grandfather. When you see him, you will say nothing, or it will be the last time that you do see him. Just confirmation that it is him, Melissa, nothing else.

I stepped from the car, led gently by Juan Marco. I knew that I had no option but to comply with his rules. He opened the door of Ramiro's limousine. I looked inside. A wave of emotion came over me as I saw my son, now on Ramiro's knee. I was sure that he also recognised me. I wanted to touch him and reached out with my hand. I felt Marco's own hand on my shoulder.

"Now is not the time. That is your son, Paulo's grandson, is it not?"

I nodded. I was unable to speak. Marco shut the car door and took my hand. As we walked away from the Mercedes, it pulled away at speed. I wanted to run after it. I had traced Danny, but now, again, had lost him.

"This will be equally difficult, Melissa."

I looked tentatively inside the back of the van. Despite the brightness outside, the interior was gloomy. In the centre, on the floor was a plain wooden box, the base of a cheap casket. The top was loose beside it. Melissa leant forward to look inside. The van's guard had seen death many times. He had no interest in what was inside. He watched attentively, however, as Melissa's short skirt rode further up my thighs. He was impressed by the length and proportion of my stockinged legs, just as others had been previously. I determined to give Melissa Grant the elbow, if ever I got home.

I was able to see within the casket. The corpse lay before me. It was the proportioned body of a caucasian male. He had been in his early forties, not an old man. I wondered what he had felt seconds before his death, or had he even known about it. These men were clinical and ruthless. He had lived by these rules and died by them. I looked at the face. It was upside down to me, the head being near to the doors of the van. I tried to turn my own head to get a better view. I looked closely at him, trying to remember the mechanic at the hotel.

The man's hair was blonde, the colour fading at the sides into grey. His eyes were closed. Through the right eye, from forehead, running vertically into his cheek, was a thin scar, a scar caused by a slashing knife wound perhaps. I looked closely and remembered that scar. As the mechanic had faced me for that short time, I had noticed something strange, not in keeping with his status. I could not initially put my finger on it. Now my memory was refreshed.

"That's him, the mechanic," I told Juan Marco as I pulled myself back from the van.

"Are you sure?"

"Yes, the scar." I ran my finger down my face as I spoke.

"Good," Marco nodded thoughtfully. "This was one of Riccione's aids. Don't forget Melissa, it could have been us in the box. He did not care about us."

"Let's go," he told the van driver as he walked back to the car.

Johnny Riccione watched the television set attentively after the departure of Paulo Ramiro and Marco. He was naturally worried about his family. He had made his decision instantly. There was no choice. His family were paramount. He would not put them at risk. The mechanic was merely a paid assassin, generally good at his job. He had paid the price of failure. Riccione was hurt at losing his prime asset. Ramiro's grandson would have remained a distinct advantage, an advantage that he had now lost.

Riccione saw the camera slowly withdraw from his wife and children. He could see the shadows of the helicopter rotors turning as the soldier backed towards the aircraft. As it gained height, he watched the people on the ground growing smaller. As the helicopter banked to pull away the picture suddenly ceased. The camera had been turned off. His last sight had been of the family guards running to find their weapons. He made a mental note to replace them. Riccione got up from his chair and walked swiftly to his car.

"Take me home, Chuck," he told his trusty assistant.

"It looks like a coffin, Brad. It's a long box but I can't see inside. The girl's looking at it right now and blocking my view. I cannot get in any closer."

The lead surveillance officer had secured an observation point upon the front of Max Pfieling's premises close to the front gate. He was virtually invisible amongst the surrounding vegetation. The binocular lenses were just visible as he peeped through the bush.

The van had not pulled up directly in front of the gates. Pfieling would not have liked, nor accepted that. The rules of his establishment were strictly kept. The Ramiro's had much respect for the man. The distance had therefore made it difficult for the Government man to see inside the van. The binoculars were strong, but the darkness within the rear reduced visibility.

Brad turned to Phil Shanks. They had both been listening to the radio transmission.

"Something big has gone down Phil. Max Pfieling is only used for matters of importance. For the two families to arrive means that serious talks have taken place. It's my guess that whoever is in the back of the van was the price that one family had to pay. I reckon it was Johnny Riccione that paid the price."

Shanks nodded. "I'm concerned about our girl Brad. What's she doing at the meeting, and what's she doing with her head in the back of the van?"

"Did she get the message when you spoke to her at the hotel?"

"I don't know. I only had a short time before the bouncer arrived. I either had to get out or kick up a fuss. I didn't have more than a few seconds. She seemed relieved to see me, but I don't know how deeply she's got herself involved. I just hope she can pull back from it."

Chapter Seventeen

Jessie Slyder now garaged his new car. He had taken some effort to remove offending items that had built up over the years. The valueless vehicles of the past had not deserved a home of their own and therefore the garage had become an extension of his home, particularly for the storage of unwanted items. He had cleaned his nearly new Pontiac three times since its purchase. He liked it. Not being too adventurous, the dirty brown of his old car had changed to a clean beige for the new. He sat proudly behind the wheel. He felt he had finally achieved something.

However, for every asset a price had to be paid and Jessie Slyder was apprehensive that the price was too high. He had accepted the initial payments from Juan Marco, little realising, at the start, that there would be no finish. He knew now that he was engulfed in the Ramiro pyre. He finally accepted the situation and decided to enjoy his demise. At that point he went out and bought the car that he had always wanted.

The telephone call, when it came, caused Slyder's heart to race and his fat face to become flushed. He sat down at his desk to allow his ventricular system to re-function. He banged his chest with his fist. He took another bite of his large bagel to calm his nerves.

Slyder felt comfortable driving his new car and pulled into the meeting place with some pride. He had expected Juan Marco. He wanted to show off his prized possession. He was somewhat deflated when Alby climbed from the Mercedes.

"The Boss sends his compliments, Jessie. We've had a couple of unfortunate deaths and want you to clear the bodies. The first is another close friend of Mr Marco who will be returned to his native Colombia. He will be flown out tomorrow night. You will arrange the paperwork from this end and ensure no difficulties arise. The second is the cousin of the young English girl, Miss Grant. The poor unfortunate man went climbing in the Andes Mountains and suffered a fatal accident. It was thanks to the resources of Mr Ramiro that she was able to locate her relation. The body will be routed from Bogota, through Miami and onward to London. The paperwork will have been completed by the Colombian authorities and you will simply have to endorse it and ensure the flight transfers run efficiently. Do you have any difficulty with these tasks?"

Had he have done so he would not have admitted it to the man mountain before him. Slyder shook his head.

"The Boss has sent you something." Alby shoved the envelope into the fat hand of the Customs man.

"It will help pay for the car." Alby smiled as he walked away.

"Have you been to South America?" Juan Marco asked me over the dinner table that evening.

"Oh fuck," I thought, but allowed Melissa to answer.

"No, no I have not." She replied.

"You will enjoy it all the more then. You must have your bags packed for tomorrow. We leave for Colombia."

"Why?" Melissa asked on behalf of us both.

"We have work to do, to prepare your cousin for his return to England and, presumably, you would wish to see your son?"

"Of course, Juan, of course I want to see Danny." I reached across the table and took his hand in mine. "But when, when will I be able to see him?"

"I don't know, Melissa. Paulo Ramiro was not pleased that he had not been told of his grandson. Tell me, Melissa, how well did you get on with Carlo."

Melissa's expression puzzled. I withdrew my hand from his.

"Why, why do you ask?"

"I am curious, Melissa. I am curious that you would wish to make love to him in the office above the warehouse. I would expect something better, for both you and Carlo."

I thought for a moment.

"It was difficult to say no to Carlo Ramiro. He was a powerful man, Juan Marco; he took what he wanted."

"And did Carlo take you, Melissa, or did you give yourself to him?"

Pain crossed my face as I relived the event. It passed quickly as I retook control of my torn emotions.

"He took me Juan, he raped me. I might have made love to him, but not there, not there in that grubby little office."

I massaged the truth. My true identity had not yet been revealed, although the expectancy was almost too much to bear. I had still to achieve my objective. If a few, further, white lies would assist in that aim, I would tell them.

"But what of Jack Knight, Melissa. Why come here and tell us of him. Why should you want Jack Knight dead, Melissa?"

"I didn't want him dead, just punished. He was responsible for inflaming Carlo. Carlo wanted me to take cocaine. I didn't want to. Knight walked into the office as I swept mine onto the floor. He told Carlo and he was upset. He took his revenge."

"And you wanted yours?"

"It was more than that, Juan," Melissa's eyes steeled. "I became pregnant as a result of Carlo's rape. Danny was the result. I have loved him and cared for him since, regardless of what his father did to me. Then what happens, he was kidnapped by the Ricciones, just to give them an edge over your family. I was convinced it was Paulo who had taken his grandson. I came out here to get him back."

"But why not tell us, why did you just not ask?"

"Do you think that Paulo Ramiro would have given me back my child if I had just asked. This is his grandson that he knew nothing about. Are you suggesting that I should have come here and just asked for him back? I don't think so, do you Juan Marco?"

The ferocity of my attack, through Melissa, caught Marco unawares. He sat back in his seat. He was not so assured as he answered.

"No, no, you're probably right. He would not have given you your son just like that, and, of course, he will not now, now that he has him."

I reached back across the table again taking Juan Marco's hand, this time in both of mine.

"That's why I need your help, Juan Marco. I would give anything to get my son, anything."

Melissa's voice was beseeching. Perhaps too beseeching. I had no doubt what I was offering. Marco had no doubt either.

"Melissa, much as I like you, I work for Paulo Ramiro. He is like a father to me. You would not ask me to betray him?"

"I don't know, Juan. I just don't know. You know what I have to do.

If there's anyway you can help me, I'd appreciate it."

"We will see Melissa, we will see."

I was tired of America and wanted desperately to return home. I knew, however, that I would and could not do so without Danny's return. I was unnerved by the turn of events. My natural instincts told me to be very careful of Juan Marco. This was a dangerous man whom I must not under-estimate.

Melissa Grant was not so restricted. She enjoyed the company of Juan Marco. She had not flirted with him; their relationship had not developed in that way. The one encounter had been spontaneous, in the back of the limousine. It had not, so far, been repeated. Juan Marco was an esoteric man. His business dealings were mainly private. Melissa had been allowed to participate only in so much as it suited Juan Marco, and his Boss, Paulo Ramiro. He would not turn against Ramiro, but perhaps he could assist in other ways.

Melissa travelled with Juan Marco and Rhino aboard a scheduled flight. She was unaware of the fourth traveller. He did not enjoy the comfort of a first-class seat, as did the others. She did not see him during the flight or after. He rested in the exclusivity of the hold, separated from the general luggage merely by a strap securing his box to the floor of the aircraft. His clearance for travel had not been through Customs. He had received special clearance by Jessie Slyder. The papers had been arranged by him and stamped by him. The mechanic travelled alone.

Jessie Slyder had not found it difficult to arrange the paperwork. Much could be excluded if he chose not to check it thoroughly. He was fortunate that his supervision was virtually non-existent. The flight had departed before his checklist was submitted.

Phil Shanks stood beside Brad Baker as they watched the aircraft through the glassed windows of the airport building. It had not been a difficult task to identify the passengers or their cargo. They had avoided the airport authorities, particularly with Slyder on duty that day, and approached the Airline direct. A simple glance at the passenger list confirmed Shanks's fear. Melissa Grant was travelling with Juan Marco to Bogota.

"I can't go with her this time." He told Baker. "I'd put both her and myself at too much risk. I'd have no control over the situation."

"Too right, Phil, the authorities out there are controlled by men like Paulo Ramiro. You could approach no one. You're better off waiting till they come back and come back they will."

"So what do we do in the meantime, Brad."

"We'll have a close look at Jessie Slyder, that's what we'll do. You know that the airline has a body on its manifest, exported by the Ramiros. I bet if we were to check it would be the one from the van outside Pfieling's."

"And Jessie Slyder's on duty today to check it out." Shanks added.

They watched the aircraft climb in the sky. Shanks felt his stomach churn with the concern he was feeling for his undercover officer.

In another part of the Airport concourse the fat man similarly watched the flight climb and felt his stomach churn, albeit with relief though. Jessie Slyder did not cope with pressure well. He wondered if the payment was sufficient recompense for his actions. He thought of his new car. Maybe it was.

The Undertaker, Pedro Ipiales, had embalmed Carlo Ramiro to the satisfaction of his father. He was further honoured to be given the job of preparing the mechanic. The body had been transported quickly but was now beginning to suffer from the heat. He had been refrigerated since his death, but the journey had returned the body to beyond room temperature. The natural bacteria within the body had returned to their active state and were rapidly devouring the interior. He knew the body should not have been transported in this state. He was unaware of Slyder's involvement in defeating international regulations.

Pedro Ipiales was an aged man, his skin leathered by the heat of the day and the dry air that filtered through. He had lived in Tunja all his life, travelling no further than Bogota, and only then when necessary. He was an undertaker, as his father had been before him. He expected that his son would continue in his footsteps. He had travelled to the airport at Bogota to collect his consignment. There were no formalities. Ramiro had seen to that. The coffin was unloaded straight from the aircraft into the back of his ageing van. It bounced slightly on the metal floor during the return journey. Ipiales cursed the roads and the authorities that failed to maintain them.

His embalming rooms were clean, the walls whitewashed. They were reminiscent of any mortuary. Only one marble slab honoured the centre of the room. He only ever worked on one body at a time. There was no need for more. He was proud of his refrigerated cabinets. They were the first to be installed in the area. He remembered his father having them fitted. The thermostat occasionally failed in exceptional heat, otherwise the bodies were well preserved. A cabinet was available for the mechanic. The chill would ease the natural emanation of decomposition.

Melissa Grant was impressed with Juan Marco's apartment. I was not so certain, although, at this point in proceedings, I had little say. It was situated in the centre of Bogota, close to the Cathedral and the Piazza Boliver. The City was founded in the sixteenth century and, in certain areas still retained an aura of colonial rule. It had suffered from a lack of investment in upkeep and the input of over four million people and had lost its early regality. Many occupants of Bogota lived in squalid, shanty, towns on the outskirts of the city. The privileged few retained the benefits that only prosperity can bring. Juan Marco was one of the few.

"This is lovely," Melissa flattered as she was shown around the apartment by Juan Marco.

She pulled open the protective shutters on the balconied windows and stepped out. The rooftops lay a tiled path before her. She turned back to her host and took his hand in hers. She led him to the balcony.

"Tell me about your town, Juan Marco."

The apartment was not large but sported several bedrooms. Melissa Grant expected that only one would be used. She was at one with this idea. It was essential to the return of my son. To this end, I agreed with her although questioned her true motives. I knew that Melissa was looking forward to it. It was the first opportunity that she had to be totally alone with Juan Marco. Alby had carried their luggage to the apartment but left soon after. He would only return when asked to do so by Marco. She presumed that no disturbance would occur to break the ambience.

Pedro Ipiales knew he had a complicated task to perform. The mechanic was not initially a heavy man, perhaps weighing eighty kilos. Ipiales could, with difficulty, create the impression that he was of heavier build, perhaps to one hundred kilos. This would allow twenty kilos of pure white cocaine to be packed tightly into the embalmed body cavities, for export to London. Once there, the drug could be expected to gross over half a million pounds. The job required precision and expertise. Ipiales had that expertise.

He carefully removed the internal organs from the body cavity and chemically cleaned and preserved the interior. He would not use the offal to feed the dogs in the street, although he knew some who did. He had a small incinerator, which coped admirably. The brain was taken from the skull. The remaining cavity would certainly receive one kilo, tightly packed.

Pedro Ipiales had respect for the dead, but more respect for the living, particularly for Paulo Ramiro. He had performed this sort of operation before and was efficient at it. He was well paid for his trouble and this provided some extra comfort for both himself and his family. He had not hesitated to agree when he had been approached by one of the Ramiro aides.

The cocaine would be delivered to him on a telephone call confirming that he had prepared the body. At the same time, he would expect the specially prepared coffin to be delivered to him. Beneath the blue satin interior, and lining the walls of the box, could be a similar amount of the valuable commodity. The regulations required the box to meet certain requirements that simply added to the weight. This left much scope for concealment.

Ipiales was again pleased with his work. The drug was delivered with the box, wrapped in individual kilo packages. Each package was, perhaps, eight inches by four inches and over an inch deep. They were securely sealed in polythene, although leakage would not affect the health of this carrier. Ipiales had to massage several of the packs into a shape to fit the cavity.

The mechanic had taken on a new form. Not the thin, aggressive man that had first glanced at Melissa Grant as he rigged the red Mercedes, this was now the overweight corpse of a different person. The chest and stomach were larger, definitely overweight. The cheeks had been puffed out to compensate. The scar on his face was now barely visible, the skin having been stretched to take up the added bulk. He was returned to the refrigerated compartment awaiting collection.

Herbie Bartlett, solicitor of the Supreme Court, watched cautiously as the custody-record of Melissa Grant began to emerge on his computer, attached to an e-mail. He had been uncertain whether he would be provided with a copy as he did not represent the person subject to that record. He had been careful not to put anything into writing for fear that he might be criticised later. He had telephoned the police station at Rotherhithe. The Custody Officer had not been helpful.

"It has been filed, you will have to contact our stores," he said.

Bartlett's third telephone call had finally been successfully routed to the erstwhile clerk.

"Why didn't you write in?" Was her immediate question.

"I do apologise, we overlooked it, a genuine mistake by my secretary. We're now running short of time. I'd be very grateful if you could assist."

"Well, I'll put a copy in the post, but you must write in confirmation."

"Of course, but we need it urgently. I wonder if you would e-mail it to me."

"This is highly irregular, but I suppose it doesn't matter. Now give me your e-mail address."

Bartlett knew the tales a custody-record could tell. He was concerned that the clerk would seek authority before sending the e-mail. She obviously did not. He breathed a sigh of relief as the final page emerged safely.

"So, Melissa Grant, what can I find out about you?" He read the document carefully.

"The Aphelion Hotel, best I pay it a visit," he mumbled thoughtfully to himself as he studied the address given.

The Night Porter at the Aphelion read the Times. The newspaper was at its best at weekends and the Porter had lots of time to enjoy the contents. He was not over-stretched. It was just after eleven, but the night had been quiet. He knew that once midnight came, he would have little to do. He might be disturbed by the occasional drunken guest, but that would be all. He watched the revolving doors turn, at the entrance to the hotel, with some disquiet. Who was arriving to breach his peace? He examined the small, balding, man as he approached. He was not impressed.

"What can I do for you, Sir?" He added it as an after-thought.

"I wonder if you can help me. I'm a solicitor. I am trying to trace a missing girl."

Herbert Bartlett handed his business card to the Night Porter. The old man studied it carefully.

"Possibly ex-army," Bartlett thought, "maybe even the Guards."

The man's bearing was upright and not weathered by age. He carried a certain authority.

"Not an officer though," Bartlett was guessing.

The Night Porter's brown uniform was properly presented. The arms of the jacket were pressed, the brass buttons shined. Bartlett could not see the man's shoes. He was sure that they would be equally clean. He had watched the man fold his newspaper as he walked towards the desk. The Porter had placed it to his side, but it was still visible. The solicitor noted that even this was formally squared.

"Well," the Man sat upright as he spoke. He had remained on his high stool behind the desk. "What can I do for you, Mr Bartlett?"

"Melissa Grant, the girl who's missing, I believe she stayed here, possibly a couple of years ago now. I wonder if you could check your registers. I have a more accurate date."

"And why should I do that, Mr Bartlett? You will be aware that all information we keep on our guests is confidential, and two years ago," he rubbed his chin. "I would have to look for that register."

"It's important, her parents are frantic. They've been unable to trace her and are concerned that she's, you know," he left the word unsaid.

"This is probably the last lead that we've got. We need your assistance. Perhaps this will assist, for your inconvenience."

Bartlett folded the twenty-pound note precisely in half before pushing it across the desk to the Night Porter. He had kept it in his top pocket, prepared for this moment. He had several identical notes lodged there, to progress the matter further, if necessary. The Night Porter slid the note away from Bartlett. It disappeared into the side pocket of his jacket.

"I'll see if the register is easily available, no promises though."

Bartlett was relieved. It was crucial that the first payment was accepted. He knew now that the information could be purchased, if it was available. He would recoup the monies four-fold from the Ramiros, ten-fold if the information was credible. He waited several minutes for the Night Porter to return. He watched as the old man walked back to his stool carrying the register. He walked slowly, although his bearing was upright. Bartlett thought he had a slight limp on his right leg. It slowed him. Bartlett did not want him any slower.

"Any luck?" He asked.

The Porter opened the book without speaking. He kept it away from Bartlett as he perused the pages. He nodded as he read them. The solicitor took another twenty-pound note from his top pocket and folded it carefully. He placed it before the Porter. The register turned towards him.

"She was a regular at that time, stayed here quite often. Not a prostitute, was she?"

"I don't know what she did to support herself, very independent, according to her parents."

Bartlett looked at the entry. Melissa Grant's name was present, but the address was sadly lacking. It was scribbled and incomplete.

"Have you any other information," Bartlett asked.

"We normally keep a file on our regular customers. I don't know if we have one for her. I could have a look."

Another twenty pounds persuaded the Porter to leave his desk and look for the guest file. While he was gone, Bartlett continued to check the register. He found other entries for Melissa. On each occasion the address was indecipherable. He found that strange.

"I found a file," the Porter told him on his return. "Not much in it though, just copies of bills and other bits and pieces, always paid in cash."

The Porter pushed the file towards Bartlett without further ado. The solicitor studied it although realising that had if it had contained useful information, it would have cost him. He handed it back to the Attendant.

"Not much in there, it looks like we've drawn a blank."

"Possibly not," smiled the Porter as he tapped his inside pocket. "A client information sheet, but this is very confidential. I'd be sacked if I showed anyone this. Not worth my job, you know."

Bartlett did not hesitate. He pulled several notes from his pocket and, this time, peeled them one by one, placing them on the desk but retaining them carefully in front of him. The Night Porter watched as the notes added in value.

"That's your lot," Bartlett told him when sixty pounds lay on the table before him. "I'm not paying more for something I've not seen."

"A hundred and its yours."

Bartlett felt he was in an Arabian flea market.

"Eighty."

He placed the final note on the desk. The Porter grabbed the money before him and reached into his pocket. The A4 sized paper was carefully folded in four. Bartlett opened it in quiet expectation.

"Best I could do, two phone numbers for contact. The first is a mobile. I don't know when we got the second. It was scribbled on a piece of paper in the file."

Bartlett grunted gratefully as he assimilated the information. He turned to leave the hotel.

"A last bit of information you can have for free, if you like," the Porter called after him.

Bartlett paused in his stride and turned to him. "What's that?"

"I've already given all this to the police, not so long ago, at that."

Bartlett was interested. "Did you get the name of the officer, not Trevellian was it?"

The man thought for a moment. "No, nothing like that. It was Knight, Jack Knight, does that help?"

He could see the solicitor nodding as he entered the revolving door to leave the hotel.

Melissa Grant gratefully accepted the invitation to the Ramiro hacienda, on my behalf. The invitation had come from Juan Marco, not from Paulo Ramiro himself. It mattered not, it would give me the opportunity to see my son.

"Do you ride?" Marco had asked as Melissa lay with him, in his bed.

I had ridden horses in my youth, but not for some years. I was concerned as to my abilities. Melissa Grant had no such inhibitions.

"Of course I do." She would blame the South American saddle, if I had problems.

Juan Marco had been brought up with the horses at Paulo Ramiro's ranch. They had been saddled prior to their arrival. Juan Marco had no need to seek permission from Paulo Ramiro. He had an open invitation. He contacted the stables directly before leaving the apartment. Alby had arrived to transport them, safely, to the ranch. The

Mercedes creaked slightly, showing its dissatisfaction at the condition of the roads.

The horses were lively animals, although Ramiro's favourites were not available to them. They were roughly broken and only responded to firm commands. Melissa Grant sat firmly in the American saddle, coping easily with the long stirrups. I probably preferred it to the short English stirrup that I had been used to. I took some time to relax, but then Melissa rode competently. Juan Marco was impressed.

"Is there anything you can't do?" He asked as we rode side by side.

"I can't see my son." Melissa spoke my thoughts.

Melissa was sharp in my reply, causing Juan Marco's silence. We rode on thoughtfully.

Apart from her obvious dilemma, Melissa enjoyed this rare opportunity to sample the pleasures of Juan Marco's lifestyle. Since our arrival both his business and Melissa's own had consumed us. With Melissa, I rode in advance of Marco, my smaller bay galloping at full pace and retaining the lead. Marco rode behind. He appeared relaxed. Melissa slowed my horse to a trot and waited for him. Whilst Marco caught up with us, I cast my mind to the previous evening and the love making that Melissa had enjoyed with Juan Marco.

"Slut?" I mused as we shared our thoughts.

Marco had been a gentle and compassionate lover. It had not been a repetition of Melissa, and his, activities in the Mercedes. On that occasion both had suffered the pressures of the occasion, merely responding to our heightened passions. Marco had dominated although Melissa Grant had not been an unwilling participant. This time we developed slowly together. It was an interesting three-some. Marco proved himself sensitive to Melissa's and my needs. Even I found his attention stimulating. The privacy of the apartment negated any need to hurry. The three of us spent much time on the white duvet covering the large double bed of Juan Marco.

Whilst I had taken a background position to Melissa Grant, I was aware and thoughtful during the love making. I knew the risks. At any time, Juan Marco could discover my disguise. I always gave much effort to ensure that I was properly dressed as Melissa Grant. Her false hairpiece was securely fitted, my own blonde tresses tight against my head. I knew that my hairdresser would have no easy task restoring it on my return, assuming that I ever did return. I was not let down. Juan

Marco commenced making love to Melissa Grant and knew no different.

I allowed Melissa's force of personality to overcome my own. Melissa Grant wanted to make love to Marco. I would only do so to further my aim, to regain my son. I knew that I should control Melissa, but it was easier not to. I saw Melissa as all that I would want to be, with much that I would not want. Her personality had developed within me, but now developed further regardless of me.

We rode back to the stables at a slow pace, allowing the horses to cool slowly. They were unsaddled for us, Marco brushing the two down before allowing the groom to take full control. Melissa ran her fingers through her hair as we walked back towards the car.

"I enjoyed that Juan, thank you." Melissa spoke on behalf of us both.

"It was my pleasure, but now we have to go back to work."

Juan Marco did not elucidate further. I knew better than to ask questions. Melissa walked towards the Mercedes.

"No, not that one. The jeep's more practical."

Melissa looked at Juan Marco. He was striding towards a maroon, hard topped, jeep parked close to them. She followed him. I wondered why but did not ask.

"Where is Alby?" Melissa asked as she climbed into the passenger seat.

"He will wait for us. We're OK, we have two little Alby's with us to protect ourselves."

Juan Marco's right hand reached above him to the roof of the vehicle. He tapped the automatic rifle secured there. At the same time, I noticed the snub of a similar rifle protruding from between the seats.

"We'll have to look after ourselves, if necessary, Melissa. Can you use one of these?"

"I'll learn quickly." Melissa replied confidently. I hoped she was right.

The Jeep pulled from the drive rapidly. I looked back towards the house knowing that my son was only yards from me but realising that the distance was again increasing. I wanted to stop Marco, to run towards the house in search of Danny. I knew that I could not, now was not the time. I turned to face forward in the seat. Juan Marco did not stop at the gate. Alby had opened it for him. He waved his hand at the loyal bodyguard as we drove through and took the road to Tunja.

The road was uneven and maintained badly. The jeep bucked occasionally when Marco failed to negotiate a pothole. Melissa looked at the tree-lined foliage to the side of the road. It was dense and overgrown. Ideal for an ambush, I thought. However, Marco drove at speed. Any aggressors would have been caught off guard.

Herbie Bartlett had traced the subscribers to the telephone numbers that he had been given. It had not been a difficult task. It was a regular occurrence, within his trade, and one that he employed others to do for him. The particular agency that he chose employed only retired policemen. Their knowledge of the system made the job easy.

"Ronny, I've got two numbers to check urgently. Can you get on to it for me?"

It was mid afternoon before Ronny rang back.

"Sorry for the delay. We had a problem with the mobile. The firm are tightening up. Still, I've got them both for you. I'll e-mail them through."

Bartlett read the e-mail on its arrival. The subscribers of the two numbers did not correspond. The mobile telephone was registered to an East-End firm. It did not interest him at this time, although he could have discovered that this was a police accommodation address. He read the second subscriber's name and address out loud,

"Katrina Marshall, now where have I heard that name before?"

I would not have remembered giving my home number to the hotel reception. It was early in my career as an undercover officer and I needed to please. My police cell-phone had given me problems and the hotel needed a contact number. I gave my home number on that one occasion. The receptionist swore that it had been destroyed soon after. Herbert Bartlett was fortunate that this was not the case.

A visit to the address in Clapham provided Bartlett with the information he required. My flat was empty. He gained no reply to his repeated knocking. The old boy on the ground floor had not forgotten the night when he had been abused by Duncan Trevellian.

"What do you want?" At first, he was abrasive as he spoke to Bartlett through his open sash window.

"I'm looking for the lady upstairs."

"Her; the first time we've had peace and quiet from her. She's gone away, don't know where."

"You've had a few problems with her then?" Bartlett tried to be friendly.

"Trouble, you bet, her yobbish friends visiting her during the night and waking up the whole street. Threatened me he did, no cause to, just threatened me."

"Yes."

"Then got herself pregnant, unmarried mother. You know what I mean? Probably end up living off the State!"

Bartlett digested the information as the man talked.

"Couldn't even keep the child. Kidnapped it was, just recently."

The final information injected instant recollection into Bartlett's mind. He had seen the newspaper reports. He remembered the case; it was in all the papers. He turned to walk away, waving his appreciation to my neighbour.

"The police were everywhere," the old man called after him. "And her a police officer as well, bloody disgusting I call it."

Herbie Bartlett had not missed the neighbour's final words, although they merely confirmed his own recollections. He would scour the newspapers to ascertain the name of the woman's son. He would already put money on the answer. It would be Danny, Danny Marshall.

Chapter Eighteen

It was not a long journey to the Undertaker. Pedro Ipiales was expecting them and was there to greet them. He shook Juan Marco's hand with diffidence.

"Good-day to you, Pedro."

I noted that Marco unclipped the rifle from the roof of the Jeep and carried it with him. Melissa followed him to the Undertaker's premises.

The mechanic was laid in state, awaiting our arrival. Ipiales was proud of his work and always showed it off to best effect. He led us straight to the coffin. I did not, at first, recognise the body of the man. It had changed completely. Apparent weight had been added and the features altered. I looked for the scar on the man's face. It was now barely visible. I felt slightly sick. Melissa remained firm before the prepared body.

"Is it finished Pedro?" Marco asked.

The Undertaker nodded.

"Then we will arrange the collection very soon."

Juan Marco took an envelope he was carrying and gave it to the Craftsman. Ipiales opened it and walked slowly away to put it safely in his desk.

"Well, Melissa Grant, what do you think of your cousin?"

"He seems to have put on weight. Has he been eating something that didn't agree with him?" Melissa smiled at Marco. The business no longer shocked Melissa. I wish it similarly had no effect on me.

"He is perhaps carrying a little extra, but I am sure his passport will reflect that."

It was unnecessary to question further. I knew that this was Melissa's test. We did not know the weight of cocaine that was concealed within the body. It was irrelevant. It was enough to know it was there.

Pedro Ipiales waved reverently as the jeep pulled away. He was happy to have satisfied the Ramiros. Much work could potentially come from them. Today's efforts would allow him to feed and clothe his family for a month.

Marco drove the vehicle carefully, though at speed. Law and order was not at its most efficient within Colombia. It was at its best within the more affluent areas of a city centre. There the residents ensured that the security agencies received a little extra for their troubles. The service deteriorated into the suburbs and countryside. Families such as the Ramiros employed their own security. Others simply fended for themselves. Marco was not fearful of travelling alone. He was cautious, however.

"You will travel with your cousin, Melissa, to ensure his safe arrival in your Country."

"I will travel with my cousin, Juan Marco, but also with my son. You know that I will not leave without him."

Juan Marco remained silent, obviously considering my words. We approached a sharp bend to the left. The road fell away to the right and to the other side was heavy vegetation. The sudden disturbance in that vegetation sounded above the low revs of the engine and was visible to Marco yards ahead. His foot naturally floored the brake pedal causing the jeep to stop immediately. It slued round in the road, Juan Marco being side on to the fault. His sharp reaction was unexpected, and I fell against the door of the vehicle, bouncing back against Marco's body. He pushed me away and reached instantly for the gun above his head. His natural reactions caused the gun to be cocked and aimed through the car window, in one continuous movement.

"Get down, Melissa," he ordered.

Melissa lowered herself in the seat of the vehicle. She reached to the rear of the vehicle, feeling with her hand for the second gun. She pulled it carefully to her. She steered it slowly into my lap and I studied the mechanism. I felt Melissa's heart flutter as she feared the ambush. Mine fluttered more.

The brown body of the tapir virtually fell on the road before them as the animal struggled to free itself from the bush. It was, perhaps eight feet long and three feet tall, a female of the species. It regained its footing in a cumbersome manner and looked around itself, still shocked at its own sudden arrival in the open. It eyed the jeep suspiciously. To Melissa the animal was mindful of a large pig, with extended snout. As we watched, a smaller, striped baby version followed its mother onto the road. She led her young past the jeep until finding another more convenient entrance to disappear back into the bush.

Melissa laughed out-loud with relief. I would have cried. She returned the gun to the back seat as Marco fastened his in its rack. He spun the powered steering back online and continued the journey. She physically saw him relax. He did not see me relax.

The flow of adrenaline and its sudden dissipation relaxed the two of them. I have not included myself in that. Melissa leaned back against the short passenger seat as the vehicle pulled back into the grounds of the Ramiro hacienda. She drew her fingers through her hair. In many ways she preferred it to my, mousy, tresses. We were not at one in these thoughts, although hers was made of genuine head hair and prepared by a principal London wig maker. It was almost indistinguishable from the real thing. She was comfortable and relaxed and smiled at the rugged profile of Juan Marco as he drove the vehicle through the gates.

Maria Ramiro held her grandson carefully as she walked from the house into the sunlight. It was many years since her own children were this small. She looked into the boy's face. She was convinced she could see Carlo in him, although accepted that this was probably just the wishes of an over-enthusiastic grandmother. She walked with him towards the corral, barely noticing the jeep as it drove through the gates.

Neither I, my alter-ego, Melissa Grant, nor Juan Marco, noticed the woman and child until the vehicle was parked. Marco helped Melissa from our seat. It was a short step to the ground and she needed no help. She was, however, flattered that Juan Marco wished to assist her. She swung towards him, almost into his arms, until the sight of my child stopped her.

Marco noticed the imperceptible change in Melissa as she saw Danny. The change occurred as I re-took control of events. My movement flowed through him and beyond as I moved slowly away from him and towards Maria. He walked behind me, catching me quickly. He took my arm, causing me to pause. My head turned, my eyes catching his. He could share my pain, the emotion passing between us. He took his hand from my arm and walked beside me as I approached. We were, perhaps, two yards from Maria, when I stopped.

"You are his mother." Maria Ramiro stated as a matter of fact.

I replied by merely nodding. Even Melissa Grant was unable to speak on this occasion. I was beyond any reaction.

"I could tell so. I knew it was you. Here, hold your son, he is truly beautiful."

She handed the child to Melissa. I was instantly at one with him.

"Now walk with me. Juan Marco, you can leave us. I have enough bodyguards around here without you as well."

Marco stood where he was as Maria and I walked slowly away from him.

"Boss, you need to make a telephone call to London. Herbie Bartlett says it's urgent." Marco had barely noticed Alby's approach. He turned and walked towards the house. The bodyguard stayed in the open to supervise the safety of the women.

I held my child close to me as I walked with Maria. He was heavier than I remembered. I sat him on my hip, causing me to walk off balance, almost to limp. He clung to me for support. He was well nourished and content. The heat of his small body mingled with my own. I felt he was home, although I recognised that he was far from being so.

"So, you are my grandson's mother, yet I do not even know your name."

"Katrina," I paused. "Katrina Marshall and this is Danny Marshall."

I had no idea why I chose this moment to dominate Melissa Grant. I knew it to be the wrong time, but somehow I felt comfortable. Too late now, I had made a spontaneous decision.

"We are now formally introduced, Danny Marshall, even though we had met before. I now also know your mother and you are a lucky boy to have such a beautiful mother."

"Thank you," I responded on behalf of my son.

"And now Katrina, I must introduce myself. I am Maria Ramiro, your son's grandmother."

We smiled at each other.

"It is a pleasure to meet you, Maria."

"And you Katrina. Now tell me, you have my son's child, perhaps you were the last to truly know Carlo. Tell me Katrina, was he a caring and compassionate man, like his father, Paulo Ramiro?"

"Indeed he was, Maria," I lied. I knew it was proper to do so. "I have only met Paulo Ramiro briefly, but I am sure that Carlo took after him."

"You are a gracious woman, Katrina Marshall. You tell me what I want to hear. I am sure that we will get on well."

We walked in silence for a moment, in the sunlight of the Ramiro home. I stroked the hair of my son with my free hand. Maria Ramiro was thoughtful.

"You did not know our son well, Katrina. Is that why you did not tell us of our grandson? He will be our only reminder of Carlo, yet we would not have known about him. Why was this?"

"There were many reasons, Maria, some too complicated to explain. But the most important, I wanted my son to grow up as an ordinary boy. He could not have done so as the son of Carlo Ramiro and the grandson of Paulo. You will surely understand that. That was the most important reason, Maria."

"I can understand, but now everybody knows. What will happen now?"

"I don't know, Maria. I want my son; he must live with me. But you are his grandmother and I would like him to know his grandmother."

The older woman touched my hand.

"These are difficult times, but we will see if the joint influence of two women together can overcome the unswerving stubbornness of an old Colombian."

Maria Ramiro was referring to her husband, Paulo, and I knew so. I had gained a valuable ally in Maria, but would that be sufficient to give my son back to me? I doubted it. The large circuit in which we were walking took us back towards the house. I watched as Juan Marco walked from the house towards us. His face was fixed and stern. He walked positively and at speed. He took my arm when he reached me. His grip was firm. He pulled me towards him, away from Maria. Both of us stopped.

"What is it, Juan?" Maria asked.

"I have to speak to Melissa alone. I am afraid she is not who we think she is."

"She is not who you think she is!" Maria Ramiro stayed with the two of us.

"I have just received a telephone call from our lawyer in England, Melissa. He has told me who you really are, a police officer. Not Melissa Grant at all, but Miss Marshall. Do I need to say more?"

"I had a job to do, Juan Marco. I had a job to do then and I have a job to do now."

"And your job led to the death of Carlo Ramiro. It was you who set him up, not Jack Knight."

"It was not me that killed Carlo. He killed himself. It is a dangerous trade and you all knew the danger. He could have given himself up to police, he did not. He chose to fight and that's what killed him. And don't forget, you had Jack Knight, a senior police officer, in your pocket. He didn't do much to save Carlo, did he? He could have walked him from the building and ensured he walked away. Jack Knight saved himself."

"I shall deal with Jack Knight separately, but now Melissa Grant, or should I still call you Melissa?"

"Katrina, Katrina Marshall." My eyes steeled beneath my disguising contact lenses. It was time for Melissa Grant to be absorbed into Katrina Marshall.

"Well, Katrina Marshall, you come with me. Maria, take the child."

My action was instantaneous and reflected my need to remain with my child. I pulled away from Juan Marco. The force of my action caught him unawares. His grip was broken. I stood still for a fraction of a second.

"Not my child, Marco. You're not having my child again."

I turned and ran from him. This was a reflex action, un-planned. I needed Melissa's keen thought. I looked around as I ran. I knew there was no escape. Juan Marco followed at a fast walk. I saw the jeep. I ran towards it. Had he left the keys in the car? I could not remember. I reached the vehicle and pulled the door open. I climbed in releasing Danny onto the passenger seat. I searched for the ignition. The keys were not there. I looked across and saw Juan Marco approaching at pace. Beyond him I saw Paulo Ramiro emerge from the house. He had heard the commotion. I reached above my head. The two guns were safely lodged in the roof. I pulled one free.

Juan Marco saw the snub-end of the automatic through the open door of the jeep. He paused in his step. I was in panic. He could not pre-judge my actions, knowing that my emotion alone might cause my finger to tighten on the trigger. Paulo Ramiro was approaching rapidly behind him. His step did not falter.

I knew that I had no final card to play. I was in a no-win situation. I was in hostile territory and surrounded by the enemy. Had I started the jeep and driven from the grounds, I did not know the area, even less, the Country. This was my last stand. To surrender would mean the permanent loss of my child, and possible my life. At this moment the latter meant nothing to me, but Danny everything. I pointed the weapon into the air and pulled the trigger. The rifle fired several times before I released the trigger. The reports were sharp and shocking. Maria put her hands over her ears and ducked her head slightly. Paulo Ramiro had reached Juan Marco and stopped beside him. Marco stood upright as if used to the sound of gunfire. Guards appeared, running, from all areas of the grounds. Within seconds the jeep was surrounded, several similar weapons focused on me.

"What is going on here?" Paulo Ramiro said loudly for me to hear.

He was talking to Marco and I awaited the answer that would seal my fate. To be denounced to Ramiro as the undercover officer who killed his son would have just one result. Juan Marco paused for a vital second. He looked towards me and our eyes fixed. I felt that something had passed between us. My heart lifted in that short glance.

"It's no problem, Paulo. She saw Maria with the child and grabbed him away from her."

"Then take the child back and get her out of here. Sort this out before I have to."

The old Colombian spun on his heel and walked back towards the house. I was grateful to Juan Marco. He had not revealed my true identity to Paulo Ramiro. However, my problems were far from over. I stood to lose my child. I knew that once I had left the ranch I would not be allowed to return.

I had failed to hear the slight click of the car door as the guard opened the passenger door behind me. Danny had not signalled his entry into the car. The first sign was when I felt the cold steel of the blade of his knife against my throat. The Colombian neck-tie, I was about to wear it. Had I been standing; my knees would have buckled. The odds were getting longer. I imagined my tongue laying on my chest. At least it would stop me talking. I lowered the gun towards Juan Marco to even the odds.

"No, Paulo Ramiro, this is not right."

The words reflected my feelings although I knew that I had not uttered them. Ramiro stopped in mid-stride and turned towards his wife.

"This is your grandson, Paulo, and your grandson's mother. The child should be with his mother. It is not right to separate them. I have spoken to the girl. She loves the child as a mother should. She also knows that the child needs his grandparents. We will see him, Paulo. He will stay with us on vacation and know us as he should, but he will not live with us. He will live with his mother in England."

Paulo Ramiro looked at his wife then turned to look at me. I held the automatic rifle firmly in my hand. The guard held his knife to my throat. One move of Ramiro's hand would signify my death. The move did not come.

"So be it." He walked back to the house. "Then take the gun away from her and find her and the child a room. They will stay here until they return to England."

I heard his words. My grip loosened on the rifle; it nearly fell from my shaking hands. I rested it on the door of the jeep. Both Juan Marco and Maria approached me. Marco took the gun from me and made it safe. The guard had disappeared as mysteriously as he had arrived. Maria opened the door of the vehicle. She pointed towards Danny.

"The child," she reminded me.

"Thank you, thank you both." Neither had revealed my alter-identity as a police officer. I knew that Paulo Ramiro's response would have been different had he found out.

"Don't thank us yet, he'll find out soon enough," Marco told me.

"Leave him to me," added Maria. "We will get you home before that happens. I will deal with Paulo. Tell me though, you did not intend Carlo to die, in the police raid, did you?"

"Of course not, Maria," I was sincere. "Nobody intended Carlo to die. He would not have done if he had surrendered."

"Perhaps you now realise that there are times when you cannot surrender, Katrina Marshall." I digested Juan Marco's words as I followed Maria towards the house.

I stayed with my son at the Ramiro ranch for just one night. An uneventful journey in the Mercedes limousine, driven by Alby, took us back to the centre of Bogota and the apartment of Juan Marco. I sat with Marco watching the day fade into evening. He sipped a Bacardi and coke, I drank Melissa's, customary, scotch and water.

Juan Marco watched me as I walked to the bathroom. I knew his thoughts. Melissa had moved on, yet I remained. My body was slim, yet well formed. Without heels my legs carried less emphasis. I shut the door behind me.

"I'll just be a minute", I told him as I did so.

Marco had finished his drink and poured another before I re-emerged. The transformation initially caught him unawares. In the privacy of the bathroom, I had removed Melissa's appearance to reveal my own. I felt the luxury of brushing my own hair. It had been held tight to my head for too long. I removed Melissa's contact lenses. My own clear lenses allowed the clear blue of my eyes to show through. I removed Melissa's clothes, dressing only in Juan Marco's white, towelling robe. It fully covered me, almost reaching the ground.

"You are beautiful whether as Melissa Grant or Katrina Marshall," Marco told me.

As we sat together Marco took my hand. He looked into my eyes and spoke to me sincerely and seriously.

"You now have an obligation to us. You might be a police officer, but you and your son are now accepted as part of the Ramiro family. You have not avoided your obligation to assist the passage of your cousin back to England. He will travel on the aircraft with you, Katrina, you realise that?"

I was silent as I thought of the consequences. I had no option but to accept the instructions. Marco's tone did not infer a choice and I therefore nodded my agreement.

As the evening drew closer Marco told me, "I have a present for you to take home with you, Katrina."

Marco got up and walked behind me. He returned with a dark wooden box, which he handed to me. I looked dubiously at him before stroking my hand across the polished mahogany. He noticed the sensitivity of my fingers as I raised the lid. The interior was satin lined. Within the material I saw a matching pair of white, bone handled, Derringer pistols. I carefully lifted one in my hand allowing it to settle in the cup of my palm. I noticed the handgrip was etched in filigree silver. It was a beautiful weapon.

“Yours and mine, Juan?”

“Just yours, Katrina.”

"They're lovely Juan, but I can't keep them. I would not be allowed to take them back into England. Your plans would be ruined, if I were to be arrested carrying these through Customs, wouldn't they?"

Marco had not thought about the English prohibitions. They existed in few other countries. He had always ignored them regardless. However, he appreciated what the girl was saying. Their cargo was too important to jeopardise its importation.

"These are yours forever, Melissa Grant. But until you can possess them, I will keep them for you. They will be here for you on your return. Meanwhile I must think of another present to send you when you return to your native England." He laughed. "And what would you like?"

"I already have everything I want Juan. I have my son back. You can give me nothing that I would want more, but perhaps I can give you something".

Marco put the gun box onto a table as I moved into his arms.

Phil Shanks had returned to England having confirmed that Melissa Grant had left Miami for Bogota. He knew he could not follow. It would be foolhardy to do so. He was now surplus to requirements in Miami. Brad Baker would continue the operation, hopefully to a successful conclusion.

Shanks and Baker parted, over beer and Bourbon, on their return to Baker's home. Brad's wife, Amy, helped them demolish the bottle of spirit. She had enjoyed the company of the English policeman and would miss him.

"We must keep in touch," she told him as she took out the empty bottle. She was unsteady on her feet although her words were clear.

"You must come and visit me in London. Let me return your hospitality."

"We'd like that."

Baker drove Shanks to the airport the following morning, although he was unsure whether he should be driving. The children had awakened Amy. She had overslept. Their breakfast had been rushed before school. Baker's head ached slightly. He drove at less than 50 mph. The speed limit did not affect him. His ability to drive did. Shanks was similarly disabled as he climbed the steps of the aircraft. As he glanced back to the Terminal buildings his fears for me were not marred by the effects of the alcohol.

Shanks could not have known that I would be making a similar journey only days later. The change of flights at Miami was a practical option. A direct flight to London would have affected more delay.

Melissa Grant was driven to Bogota Airport in the Mercedes-Benz. Juan Marco escorted her and Danny into the Terminal building. They were to fly first-class thanks to the Ramiro family and had access to the private lounge prior to take-off. Alby stayed at the door of the lounge, as ever protecting the inhabitants. Melissa again dominated me. Only her passport had travelled with me through to the United States and therefore, only Melissa Grant could fly home. Danny was a more difficult problem. He had entered the States on false papers and was not contained within Melissa's passport. The authorities at Bogota were no problem, they were simply bought off. Juan Marco recognised that the detour through Miami might lead to unnecessary questioning. However, that was the route that had been planned for the emigrant mechanic, and that was the route that must be taken. It was another problem for Jessie Slyder to sort out. He was contacted by Alby and informed accordingly.

Melissa held Danny close to her. He was initially reluctant until the sound of my voice again confirmed me to be his mother.

"Goodbye, Juan, and thank you," I told him as the Flight was called.

"It is too soon to say goodbye, Melissa Grant, or perhaps I should say goodbye to Melissa Grant and hello to Katrina Marshall."

"Maybe."

"We will meet again soon. You must bring Paulo's grandson to see him. But first you will ensure that the body of your cousin, the mechanic, is safely delivered to your Country, yes?"

"I will do what I can, Juan, you know that."

"It is the price you pay."

He took my free hand in his and kissed it gently. He did not release it. He pulled me to him slowly. Danny still sat, contented, on my hip. Juan Marco moved to the other side to allow him room. He kissed Melissa fully on the lips. Both she and I responded before pulling back. I knew that I had won over Juan Marco, whether as Melissa Grant or Katrina Marshall. Maria Ramiro had also given me support. But for how long would they be on my side, particularly if the load, designated as my cousin, was not delivered.

"Juan, I must go, otherwise I'll miss the Flight."

Juan Marco did not wait to see the Flight leave. He beckoned to Alby to follow as he strode towards the car. He need not have done; the Bodyguard was instantly at his side regardless.

The flight to Miami was short and effortless. I knew that neither Melissa nor I could relax until we had safely landed at London Heathrow. Until then Melissa had the worry of my son, and also the worry of her cousin who travelled in the hold. She had no hesitation in accepting the miniature scotch offered by the hostess.

We were delayed only a short time in the transit lounge at Miami International before boarding the connecting flight to London. No questions were asked regarding Danny's identity. He had been provided, at short notice, with documentation. It seemed that the Ramiro's influence in Bogota knew no bounds. Melissa assumed that the luggage, and thus her unwanted cousin had been similarly satisfactorily transferred. She asked no questions and no questions were asked of her. It was only after an hour into her final flight that she finally fell asleep and I allowed myself to join her. Danny had drifted off long before having sampled the delights of a microwaved in-flight bottle. I did not dream; my sleep was not that deep.

Chapter Nineteen

Jessie Slyder sat on the swivel chair in the corner of the secure room within the Federal Building. A plain clothed officer stood guard by the locked door. He had said nothing to Slyder. Jessie's attempts to communicate had been blocked by silence. He was now silent himself. He rocked slightly on the chair. The slight movement caused the chair to squeak. It was a rhythmic, annoying, sound. He hoped it would disturb his guard and cause him to speak. It did not. The man was well trained.

Slyder was hungry. He had eaten his, customary, bagels prior to his arrest but had consumed nothing since. His stomach was not used to being empty. It reacted badly. It sounded off at regular intervals, intermingling with the squeaking chair.

The Customs man knew that he was finished. His new car would have to be sold. He would probably be imprisoned, although he was currently trying to avoid this probability. His lawyer was negotiating with the Government agent, Brad Baker. They had left him some time ago to consider his plight. He looked at his watch, or where his watch should have been. It was no longer on his wrist. It had been seized, along with his other property. Jessie Slyder was fidgety. He was a worried man.

His problem had begun the previous day. The coffin had arrived, as he was pre-warned, on a routine flight from Bogota. The papers were correct. They appeared genuine. As he was required to do, Jessie Slyder processed the paperwork and inspected the consignment. He endorsed it as correct and passed it for its onward journey to London. To endorse Melissa and Danny's papers as correct was a simpler task.

Slyder was arrested soon afterwards. He was taken to the Federal Building and locked in a cell overnight. He had protested his innocence, but nobody had been prepared to listen.

"What have I done wrong, I am innocent," he shouted on more than one occasion. Nobody came to his cell.

The following morning found Slyder curled up under a blanket. He was in a light sleep, more of a doze. The bench on which he lay was hard and unyielding, the mattress thin. He was uncomfortable and tired. The tiredness finally overwhelmed all other emotion and he drifted off.

Brad Baker was not an unreasonable man. He entered the cell and introduced himself.

"Are you hungry, Jessie? Can I get you something to eat? This might prove to be a long day for both of us."

Slyder did not reject the offer. His aggressive confidence having returned, he instructed the officer of the fillings he required in his bagels and demanded his immediate release. He now realised his fortune in being allowed one of his demands. The bagels had staved his hunger but were insufficient to last the day.

Jessie Slyder knew the Miranda caution. He had given it many times to errant importers of contraband. He knew of his entitlement to a lawyer, but initially rejected this in the confidence that there would be no evidence against him. Baker's first interview was not difficult for Slyder. The officer explained that their search of the coffin and body revealed a large quantity of concealed cocaine. The substance would be subjected to laboratory analysis to confirm the result.

"But what's this got to do with me," the Customs man asked.

"We believe that you knew the cocaine was there and that you had been paid off."

"What, how can you say that? I had no idea. I checked it out. It looked fine to me."

Slyder feigned innocence with some persuasion. He thought he was probably winning over the Federal agent.

Baker asked him about his training and background. He had trouble remembering accurately how long he had worked at the Airport. He explained the procedure involved in his work. That was easy, he knew it backwards.

He was less comfortable with the questioning concerning the consignment itself. He accepted that he should have paid special attention to the transfer from Bogota. Yes, he knew that cocaine was prolific in Colombia. He was aware of the many and various methods used by the producers to transport their illicit goods abroad. No, he could find no fault in the paperwork. No, his suspicions were not roused when he inspected the content. He did not know the dead man and had never seen him before. How could he have done? The man was an Englishman who had died in Colombia.

After his first interview, Jessie Slyder was confident that the Federal man had nothing against him. His had answered the questions and shown himself to be an innocent man. He expected to be released soon. He lay on his back, in the cell, with his arms behind his back. His worries had dispersed.

The second interview commenced with a demand from Slyder that he be released immediately.

"Not just now," Mr Slyder, Baker told him, "I've just a few more questions to put to you."

Again, Baker reminded Slyder of his right to silence. Again, he rejected the offer of a lawyer.

"Mr Slyder, Jessie,"

"Mr Slyder!" The suspect corrected the officer.

"Mr Slyder, you have told me that you knew nothing about the cocaine concealed within the coffin and were not involved with its transfer on to London. Is that right?"

"Yes, of course that's right. Now, if that's all I'd like to go home."

"Do you know Paulo Ramiro, Mr Slyder?"

Slyder thought for a moment. "I know of Paulo Ramiro. He is a Colombian drugs dealer. We all know of him. I don't know him personally."

"We believe that Paulo Ramiro is responsible for this consignment."

"That's possible. I wouldn't know. It's nothing to do with me."

"That's what I'm not so sure of Jessie. I'd like you to listen to a couple of recordings."

It was soon after this that Jessie Slyder exercised his right to legal representation. The recordings of his meetings at the Orange Bowl were supported by the photographic evidence confirming his presence. He stumbled slightly as the first photograph was shown then realised the common sense of exercising his right to silence. He adopted that course.

Brad Baker had planned his strategy for interview. He wanted Slyder's initial story recorded and got it. It was only then that he would present his full, damning evidence. He watched carefully as Slyder's face reddened. His blood was pumping. Slyder did not see Baker's raised eyebrow of acknowledgement to his interviewing colleague.

Slyder's lawyer was a public defender. Having not specified a lawyer, and having no funds to privately pay, his defence was conducted by the State. Herbie Bartlett was a high roller in comparison. The Marlborough cigarette hung low from the corner of the man's mouth. It remained unlit until the opportunity arose for him to leave the building. His hair was greying; his suit was greying also. The public defender's office did not pay well.

The Lawyer had discussed the evidence with Brad Baker for over an hour. He had seen the pictures and listened to the recordings. He was direct with Jessie Slyder.

"You've got two choices, Jessie; serve ten to twenty or sing like a canary. What's it going to be?"

So it was that Slyder remained perched in the corner of the room waiting for Baker's return. He had, indeed, been singing and would continue to do so. He had told all, held nothing back. He had explained his meetings at the Orange Bowl and explained his involvement with the Ramiros. He had been threatened by them and only acted through immediate fear for himself and his family. This was his Lawyer's only worthwhile contribution; the timeless defence of duress was resurrected once again.

Jessie Slyder was relieved when the door to his cell finally opened and Brad Baker and the Lawyer re-entered. The guard had not been the best company. Slyder's nerves had not been assuaged by the lack of conversation. Baker walked up to him and spoke directly.

"Do you think that you could persuade a Grand Jury, Jessie?"

The man looked at his Lawyer before shrugging his shoulders. He knew he must agree. As a result of his response, warrants of arrest were sworn out for Paulo Ramiro and Juan Marco.

Pedro Ipiales was pleased with his recent income. The Ramiro family, through Juan Marco, had recompensed him well for his hard work. It had allowed him to care properly for his own family and even to treat himself to an extra bottle of Aguardiente, which he now kept within his work-place, on an upper shelf, beyond the reach of other interested parties, whether dead or alive.

Ipiales had enjoyed the local brew for many a good year. The locally produced Guaro was initially over forty per-cent proof but due to local taxation had reduced to twenty-nine per-cent. As Pedro had aged, he preferred his drink at the lesser proof. It was unusual for Pedro Ipiales to be employed during darkness hours and it took three shots of the clear liquid to give him the continued energy to work through the night.

Pedro had opened his small mortuary having been visited by Alby and told that the Ramiros required his urgent services. He knew that he would be well rewarded for his efforts and was pleased to comply. As he unlocked the door, he checked the lights to ensure that the electricity supply still continued to provide. All was well. That pleased Ipiales as he retained one local resident in the refrigerated locker, awaiting burial in the next couple of days.

He was gently sipping his third glass of Aquardiente when Alby returned with the delivery and instructions from Juan Marco. Ipiales was surprised at the return of the mechanic but even more surprised at the instructions given by Juan Marco. He recognised that it was not for him to argue and therefore he simply prepared his instruments whilst Alby removed the heavy corpse from the coffin. As I slept at the Ramiro ranch, having finally found the location of my son, Danny, and being re-connected to him, Ipiales began his night's work.

Ipiales began at the head of the corpse. Before removing the face, he had to ease away the stitching that he had introduced when repairing the body in the first instance. He took much care not to damage the remaining flesh as his repair work would have to be repeated and he knew that it was never easy second time round. The top of the mechanic's skull had been replaced in position and held in place by the lodged cocaine package. The Undertaker had done a fine job in placing the cocaine in the vacant cavity. The task to remove it was more difficult. Ipiales had manipulated the package to fit the cavity and, in doing so, had taken care not to split the polythene wrapping. In removing the package, he took even more care. He was not a user of the drug, albeit that he had chewed the natural coca leaf in the past. He pulled on rubber gloves and donned a facemask to protect himself, should the wrapping rupture during the procedure. The first package was safely removed. He stowed it carefully, ready for return to the Ramiro family, in due course.

Prior to his work commencing, the Undertaker had been provided with a large bag of ground chalk by Alby. He followed his employer's instructions in wrapping a quantity of the chalk in fresh polythene prior to placing it in the vacated skull aperture. His kitchen weighing machine gave him close to a kilo of the substance which, when wrapped, closely resembled a similar weight of cocaine. Having substituted the cocaine, Ipiales carefully replaced and repaired the face.

"Not bad," he mumbled in his native Spanish.

He paused for another shot of Aguardiente.

The removal of the cocaine from the body orifice was a similarly difficult task. Pedro had been efficient and competent in his initial task. He knew that the body was to be exported elsewhere and therefore wished it to pass muster. To where it would travel was indifferent to Ipiales. The fact that it had to pass through Customs controls was important and remained so. The individual packages of cocaine were carefully removed from the body and replaced with the chalk. Once the corpse had been cleaned, Ipiales set about the easier task of removing the additional packages from the coffin itself. The chalk packages again replaced the drug.

It was the early hours of the morning before Ipiales had finally completed the job. He contacted Alby by cell-phone to alert him as to collection. Whilst awaiting Alby's arrival he re-filled his glass with Aquardiente. The bottle was almost empty. It had seen him through the night.

Alby grunted his approval before lifting the mechanic's body and replacing it in the coffin. Both that and the extracted drug were then loaded onto his truck for onward transport to the Ramiro ranch. He thrust an envelope into the caretaker's hand before leaving. Ipiales simply weighed the envelope in his hand. That alone showed it to be more than ample payment for his work. He smiled as he turned off the lights and locked the door. He walked the short distance to his home. He would sleep soundly that day.

"I have taken steps to safeguard our investment." Marco explained to Paulo Ramiro as they took coffee together prior to breakfast.

They both were early risers and sat together on the patio overlooking the ranch. The large umbrella protected them from the heat of the day, although the purpose of their early coffee together was to avoid such heat.

"So what have you done?" Paulo wanted more definition.

“I was not happy with the proposed exportation. I do not trust the girl to complete the job, not do I trust Slyder or Knight. If any one of them fails, then we stand to lose a significant investment. I decided to safeguard the substance and treat this as a test run.”

Through habit, Juan Marco did not refer to the drug by name, preferring the investment or the substance. He had been trained that others could be listening at any time.

“So what are we exporting?”

“The girl will still be taking her cousin home. He is still relatively heavy but merely supported a legal, not illegal substance. They both will pass through Miami, with her child. It will be interesting to test Slyder further before trusting him. If Slyder achieves, then we can put Knight on the final importation and see how he performs.”

“And where is our investment?”

“Where it should be, here with us.”

Both men smiled as they picked up their coffee cups to sip the content.

Brad Baker was unaware of Marco’s action when interviewing Slyder. Slyder’s subsequent arrest did not trouble the two Colombians. The warrants would be easily overturned by their Miami-based Lawyers. They knew that Slyder would not give evidence before any jury, let alone a Grand Jury. They had been properly safeguarded by Marco’s actions allowing their businesses to continue with only limited hindrance.

Jack Knight walked by the side of the River Thames close to Kingston Bridge. He was in a relaxed mood. It was before lunch and soon time for his first drink of the day. The public house he had chosen was a few hundred yards away and fronted the river. The sun was warm, but not too warm to sit outside. It was an ideal day to take lunch by the river.

Knight had heard of the Miami drugs seizure. The warrants of arrest were now public knowledge and had been reported in the press and on television. Jack Knight had considered his position with the Ramiros. His relationship with Carlo Ramiro had been acceptable. Carlo paid him the respect that he deserved. Juan Marco had not been the same. Knight was sick of dealing with hired underlings. He despised the lawyer Herbie Bartlett. It was time to break from the

Ramiro fraternity and the ideal opportunity for that break had been created for him. He was pleased that he had developed a working relationship with the Ricciones. It would fill the monetary void left by the Ramiros. He would also extend his working relationship with Rupert Veneer. He was pleased to have control of the Politician. It would pay dividends in the future.

Knight continued to mull over his good fortune as he walked. His own thoughts engulfed him, and he did not notice the small, middle-aged, dark-skinned, man who approached from the opposite direction, until it was too late. The collision between the two initially left Knight breathless. The contact was glancing but firm. The man's protruding elbow caught Knight in the solar plexus, winding him. He paused in his step to catch his breath. He turned towards the man as he walked rapidly away.

"Bloody fool," he shouted after him. The man did not look back.

Jack Knight paid no attention to the lady who passed close to the two men as they collided. As he turned, she continued to walk in his direction, passing on his blind side. Knight regained his composure as he entered the door of the riverside pub.

"A pint of lager," he ordered as he approached the bar.

The darkness of the interior contrasted starkly with the daylight outside. Despite the attempts of the multi-national owner, the light-wood, interior, design was not sufficient to lighten the ambience.

"It's too nice to sit in here," Knight said to the barman as he paid.

"I wish I wasn't here; I can tell you."

Jack Knight walked back into the daylight, finding a vacant table, overlooking the river, and placing his pint on it. He pulled himself into the connected bench. He rubbed his right thigh, close to the buttock as he took his seat. It had been aching since his contact with the lout on the footway, he remembered.

As Knight sipped the refreshing liquid from his pint glass, he allowed his eyes to relax, surveying the gently flowing River Thames. A double skiff was pulled, rapidly, by two oarsmen. Too energetic, Knight thought. The effect of viewing the river became strangely relaxing. He watched the water, the light reflecting magically on the small, jumping, waves. Those waves became larger, like small dancing figures. They grew to dramatic proportions, they were dancers, ballet-dancers on stage. The house-lights lit their white costumes as they turned and moved so gracefully. But the light grew brighter, its glare slowly overtaking the characters within. He could just see their figures, beckoning him to join them.

Had Knight known of the gas injected drug that had infiltrated his body, there would have been little he could have done about it. It was a carefully planned and executed operation, carried out by the couple on previous occasions. It was so simple, yet they had never been caught. The man distracted the target by colliding heavily with him. The force of the collision disturbed the target, possibly causing him physical pain. The woman imparted the drug through gas injection as she approached from behind at the same instant. The drug was a derivative of Curare, its effects concentrated and powerful.

In due course the drug would alone have caused the death of Jack Knight. The couple had other plans, however. Whilst Knight sat, unmoving the swarthy South American walked behind him. His hand movement was swift, evading the eye of other customers. The knife was drawn across the throat of Jack Knight, only a slight 'swoosh' was heard as the honed blade seared flesh and muscle alike. In seemingly one movement his aggressor reached inside the gaping wound and drew Knight's tongue from his throat. He balanced Knight carefully. The Superintendent remained seated. His Colombian neck-tie would only be noticed when he fell forward gracefully from his chair. By that time the couple had departed.

"Adios," said the South-American as he walked quickly away.

There was no pain as Knight's head struck the firm wooden slats of the table. His beer jumped slightly at the impact but did not spill. Other customers ignored him as just another lunchtime drunk asleep at the table. It was only when the barman collected the glasses that his death was discovered.

The couple had initially trained as pickpockets in their South-American upbringing. They had diversified, in their expertise, and were now a closely bound team both in their private and business life. They could not afford to be otherwise, the rewards being too great, yet the penalties also. The woman waited for the man to join her before walking to the town centre to disappear among the throng of enthusiastic shoppers. The gas-gun was secreted in a rubbish bin, sufficiently far from the incident to make its discovery unlikely. If it was found, it would never be traced.

Sir Matt Stephens, Cecil Parkes, his Assistant Commissioner and Michael Farrar, the Home Secretary, met the following week at Knight's funeral. They had spoken several times on the telephone since the untimely death of the Superintendent.

"How did Mrs Knight take it?" Farrar asked as they stood outside the small, almost countrified church, in the heart of the Surrey commuter belt.

"All right, but it took some explaining. She still doesn't know the whole truth."

"Who conducted the post-mortem?"

"Henry Clayman, excellent man. He wasn't happy about suppressing the cause of death though. I had great difficulty in getting him to sign the death certificate. Coronary failure, we agreed upon."

"Best thing, don't you think? The repercussions of a murder enquiry could have been horrendous."

"Yes, we've got the full autopsy report, if we need it, but I think that's unlikely. This was a professional hit. We know of the technique, but not those responsible. We have the body samples, if we ever need that evidence."

"So his wife accepted a heart attack, did she?"

"Just about, we had to explain that an enquiry would do nothing for her or the family. It would highlight his past abuses and simply reflect badly on him. She knew that there was no chance of a further investigation succeeding. She finally accepted it as best for everyone."

"And how's your girl?"

Cecil Parkes entered the conversation. "All right, she got her boy back, which was what she wanted. We've put her out to a safe house at the moment, a place in the country. We've got to debrief her properly and work out what we're going to do with her."

"We were fortunate that the Americans played their part, arresting the Customs man and seizing the body."

"The headlines were good for us: 'Successful joint operation between US and English police, undercover cop foils Colombian drug deal'. All good stuff, and we're making the most of it. We are fortunate that the full truth will never come out though."

"And fortunate that the drugs never made it to England. What would she have done? Would she have tried to get the body through?"

"We might never know. She certainly hasn't answered that one yet and it's my bet she never will. Maybe its best we don't know."

The Home Secretary nodded. "Have we thanked the Americans for their help? It was very important, you know."

"Yes we have. It's time to get into the church. The hearse is approaching."

The Commissioner led the three men through the graveyard, along the gravelled path, towards the small church. He walked ahead with the Home Secretary. Cecil Parkes followed a few steps behind.

Sir Matt Stephen's took a rectangular parcel from his pocket and handed it to the Home Secretary.

"The recording I promised you Michael. Found it in Knight's desk when we were clearing it. Not good viewing, your man Veneer does not come out well. Still, you knew that didn't you? I'll leave that problem in your hands."

"Thank you Matt, I appreciate that. I owe you one."

"I think we probably both owe each other by now."

A knowing smile passed between the two men as they passed into the darkness of the church.

The Under-Secretary of State took his position before the despatch box for the last time. It would certainly be the last time during this parliamentary session, possibly during his political career. His summons to appear before Michael Farrar had not been totally unexpected. He had been on tenterhooks since the death of Jack Knight.

Rupert Veneer had read of the death of the Detective Superintendent in the newspaper at the House of Commons. It had not made front-page news and was of little interest to those not involved with the man. The death by heart failure was not newsworthy in itself. The fact that he died at a riverside pub in the suburbs allowed it to enter an inner page. Had the truth been known, it would, of course, have been front-page news.

Veneer did not know the truth of Knight's death but regardless felt no sympathy for him. Indeed, as he read the news, a large sigh of relief exited his body. Rupert Veneer's political career had been entirely compromised by the corrupt police officer. His own corruption had been classic. He had been enticed by sex, the prospect of a free and exciting night with a free and exciting woman. The use of cocaine had been an ancillary relief, yet a relief that would be damning if publicised. The recording of the event was all that Knight needed to influence Veneer.

Rupert Veneer had passed little information to Jack Knight. His death had been timely in that his demands were becoming more forthcoming. Rupert Veneer had fed titbits of Home Office information to avoid publication of his misdemeanours. Knight had made his intentions clear.

"Unless you give me something useful, it's going to the highest bidder. The Press would love this recording. You can imagine the headlines now. Get your finger out Veneer. I want information that I can sell, that will give me the profit I could make from your recording."

A weight had lifted from Veneer when he had heard of Knight's death, although he knew that he was not in the clear. Whilst he had been given a copy of the recording of his activities, he knew that Knight had retained the original. He did not know where. He had neither the knowledge nor ability to track down the original. He simply had to hope that it would not fall into enemy hands.

Michael Farrar looked serious as Veneer had walked into the confines of his parliamentary office.

"Well Rupert, have you seen this?"

The Home Secretary had uploaded the recording to a secure and personal computer. He played part for Veneer to view.

"Yes Sir, I have. It seems like I cocked up, doesn't it?"

"It certainly does. I had high hopes for you Rupert, but this! I warned you of such things, indeed, your mother warned you before that."

"I know, what do you propose?"

"I don't think we want to upset the Prime Minister with this. We don't want to create any unnecessary fuss. But we have a problem. We don't know if we now have all the copies of this recording. We also have a girl out there who could floor you if she goes to the Press. You know what they're like, they'll find evidence where none exists."

"I hope not."

"I hope not, as well Rupert, but I can't take that chance. The integrity of the Home Office is vital to the Government and, more importantly, vital to my career. I'm not going down with you. You're on your own. You can stand and fight if you wish. Under those circumstances I'd have to tell the Prime Minister and show him the recording. I have no doubt that you'd be fired as Minister and that would be the end of your career."

"My other option?"

"To resign your current position and to return to the back- bench. With that option you can have both copies of the recording and keep your fingers crossed. With luck you might get another offer in the next re-shuffle. I leave it to you."

"My mind's already made up. You'll have my resignation within the hour."

The morning's activities had drained Rupert Veneer. The House was almost empty for the afternoon session. The Member for North Forsythe was slightly slumped in his seat. He had a full and comforting lunch. The port had made his eyes heavy. His breathing was deep. Had he been able to focus he would have noticed Veneer's colour was paler than usual.

Before speaking, Veneer ensured that his hands were firmly placed on the despatch box. They must not be seen to shake. He took a deep breath. He wished he had heeded his mother's words. Jack Knight had been a two-legged horse and Veneer had chosen to ride him. It had been a clear mistake that could not be remedied. It had cost Veneer his position and possibly his career. Knight had paid more heavily. He deserved to.

Rupert Veneer emptied his full lungs on his first words. He hoped they would not be his last.

"We are the party of Law and Order."

Danny lay on me as I relaxed before the small coal fire in the lounge of the small cottage. I had moved home since returning to England. I could no longer trust the security of my Clapham flat and sought solitude elsewhere. Trevellian knew my address and visited regularly. We were close friends, but I doubted that the relationship could ever develop further. On his frequent visits he would play with Danny in the walled garden of the cottage. I appreciated that I was an over vigilant mother. I had earned the right to be so.

I had not been suspended from the Metropolitan Police, although I had expected to be. Detective Chief Inspector Shanks had listened carefully to my full account and thoughtfully filled in some of the gaps. Trevellian had told me the rest. It had been suggested that a period of sickness would be appropriate. I gratefully accepted. The Police Doctor had no hesitation in signing the certificate.

I had moved to a new house in record time with the assistance of Metropolitan Police lawyers. My cottage was beyond London, in the subdued atmosphere of the Surrey countryside. I had neighbours, but they were unassuming folk who kept themselves to themselves. I was happy with that. I preferred it that way.

I missed the hustle and bustle of London. I missed the opportunity to shop in my lunch hour. I missed the black London cab and the nightclubs open till the early hours. I valued my solitude and safety and particularly that of my son. The rest paled into insignificance.

Danny gently rolled from my stomach onto the settee. He was a contented child, unlike his father. He had recently taken his first steps. I was convinced that he would talk soon. I wondered what his first words would be. I hoped he would not speak Spanish.

The doorbell rang. I was still suspicious of unexpected visitors, although I doubted that there was reason to be so. I had no contact with Danny's grandparents since my return to London. I knew that both Paulo Ramiro and Juan Marco were still wanted by police in both America and England but was equally aware that the warrant could not be executed whilst they remained in Colombia. I had fond memories of Juan Marco, with good reason.

I presumed that the Riccione family interest in Danny had finished in Miami. Johnny Riccione had his own family to protect. They would come first although business would always run in parallel. I would not forget the threat, however, and took what precautions I felt appropriate.

I went to the front door, leaving Danny playing with toys on the carpet. He was not interested in the visitor. I had bought too many toys for him on his return. He had barely experienced half of them.

I secured the safety chain before looking through the peephole. The small scope distorted the visitors face. He was a young man perhaps in his twenties. His cheeks appeared bloated; his whole body shortened. He carried a small box in coloured paper. I saw no immediate threat. He could not see the loaded shotgun standing to the side of the door. I had obtained a licence, on my return. The safety catch was on to safeguard Danny. I had learned to switch it off as I swung the gun to my hip. I was not a good shot. From close range I did not have to be.

The End (or is it?)

Printed in Great Britain
by Amazon

32560925R00169